ROGUE MISSION

A NEW JORDAN SANDOR THRILLER

FROM BESTSELLING AUTHOR

JEFFREY S. STEPHENS

A POST HILL PRESS BOOK

ISBN (Hardcover): 978-1-61868-813-2
ISBN (eBook): 978-1-61868-812-5

ROGUE MISSION
A Jordan Sandor Thriller
© 2016 by Jeffrey S. Stephens
All Rights Reserved

Cover Design by Dean Samed, Conzpiracy Digital Arts

Post Hill
PRESS

Post Hill Press
275 Madison Avenue, 14th Floor
New York, NY 10016
posthillpress.com

with sincere appreciation to Larry Garinger

PROLOGUE

Hartford, Connecticut

By the time darkness fell over the blunt silhouette of the federal courthouse in Hartford, the building was all but abandoned. Now, one by one, the men and women who worked the janitorial night shift were arriving.

The cleaning crew was well known to the two federal officers manning the front door. The marshals would glimpse at the familiar I.D.'s, check handbags and backpacks, send the workers through the metal detector and off to their assigned areas.

Inside, long corridors led to courtrooms, judges' chambers and a labyrinth of other offices. There were floors to be mopped and waxed, wastebaskets to be emptied, desks and cabinets to be dusted, and other chores to be performed, a monotonous routine that was followed night after night as the building was prepared for the next day's business.

"Evenin' Dorothy," one of the U.S. Marshals greeted a middle-aged black woman as she placed her handbag on the conveyor belt that passed through the x-ray machine. "How you feeling?"

"Old and tired," she said with a short laugh.

"You and me both," he replied.

She stepped through the scanner, picked up her purse, and slowly headed down the hallway.

The next worker to come through the front door was a stranger to both marshals. He looked to be in his early thirties, a light-skinned African American, about six feet tall, well built, with a shaved head and a friendly face. No one had seen him standing across the street for the past twenty minutes, waiting in the shadows until Dorothy got there.

"Can I help you?" the senior guard asked him.

The man reached into his pocket and produced a piece of paper together with an identity card. "Preston came down with some sort of bug," he explained as he handed over the documents. "They called me in at the last minute."

The marshal checked the work order, then read his name off the plastic card. "David Prince."

"It's pronounced Daveed," the young man corrected him.

The marshal nodded. "Never seen you here before."

David Prince shrugged. "Been here a couple of times. I know my way around."

The Marshal called out to Dorothy and asked her to come back. "Just the same," he said, turning back to David, "Dorothy'll show you where to go. You're working for Preston, she's the one to let you know what you've gotta do."

David nodded. "That'll be great."

They had him empty his pockets, which contained nothing but a wallet, key ring and some chewing gum, then had him remove his belt. After David passed thought the metal detector, the marshal handed everything back, along with his identity card, but held onto the work order.

By now Dorothy had returned to the security desk. The marshal told her, "This is David Prince, filling in for Preston. You show him where to go and what to do."

Dorothy gave David a once over and sighed, as if to say this was just one more thing she didn't want to be bothered with.

"We got a big day here tomorrow," the guard reminded her with a smile.

"Don't I know it," Dorothy replied. Then she turned to David. "Come on, young fella. Preston does my heavy lifting, you get that honor tonight."

As they walked off, members of the night shift continued to show up and make their way to other sections of the building.

◉

A few hours later, after completing their assignments on the third floor and most of the second, Dorothy led David toward one of the larger courtrooms.

"They're having a ceremony in there tomorrow morning," she said.

The young man nodded, then politely volunteered to do whatever was needed to get it into shape.

"Got to have everything spic 'n span," she told him.

When they entered the large courtroom, David took a quick glance around.

"Looks pretty clean already."

Dorothy shook her head and fixed him with a disapproving stare.

David responded with a smile. "I'll go get the mop and pail."

"You know where the utility room is on this floor?"

"Sure do," he told her, then headed down the hall and found the supply closet. He entered the small space, switched on the light and pulled the door closed behind him.

Attaching a hose to the faucet, he began to fill the large bucket that sat on wheels beside the sink. Then he moved aside some boxes on the metal shelves to the right until he found what he was looking for.

Two days before, there had been a scheduled delivery of cleaning fluids and compounds. Secreted within those boxes were the deadly materials he was seeking: plastic explosives that had been molded so they could be hidden inside a drum of floor wax; two bottles disguised as glass cleaner, each containing a different colorless liquid which, when combined, formed a highly flammable explosive; and timing devices, more difficult to conceal, that had been taken apart, their pieces stowed amidst the packing materials and inside the handles of two new brushes.

David carefully placed the two clear bottles inside the large bucket, where they all but disappeared from view under the water. He placed the packets of C-4 explosives in the roomy back pockets of his overalls. Then he began assembling the detonators.

He was concentrating on the components of these timing devices, with the water still running, so he did not hear the door open behind him.

"What's taking you so . . . ," Dorothy began, but then stopped as she watched him at work on the small counter. "What the hell are those?"

David's plan was to convince the old lady to leave him in the courtroom, promising her that he would scrub the floors until they shined. He had no interest in killing her, since that would just create an unneeded complication. Just ten minutes alone was all he needed to accomplish what he had come there to do. After that he would finish the shift with her and they could walk out of the building together.

That was no longer an option.

When he turned to face her, the look in his eyes instantly told her all she needed to know. She made a move to back away and began to cry out, but he was too fast and too strong. He leapt at her with feline quickness, giving her shoulders a violent twist so he could grab her throat from behind, his muscular arm immediately beginning to choke the breath out of her.

Dorothy responded on instinct, the absolute wrong counter-measure. Instead of reaching back and trying to claw at his eyes, or punching down towards his groin, or even stamping her heel onto his foot, she reflexively reached up with both hands in an attempt to free herself from his grasp.

She had no chance against his brute strength.

David increased the pressure, his forearm so tight against her throat she could neither breathe nor scream. The more she struggled the sooner she ran out of oxygen. When her arms finally fell to her sides and her body went limp, he held on for another few seconds, then gave her head a powerful twist and snapped her neck.

Certain she was dead, he let go, her corpse sliding from his grip onto the floor.

"Damn," he snarled aloud, faced with two unexpected problems.

First, he had to find a place to hide her. Second, when he exited the building he would need a plausible explanation why he and Dorothy were not leaving together. He could not afford to arouse suspicion.

He shook his head. He would worry about his departure later. Right now he had to attend to the issue at hand—finding a place for her body. He turned off the water and threw a large rag over the detonators. He leaned down, took Dorothy under the arms, jerked her up and slung her over his right shoulder like a large sack of potatoes. Then he carried her across the hall.

The judicial ceremony would be in full swing by eleven the next morning. Wherever he put her, David had to be sure her corpse was not discovered before then. Using the passkey hanging from Dorothy's apron, he entered the warren of offices opposite the courtroom entrance.

He moved swiftly, even under the weight of Dorothy's inert form. He knew the other members of the cleaning crew were unlikely to venture into this part of the building, but there was always the chance one of the marshals might decide to come by on patrol, especially since they had never seen him before. He had to act fast.

He looked behind various large desks and tall cabinets, then spotted a storage closet toward the rear of the file rooms. He opened it and found dozens of dusty old boxes piled high, not a place that was likely to be visited any time soon. Dropping her body to the floor, he moved a stack of cartons out of the way, making enough room to lay Dorothy down. He then dragged her behind the cartons, replaced them, and had a look at his handiwork.

She was not visible, not unless someone stepped inside and moved the boxes aside. He pulled a rag from his pocket and wiped at the footprints he had made in the dust. Then he stood again and nodded to himself. It was the best he could do, so he shut the door and hurried out to the corridor and back inside the utility closet— this time locking himself in. If someone else was going to come looking for him this time, at least he would hear the key in the door.

He finished putting together the timing devices, gathered up a few other items that had been included in the lethal shipment, shoved them in his pockets, and opened the door. Mop in hand he wheeled the pail toward the courtroom.

Not making the same mistake twice, he locked himself inside, standing at the counsel tables in the middle of the spacious, high-ceilinged room, David pulled the two glass jars from the bucket of water, wiped them off and set them down. One contained polystyrene, the other benzene. Combined, they formed what is commonly known as napalm 2, a highly combustible substance that not only does tremendous damage to buildings and property but, when ignited, will cover its victims in a thick, fiery hail that clings and burns and kills.

He expertly blended the lethal mixture in three equal amounts, then poured the fluid into three clear plastic bags. Putting those carefully aside, he went about setting the timers on the triggering devices and connected each of those to a portion of the C4 *plastique*. That done, he placed each of the three armed detonators, together with the bags of fluid, into a second, thicker plastic bag, to help defeat any last-minute sweep by bomb sniffing dogs, although any such precaution would be highly unusual.

Americans are absurdly confident that their courthouses are safe places, he noted with contempt.

Next, he pulled out several adhesive strips that had also been left for him in the utility closet, and secured the three devices in the locations he had already chosen throughout the room.

He affixed the first beneath the judge's desk, all the way in the back, behind the drawer. He taped the second beneath one of the counsel tables, in the middle of the room. He hid the third under the front row of benches, in the area where spectators would sit.

Having a look around, David was satisfied everything was in order and no traces of his handiwork remained in evidence. He unlocked the door to the courtroom and went about the business of mopping the floor.

That was when he heard someone come in behind him.

"How you doin', young fella?"

David spun around and found himself facing the senior guard. "I'm good," he said.

The guard nodded, then asked, "Where's Dorothy? Didn't see her in the hallway."

David did his best to appear embarrassed. "You didn't see her leave?"

"She left?"

The young man shrugged. "She wasn't feeling all that well. We had most everything done, I told her I would finish up here." He grinned. "Had the sense she might try and slip out, maybe trying not to get docked."

The marshal looked more puzzled than upset. "That's not like Dorothy."

"Don't know what to tell you," David said. He was standing with the mop in hand, water dripping around his boots. "All right if I keep at this?"

"Sure, sure," the marshal replied. "How long ago did she leave?"

David was back to mopping, and didn't look up as he said, "Not that long."

The marshal turned and left the room, leaving David to do just as he had promised Dorothy—the floor would shine for the dignitaries who would be arriving in just a few hours.

PART ONE

CHAPTER 1

Hartford, Connecticut

Dressed in a navy blue suit, white shirt and red tie, Jordan Sandor left his brownstone apartment on West 76th Street in Manhattan, climbed into his weathered but reliable Land Rover, and headed to Hartford.

Sandor did not typically attend this sort of event for at least three reasons. First, in the world of clandestine operations he inhabited, anonymity was a priceless asset. Second, Sandor harbored a general distrust of authority and all its trappings. Third, he just hated the damn things because they were always boring and inevitably ran too long.

But today was different. Today was about Jim O'Hara, the man who served as Sandor's commanding officer in Iraq and who became so much more to him than that. O'Hara was being honored for his promotion from federal trial judge in Connecticut to the Court of Appeals in Manhattan, and Sandor was not going to miss it.

Unfortunately, by the time Sandor reached I-91 the morning rush hour was a brutal mess, and he cursed himself for not leaving earlier. He began weaving in and out of the slow moving traffic, doing all he could to arrive in time for the formal part of the proceedings. When he finally reached the Main Street exit, he knew it was going to be close. As he worried over his lousy timing, his cell phone rang.

"Sandor," he said, keeping his eyes on the road.

"Where the hell are you?" the familiar voice barked.

"Nearly there, sir," he told O'Hara. "Got tangled up a bit on the highway."

"Damnit son, haven't I taught you to prepare for every possible contingency in life? Didn't you have enough sense to realize there'd be rush hour traffic this time of the day?"

"Sorry sir, pulling into a parking lot right now."

"We've got judges, lawyers, even congressmen here. They all managed to arrive on time."

Sandor pulled his Rover to a stop in the first space he saw, ignored the parking meter as he jumped out and, with the phone to his ear, began running toward the building, "Almost at the front door," he reported as he raced across the empty plaza.

O'Hara began chuckling softly into the phone. "They're telling me they want to get this clambake fired up, but I didn't want to start without you. Had to be sure you were on your way."

"Almost there, just across the street now."

"All right," O'Hara said. "Get your ass up here." Then he signed off.

There were three Marshals on duty at the entrance, one manning the body scanner, one handling the search of bags and briefcases, the third added to the detail because of the VIPs in attendance.

Sandor already had pulled out his credentials—he was using his standard State Department cover—and, as held them up, he said, "I'm here for Judge O'Hara. Running a little late."

"Empty your pockets," the Marshal sitting at the desk told him.

Sandor quickly complied, then reached under his suit jacket and withdrew the Walther PPK from its holster at the small of his back. "My carry license is in there," he said, pointing to the billfold he had placed in the small tray on the table.

"Not any good in here," the marshal said. "Not today."

"You want to check my papers again?"

"I looked, don't need to check it again," the man said. "Since when does a State Department attaché need to carry?"

"It's a dangerous world out there," he said.

"Not in here," the marshal told him. "You want to go upstairs, you leave the gun with us."

Sandor didn't have time for a pointless debate. "Your rules pal."

The marshal took his time filling out a receipt, then had Sandor pass through the metal detector.

Shoving his billfold back in his pocket, Sandor asked, "Want to tell me where O'Hara's courtroom is, or is that a state secret?"

The guard at the desk didn't respond, but the man standing behind him said, "Second floor. If you take those stairs to your left it'll be faster than the elevator."

"Thanks," Sandor said, then raced for the stairway, taking them two at a time till he reached the landing where he saw the sign for the courtroom of James J. O'Hara, District Judge.

Sandor took a deep breath as he approached the oak door. It had a small window and, looking inside, he could see O'Hara standing behind the bench, talking to the large group assembled before him. Sandor smiled and began to pull the door open.

Later, he would not remember the sound of the explosion, the flash of lights, or being knocked backward across the corridor. All he would remember is looking through that small window and seeing the Old Man.

CHAPTER 2

Hartford, Connecticut

The celebratory scene inside the courtroom instantly turned to chaos. Fire engulfed parts of the room as shards of broken wood and chunks of plaster rained down on the attendees. The sprinkler system went on, but the main damage had already been done. Some people managed to scramble for the door. Others screamed in agony, rolling on the floor, their clothing and hair alight with the fiery napalm. The concussive force of the three blasts had injured some, knocked others unconscious and left most of the group dazed and disoriented.

Four people were already dead, including James J. O'Hara and his law clerk, who were both standing behind the judge's bench when the first explosion ripped them to shreds. Marshals and federal agents on duty in other parts of the building came running when they heard the blasts. Emergency calls were immediately made for armed backup and to Hartford Hospital for as much mobile help as they could arrange.

The hallway outside the courtroom became the staging area for improvised triage, looking more like a medical response after an attack in Afghanistan than a government facility in Connecticut. Blood and smoke were everywhere as the fires were brought under control by a combination of the sprinklers, extinguishers and every available blanket, coat and tarp that could be found.

All the while, cries of intense pain echoed along the marble corridor.

Ambulances and EMT vans arrived, pulling onto the sidewalk and into the plaza outside the front entrance. Stretchers were carried up to the second floor where victims were being removed in order of the severity of their injuries.

One of the first responders pointed to the inert form lying off to the side of the corridor, unconscious and bleeding from his head and left leg. They hurried over, lifted Jordan Sandor onto a stretcher, and carried him out.

The top floors of the building, several flights above Judge O'Hara's courtroom, housed various local federal offices, including Homeland Security and the FBI. Their local assistant directors were already tied into Washington on a teleconference. The questions from their superiors were coming faster than information could be assembled.

Where did the explosives come from and how had they been hidden inside the courtroom?

What sort of devices had been used?

Was this the work of a terrorist group or a lone madman?

What was being done to scour the area for a possible second assault?

Had they locked down the building, preventing anyone but the injured from leaving?

What sort of perimeter was being established outside the building?

Who was dealing with the media already gathering on Main Street?

Did anyone have a list of those present for the ceremony?

Could they put together a list of everyone who had been in and out of the building in the past three days?

How many hurt, how many dead?

While those exchanges were taking place between Hartford and Washington, an agent at CIA headquarters in Langley received a Code Red on her computer screen. She printed the notification and hurried upstairs, where she was immediately shown into the office of Deputy Director Mark Byrnes.

The notice indicated that one of the victims of the Hartford attack had been identified in the hospital emergency room by his State Department credentials. His I.D. carried a special number that routed the alert away from Foggy Bottom and to Langley.

Jordan Sandor was down, and Byrnes acted swiftly, putting a team in motion.

CHAPTER 3

Hartford, Connecticut

Hartford Hospital was overwhelmed with incoming casualties, EMT's and accompanying law enforcement personnel. The frenetic pace of the ensuing activity was being organized by a simple principle known to anyone who has ever worked in an emergency room—treat the most seriously injured first.

Today, that assessment was difficult to make. Several victims were still unconscious. Many were bleeding. Others had suffered third degree burns, and had to be prepared for transport to the nearest burn facilities. Those with concussions and broken bones were still being evaluated.

Dr. Robert Jamieson, an elegant looking man with silver hair and a demeanor that retained its calm even in the middle of this melee, was the senior physician on duty in the E.R. He was soon joined by department chiefs from a variety of disciplines. Head trauma, cardiac arrest, orthopedic issues and all types of organ damage needed to be appraised post haste.

This had become a war zone, and no one on staff was prepared for it.

"Who's attending this patient?" Dr. Jamieson called out as he approached the gurney holding the still insensible Jordan Sandor.

An intern hustled across the room. "Dr. Yang assigned me to watch him," the young man explained, "but I was called away for a moment."

Jamieson read the chart, then had a look at the damage. A surface wound to Sandor's head bore a large bandage, the bleeding from his left leg had been stopped, and x-rays had been ordered for his leg and shoulder. Right now, however, Jamieson's concern was that the patient was still unconscious, and the blow to his skull might be causing him to slip into a coma.

"Anyone see how his injuries were sustained?"

The intern shook his head. "Not sure. One of the guards who responded to the scene recognized him. Said he arrived late, had enough time to get upstairs and reach the courtroom when the first explosion went off. Based on where he was found, they think the door might have blown open and knocked him clear across the hallway."

Jamieson nodded as he took out his small flashlight, pulled back Sandor's right eyelid and had a look, then repeated the examination of his other eye. "This man may have internal cranial bleeding, could be putting pressure on his brain. Get Dr. Yang over here, we need to get him into the O.R., stat."

The intern, too overwhelmed by the circumstances to be worried about decorum in dealing with a senior staff physician, bluntly told him, "There are no O.R.'s available. We've got patients lined up in the hallways waiting for one."

A voice from behind them said, "Well then, find a place to do what you need to do, and get it done now."

As Jamieson turned, he found himself facing a tall, uniformed U.S. Marshal.

"I understand this is a difficult time for everyone," Jamieson responded politely, "but I don't think you should be involving yourself in medical procedures."

The marshal shook his head, as if the doctor was having trouble with the English language. "We just received notification from Washington to find a patient. Name is Jordan Sandor. This is him, right?"

Jamieson nodded.

"We have orders to get him treated immediately and keep him in protective custody. Incommunicado."

Jamieson's eyes widened. "Are you telling me this man is a suspect in the . . ."

"Exactly the opposite," the marshal interrupted. "I'm telling you we've been ordered to give this man the V.I.P. treatment until a team arrives from D.C."

Jamieson rocked back as if he had been hit with a short left jab. "V.I.P. treatment? Do you see who we've got here? Judges. State senators. A United States Congressman."

"And this guy Sandor," the marshal said, as if completing a list. "So please, do whatever you've got to do for him, and do it right now."

◉

There were any number of reasons that DD Byrnes of the CIA acted with such dispatch to ensure that Jordan Sandor was sequestered, treated and kept under wraps. Not the least of these was the need to preserve state secrets. A covert operative rendered unconscious, who is then revived in strange surroundings under heavy medication, is not someone the Agency wants engaging in idle conversation with anyone not cleared at the proper levels. Sandor had not been knocked out in a fist fight, he had been badly injured in a massive explosion, and he needed to be treated with special care.

The irony of the situation was not lost on Byrnes as he reviewed an email with a preliminary report on his agent's condition. If Sandor had died in the blast, the Agency would not even acknowledge they knew him. Dead, Sandor posed no risk. Alive and injured, his recovery needed to be managed.

⊙

Less than four hours after the explosions had been ignited, three men in suits, flashing federal credentials, arrived in the emergency room and asked who was in charge. They were pointed in the direction of Dr. Jamieson.

The tallest of the three men strode across the room and introduced himself. Craig Raabe was in his late thirties. He was tall, his face and scalp clean-shaven, his gait athletic. He was one of Sandor's closest friends, the agent he trusted more than any other when the shooting started. When Raabe gave his name to Dr Jamieson, it was in a voice so quiet it was almost a whisper.

Then he said, "You have a patient here, Jordan Sandor. We're here to take him to Washington."

Jamieson already had enough of this man Sandor to last him a lifetime, and shipping him off to D.C. sounded like a good idea. Still, he was obliged to say, "He's only been out of surgery for an hour."

Raabe called for the other two men to join them. The place was still jammed with patients, nurses and doctors, many of whom were now interested to learn if these three men had anything to do with the mystery patient that had been receiving such special care. Raabe, as if he owned the hospital, led his two colleagues and Dr. Jamieson to a small consulting room he spotted in a corner to his left. One of them, Raabe explained, was a doctor who had come to oversee Sandor's transfer.

The physician told Jamieson, "I've been briefed on the surgery. Any reason you feel a move would be dangerous?"

"Dangerous?" Jamieson asked. "We've only just been able to stop a cranial bleed that was about to mimic a stroke. His vital signs are stable, but the next few hours will be critical to his recovery. How do you plan to get him to Washington?"

Craig Raabe told him, "A medivac chopper on the roof will take us back to Bradley. We have a plane waiting for us there."

Jamieson treated them each to a look of incredulity. Then he said, "Gentlemen, I don't know who the hell this Sandor is, but I've got an E.R. that's filled with patients who have yet to receive any treatment beyond bandages and pain-killers." Then he turned to the doctor who would be taking charge of the case. "If you're willing to sign the release forms, and you think it makes sense to put this man on a helicopter and an airplane, then good luck to all of you."

Jamieson was about to walk away when Raabe held up his hand to stop him. "Doctor, I know you're doing your job here. We appreciate that. It's a tough day for all of us. But if Sandor's vital signs are stable, a chopper ride and a flight to Washington are not going to be an issue for him."

Jamieson responded with a deadly serious look. "He's still unconscious, you understand that?"

"I do."

"All right," Jamieson said. "Sign the papers and we'll release him."

"We'll sign," Raabe said. "Then you'll need to give us his chart and any other paperwork you have with his name on it."

The way he said it, Jamieson knew it was more than a request. He also knew this conversation was over.

CHAPTER 4

Hamilton, Bermuda

Corinne Stansbury was a bright young woman on the fast track to success in the world of international finance, but not every such path is without detours. Several months ago her superiors at Randolph Securities suggested she move from their headquarters in Great Britain to "cover the desk in Hamilton," as they phrased it.

She agreed.

Corinne knew that she was being shipped off to one of the firm's secondary locations, but there were reasons she was willing to put some time in there. The upgrade in lifestyle was undeniable, as she traded the cold gray skies and urban tensions of London for warm pink sand and the relaxed attitude of Bermuda. Her apartment, in a luxury building, was twice the size of her flat in Knightsbridge, and had a sensational view of the ocean. And there was the all-important increase in authority, at least locally, which in the long term should enhance an already impressive résumé.

Then, of course, there was the opportunity to escape the rumors of those extra-curricular activities her detractors claimed had helped advance her career back home.

It was not surprising that a single woman with Corinne's charms and intellect would become involved with men in her profession. Nearing her thirty-fifth birthday, she possessed assets beyond an extensive knowledge of global markets, currency trading and arbitrage. Her lovely face was framed by brunette hair that contrasted beautifully with an alabaster complexion she maintained even under the brilliant island sun. Her eyes were a rich brown, and she could adjust her gaze from cool intensity to tender vulnerability, as the situation required. Then there was her shapely figure, which one of her colleagues had judged "built for pleasure."

In many ways it was not easy being an attractive woman in a business dominated by alpha males. When the assignment in Hamilton was suggested, Corinne understood that the man at the top of Randolph Securities was doing her a favor, and she knew that declining the offer was out of the question. She accepted, even though it temporarily removed her from the center of the firm's operations. Her plan was to excel at this new post and then be welcomed back to London at a higher level of responsibility.

After just a few boring weeks living and working in the tranquil environs of Bermuda, she hoped her return to the U.K. came sooner rather than later.

Tonight, however, she was looking forward to dinner with a highly placed fund trader who was in town for a few days to compare off-shore investment opportunities in the Cayman Islands, the Jersey Islands and elsewhere. Both he and Corinne saw the possibility of an alliance of one sort or another.

In preparation for the evening ahead she chose an appropriate outfit. This was not an occasion for a corporate pants suit.

She started with a black thong, then selected a matching bra that comfortably augmented her ample cleavage. She slipped into a slinky, navy blue dress, the décolletage working well with the bra, the fabric clinging to her ass as if it was painted on, the hem short enough to show off most of her long legs. Then she sat at the dressing table in her bedroom to apply her makeup as she caught up with the headlines from CNN.

Corinne was absently listening to the report of an explosion at a courthouse in Hartford, Connecticut when they began to name some of the V.I.P.'s who were in attendance. One of those injured was being identified as a Saudi diplomat believed to be a Director of Finance for the World Health Institute. She put her mascara brush down and turned to the television, waiting for a name, until the reporter announced that officials were not prepared to release any further information about the man at this time.

She picked up her cell phone, punched in the speed-dial number, and listened as the call went directly into voicemail. She decided not to leave a message, rang off, and sat there staring at the television screen when she was surprised by the doorbell. She glanced at the clock—if it was her date, he was early.

She hastily painted on some lipstick, fluffed her hair and went to the door. She was surprised to find two men there she had never seen before, one of whom was displaying a badge.

"Miss Stansbury?"

"Yes."

Holding up the I.D. so she could have a better look, he said, "We need a word with you." Corinne remained standing in the doorway. "About what?"

"As you can see, we're with Interpol. We're investigating a series of currency transactions." He gave a theatrical look up and down the corridor. "You really want to have this conversation here, in your hallway?"

Corinne took a quick peek, as if expecting a neighbor to be eavesdropping on their discussion. There was no one else there. "Isn't this a rather odd time and place to be dropping by?"

The two men exchanged a quick glance. Then the first man said, "We have no interest in advertising the fact that we're conducting this inquiry, and since you're not a target we thought it would be less embarrassing for you if we spoke here. If you prefer, we could come to your office in the morning."

Corinne hesitated, feeling more suspicious than nervous.

"All right," she said and stepped aside. "But I'm expecting company very shortly."

"This will only take a few minutes," the first man assured her as he walked in, followed by his associate.

Corinne shut the door and led them toward the living room. Even before they had walked the length of the foyer, however, the second man moved forward. He had been holding a syringe, out of view, and now plunged the slender needle into her left thigh.

"What the hell . . . ," Corinne began, but the first man swiftly covered her mouth with his hand, taking her around the throat with his other arm. He was careful not to apply too much pressure. They wanted no bruises, no sign of a struggle.

Corinne twisted against his tight grip, but the second man was already lifting her legs in the air as they carried her inside.

"We're going to sit you down here. No harm will come to you," the first man assured her. "We just need to ask some questions and the drug we administered will make it certain you are going to tell us the truth."

Corinne was already feeling disoriented, her strength seeming to flow out of her as they lowered her onto the couch. When he removed his hand from her mouth she wanted to scream, but could not. All she felt was a violent pounding in her chest, her heartbeat accelerating as if she were running a mad dash to nowhere.

The first man sat beside her, doing his best to keep her upright. "You'll be just fine in a few moments," he told her, but now Corinne could barely make out what he was saying. She was beginning to convulse, her racing heart reaching a crescendo until it seemed to explode in a painful spasm that left her gasping for air. Then she slumped forward.

The first man felt for her carotid artery. She was dead.

The second man took a prescription bottle from his pocket and placed it in Corinne's lifeless hand. Pressing her fingers together to ensure her fingerprints would be all over the container, he then removed it with a handkerchief and walked it into her bedroom, where he placed it on her dressing table. "In here," he called out to the first man.

Leaving Corinne on the couch, he joined his accomplice in the bedroom.

"Looks like she was getting ready for a night out."

"Perfect," the first man said.

They went back to the living room, lifted Corinne, and carried her inside. There, they sat her on the seat in front of the vanity. Holding her in place, they smoothed out her dress and hair, then let go, allowing her to tumble onto the floor, the victim of a heart attack brought on by the use of too many amphetamines.

They wiped the entire place clean of their fingerprints, including everywhere they had touched Corinne.

Then they left.

CHAPTER 5

London

Charles Colville was the office manager of Randolph Securities Ltd. in London, a position he held not because of his administrative brilliance, but because he was the nephew of the company's founder and Chief Executive Officer, Alfred Randolph Colville. RSL was an international investment firm with posh offices around the world, a collection of elite clients, and a roster of talented traders with large expense accounts and even larger egos.

Charles was not one of those making the critical financial decisions that are the lifeblood of RSL's success. His job was to oversee the ministerial tasks his uncle entrusted to him. Unfortunately, as is often the case in such nepotistic arrangements, the caterpillar ultimately becomes dissatisfied with his comfortable sinecure and longs to be a butterfly.

Lately, Charles had been making moves to realize that ambition. As he told one of his recent bedmates—an up and coming assistant trader with large breasts, an inviting look, and a willing nature—one cannot sit in the middle of these huge financial transactions without developing a certain know-how about how successful trades are made. Charles was convinced osmosis alone had imbued him with the ability to successfully play in this arena. After too much claret and too little discretion, Charles bragged to the young woman that he had figured out how some of the smartest operators in the firm were making large scores buying and selling currencies—arbitrage, as it was called—and he had begun mimicking their actions through an account he opened in an independent brokerage firm. He even went so far as to offer some of this insider information to the woman, if she was interested.

She was and, foolishly, he did.

Ironically, the person Charles really wanted to tell about his newfound wisdom was his uncle, but he realized that would be an even bigger blunder than the mistake he had made in sharing it with the shapely woman from the trading desk. Alfred Randolph Colville—Freddie, as he was known to those closest to him— repeatedly told his nephew that he didn't want him to be clever, he merely wanted him to be his eyes and ears in the London office.

Charles was therefore obliged to keep his cleverness to himself. Most of the time. He had made a small killing over the past week by shorting Euros, and tonight he was treating himself to a date with a luscious Russian girl—tall, blond and, according to the friend who had introduced them over drinks, an aspiring model. They would have dinner at Annabel's, do some gambling at one of the private clubs where his uncle maintained a membership, and then back to his flat.

Before he left the office, Charles logged into his travel account to check on the flights he had booked to and from Bermuda the following week. Even as he tried to focus on Corinne and what awaited him there, he still found himself thinking of this Russian girl—did she say she liked to be called Natasha or Natalia, suddenly he couldn't recall—remembering the photo she had sent him, envisioning her impossibly long legs, full lips and bedroom eyes.

He held that image in mind as he rode down on the lift, already becoming aroused as he stepped onto Jermyn Street and looked for the car that should have already picked her up and would by now be taking them to the restaurant. When he spotted the driver across the street he gave a brief nod and stepped off the curb. Suddenly, a dark sedan to his right accelerated so quickly that he never had a chance to get out of the way. It struck him without ever hitting the brakes, tossing him in the air and leaving him for dead as it sped off.

As Charles lay in the gutter, painfully struggling to draw his last breath, the driver of the limousine across the way slowly pulled away and departed the scene.

CHAPTER 6

Washington, D.C.

A week after the bombing, Jordan Sandor was being released from Walter Reed Medical Center. As the doctors cautioned him, he was still far from healed. The explosion had damaged his previously injured left leg, and caused various lacerations, but those wounds would mend in their normal course. It was the seriousness of his neurological injuries that concerned them. Not only had the blast created a major concussive force, but the heavy oak door Sandor was opening when the blast occurred was driven off its hinges, striking him in the head and forcing him across the wide corridor, knocking him senseless. He had remained unconscious for nearly twenty-four hours, with the full repercussions yet to be determined. His recovery was a work in progress. His fellow agent, Craig Raabe, came to collect him and give him a ride, offering the guest room in his D.C. apartment as a place to pursue his recovery. It was a high rise with a well-equipped fitness center in the basement, but Sandor refused.

"Time for me to go home," he said.

Home for Sandor was a third-floor walkup in a Manhattan brownstone.

"Use some sense," Raabe said. "Getting up and down the stairs on your bum leg is not going to be fun. I've got an elevator and a gym right there in the building where you can do your rehab."

Sandor shook him off. "Thanks, but I need to be home."

Raabe knew his friend well enough not to waste any more time on the debate. "All right, I'll help you get to New York," he said, then watched as the nurse on duty insisted that Sandor climb into a wheelchair.

"Is this really necessary?" Sandor asked the attractive young black woman who was doing the insisting.

"Couldn't find any roller skates your size," she told him.

Sandor responded with a frown.

"S.O.P.," she said. "Don't want you falling on your way out. Liability is a bitch."

"And after that?"

Now she smiled. "After that, you're on your own."

Sandor reluctantly lowered himself in the seat, and Craig walked alongside as the nurse pushed the chair. "Before we get out of here, you should know someone is waiting to see you."

Sandor looked up. "Byrnes?"

"Oh yeah. You should also know that he came by a couple of times to have a look at you when you were doing your Rip Van Winkle."

"Stopped by to tuck me in?"

"Probably making sure you weren't talking in your sleep."

"What a guy."

"You caught a serious shot to the head, Jordan. The doctors say you need to take this seriously."

"All right, mom," Sandor said. "I'll go home and rest my brain. Won't even watch *Jeopardy!*"

Raabe turned to the nurse. "Why not let me just push him down a flight of stairs?"

Instead, they rode down in the elevator, then entered the spacious lobby where they spotted Deputy Director Byrnes and one of his assistants waiting near the front.

"I'll take it from here," Raabe told the nurse.

"Procedures . . . ," she began, but Raabe held up his hand.

"It'll be okay," he told her, then moved her aside and began rolling Sandor away.

"Bye gorgeous," Sandor called over his shoulder. "Don't forget to write."

When they reached Byrnes, the first thing the DD asked was whether the wheelchair was necessary.

Sandor stood up and grabbed hold of the cane Raabe was carrying for him. "Exactly what I wanted to know."

"You okay to walk?"

"Yes sir."

"Good. My car's out front, we need to have a private conversation."

As they stepped outside, Byrnes asked Sandor how he felt.

"As good as I could expect."

Byrnes nodded. "Take all the time you need to recover."

"I'll be ready to get back in the saddle sooner than you think."

"We'll see," the DD said. When they reached his car, he told Sandor and Raabe to get in the back, excusing his assistant and driver so he could be alone with his two agents.

He climbed in the front passenger seat and turned to face them. "I'm going to be blunt here. I'm concerned about the comments I received from your neurologist."

Sandor feigned outrage. "You spoke with my doctor? Ever hear of patient confidentiality?"

Byrnes treated Sandor to one of his patented frowns. "Your health is a security issue. I have every right to know your condition so I can be certain the Agency is not at risk. For that matter, as long as I consider you one of our assets, I have no intention of putting *you* at risk." He paused, then added, "I also won't sit still for you doing anything irresponsible."

"Meaning what?"

"Meaning I know how close you were to Jim O'Hara, and I know you're going to want to involve yourself in the investigation of this attack. But I don't have to remind you—"

Sandor cut him off. "I'm not that fuzzy-headed anymore, sir. You're going to tell me this is a domestic crime, that the Agency has no jurisdiction, and that I'll be in a world of trouble if I start poking around in any way that takes advantage of my federal credentials. That about right?"

"It appears you're recovering faster than predicted."

"Okay, so I've been warned. Now, do you really expect me to sit around and do nothing about this?"

"That's exactly what I expect. And by the way, given your condition, sitting around is absolutely the best thing you could do for yourself." He looked at Raabe. "We'll line up a topnotch rehab program for him in New York."

Sandor was not interested in discussing a workout program. "May I remind you, sir, that in addition to murdering Jim, these bastards killed several other fairly important people, injured dozens and almost put me in the morgue, just in case any of that wasn't in the report."

"I'm fully aware of the situation."

"Good. So, while I've been laid up for a week being drugged and poked and prodded, has anyone come up with a theory why O'Hara would have been the target of a terrorist attack? Or who was responsible?"

"No to both of those questions. Not yet. If you have any ideas I'd be happy to hear them."

"As you say, not yet."

Byrnes shook his head. "If you have any bright notions, let me know, but I don't want you doing anything more than thinking about it."

They were quiet for a moment, then Sandor asked, "Any word on how his wife is doing?"

Byrnes nodded. "She was nowhere near him at the time of the explosion. Her physical injuries were minor, but she saw him torn to shreds. Not good."

Sandor took a deep breath to steady himself. "I should go and see her."

"Not yet, Jordan. She's still confined to bed. They're doing what they can for her, but it's not good."

The sadness in his eyes turned to anger. "So you said. And you just want me to sit back and do nothing."

"You know the deal here, don't screw with this. I won't be able to do a thing to bail you out of trouble if you start coloring outside the lines." When Sandor managed a look of unreserved innocence, Byrnes turned to Raabe. "Get him to bed will you? Maybe someplace he can be strapped in."

CHAPTER 7

London

Freddie Colville was seated behind his large desk, an impressive rectangular slab of polished marble that sat on four narrow chrome legs. It had no drawers or other functional accessories, its sole purpose being the imposition of an appropriate distance between its owner and anyone occupying the chairs facing him. This afternoon, his visitors were Mark Killian and Eduardo Cristo from the World Health Institute, the largest client of Randolph Securities. Colville, as he approached sixty-five, remained trim and elegant, his generous head of silver hair framing a face that featured an aquiline nose, prominent jaw and steel-gray eyes. His appearance suited both his position and upbringing—his bespoke suit was from Saville Row, his handcrafted shoes from John Lobb, his made-to-measure shirts from Turnbull & Asser, his attitude entitled.

He was normally a cheerful man but today, as he continued to struggle with the deaths of his nephew Charles and his protégé Corinne Stansbury, his mood was uncharacteristically somber.

Killian, who ran the not-for-profit international organization known as WHI, was a tall, red-haired man, with broad shoulders and a rough-hewn look that was in stark contrast to Colville's gentile style. However, his lumberjack looks were never going to fool anyone for long. He was a worldly man who had the ability to move comfortably through the upper echelons of society, and an understanding of how to get things done in those rarified environs. As he would remind whatever doubters might still exist, one does not raise hundreds of millions of dollars for a humanitarian cause without knowing how to play the money game at the highest levels.

Eduardo Cristo was WHI's top financial officer, a board certified physician who became more interested in the business of medicine than its actual practice. He held various positions in biotechnology companies before being tapped by Killian to head their investment department.

Over the course of time, through their numerous dealings, Colville, Killian, and Cristo had become friends as well as business associates, and they had gathered to discuss both aspects of those relationships. Killian and Cristo had met Freddie's nephew Charles any number of times, and both had dealings with Corinne. They shared their thoughts about these tragedies, including the predictable observations about two young people who had been taken far too soon. Then Killian got down to the matter of how these events might impact pending transactions involving WHI.

"Before we deal with that," Freddie Colville asked, "have you any further word on Hassan?"

Shahid Hassan, a member of the Saudi royal family, was one of those injured in the Hartford bombing. He was not only a diplomat working on behalf of his government, he was also a key envoy for

WHI. The United States government had just released the names of those killed and injured in the attack, and Hassan was included in the latter group.

"He's all right," Killian replied. "We've been in touch. He'll be at the United Nations function."

"Good," Colville said. "Does he still intend to accompany the mission to Iraq?"

"So he says," Killian reported.

Colville nodded, "Good," he repeated, appearing for the moment to be distracted by something. "Threes," he said. "They say bad news comes in threes." The other two men waited.

"Well," Colville said, prepared to return to the real purpose of their discussion. "I can assure you that my nephew's death, sad as it is for me, will have no bearing on any of your outstanding trades. Charles oversaw administration, he was not involved in the other aspects of our business."

Killian turned to Cristo, who picked up the cue.

"Are you certain?" he asked.

Freddie Colville blinked. "I'm not sure I understand."

"Go ahead," Killian encouraged Cristo. "We're all on the same team here."

Cristo leaned forward, although the expanse of the large marble desk between them defeated any effort at intimacy. "We have information regarding financial activities in which your nephew was engaged. We were compiling the data with the intention of bringing it to you.

Then of course . . . ," He left the last part unspoken.

"What sort of financial activities?"

"It appears Charles opened up accounts at two outside brokerage houses. He was tracking trades being made here at RSL, mimicking them for his own benefit."

Colville leaned back, stared up at the ceiling and emitted a long sigh.

"I believe that would be a breach of protocol on at least two fronts," Killian weighed in.

Still looking upward, Colville agreed. "Indeed it would. Given his position, he was prohibited from owning outside accounts."

"Yes," Killian agreed. "Then there is the more serious matter of co-opting proprietary information from your traders, without their knowledge, and using it for his personal gain."

Colville slowly lowered his head, and met Killian's gaze. "Most disturbing."

"Which brings us to the matter of Fronique. What do we do about that?" Killian asked.

Fronique was a French manufacturer of highly advanced technological equipment. The company had an extremely low profile in the investment community, but Corinne Stansbury had done her homework and encouraged Freddie Colville to take a large financial position in the company on behalf of WHI. That created a potential public relations issue when they discovered Fronique was not only working on UAV's designed strictly for surveillance, but they were also developing military-style drones with strike capabilities. The obvious solution was to have WHI divest itself of the asset, but they were all convinced the advances being made at Fronique would become incredibly lucrative. Corinne had therefore set up a complex matrix of offshore companies to shield WHI from any embarrassing connection to the French manufacturer.

Whether Killian and Cristo were comfortable with the arrangement was a matter for conjecture. With Corinne's death, several questions would inevitably need to be answered. The most obvious, of course, was the one just posed by Killian—now that Corinne was not around to run interference for them, what should they do about Fronique?

"I don't think we have to do anything, at least not yet," Colville replied. "Corinne had things well organized, and Charles had nothing to do with Fronique."

Killian nodded at Cristo, calling on him once again to deliver the bad news. "To the contrary, I'm afraid. In at least one of his outside accounts, Charles purchased shares of Fronique. And then— forgive me for being indelicate—there is the matter of the personal relationship between your nephew and Corinne."

Colville blinked. "That was over some time ago."

"Perhaps," Killian said, sounding unconvinced. "But someone passed him enough information to motivate him to buy stock in an obscure company."

"Your point is well made," Colville conceded. "However, Charles is gone now."

"Sadly, yes. But we need to unravel those accounts of his as quietly as possible. More important, perhaps, we need to know who *he* might have spoken to about Fronique."

"What makes you think he would have been foolish enough to tell anyone what he was up to?"

Killian gave him a look that suggested he did not want to speak badly of the recently departed. "Let's just say that your nephew's propensity for boasting about his brilliant trades is how we discovered what he was doing in the first place."

Colville groaned. "It's upsetting enough to learn that Charles has been disloyal, but to imagine he shared the information with someone else is unconscionable." He stopped for a moment, trying to get his mind around what an imbecile his late brother's son had turned out to be. "Who did he speak to?"

"Girls," Cristo said.

"Girls? As in the plural?"

"Yes. Women he took out."

Colville uttered a bitter laugh. "His models," he said derisively.

"And one of the women you have working here," Cristo added.

Colville stared at Cristo. "You've been in contact with these women?"

"Let's just say I'm acquainted with some of the young ladies he found attractive as companions."

"My God, you set him up with these women?"

Cristo, remaining unruffled, said, "Your nephew called on me from time to time to make introductions."

Killian intervened. "The important thing is that Eduardo can handle the damage on that front. The real issue is what to do with the structure Corinne created. We need to know who will be picking up the pieces."

Colville assured them he would put his top manager in charge of the transition.

"Good," Killian said. "Coordinate anything you need through my office." It was not an offer, it was an order.

"Of course," Colville agreed.

"Our biggest fear right now," Killian reminded him, "is the possibility that any one of a number of regulatory agencies might delve into these businesses. The timing of the deaths of Charles and Corinne will increase that likelihood."

Colville, having been knocked about enough for one day, said, "You have absolutely nothing to fear on that score. Every transaction ever made on your behalf has been above board."

"I know that, Freddie," Killian told him. "We're concerned about image rather than substance right now."

"Exactly," Cristo said.

Colville decided to change the subject. "Are you both going to attend the affair at the U.N.?"

"I'll be going," Killian said. "Eduardo is going to stay here and work on these issues."

"Sorry you'll miss it, I'm sure Hassan will be sorry you're not there," Colville said. Then he turned back to Killian. "I can give you a lift on the company plane."

"That would be excellent. We'll need to come back here right afterward, too much to do."

"Of course," Colville said, "I completely agree."

CHAPTER 8

New York City

Ten days after his release from the hospital, Jordan Sandor was engaged in a rigorous workout at the health club he used near his apartment. Notwithstanding the instructions given by DD Byrnes, he was not about to trust his rehabilitation to a physical therapist assigned by the Agency. Over the years Sandor had suffered a number of serious injuries, in too many clandestine missions to name, and he knew his body better than anyone. He engaged the help of a trainer he knew at the gym on Amsterdam Avenue, but was primarily on his own as he struggled to recover his strength and stamina.

Sandor pushed himself hard, determined to get back into combat-ready condition as soon as possible so he could avenge the death of the man who had been so influential in shaping his life.

When Sandor was in the Army, he served a tour in a hot zone in Iraq, and Col. James O'Hara was the officer in charge. From the outset, Sandor challenged his C.O. with his inherent distrust of authority and a willingness to voice those doubts.

He soon found that O'Hara was no one to be trifled with.

A graduate of West Point and Yale Law School, O'Hara ignored the easy route made available to him, refusing an offer to join the staff of the Judge Advocate General, choosing instead to serve in combat. By his reasoning, he was trained at the Point, and he owed his country more than a couple of years shoving legal papers around.

O'Hara had a talent for leadership, including an innate ability to make friends without creating enemies. Unlike some who possess that skill, O'Hara was no glad-hander. He could read people and had no qualms telling them what he thought, whether or not they wanted to hear it. Yet somehow he could do it in a way that was neither accusatory nor judgmental. He never sought to make anyone feel wrong or inadequate. He tried instead to inspire by his words and his example, always allowing people a back door if they needed one. People learned that they could count on him for the truth, and he was respected rather than disliked for that quality.

Managing his young lieutenant was therefore no problem.

O'Hara found ways to deal with Sandor's behavior that other officers would have had neither the ability nor the interest to try. He learned about Sandor's background—his father's death in Vietnam; his mother's mysterious disappearance; and the fact that he was raised by grandparents who were never quite sure how to handle the bright, athletic, brooding boy.

Through the prism of Sandor's personal history, O'Hara saw the young man's potential, recognizing instincts that cannot be taught, an aptitude for skills that can, and a primal need for someone to set him on a path that would exploit those talents.

O'Hara also saw that the young lieutenant, whatever his personal issues might be, never failed in his performance as a soldier, and never put his men at risk. While off-duty, Sandor found time for girls, alcohol, and the occasional fistfight—but O'Hara understood that was all part of what occurred when tension, fear and testosterone levels ran high. Still, whenever the starting bell rang, Sandor was ready for action, and his performance as a soldier was exemplary.

Rather than trying to break Sandor's spirit, O'Hara managed to harness his energy and refocus his anger, leaving enough of the grit intact so he could pursue the career O'Hara was convinced he was born for. When their tour was over and O'Hara was chosen for a stint with Army Intelligence, he took Sandor with him. Soon thereafter, O'Hara spoke with former classmates who were now highly placed in Washington. That was when he arranged an invitation for Sandor to meet with recruiters for the Central Intelligence Agency.

Not long after that, O'Hara and Sandor lost touch, which is standard operating procedure for someone being inducted into Clandestine Services. Your past has to evaporate into the ether as a new life is created. O'Hara moved from Intelligence to his role as a prosecutor, and then to the federal bench. Sandor became a fast-moving shadow for the CIA, and although his one-time C.O. did what he could to keep an eye on his progress, O'Hara knew enough not to ask too many questions. He and his wife never had children, so O'Hara retained a special affection for his former junior officer, even if their contact was now only on rare occasions. O'Hara was a jurist who needed to keep his distance, and Sandor inhabited a world where friends are the rarest and most dangerous of commodities.

This morning, as Sandor remembered his days with O'Hara, he continued to test himself in his workout. Yesterday he had concentrated on exercises for his injured leg, so today he focused on his upper body, particularly his damaged shoulder. Lying on a bench, he was into his second set of reps pressing a barbell, when he heard someone come up from behind and ask, "That the best you can do?"

Sandor lowered the weight into its brackets and twisted around, stunned to see his old friend Howard Lerner standing there, the familiar smile in place. "Joey Sax?"

Lerner laughed. "No one has called me that in a long time, buddy."

Sandor sat up, grabbed his towel and wiped off his face. "How long?"

"Don't start counting, you'll only depress me."

Lerner was average in height and build, with a wiry physique and lousy posture that always made him seem even shorter than he was. He had dark hair that was so curly it looked perpetually uncombed. He had an even nose, brown eyes, and an expressive mouth that could display any number of attitudes, ranging from curiosity to outrage to humor, sometimes all at once. He was, among other talents, a gifted musician, hence the nickname from years past.

"You don't look any the worse for wear," Sandor told him.

"Wish I could say the same about you. You okay?"

"Tough workout," Sandor said, then got to his feet and held out his hand. "Too sweaty to give you a hug."

"You were never my type anyway."

Sandor had a look at his friend's suit and tie. "You're obviously not here to run the track. To what do I owe this pleasure?"

"I needed to speak with you. In person."

"You make that sound fairly ominous. No 'How are you?' 'How's life?' None of the usual banter?"

"We'll have time for that later, but this is not the time or the place."

"How did you find me here?"

"I've got connections." When Sandor did not reply. Lerner shrugged. "I stopped by your building. You weren't home so I rang some bells. One of your neighbors said you might be here."

"You could've called."

"Like I said, I needed to see you in person."

Sandor nodded. "Damn, it really has been a long time."

"It sure has."

"Last time we spoke, you were circling the globe like a modern-day Magellan. Where you headquartered nowadays?"

"London, mostly. For the moment I'm here in New York, staying at the St. Regis. I've got a couple of things to do this morning, but I was hoping you could meet me there, at the King Cole Bar. Say two o'clock?"

Sandor gave him a long, searching look. "That's it? That's all I get for now, after all this time?"

"Can you make it?"

"Sure," Sandor said. "I'll be there."

The King Cole is one of New York's finest watering holes. Some complain that it has become a bit *tourista*, a case of popularity destroying the cachet, but Sandor believed places only become famous because they are worthy of it, for one reason or another. The Statue of Liberty, Rockefeller Center and the Empire State Building—they're no less majestic because people from out-of-town want to stop by and gawk at them.

Sandor arrived just after two, and found his old friend already seated at a quiet table in the corner of the room, facing the large mural behind the bar. Making his way across the floor, he did what he could to disguise the slight limp that yet persisted, but could not avoid wincing as he lowered himself onto the banquette.

"Pull a muscle in your workout?"

"No," Sandor said, "just a little banged up is all. You heard about Hartford."

"Of course."

"I was there."

"You were with the Old Man?"

"Not exactly. I got there late, walked in just in time to catch a door with my face." Sandor shook his head.

"My God, I had no idea."

"Yeah, lucky me," Sandor said.

"From what I saw on television, you *are* lucky."

"Maybe so." Sandor gave him a look that said he didn't want to talk about it, at least not now.

The waiter came by and Sandor ordered a ginger ale.

"No Jack Daniels?" Lerner asked.

"Doesn't work all that well with painkillers," Sandor said. What he did not say, was that he was not actually taking any of the drugs the doctors had prescribed for him. He was still dealing with the after-effects of the head trauma, and that was the reason he was passing on a cocktail. "Getting over a nasty bump to the head."

Lerner gave him a look of real concern. "But you're basically okay?"

"Basically."

"Well, please forgive me buddy, I ordered a Black Label on the rocks."

Sandor smiled. "Just like old times," he said.

Lerner and Sandor had served together in Iraq, right out of college, a couple of gung ho patriots from military families. Lerner's father was an enlisted lifer who finally retired as a master sergeant several years back. Sandor's father was a lieutenant, killed in the line of duty at the very end of the war in Vietnam. He was leading a patrol along the periphery of the DMZ when the corporal just behind him stepped on a land mine. Sandor had just been born, and so his father never even got to see him.

After Lerner and Sandor completed their tour of duty together, Jordan was assigned to intelligence by O'Hara, and re-upped. Lerner headed back to school, earned an MBA at Wharton, a doctorate at

Harvard, and since then became wealthy as a renowned brainiac in finance. He married young and divorced after a few years, leaving behind two daughters who were now living in Southern California with his ex-wife.

As often happens, comrades-in-arms stay in touch for a while, then their life paths diverge, but never lose the bond forged in battle.

Sandor asked about the girls. "I haven't seen them since they were babies," Sandor said.

"Wouldn't let the likes of you anywhere near them now," Lerner said. "They're beautiful." He pulled out his cell phone and gave Sandor a look at several flattering pictures of two dark-haired girls in their early teens.

"They really are beautiful. Good thing Carmella was a looker."

"Did you say the former Mrs. Lerner was a hooker? I knew I was lucky to get rid of her."

Sandor handed back the phone, realizing again how much time had passed since they last saw each other.

"It's been nearly ten years," Lerner said, reading his friend's mind.

Sandor nodded. "Looks as if life's been good to you." He cast an approving eye at Lerner's outfit. "Custom made suit, probably English. Tie is definitely French, shoes are Italian. Appears you're a one man support system for the global economy."

"Money buys things," Lerner said without any enthusiasm for the concept.

"So they tell me."

"Including trouble."

"Aha."

The waiter returned, and they remained silent until their drinks were served and they were left alone again. Then Sandor said, "It appears the time has come for you to explain the reason for this reunion." He lifted his soda and said *"Cent'anni."* They clinked glasses and he took a drink. Then Sandor fixed his friend with a serious look and said, "The floor is yours."

CHAPTER 9

CIA Headquarters, Langley, Virginia

Deputy Director Mark Byrnes was in his office on a videoconference, receiving an update from the FBI on their investigation into the attack in Hartford. The call included representatives of the Department of Homeland Security and the National Security Agency.

New information indicated that the group responsible for the explosion was a fringe terrorist organization out of North Africa calling itself Ansar al-Thar. Byrnes suggested they get some background information from a member of his team, and asked Gabe Somerset to join them.

Somerset had recently returned from assignment in Algeria and then Niger, where he represented the CIA as the American drone base in Niamey was being created. He was knowledgeable about various splinter groups spawned by al Qaeda and ISIS. He was also a vocal advocate for the new UAV technology—eyes-in-the-sky with strike capabilities—over the old-fashioned "boots on the ground" approach.

He was shown into Byrnes' office, and the DD asked him to share whatever intel he had on Ansar al-Thar.

"Relatively new band of renegades," Somerset told them. "Small, not well-financed, and very violent. Sympathetic to ISIS. Led by a Syrian, name of Nizan Farashi. We're still gathering details on his personal history, but we know that he's a radical, even by the standards of Islamic extremists. His followers believe they are the true acolytes of bin Laden. No action is too cruel or too brutal, far as they're concerned."

Richard Bebon, Deputy Director from the FBI, asked, "Have they actually claimed responsibility for Hartford?"

"Not directly, no," Somerset admitted. "However, the chatter we've been monitoring points to Ansar al-Thar as the group behind the attack."

The man from the NSA agreed. "We have the same intel."

There was a knock at the door and Craig Raabe entered, carrying a copy of the newly developed forensic data from Hartford, just received at Langley. He passed out copies and Byrnes asked him to give everyone an overview.

Raabe remained standing as he summarized the information. "There were three blasts, almost simultaneous, which is consistent with eyewitness accounts. The charges were set around the perimeter of the courtroom, two where guests would be sitting and the third underneath Judge O'Hara's desk. The lab confirms there were timing devices that set off C4, which in turn ignited an anti-personnel substance. That compound was a crude form of napalm B, a mixture of polystyrene and benzene, mixed with gasoline. All indications are that the napalm B was mixed on-site."

One of the women from Homeland Security cursed aloud. Byrnes told Raabe to continue.

"As you probably know, napalm B is different than its predecessor. It is less prone to accidental detonation, easier to mix and safer to handle. Once it was ignited, the concussive force of the explosions was followed by a fiery shower that rained down on the people there, sticking to their skin and clothes."

"How the hell did they get that crap in the building?" the woman from the NSA demanded.

"Not sure, sir," Raabe replied. "The FBI in Hartford has pieced together a likely scenario."

"We're listening."

Raabe described how a replacement worker showed up to work the janitorial shift the night before O'Hara's ceremony. "He had identification, name of David Prince. Said he was filling in for Preston Brown. Claimed Brown was ill."

Local authorities had since learned that Preston Brown was kidnapped that evening. He had apparently been attacked from behind as he left for work and was about to get in his car. The police found his body in a vacant lot outside Glastonbury. His hands were bound behind him and a hood was pulled over his his head. He had been shot twice in the back and once in the left temple, all from close range.

"They did their homework beforehand," Raabe went on. "Seems this man, Brown, usually worked with a woman named Dorothy, and they were assigned to the part of the building where Judge O'Hara's courtroom was located."

"Perfect."

"As we already know, this woman Dorothy was murdered, her body discovered the day of the attack, when the entire building was searched."

"Didn't the guards question this David Prince at the end of his shift when Dorothy wasn't with him?"

"One of the marshals spoke with him. Prince told him Dorothy left early."

"Wouldn't the guards have seen that?" Byrnes asked.

"Not necessarily," Raabe explained. "They go on patrols of the building once the entire crew is on site. Doors are locked so no one can get in, but it's fairly easy for someone to leave."

Byrnes frowned. "Didn't it raise any red flags for the security detail?"

Raabe shrugged. "Way it appears, they didn't want to get her in trouble." The woman from NSA cursed again.

"The video from the security checkpoint shows this man Prince," Raabe told them. "It seems obvious he was the one who placed the explosives and strangled Dorothy. The FBI is tracking leads on his identity. He came into the courthouse empty-handed. Assuming he did the mixing and placing of the explosives," he continued, "we still don't have an answer to your question as to how the various chemicals were brought into the building. As I say, nothing in the tape shows him carrying anything with him. It's possible he could have smuggled the C4 *plastique* somewhere inside his clothing, but the amount of polystyrene, benzene and gasoline that was used must have been delivered before that night and hidden somewhere inside the courthouse."

The group moved away from the forensic results and the lax security, focusing on the intentions of the terrorists, particularly the placement of the charges. How did the terrorist know who would be standing where? If O'Hara was the primary target, why? And, if he was, why place explosives in the back of the room, since he would obviously be standing up front?

Or, was this simply a random attack designed to injure and kill as many people as possible?

Raabe pointed them to the section of the report on the identity of the victims. One of those injured was a diplomat named Hassan, from Saudi Arabia. That was when Byrnes stepped in.

"I realize the FBI and DHS have the key roles here, but my agency wants to support those efforts. As Agent Raabe pointed out, the attack involved a Saudi minister, and was likely the work of a foreign terrorist group, Ansar al-Thar. I hope you all agree that the CIA has a measure of jurisdiction."

Bebon from the FBI said, "Speaking for the Bureau, we'll take all the help we can get." The others agreed, although some less enthusiastically than others.

Somerset said, "In addition to his ties to the royal family in Riyadh, Hassan works with the World Health Institute. He was in the New York area in connection with a humanitarian mission. There's an event related to that work at the U.N. tonight."

"Why is that relevant?" Bebon asked.

"Well, for one thing the WHI is an international presence with ties to the Saudis. And for another, it's refreshing to find a wealthy Arab who's one of the good guys, instead of having oil running through his veins."

No one was amused, and Byrnes shot his subordinate a disapproving glance. "I believe the real point," the DD said, "is that it's possible Hassan was a target of the attack."

"Which means," Bebon said, finishing the thought, "security better be tighter than usual in New York tonight."

CHAPTER 10

New York City

Lerner took his time describing the sort of investing he had engaged in over the past few years. His work consisted primarily in trading international currencies.

"Your comment about my wardrobe was not far off. I work with everything from Chinese renminbi to Euros to Swiss francs. I'm the number two trader in Randolph Securities. You've heard of it?"

"I recognize the name," Sandor said.

"It's a very successful shop and, until recently, I felt good about the place. But we'll get to that later," Lerner said. "Staying with arbitrage, you need to know it's a peculiar game. It doesn't matter if markets go up or down. Betting on currency allows you to make money coming or going."

"Allows *you* to make money," Sandor reminded him. "First you have to understand how the game is played, then you have to be smarter than almost anyone else playing it."

"Fair enough. In fact, some things have been happening lately that make no sense, not even to me. And remember, I do this all day long."

"Before we get too deeply into the business of currency trading, you obviously came to see me because you need my help. How about you provide a little context for that?"

Lerner nodded. "Information is the lifeblood of my business, all kinds of information. I work with a lot of highly placed people because, obviously, the closer the source is to the top, the more valuable the intelligence."

"You're not going to give me some half-assed justification for insider trading, are you?"

"Don't be naïve. It's *all* insider trading. When your friend tells you about a certain stock, where do you think he got the tip? It may be third-hand information by the time it comes to you, but you don't ask, right?"

"I'm not in the stock buying demographic, pal."

Lerner responded with a doubtful look. "Okay, just pretend you are for the moment. The point is, someone hears something, passes on the information, then you're having dinner with a friend and he passes it to you."

"I get the concept."

"Good. Now take my situation. When I'm having dinner, it might be with the CEO of a major company. We share stories, nothing secretive or anything, but the next day the markets move and I'm ahead of the curve. It's the same concept, just at a different level. We live in the electronic age; information is the currency we all trade in."

"Still sounds like rationalization to me."

"You think so?" Lerner shook his head as if frustrated by a backward student. "The data is out there, it's all about how far up the food chain you are when you get access, and how quickly you can react."

"That's a bit cynical, don't you think?"

"No, I don't. In life, we all base our decisions on the intelligence we gather, particularly in business. For instance, I have a fairly good idea what you do nowadays. I would say that information is also the currency of your profession, even if the nature of that data is different than the sort I look for. The key issue is how soon you get the leads and how quickly you move on them." Sandor remained silent. "Since we last met, I understand you've developed an unusual skill set."

"I work for the federal government," Sandor began, but Lerner cut him off.

"Please Jordan, we've been through too much together for you to give me some malarkey about the State Department or the Diplomatic Corps or the damned Budget Office. I know you're with the Company," he said, then lowered his voice as he added, "and I know you're CS. That's one of the reasons I'm here."

Sandor had never told Lerner that he was recruited by the CIA, much less its Clandestine Service. "I'm still listening," he said.

"Good, because you're on a very short list."

"Short list?"

"Yes Jordan. The list of people I trust."

Sandor nodded. Howard Lerner had always been prone to conspiracy theories, and Sandor had to balance his friend's suspicious tendencies with the occasional accuracy of those instincts. When they served their tour together in Iraq, some in the unit teased Lerner about his paranoia but, as it turned out, he saved their asses more than once when they followed his hunches.

"Okay," Sandor said. "I'm flattered by your confidence in me, regardless of your misguided notions about my career. Now let's get down to the nitty-gritty, shall we?"

Lerner nodded. "There was a young woman I worked with at Randolph. Smart. Good looking." He paused. "A couple of months ago they transferred her to our office in Bermuda." He stopped to take a drink of his scotch. "There was a lot of scuttlebutt about the move, but for now the important headline is that she's dead."

"How did she die?"

"Not sure. Word is that Corinne had some sort of coronary brought on by amphetamines, but I know that's total bullshit." Lerner paused. "I knew her. She was about as likely to use that crap as you are."

"I see."

"No, you don't, because there's more." Then Lerner told him about the hit and run that killed Charles Colville.

Sandor called for the waiter, ordered Lerner another Black Label and asked for a Jack Daniels on the rocks. Lerner smiled. "Time for that drink, huh?"

"You know me pal," Sandor said. "I don't believe in coincidences."

"I spend my life doing mathematical computations and analyzing algorithms. And I know for a *fact* there are no such things as coincidences."

"All right, so how do these two deaths figure into your life?"

Lerner paused. "I believe these deaths are related to a series of strange trades running through some of our major accounts."

"Such as?"

"I need to give you a lot more detail, but not here and not now."

"When?"

Lerner lowered his voice. "I bought a laptop when I got to town last night. Need to set it up and load some data. I couldn't risk using my own computer, for reasons that'll become obvious. Meet me in my room here at six. That okay?"

Sandor agreed.

"And dust off your tuxedo, we need to attend a black tie dinner at the U.N. tonight."

"What?"

"Trust me on this one—have I ever let you down?"

"Not including the redhead in Baghdad?"

Their drinks came and Sandor had a sip of the whisky, the first he'd had since before the attack in Hartford. "Give me one good reason I need to go to the U.N."

"You'll get to meet a couple of the players involved."

"For instance."

"You'll see when we get there." When Sandor frowned, he added, "I'll fill you in when we meet at six. I promise it'll be worth going."

Sandor took another sip and placed his glass on the table. "All right," he said, "but no matter what happens, I'm not dancing with you."

⊙

One of the men assigned to track their movements decided it was time to report in. After making a final pass near the entrance to the King Cole barroom, he went out onto Fifty-fifth Street and placed the call.

He had already taken photos and forwarded them for identification. He was now told that the man was Jordan Sandor, a State Department attaché who had served in the military with Lerner over a decade ago. It was likely their conversation was more than just two former platoon mates reuniting to talk over old times.

Their superior intervened, telling them not to concern themselves with the background data. At this point they would both need to be taken out. "Keep an eye on them, and call in the sweepers," he ordered.

CHAPTER 11

New York City

As Sandor strolled back to his apartment, he was disappointed to feel a wave of fatigue wash over him. Up to now his day had consisted of a workout in the morning, his discussion with Lerner, and one Jack Daniels. It was not much exertion for a man accustomed to action, and yet he was feeling it.

He intended to walk all the way home, figuring the fresh air would do him some good and knowing his leg needed the work, but by the time he reached Central Park South he thought better of the idea. It was not just the lingering effects of his injuries that concerned him.

His trained instincts warned him he was being followed.

Sandor had the sense he and Lerner were being watched shortly after he arrived at the King Cole Bar. At first he shook it off. He had been out of action for a couple of weeks, which might cause him to read too much into things, and the unexpected arrival of his old friend ratcheted up his internal radar. But then he saw a nondescript man of about thirty-five stroll slowly past the entrance to the barroom for at least the second time, and that was certainly not his imagination at work.

As Sandor walked cross-town, he became convinced he was being tailed, and he did not hesitate. He hailed a cab, jumped in, and headed to Central Park West, where he had the driver make a right and drive north. As they approached his street, Sandor told the cabbie to continue on to 86th Street, where they turned left and kept going until they reached Broadway.

Sandor jumped out at the corner, made for the subway entrance, and hurried down the steps. Rather than enter the station, he raced directly across the underground plaza, coming up the stairs on the west side of Broadway. Without waiting, he flagged down another taxi and headed south to 76th Street.

"Just pull over," Sandor told the driver. His hope was that he had gotten ahead of whoever was chasing him, which would give him the edge, but after three minutes he was persuaded he had lost the man.

"No offense buddy," the driver said over his shoulder, "but are we going somewhere or are you planning on moving in here?"

Sandor paid, got out, and began strolling north at a normal pace, mindful of the activity around him, watching to see if any other cabs came to a stop. He walked east, circling the entire block before reaching his brownstone. He had a quick look up and down the street, then headed up the stairs. He was sure he had lost the tail, and now it would only be a matter of whether the man knew where Sandor lived, or whether the operation was what is sometimes referred to as blind surveillance.

Inside his apartment, Sandor stopped in the kitchen and glanced at the pain medication that had been prescribed for him. Just looking at the bottles sent a shooting pain up his leg, but he left the drugs sitting on the kitchen counter and went into the bedroom.

The dinner at the United Nations was a black tie event, and Sandor would have to dress for that. He would take his State Department credentials, carry his Walther and, just for good measure, strap a second weapon to his ankle. He realized they would force him to give up the weapons when he entered the U.N. but, the way things were going, he wanted to be prepared for any surprises that might arise before or after.

For now, he decided he would make a quick call to Craig Raabe, then rest before he prepared to meet Lerner again. He sat on the bed and placed his automatic beside him.

⊙

The man who had been trailing Sandor lost him on 78th Street and Columbus Avenue. Between the heavy afternoon traffic and a missed light, Sandor's taxi had gotten too far ahead, then turned out of view.

He had his driver pull over and got out. After a quick look up and down a couple of streets he phoned in. "I lost him," he reported.

"Too bad," came the response.

"I think he made me. I think he had his cab take evasive action."

"Not surprising." There was a pause. "We will follow up on this end to find an address for him. Go back to the hotel and wait there."

"On my way."

"Try to stay out of sight. You will have a secondary role when we send in the new team.

If he spotted you, we cannot afford to have him see you again."

"Understood."

"I hope so," came the reply, then the line went dead.

CHAPTER 12

New York City

A few hours later, on the cab ride from his apartment back to the hotel, Sandor saw no indication he was being followed, which meant that possibly Lerner, not he, was the primary target of the surveillance.

He thought about arranging backup by calling in a favor from someone he knew in the local agency office, but he realized that would get back to Byrnes, which was a complication he did not want right now. His only security at the moment consisted of the automatic fitted snugly at the small of his back and the Rohrbaugh R9 secured against his right ankle.

At the St. Regis, Sandor stopped at the front desk where they called to confirm he was an approved guest. Then he took the elevator up to his friend's suite.

Lerner was waiting at the door and showed Sandor into a large sitting room.

"Nice crash pad," Sandor said.

The room was furnished in opulent style, featuring soft grey wall coverings made of silk, Waterford chandeliers, and legacy pieces that celebrated Louis XVI sophistication in a comfortable, modern setting.

"Home away from home," Lerner said. "Drink?"

Sandor shook him off. "Maybe later."

Lerner took the couch, Sandor chose an armchair facing him, and they picked up where they left off, Lerner continuing his tutorial on how currency trading works.

As a case study, Lerner described how arbitragers benefited from the fiscal collapse in Greece, and why the Euro would be a vulnerable currency if a lineup of powerful multi-national corporations decided to play with its valuation. China, fast becoming the world's most important economic influence, had a stake in keeping the European Union on an even keel—the EU represented the second largest foreign market for its products, after the United States. On the other hand, if a domino effect began, and the fall of Greece was repeated in Italy and then France and so forth, China's motives might be altered.

"Are you saying that China is behind the currency fluctuations?" Sandor asked.

"To the contrary. As I've said, the Chinese played some of those games ten years ago, but now they have every reason to stop the volatility, to the extent they can. No, it's not the Chinese government. The moving forces in these currency swings are large companies and the men who run them."

"Companies move national currencies?"

"Of course," Lerner said, as if the concept was something that should be obvious to anyone. "These corporations already rule the world. Moving the value of the dollar or the Euro is child's play." Lerner leaned forward and began tapping away at the laptop that sat between them on the coffee table. Then he spun it around to show Sandor some graphics. "These are charts tracking the movement of currency valuations over the past three years. See here? This is the dollar, the Euro, the yen, the RMB." Lerner stood and came around to sit in the chair beside Sandor, then went back to work at the keyboard. He overlaid the graph displaying currency valuations with a series of dates representing major trades made by various companies in Bermuda, the Cayman Islands, and the Channel Islands. "These are all shell companies owned through a matrix of other corporations. The accounts are traded by my company, RSL."

Sandor studied the overlays, seeing how the timing of these trades anticipated drops in various currencies. "So your clients took short positions in each of these instances, just before the values fell."

Lerner turned to his friend. "Exactly. And Corinne Stansbury was one of the traders I relied on for that real-time information. Sometimes she even ran the trades for me."

"Always in currency?"

"No, there were also plays made in market indexes."

"I assume the timing worked out on those too?"

"Very much so."

"Do all these transactions anticipate downward turns in the markets?"

"Not all. But even some of the positive buys are sketchy. For instance, she took some large positions in a French technology company doing state-of-the-art work on drones. Fronique is the name. Underneath all of the layers of ownership, the ultimate holder of the interest she bought is our biggest client, WHI."

"The World Health Institute? Don't you think a humanitarian organization investing in drone technology is a bit counter-intuitive?"

"The party line is that the drones being developed there are strictly informational," Lerner explained. "Photographs, video links . . . ,"

"Illegal surveillance, armed UAV's," Sandor finished the thought.

"No doubt it's a questionable investment for WHI, which is another reason for my concerns. Especially after what happened to . . ."

"I got it. But your girlfriend Corinne wasn't doing this on her own. People at WHI had to know what she was buying for them."

"I never said she was my girlfriend."

"You also never mentioned how great I look in this tux. Some things just don't need to be said."

Lerner leaned back in the comfortable chair and allowed himself a moment to reflect on Corinne. "We had our time together, let's leave it at that."

"I'm happy not to get into the details of your love life, believe me. So who was she dealing with at your company and at WHI?"

"She reported directly to Freddie Colville, who essentially owns RSL, and she also met all the key players at WHI. Mark Killian, tough customer who runs the fund. Shahid Hassan, from the Saudi royal family, smooth operator who raises truckloads of money for the Institute.

Eduardo Cristo. They made him financial director not so long ago, and he's energized their portfolio. Very smart, very market savvy, and absolutely determined to grow the resources of the Institute."

"So, as good as their intentions and mission may be, you're telling me the boys at WHI don't care what sort of company they invest in. This French company, for instance."

"Not sure that's how they see it, or if they've even focused on that position. Just thought I should mention Fronique, since it was a big play for Corinne. Not to mention a complicated gambit."

"As evidenced by all the shell companies she ran it through."

"Right."

"And now she's dead, along with Charles Colville."

"Correct."

"Did Charles Colville have anything to do with Fronique?" Sandor asked.

"Not that I knew anything about. But in the past week there's a rumor circulating that he was tracking some of the big trades made at RSL, then making the same investments for his own account in another firm."

"I'm guessing that was a rule-breaker."

"No kidding."

"What about Corinne?"

"She wasn't mimicking the trades, she was involved in the actual transactions. Charlie was just on the administrative side, so he was effectively stealing the information and profiting from it. Or that's the latest word on him."

"But Corinne was also profiting from it," Sandor said.

"No doubt."

"All right. So I assume there's more to your graphs and bar charts than what you've showed me so far."

Lerner leaned forward and went back to work on the computer, adding two more variables. The patterns revealed by the new overlays became even more impressive. They included various terrorist attacks and other world events that depressed markets, sending stock and currency values tumbling. "Have a look at these. When you analyze all the data, it's as if the group taking these short positions knew the currencies were about to fall."

"Just like bin Laden's people, who shorted airline stocks before Nine-Eleven," Sandor said.

"Correct. If you know something terrible is going to happen in an industry or a company or a market sector, it's as valuable as knowing the result of a horse race before it's run."

"And you're saying there were people inside RSL who knew about these events in advance."

"I'm not sure, but these graphics certainly make it appear that way," Lerner said. "And if they did, then it gets even worse. Not only did they know about it, but when it was discovered that Corinne and Charles recognized the patterns . . ."

"They were removed," Sandor finished the thought.

Lerner nodded slowly.

"But you've also seen these patterns, and you've also made a determination about what they were doing."

"Which is why I'm here."

"And you have connections to both Corinne and Charles."

"Corinne for sure. I had no idea what Charlie was up to."

"All right then, if I'm going to be able to help, I'm going to need a lot more information about the players involved."

Lerner took a thumb drive from his coat pocket and handed it to Sandor. "I know I don't have to say this again, but you are the only person I can trust on this. This is both information and insurance."

"Understood," Sandor said. "I take it this is for later viewing, if and when it becomes necessary."

"Only then," Lerner said.

Sandor placed the device in his pocket. "Now are you going to tell me something about this dinner tonight?"

"You need to know about the players involved." He grinned. "Several of them will be there tonight, and I don't want you to miss the opportunity of meeting them."

CHAPTER 13

United Nations, New York City

The formal affair at the United Nations was being held to showcase a delegation leaving for North Africa in two days. The reception was taking place in the Dag Hammarskjold Library, to be followed by a banquet in the grand ballroom.

The group being honored was embarking on a humanitarian mission jointly sponsored by the U.N. and the World Health Institute. The headliners had each earned the right to be called a superstar, and had each been a long-time supporter of these organizations. The American actress Amanda Jensen was perhaps the most famous woman in the world. The international rock star from Ireland known as Dedalus shared a similar level of acclaim. They had given generously of their time and money to programs dedicated to providing clean water, food, and health care to the most impoverished corners of the globe. Now they were going on the road together to promote those causes.

Given the involvement of Jensen and Dedalus, the turnout was large, luminous, and well funded. Various diplomats and government types were present, along with top representatives of the media and a gaggle of other celebrities, all of whom had paid dearly— personally or through their companies—for the opportunity to be part of this elite crowd.

In light of the roster of attendees, and the recent attack in Hartford, security was extremely tight, even by the standards of a gala function at the U.N. Armed guards were in evidence, from the entrance on the main floor, throughout the building and in the library. Many were in uniform. Others attempted plain-clothes discretion, but armed security personnel in ill-fitting tuxedoes simply do not look like movie producers from Los Angeles or national newscasters from New York in custom-made dinnerwear.

At the first checkpoint, Lerner produced his invitation for two. While their right to be there was being authenticated, Sandor looked around, wondering if there was any sort of gathering he disliked more than this. If so, he would be hard pressed to name it.

When his turn came to pass through the metal detector, he produced his two weapons and displayed his State Department credentials.

Lerner reacted to the sight of the two guns with a wry grin. "Things must be getting rough over at Foggy Bottom," he said.

The guard facing Sandor told him he would have to leave his weapons behind if he wanted to be allowed inside, a painful reminder of that same discussion the morning he entered the courthouse on Main Street in Hartford. The result of his protest here was also the same. The only difference tonight was a stern reminder that, "You are on United Nations property now, sir."

"Tell that to the New York City taxpayers," Sandor replied as he accepted a receipt for the two automatics.

Sandor's level of discomfort was heightened, not only by the vulnerability he felt any time he was unarmed, but because he was a CIA agent assigned to the division of Clandestine Services. In his line of work, shadows were preferable to the spotlight, and public appearances of this sort simply run counter to the nature of his profession.

Sandor was impressed to see that Lerner, on the other hand, appeared very much at home in these surroundings. His friend had come a long way since his wise-cracking days as Joey Sax. He moved comfortably through the well-dressed throng, introducing Sandor to various personalities and dignitaries. Many of the faces were well-known, some as familiar as that of a close friend, but the glamour was wasted on Sandor.

There was, however, one person he was pleased to see—Beth Sharrow.

Beth was an analyst assigned to the CIA's New York City office, where she and Sandor met years before. They had dated on and off until their relationship veered dangerously close to a serious love affair. That sort of connection was something Sandor believed he could not afford, mainly for fear of putting Beth at risk. Still, they remained in touch, and that contact was enough to create the nightmare scenario Sandor had hoped to prevent.

One evening, in a gruesome twist of fate, Beth was accosted, beaten, and nearly murdered by an assassin who was determined to find Sandor, and was convinced that she could lead him there.

Beth recovered from the assault, never blaming Sandor for what happened. As she told her superiors, it was all part of the risk she accepted in working for the Company. Nevertheless, she had kept her distance since then, and Sandor respected the decision.

Tonight, Sandor spotted her across the room, standing beside a tall, dark-haired man. Sandor had learned from his best friend, Bill Sternlich, that Beth had begun seeing someone in the diplomatic corps—Sternlich and his wife remained close with Beth after she and Sandor were no longer an item—but Sandor was not about to be put off by her new romance. He excused himself from Lerner and strode across the room.

When Beth saw him coming, her reaction was a mixture of surprise and pleasure, which she blended into the briefest of smiles. "Well," she said when he reached them, "seems just anyone can get into these events nowadays." Without waiting for a reply she turned to her left. "Robert, this is an old friend, Jordan Sandor. Jordan, Robert Pergament."

Sandor extended his hand.

"Good to see you," he said.

Pergament nodded.

Turning back to Beth, Sandor said, "You look great." And she did. Her hazel eyes shone, her lips were pursed in the bemused attitude he knew so well, and her skin gave off a healthy glow beneath the recessed lights above. He noted that she still wore her chestnut colored hair at the length she used to describe as "sensible"—short enough to manage for work, stylish enough for casual moments, and long enough to be fashioned into something sexy, as she had done for this event.

Beth took a moment to give him the once over. "I have to admit, you look a little thin," she told him.

Sandor grinned, then said to Pergament, "I've been on one of those extreme diets. Thought I might get into marathon running or something . . . but then I came to my senses."

Pergament was apparently not the jovial type, but he knew when to give a couple of old friends a moment to catch up. "Why don't I get us a couple of glasses of wine? You want anything Sandor?"

"No, I'm good thanks."

Pergament told them he would be right back, then headed off to a makeshift bar in the far corner of the spacious library.

"So," Beth said, "you really do look a little beat up. You all right?"

"It's been a tough couple of weeks."

She nodded. "You chose a tough line of work." If she had any information from inside the agency about Sandor's injuries, she was not saying.

"Some days are worse than others," he said. "So what brings you to this gathering of the rich and famous?"

"Not *what*, Jordan, *who*. Robert and I have been seeing each other."

"Uh huh."

"He was invited, he's with the diplomatic corps."

Sandor nodded. "I'll admit it was diplomatic of him to give us a moment alone. Must be good at his job."

She frowned.

"I'm really happy to see you," he said.

"Me too."

"We should get together some time, catch up." Before she had a chance to demur, he added, "Coffee or something. Maybe at that bakery on Grand Street we used to visit early in the morning."

Beth could not suppress a smile at the memory of those dawn runs in Soho. "Maybe," she said. "But only coffee. Hot cross buns would be out of the question at this point."

"That's too bad," he said, forcing a look of disappointment. "You know how I feel about hot buns."

Beth laughed. "You did say you were on an extreme diet, didn't you?"

"You have no idea."

"So, have you spoken with Bill lately?"

"I haven't, actually."

"He's here tonight."

"Really?"

"He's covering this mission for the paper. Going with them to Iraq."

"You're kidding."

"He said he hasn't spoken with you for a couple of weeks, but I just thought you would know."

Sandor saw that Beth's escort was on the way back. "I'm going to go find him. Meanwhile, we have a date? Just coffee?"

"We'll see," she said.

"I'll give you a call."

"I doubt it," she replied with a smile. "By the way, you haven't told me what you're doing here."

As Pergament approached, Sandor said, "I'm doing a favor for a friend, and I see him waving me down right now."

Sandor rejoined Lerner, who was standing beside two men, one an elegant looking Arab, the other a tall man with a generous head of silver hair, stylishly dressed in a peak lapel tuxedo.

"Jordan, I want you to meet the head of my firm, Freddie Colville," Lerner said, gesturing to the tall Englishman. "And this is our good friend Shahid Hassan, both a diplomat as well as an ambassador for the World Health Institute. Gentlemen, this is my old Army pal, Jordan Sandor." As the men shook hands, Lerner told Hassan, "It appears you and Jordan have something in common."

The Saudi responded with a curious look.

Lerner first mentioned Hassan, earlier in the day, and Sandor immediately recalled the name from the list of those injured in Hartford. Although the DD forbid Sandor from embarking on an unauthorized vendetta following the attack, he did send him the list of attendees at O'Hara's robing ceremony, including details on those injured and killed. Given Sandor's closeness to the judge, Byrnes thought there might be value in having him review the information.

Sandor did not tell Lerner that he recognized Hassan's name, nor did he admit that he wondered about the connection between James O'Hara and a member of the Saudi royal family. Instead, he called Craig Raabe when he got back to his apartment and asked him to check it out.

Based on a quick rundown, it turned out that the two men had dealings when O'Hara was a prosecutor with the Justice Department in Washington. Raabe told him there might be more to it than that, he just needed time to peel back the layers.

Later, when Sandor returned to the hotel, Lerner provided him background on the people they were likely to run into at the U.N. that night. He described Hassan as a major financial advisor and fund raiser for the World Health Institute. Since Lerner had also revealed that WHI had benefitted from some of the trades that were now worrying him, it appeared to Sandor there might be angles to the O'Hara-Hassan affiliation he would need to explore.

Sandor put those thoughts aside as Lerner said, "You two were both part of that tragedy in Hartford."

Hassan turned to Sandor. "My apologies, I do not recall our meeting that day."

"No reason to apologize," Sandor said. "I was last to arrive. Got there just in time for the courtroom door to explode in my face."

Hassan responded with a solemn nod. "Were you badly injured?"

"Not really. As Lerner mentioned, we were in the Army together. I've been through worse."

"Well, whatever your injuries, I'm pleased to see that you appear to have recovered."

"And you?"

"I am also one of the lucky ones. Like you, I survived." Hassan appeared to be turning over an idea he was not sure he wanted to share. "I knew very few of the other people present, but I was pleased to attend the ceremony for my friend Jim O'Hara. I still cannot believe he's gone."

"Neither can I," Sandor agreed.

Again, there was something in the Saudi's eyes, as if he wanted to share a thought but decided not to. A cautious man, Sandor noted, as Hassan asked, "You knew him well?"

"We both did," Lerner replied. "He was our C.O. in Iraq."

"I see. I'm sure he was a fine leader."

"Yes, he was," Sandor said. "I did a lot of growing up during that tour."

Hassan allowed himself a respectful smile. "That was one of his many talents, I believe. He made people around him want to be better. Do you agree?"

Sandor smiled. Generally speaking, anybody who liked O'Hara was okay with him, but this Hassan was going to be tough to read. "Yes," he replied simply. "He was an inspirational leader."

When it seemed no one was going to volunteer anything else about James O'Hara, Freddie Colville said, "I never had the privilege of meeting the judge, but I can see you all feel his loss quite keenly."

"Very much so," Hassan told him.

After another uncomfortable moment, Lerner said to his boss, "You didn't fly from London to listen to us reminisce about Jim O'Hara. Why don't we all go get ourselves a drink."

CHAPTER 14

United Nations, New York City

The buffet dinner laid out in the upstairs ballroom was all but ignored as crowds circled around Amanda Jensen in one corner of the room, and Dedalus in another, each a sun around whom too many planets were orbiting.

Or so Sandor saw it. He could not think of anything more useless than wading through a mob of sycophants for the sole purpose of shaking hands with a celebrity who would have no idea who you were and even less interest. He did his best to keep his distance, instead trying to spot Bill Sternlich in the crowd while focusing on what he might do to aid Lerner which, he reminded himself, was the only reason he agreed to attend this shindig in the first place.

He was again standing with Colville, Hassan and Lerner, when another man joined them.

Mark Killian was tall, broad-shouldered, red-haired, with features as blunt as his manner. He was introduced as the head of WHI and, once he joined their discussion, it was clear where the epicenter of this power group was located.

Colville did his best to maintain his stiff spine and upper lip but, for all his British swagger, was quick to defer to the burly American.

Lerner was not so much a supplicant in this court as a knight errant. He was there to do the bidding of both Colville and Killian, since pleasing them funded his extravagant lifestyle.

Hassan was another matter entirely. Although he provided counsel and contacts to WHI, it was clear to Sandor that he worked *with* the company and not *for* it, and was not in any way beholden to any of the others. He appeared to be a true believer in WHI's purpose and programs, and as an Arab with Western tastes and a British education, he deftly spanned a wide cultural divide, someone who was as welcome in the Court of Saint James as he was in the House of Saud. It was evident to Sandor that he brought access to great wealth which, in the world of charitable organizations, is the name of the game. But Hassan also exuded integrity and grace, all the while displaying something in his gaze that told Sandor he was no one to trifle with.

The four men engaged in shop talk until one of them mentioned the tragic loss of Corinne Stansbury. Their reactions varied, and Sandor became ever more curious about this woman and the various roles she had played in the business and personal lives of these men. Unfortunately, the subject was exhausted rather quickly, and three of them moved off to discuss world events with a group of European investment bankers standing nearby. Hassan stayed behind. He mentioned to Sandor that he was included in the delegation leaving for Mosul in two days.

"So," Sandor said, "you're part of the road show."

"Yes," Hassan told him, his diffident smile appearing to be as amused as he allowed himself to become. "I thought someone in the group ought to be able to speak the language."

Sandor laughed. "But you're not hanging out with the two big stars tonight."

"No, I'm not. I am certain we will see quite enough of each other over the coming days." His expression became more serious as he added, "I also find your company—how shall I say this—more intriguing."

"Intriguing? I'll take that as a compliment, coming from a man as accomplished as you."

"A compliment? Perhaps. I would say it's more an observation."

"All right, now I'm the one who's intrigued."

Hassan nodded. "From the moment we were introduced I have noticed several things about you. First, you are an excellent listener, an admirable quality in anyone, and far too rare, especially in a gathering such as this. Second, you are extremely observant. I can see it in your demeanor and comments. Third, you have said almost nothing about yourself, while collecting information about all of the rest of us."

"You make me sound like quite the snoop."

Hassan responded with a knowing look. "Then there is the very fact of your presence here."

"Like you said, I'm a good listener. Go on."

"I know Mr. Lerner reasonably well from our dealings at Randolph Securities. An opportunity like this, a star-studded event when he could have brought and impressed a beautiful young woman, is something he relishes. Instead he chose as his escort someone he describes as an old army pal. Not Howard's normal *modus operandi*."

"You haven't seen my legs."

Hassan showed him that smile again. "Come, come, Mr. Sandor. I have already concluded that you employ humor as a means of deflection, and I'm interested in a serious discussion."

"All right."

Hassan nodded. "I have noted your interest in the discussion about our deceased colleague, Corinne Stansbury."

"Very sad."

Hassan frowned. "As with humor, it is equally clear that you are adept at stating the obvious to redirect the flow of conversation. For the moment it is only the two of us, so I ask that you indulge me as I pose a simple question. Why are you really here?"

Sandor stared at the man without speaking.

"I believe it is not mere happenstance that we were both at Jim O'Hara's ceremony in Hartford and now find ourselves together tonight. I also believe your interest in Ms. Stansbury is more than casual curiosity. I believe that Howard has expressed concerns to you, and that he feels you possess the talent to address those concerns." When Sandor remained silent, Hassan asked, "Would you say those are fair statements?"

"I would say you are also an observant man."

"Would it interest you to know that Corinne was a friend of mine?"

"That would depend on how close your friendship was."

"Let us say, close enough that her death is a personal tragedy for me."

"I see."

"Perhaps you do, and perhaps you do not. But in time you will, I am convinced of that. As a consequence, I would like *us* to be friends. I would also like you to know that I am not Howard's enemy."

Sandor fixed him with a serious stare. "Why would you feel the need to tell me that?"

"You already know that answer, Mr. Sandor, or I have badly misjudged you."

"I take it, then, that this is a warning that Howard has enemies, perhaps several."

Hassan responded with a slight bow. "I am afraid that may be so. I consider myself his friend, and an admirer of his financial acumen. I have no way of knowing how many enemies he may have, but I wanted you to be clear that I should not be counted among them."

"I'm glad to hear that. Especially since you were a friend of Jim O'Hara's."

"I was. As to Corinne, I have seen the confidential report, which suggests she died of a heart attack induced by the use of drugs." He shook his head slowly. "She had certain vices, Mr. Sandor, but the use of narcotics or other such substances was not among them. Whatever you are up to, whatever Howard is asking of you, I would consider it a personal favor to me if you would begin there."

"With Ms. Stansbury's death?"

"Yes." Hassan drew a deep breath and exhaled slowly, as if he had completed some difficult business. "Now I really must join the others in the delegation where I am to endure the embarrassment of being praised for something we have not yet done, and which everyone should join in doing anyway." The slight smile appeared again. "It should be obvious, I think, but I would prefer this discussion be kept between us."

"You mean, in particular, I should not mention it to Lerner."

Hassan made a slight bow. "I will leave it to your discretion," he said. "Now forgive me, but it is time for me to suffer the slings and arrows of undeserved praise."

Sandor made his way to the bar, where he ordered a Jack Daniels on the rocks and took another moment to survey the room once more in search of Sternlich.

"Quite a gathering," the man standing beside him said. He looked to be about fifty, too well groomed and too tanned to be from anywhere but California.

"Yes," Sandor agreed. "It is."

"Looks more like the Golden Globe Awards than a U.N. event."

"Wouldn't know," Sandor replied. "Never seen the Golden Globes."

"Not even on TV?"

"Never."

The man stuck out his lower lip, as if the concept deserved serious thought. "Never?"

"Not even once."

The man looked him up and down. "First time for everything."

"So they say."

The man took a sip of his drink, which Sandor gave a disapproving look, figuring it to be a white wine spritzer. "Some good looking women here," the man observed.

"I've noticed."

"What do you think of Amanda?" The man used her first name as if that were the sort of relationship they had.

"Never met her."

The man laughed a friendly sort of laugh. "Well I'm sure you've noticed she's here. Haven't you taken the time to say hello?"

"Figured I'd wait until she built up the courage to introduce herself to me."

The man laughed again. "I take it you're not much for celebrities."

"Not the Hollywood type, no."

"Is there another kind?"

Sandor stared at him.

"You don't think what Amanda and Dedalus are doing is commendable?"

"Commendable? That's an interesting word." Sandor had a drink of his whisky. "I think it's helpful when famous people bring attention to worthy causes, even if their real motive is self-aggrandizement."

"That's a bit cynical, don't you think?"

Sandor shrugged. "I'm not criticizing, I'm just observing. People in show business are all about blowing their own trumpets. Am I wrong?"

"Sometimes."

"All right, I'll concede there are guys like Denzel Washington who do what they do and keep it quiet. But most of them care more about the media attention than the results of what they're supposed to be accomplishing."

The man's gleaming white smile, which up to now appeared to be permanently affixed to his face, finally dimmed. "So then, when celebrities engage in charitable activities, you don't believe they're entitled to be praised?"

"I really don't care one way or another," Sandor told him, then had another pull at his drink. "But there are a lot of anonymous people who work hard to see that things get done properly, while the rich and famous are protected and coddled and then take the bows. As far as I'm concerned, the folks behind the scenes are the ones who should be receiving the praise. Your celebrities should just do their best not to get in the way."

CHAPTER 15

New York City

The festivities finally appeared to be wrapping up with a string of self-congratulatory speeches that were repeatedly interrupted by obligatory rounds of applause.

Sandor wondered if subjecting someone to an event like this could be considered an enhanced interrogation technique.

The last speaker was Amanda Jensen and, despite his general attitude toward movie stars, Sandor had to admit she was even more beautiful in person than what little he had seen of her on the screen. He listened for a while as she discussed the suffering of the refugees they intended to help, then he resumed his study of the people around him.

He took some final mental notes on the men at his table, particularly Killian and Colville. Whatever he was going to do for Lerner, he already knew that the trail would either begin or end with one of them. He also noticed there were others watching his group from elsewhere in the room. An experienced field agent, he was trained to continually assess his surroundings and those populating the scene. Tonight there was a personal component as well, since he had come at Lerner's invitation to gather background on a situation that was becoming increasingly complicated and possibly dangerous. When the completion of Jensen's remarks was greeted by a predictable standing ovation, several people stopped by to bid good night to Killian and Colville.

Later, Sandor would have questions for Lerner about who each of them was and how they fit into the WHI and RSL orbits. He had already decided he would keep what Hassan had said to himself.

Once everyone finally began filing toward the exits, Lerner invited his boss and Killian back to the St. Regis for a nightcap. They declined, explaining that the company jet was waiting to whisk them back to the U.K. Colville offered Lerner a seat on the flight, but he told them he still had business in New York and would be back in London in a couple of days. They said their good-nights and went on their way.

Downstairs Sandor stopped at the security office to retrieve his weapons. Then he and Lerner walked outside to First Avenue and began to stroll west toward the St. Regis

"So, what do you think?" Lerner asked.

"About what, precisely?"

"Start with Freddie Colville."

Sandor shrugged. "Obviously very polished. Knows how to take a back seat to his big client."

"Killian."

Sandor nodded. "Killian is the powerhouse in that duo. Colville has the British pedigree, Killian is a bit rough around the edges, but he's the real deal."

"Fair enough. Just remember, those two are as thick as thieves."

Sandor nodded but said nothing.

"Any feeling about how they might connect with what I've explained to you so far?"

"Too early to draw any conclusions."

"Fair enough." After they had walked on a bit, Lerner asked, "What'd you make of Hassan?"

"Class act. Intelligent. Cautious." Sandor hesitated before adding, "He has some sort of hidden agenda I can't read yet."

"That's what I see too," Lerner said, then dropped the subject.

◉

Back at the hotel they bypassed the bar and headed upstairs. Lerner said there was more he wanted to explain on the computer, particularly now that Sandor had met three of the key players. When they reached his suite Lerner called room service and ordered up cocktails, then fired up his new laptop.

Lerner began providing more detail on the various transactions that were causing him concern. He went through some of the short sales that occurred just before major market corrections, and Sandor immediately recognized some of the dates because they coincided with events overseas in which he had been involved. One of those was an attack on a shopping center in Nairobi.

"That was certainly a lucrative bit of timing for your traders," Sandor observed.

"More than just good luck, you mean."

Sandor was still looking at the computer screen when the bell rang.

"Got it," Lerner said, then went to the door and opened it, allowing a stocky man in a waistcoat to wheel in a table holding a silver bucket with ice, two crystal glasses, a bottle of Balvenie, a bottle of Jack Daniels, and a tray of hors d'oeuvres.

Sandor did not pay much attention until he saw a second waiter follow the first man in and shut the door behind him. That's when he leapt to his feet.

A room service delivery of liquor and canapés at one in the morning is not a two man job.

Before Lerner realized what was happening, the first man drove his left elbow into his gut, doubling Lerner over, then knocking him to the floor with a hard chop to the back of his neck. The second man, taller and trimmer than the first, had already advanced into the sitting room, coming towards Sandor. His right hand, which had been at his side, was now raised, holding an automatic with a lengthy suppressor attached to the barrel.

Sandor saw the weapon and, before the assailant could take aim, dove to his left. He pulled the Walther from the holster at the small of his back as he rolled on the floor behind an armchair, then came up on one knee, using the chair for cover.

The tall man had begun firing, and Sandor heard the spitting sound of three silenced shots as they lodged in the thick upholstery.

Sandor's only advantage was that the shooter did not know he was armed. Sandor drove his left shoulder into the back of the chair, toppling it forward as he lunged to his right. The assassin, who had been moving toward him, was pushed off balance by the chair. Sandor did not hesitate, coming up and firing four shots into the shooter's chest.

The loud report of the shots from the Walther echoed throughout the room as the man dropped his weapon and clutched at his shirt, ripping it open as he fell backward, blood spreading across his upper torso.

Sandor kept moving, now finding cover behind the couch. He had seen that the first man was still standing over Lerner, holding an automatic pointed at his friend's head.

Sandor hollered, "Drop your weapon! Now!"

"You want your friend to die?" the man responded in a raspy voice.

"If he does, you do too," Sandor warned him. "You've only got one way to live through this. Throw your gun on the floor and put your hands on top of your head."

"You want your friend to die?" the man asked again.

From his line of sight behind the couch Sandor could see that the burly man had Lerner's shirt collar in his left hand, his right holding the gun tight against Lerner's temple. If Sandor fired, there was no chance the man would not pull the trigger, and Lerner would be gone.

Sandor spotted a vase that had rolled onto the floor in the brief scuffle. He reached for it and hurled it against the far wall of the sitting room.

The sound was loud as a gunshot and the shooter instinctively turned in the direction of the noise, momentarily pulling the gun away from Lerner's head. It was just enough of a distraction for Sandor to make his move.

He shouted "Lerner!" as he rose on his knee from behind the sofa.

His friend reacted by making a desperate attempt to yank himself free, just as Sandor fired three shots at the assassin's head. The force of the shots knocked the man backward, but he was able to get off two reflexive rounds. The first bullet hit the ceiling, but the second grazed Lerner's shoulder.

Then the shooter crumpled into a lifeless heap on the floor, the weapon still in his hand.

Sandor scrambled to his feet, the weakness in his left leg forcing him to brace himself with his hand. This was the first action he had seen since he suffered his injuries in Hartford, and he was reminded that a strenuous workout in the gym is not the same as actual combat. Not only had his leg almost given out, but he was suddenly aware his head was not as clear as it should have been—and two Jack Daniels over the past five hours could not be blamed.

"Damn," he spat out as he steadied himself.

"What the hell are you cursing at?" Lerner asked. He was sitting now, slumped against the wall, holding the top of his right shoulder. "I'm the one who got shot."

Sandor took his time checking the two intruders, feeling for their carotid arteries. They were both dead. "You all right?" he finally asked.

"I've been beat up and shot," Lerner said. "I don't know if that qualifies as all right."

"Let's have a look." Sandor kneeled down, opened his friend's shirt and checked his shoulder. "Lucky. Just a flesh wound."

"Why don't I feel lucky? Stings like a mother."

"I've seen you in worse shape after a bar fight." Sandor stood, held out a hand and said, "Come on."

"Come on where? I'm bleeding, in case you missed that part."

Sandor nodded. "I'll get that taken care of, but we have to assume our two visitors have spotters downstairs, and there'll be police and hotel security showing up any minute now. We need to get out, and we need to get out now."

Lerner took hold of Sandor's hand and stood.

"Grab your computer," Sandor told him as he had a look around. "Anything else you absolutely need to take?"

Lerner looked into Sandor's eyes. "I guess I don't have time to pack."

"If you can throw a couple of things in a bag, okay, but we've got to move."

Lerner did as he was told, tossing some clothes into a carry-on satchel in the bedroom.

Sandor collected the two automatics the shooters had used and threw them in the bag.

"Just in case," he explained.

Lerner nodded. "I knew I had problems," he said as he zipped the case closed. "I just can't believe anyone wants me dead."

"They don't," Sandor told him.

"What?"

Sandor didn't respond. He grabbed a hand towel from the bathroom, shoved it under Lerner's shirt and pressed hard. "Keep this in place," he said. Then he helped him pull on his tuxedo jacket to cover the growing bloodstain on his white dress shirt, then put on his own. He grabbed Lerner's bag and headed for the entrance of the suite, stepping past the bloody corpses. Opening the door he had a careful look up and down the corridor. "All right," he said. "Let's go." Lerner followed him down the hallway, hurrying past the bank of elevators and into the stairwell. "We'll grab the elevator a couple of floors down."

Lerner stayed right behind him. "I'm asking you a question, Jordan. If they didn't want to kill me, what was all that about?"

Sandor stopped and turned to him. "If they wanted you dead they could have shot you as soon as you opened the door, right? But they didn't. They shot at me, remember? I was in their way, so they figured me for collateral damage."

"Then what were they doing there?"

"It's only a guess, but I think they were there to take you someplace."

"Where? Why?"

"Hell if I know, but we're going to find out."

CHAPTER 16

New York City

Two men slipping out of a hotel after one in the morning carrying a small suitcase would have drawn unwanted attention in almost any city in the world, but not in New York. Clad in their tuxedos, Lerner and Sandor looked like a couple of musicians heading home after a club gig, and that's exactly how Sandor wanted it.

When they stepped off the elevator there were people in the lobby, in the bar and out on the street, but there was no sign anyone was reacting to the battle upstairs. At least not yet. Someone on their floor had certainly heard the shots and by now must have called the front desk—or the police—but those at ground level were apparently oblivious to what had occurred twelve floors above them. For the moment, Sandor's main concern was the possibility the two thugs in Lerner's suite might have accomplices waiting for them down here.

He was wary of everyone they passed as he moved away from the main entrance and exited through a side door onto 55th Street. Sirens were wailing in the distance now, which is also nothing extraordinary in New York at that hour, but Sandor could tell they were heading in his direction.

"Come on," he said as took Lerner by the arm and led him toward Madison Avenue.

"I'm doing the best I can, old buddy, but I have to tell you, I'm not a hundred percent."

"Well suck it up," Sandor said. "Neither am I." He had a look around. "We're not risking a hospital visit for that little scratch on your shoulder. Just breathe deep and keep walking."

They grabbed a cab at the corner of Madison and headed to a club behind Carnegie Hall where Sandor knew the bartender. He sat Lerner in a comfortable chair at a corner table, ordered drinks and put them down, then borrowed the house phone and made a call. When he was done he rejoined Lerner, who had polished off his double shot of scotch and was looking better for it.

"Nothing a little single malt won't help," Lerner said with a forced smile.

Sandor sat beside him and had a swallow of his bourbon. "Listen up partner. I've got to get you someplace safe while I sort things out. I've made the arrangements for that, and for a doctor to patch up your shoulder."

Lerner nodded, the combination of gunshot wound and whiskey having slowed his normal rhythm by a few RPMs. "Someplace safe would be good."

"I'm glad you agree."

Lerner hesitated. "What the hell do you really think that was about?"

"Not sure yet," Sandor said. "But they were watching us when we had drinks earlier today. One of their pals followed me home."

"Really?"

Sandor responded with a look that made it clear he was all business now. "You said you had an idea what I do."

Lerner nodded again, this time his head appeared to be on a spring. "I have a pretty good idea, yeah."

"Well I've got some friends who are going to take care of you. Experienced and well-armed men."

"From your office in the State Department?" Lerner asked with a crooked grin.

"No wise-guy, these men are freelancers." Sandor had any number of contacts outside the Agency, private contractors he respected. Now that it was evident Lerner had not exaggerated his concerns, he had to take his friend out of circulation so he could get to work.

"These are men who fly below the radar, if you know what I mean."

"Speaking of flying, how about another drink?"

"You okay to handle it?"

The grin reappeared and he was looking more like Joey Sax than he had all day. "Okay as I'll ever be."

Sandor gave the bartender a signal for another round. "These men are going to hide you and guard you. Just for a few days at the most. I told them you can afford Secret Service level coverage, because that's what you need."

Lerner's eyes cleared up a bit. "You really are serious."

"As a heart attack. Whatever they're after, you just saw how far they're willing to go. And by the way, I also need these people to cover *my* back. What I'm going to do is totally outside the ropes, you understand that?"

"I do. That's why I came to you."

"Because I have to tell you, we have another option. I can call the authorities and turn it over to them."

Lerner gave his head a vigorous shake, then winced. Disagreeing apparently required a more painful gesture than nodding. "I could have called them myself, chrissake. I go to the feds and I'll be ruined on sixteen different levels."

"I assumed that's what you'd say. So now this is all about trust. I'm going to take the information you gave me and get some answers for you, and you have to believe that I'll do whatever I can to protect you and to act in your best interests. But once I turn you over to these men, your deal is to do exactly as they tell you. You clear on that?"

"I'm clear, I'm clear. Where's my other cocktail?"

The second round of drinks arrived, much to Lerner's relief. The scotch was dulling both the pain in his shoulder and the fear in his eyes.

"We're going to be picked up here and you'll be taken to a doctor. After you get fixed up, you'll be escorted to a safe house on City Island in the Bronx. You can keep your computer, but no phone calls, no emails, no internet connection, nothing that would enable anyone to track your location. You got that?"

"Not even wifi? I'll be out of business."

"You'll be dead if you use it. You can miss a couple of days."

Lerner sighed. "Got it."

"Whether you think someone is a friend or an enemy at this point, it doesn't matter. You're not to have contact with anyone but me and my people. I'll reach out for you, not the other way around. If you need to notify your office that you'll be away for a few days, I'll handle it. All right?"

"All right."

They were quiet for a minute. "You never told me why you weren't at the old man's ceremony. You were invited, right?"

"Oh sure," Lerner said as he took a gulp of the whisky. "Sure I was invited, but I was out of town. "

Sandor nodded. "Your pal Hassan made it. You had to be pretty far out of town to miss something like that for O'Hara."

A sad looked passed over Lerner's face. "Yeah, sorry I never got to see him again."

"So where were you?"

"France," Lerner said with a shrug.

"France?" Sandor gave him a searching look.

"I was at a meeting at the place I told you about."

"Fronique."

Lerner nodded, then had another go at his drink.

"Well then, it seems we have more to discuss."

CHAPTER 17

New York City

Half an hour later a three man crew pulled up on 56th Street in a Suburban. The driver stayed at the wheel as the other men entered the bar and asked Sandor to join them on the street. After a brief discussion, Sandor went back inside to help Lerner to his feet, then led him out and into the back of the waiting SUV.

Sandor leaned inside and told his friend, "You do whatever they say," then handed him his bag.

Lerner nodded as the two men, who had been standing watch, quickly climbed into the back, on either side of him. Before they had pulled the doors closed, the driver put the car in gear and sped off.

Sandor returned to the bar, paid the bill, then took a cab back to his place, eager to sleep off the long day and night.

When he reached his apartment he was certain he had not been followed, but as soon as he unlocked the door he knew instantly that something was wrong.

It was nothing obvious, just a subtle tell he employed, even at times when he was not on active duty, such as now. His foyer had a small, colorful, oriental carpet. In the center, he used a small amount of beige powder—virtually invisible to anyone else since it matched the field of the rug. He always walked around it when he came home, something that had become a habit.

Now, however, the faintest outline of a partial footprint was visible.

As he stepped inside he could see that no table had been overturned or drawer left open, and yet he was certain the place had been searched—not tossed, just gone over. It was a professional job with almost nothing left out of its original position. He drew his weapon, pulled the door closed behind him, and began a search to ensure no one was waiting there to greet him on his return.

He moved slowly from room to room, checking closets, behind doors and in the tub.

The place was clear.

Then he checked the hidden compartment in the ceiling of his bedroom closet.

It had not been discovered, which was a relief. There was nothing else in the apartment they could have seen or taken that would matter.

He pulled his go-bag from the hidden shelf, placed it on the dresser, then sat on the edge of his bed and tried to make sense of things.

Someone had arranged to keep tabs on Lerner. First there was the spotter he saw outside the King Cole bar in the afternoon. Then there was the tail on his way home. It was only surveillance, no attempt was made to take him out at that point, which seemed to confirm that Lerner, not he, had been the target. They probably wanted to know who he was and where he was going after he left, but Sandor had been careful, having the taxi drop him two blocks away, then circling back on foot to be sure he had lost the tail. Even with that, if someone saw the building he entered, finding his apartment would still not be easy. He had no name on the mailbox or door.

Locating and breaking into his apartment therefore raised the stakes.

After failing to follow him all the way to his door, they must have gotten the information from another source. Given his State Department cover and the layers of security that protected his identity, someone had to have seriously deep connections to find their way here.

It makes no sense, Sandor told himself. Why would they need to search the apartment? Especially since they were tracking Lerner and made their play at the hotel? *What the hell would they be looking for here?*

In the hotel room, they were willing to kill Sandor, but they obviously wanted Lerner alive.

Why?

Sandor checked his watch. It was nearly three. He had to call Bobby Ferriello, an NYPD Lieutenant he had worked with in preventing a terrorist plot in midtown. He preferred to wait until morning, but by then there would already be an APB issued with a BOLO for Howard Lerner, occupant of a luxury hotel suite where two bullet-riddled bodies had been found. He had no choice.

Sandor took a clean phone from the leather bag, entered the activation code and punched in the numbers.

Ferriello picked up his cell phone call on the fourth ring and mumbled something that sounded like, "What?"

"It's Sandor."

"Sandor? What the hell . . ."

"I wouldn't call you at this hour if I didn't have to."

"Uh huh," the detective replied as he roused himself to full consciousness. "Well that's cold comfort since *this hour* happens to be the middle of the night, just in case you hadn't noticed."

"There was a shooting tonight," Sandor told him, then provided the headlines.

By the time he was done, Ferriello was fully awake. He said, "I'm in Brooklyn narcotics, Sandor, you need to get in touch with the boys in midtown homicide."

"You wouldn't want me to call a complete stranger about something like this, would you?"

"Why didn't you call the police from the scene?"

"And sit around to see if the shooters had friends backing them up?"

The policeman grunted. He knew Sandor made sense on that score.

"You remember what I do, right? It's not my job to sit around and wait for the cavalry to show up."

Ferriello said, "Hold on," then engaged in a short dialogue with his wife, something to the effect that he was on the line with a friend in trouble, and would be done soon. "All right," he said as he returned his attention to Sandor, "what do you want from me?"

"I need you to contact the homicide squad that handles this. Tell them you and I have worked together, that I'll come in and make a statement later. But for now they've got to lay off Lerner and me."

"You're joking, right?"

"Just let them know I'm a federal agent, nothing more than that. This was a clear case of self-defense, the way the room was shot up their forensics team will see that in a heartbeat. All I need is a little time."

There was silence. Then Ferriello said, "Let me make some calls. Where can I reach you?"

"I'll get back to you, but take this down." He then recited a phone number in Washington. "You remember Craig Raabe? If you get pushback on this, he's the guy to call, he'll make it right."

"Okay, let me see what I can do."

"There's just one more thing."

"Naturally."

Sandor told him about his apartment. "I don't want to file a formal report, I just need a discreet investigation, see if anyone in the neighborhood or my building witnessed anything."

"You don't want your own people doing that?"

"I don't even want them knowing."

"And I shouldn't ask why."

"I would appreciate it if you didn't."

"Uh huh. All right, let me see what I can do about that. Just one more thing for me, then."

"Name it."

"Any chance I can buy back my introduction to you?"

After he signed off with Ferriello, Sandor knew he would have to leave the apartment and check into a hotel. First, however, he called Beth Sharrow.

"It's Sandor," he announced in response to her sleepy-voiced hello.

"What a pleasant surprise."

"Hope I didn't wake your boyfriend."

"Cute," she replied, but did not say whether or not she was alone. "You better have a good reason for this call Jordan."

"I do. I've got a problem and I need your help." Then he shared with her what he told Ferriello.

"I remember you mentioning your friend Lerner. Actually, I can understand why someone would want to shoot *you*, but . . ."

"They were after him, not me," Sandor interrupted.

"I see. You want to tell me why?"

"I'm not sure yet."

"And the help you need?"

"I'm on leave. Had a little accident and Byrnes has me on R & R, so I'm strictly on my own here, can't use the resources at Langley. Once I sort some things out I'm going to need information on a number of people."

"And you want me to get it for you."

"Look how sharp you are, even in the middle of the night. By the way, this conversation isn't disturbing the diplomat's sleep, is it?"

"Are you asking for my help or are you trying to provoke me into hanging up?"

"Help would be good."

"All right, you let me know what you need and I'll decide what I'm willing to do."

"That's great, I'll get back to you in the morning."

"Good," she said, "because now I'm going to try to get back to sleep."

"Thanks Beth."

She paused. "Same old Jordan."

"It's what I do," he said.

"You sure you're all right for now?"

"I'm hanging in there."

"Well whatever you're up to, be careful. And be sure to take your meds." Then she hung up.

Sandor smiled, knowing that last line was a message. *Wonder who told her I'm supposed to be taking medication?*

CHAPTER 18

CIA Headquarters, Langley, Virginia

Lieutenant Ferriello made the phone call Sandor requested, which led to several irritating transfers before he was finally put through to the officer in charge in the 17th Precinct. The captain there told Ferriello they had already received word of the shootings at the St. Regis, had dispatched a pair of detectives, a forensics team, and the coroner's office. When Ferriello explained what he wanted, the man actually laughed out loud.

"I want to get this straight," the captain said, "just in case I keep my job long enough to have to write a report. You're telling me you know the identity of the perp who left these two stiffs behind. That this shooter is not the guy who was renting the suite, but a spook working out of some alphabet agency in D.C., and you're asking me to hold off on putting out an arrest warrant, or to even start looking for either of these two jokers, until the feds get back to me. Do I have this right?"

Ferriello let out a long, audible sigh. He had worked with Sandor twice before and, compared to some of the things he had been called upon to do in the past, this didn't even seem like a big deal. "That's exactly what I want, and I wouldn't be asking if I didn't know who I was dealing with. Just give me an hour or two, I'm sure I can get Washington to confirm."

"You at least going to give me the guy's name?"

"I can't do that, not yet. But ask around the department about me, I'm not someone who's going to hang you out to dry on this."

"Ask around? It's four in morning, for godssake. Who am I gonna ask?"

"Just give me a couple of hours, that's all I need."

There was silence, then the captain asked, "How high up does this spook go?"

"High enough," Ferriello told him.

"All right," the captain said. "My men are already at the crime scene, so I'm covered there. I'll have them take their time. You've got two hours, provided I have your word you're going to hand over this information later today."

"You've got it," Ferriello said, thanked him, then called Craig Raabe on the number Sandor had provided.

"What?" a sleepy voice answered.

"No reason for you to be getting your beauty sleep while Sandor has everyone else up," Ferriello said, then filled him in.

Raabe was fully alert now, asked a few short questions, then told him, "I got it. Who do I need to call in NYPD homicide to cover your ass?"

⊙

94

In the Information Age, intelligence moves up and down the food chain with lightning speed. By the time Raabe arrived at his office at Langley, just as the sun was rising, the CIA, FBI, NSA and NYPD were aware of the shootings at the St. Regis; the likely participation in that event of an unidentified federal agent; and the disappearance of an international financier by the name of Howard Lerner, who was wanted for questioning in connection with the incident.

Just a few hours before, Sandor checked into a boutique hotel he sometimes used, on Madison Avenue and 76th Street, and had barely entered the REM realm of sleep when his secure cell phone buzzed him back into consciousness.

He picked it up and said, "Sandor."

"Good morning sunshine," the familiar voice greeted him. "Seems like you've been awfully busy for a guy on medical leave."

"Ferriello called you."

"He did," Raabe said. "He took care of the homicide squad, kept your name out of it for now, and I followed up to be sure we've got his back. But people are looking for this friend of yours. They had his name as the occupant of the suite, nothing we could do about that."

"You on a secure line?"

"I am."

Sandor sat up in bed and took a swallow of water from the bottle on his nightstand. Then he told Raabe everything he had learned from Howard Lerner, and everything that had occurred since the prior morning, right through the shootings. "I'm going to need help on this."

"You think?" When Sandor did not respond, Raabe said, "You've got to come in and see Byrnes."

"This is not company business, Craig. I'm on leave doing a favor for a friend."

"Maybe so, but there are things I need to tell *you* about what happened last night. First, you were identified in surveillance video taken at that U.N. soiree last night, clearly seen accompanying the now-missing Howard Lerner. By the way, you're moving around pretty well for a guy on one leg."

"Man's got to get out on the town once in a while."

"Well, when you put together that sighting with the man who was renting the suite that became a war zone, and the fact that your pal Ferriello was the cop who intervened after the fact, our friends downstairs have already concluded you were responsible for the scene at the St. Regis."

Sandor yawned. "I get blamed for everything."

"Second, the two hostiles you took out have been preliminarily identified as members of a cell run by Ansar al-Thar."

"Splinter group of ISIS."

"Bingo. But hold on, there's more."

"I was hoping."

"My third news flash is about the Hartford bombing. No one ever took responsibility, as you know, but the boys in DI believe they've identified the group."

"Ansar al-Thar?"

"Give that man a gold star. Incidentally, NSA is working on the same theory."

"What the hell would a terrorist group want with Jim O'Hara or Howie Lerner?"

"No idea, but in case you forgot, you're not supposed to be involved in investigating the Hartford attack."

"I'm not."

"Then you better spend some energy figuring out how to explain that you just took out two men from the same cell that —"

"I get the point," Sandor said. "Man, the last thing I need right now is trouble with Byrnes."

Raabe laughed. "I think we're way past that. He already called, he's on his way in, and he wants to see you as fast as you can get down here."

"Damn."

"You know how he feels about getting up early."

"Early? I haven't even been to sleep yet."

"Welcome to the club," Raabe said. "What do you really make of this?"

"Not sure," Sandor admitted. "I'm still trying to piece together what Lerner's told me so far." Sandor paused. "I realize it's going to sound crazy, but the one thing I keep coming back to is the idea that O'Hara wasn't the target of the blast."

"We've been looking at that theory," Raabe said. "Remember, there were three bombs with all sorts of possible victims. This wasn't a sniper shot, this was C4 and napalm B."

"That's my point. Suppose they chose that form of attack as a cover-up? What if the reason they used explosives was to hide the identity of the intended victim?"

"Not very efficient. Who's to even say they got their man? Or woman? When those blasts went off, there was no way to know who would be standing where, except O'Hara. He was standing up front, and there was a large chunk of the explosive right under his desk."

"Don't remind me, Byrnes let me read the preliminary report," Sandor said. "Can't get the image out of my mind."

"Sorry," Raabe said. "So, you have any theories on who they might have been after?"

"Maybe. I need you to get me a copy of the complete file the FBI put together on the blast patterns, the seating chart, all of that."

"Whoa cowboy, sounds to me like someone's got to read you the Posse Comitatus Act for the six hundredth time."

"Hey, I just want to see what we have so far. I was a victim, for Chrissake."

"We've got some new data from analytics, I'll see what I can do. Meanwhile you need to come in."

Sandor thought it over. "All right, but I'm not flying. I'll grab a first class seat on the next Amtrak. At least I can get a couple hours sleep that way."

CHAPTER 19

North Africa

In a camp less than one hundred miles east of Benghazi in Libya, a group of men sat inside a low-slung white building consisting of a single room. One of the walls was covered with maps and charts, in front of which stood the leader of the gathering, a Syrian named Nizan Farashi. The others sat on mats and rugs placed on the dirt floor, listening as Farashi explained their objectives.

"There will be far too much protection at the airport. We must wait until they have been loaded onto their trucks and buses with the supplies. Even though their route has not been disclosed, the convoy is laden with supplies and will move slowly as a matter of necessity. We will disrupt their progress here," he said, pointing to a spot on the largest of the maps.

One of the men, seated closest to Farashi, asked, "Have we any information of the security that will accompany their expedition?"

Farashi turned to his most trusted aide, a young man by the name of Gabir. "Tell them how we are approaching that issue."

Gabir stood and faced the others. "We have no specific information yet. However, the United Nations deplores the use of force, so we are basing our assumptions on prior experience. There will undoubtedly be armed guards accompanying the group, but we have received confirmation that a military presence has been forbidden. The actress and the singer will likely have personal bodyguards, but we do not yet know how many, how well trained they are, or what level of preparation they have made for such contingencies. We have people in place who will be sending us updated information before they set out from Mosul for the camp."

Another of his men asked if he was certain the targeted individuals would be part of the mission.

"Yes," Farashi said, pointing to a group of photographs on the board behind him. "Once we create the initial distraction, the most important thing is to assure them that we mean their people no harm. Faced with the choice of fighting or being taken alive, westerners will always opt for survival."

There were expressions of assent from the attendees, with a few comments about the weakness of the west in general and Americans in particular.

"They will want to live," Farashi interrupted, "and we will provide them that choice. Proceed Gabir."

The younger man went on, "The critical element for this phase of the operation is to create separation between those we will take as hostages and the others. Those people are not important to us, and it will be preferable if we can simply set them free. We will disable their vehicles, but we have no use for dozens of hostages. That will only create unwanted complications."

An elder in the back of the room spoke up. "What if these others resist?"

Farashi nodded slowly, as if this were some unpleasant detail he had already been obliged to consider. "We may be forced to make examples of anyone in their party with heroic intent."

"We are authorized to kill them?"

"As it becomes necessary, yes," Farashi replied. "Battlefield conditions will dictate such decisions, but only on my order."

If anyone in the room saw the irony of referring to an unprovoked attack on a humanitarian mission as a battlefield, no one said so.

"However," Gabir continued, "the key people we have identified are to be protected at all costs." He pointed to the photographs behind Farashi. "If any of these individuals are harmed during this first phase, it is likely to incite an immediate military response. Only if we demonstrate these people are safe will our enemies hold off on such action and try to negotiate their release. If it appears we are randomly killing them, our enemies will mount a counteroffensive, and we will have failed."

Farashi agreed with the importance of this approach. "We cannot allow our emotions to get the better of us as we confront these infidels. We cannot wantonly kill or injure the very people who are central to our plan."

Another of the older members in the group raised an issue about a critical aspect of the plan that had been troubling many of them. They were a collection of radicals who had fought for the glory of Allah using the crude and brutal tools of terrorism they understood, all of which were well-known to them and had become all too familiar to the world at large. Now Farashi had formulated a complex scheme relying on technology none of them had ever used before.

"What of your other plan?" the man asked. "Is everything in place?"

Farashi hesitated before responding. "My brothers, we have not come this far without every calculation having been properly made. We have received the necessary assurances that, provided we complete our tasks, our objectives will be achieved."

There were some other exchanges among the rank and file until Farashi brought them back to order.

"Please do not concern yourselves," he told them. "Our task is to capture these faithless people, and in the name of Allah we will succeed." Then he began chanting "*Allahu Akbar*," and, as the others joined him, he turned to have a look at the photographs behind him, his attention focused on the picture of Shahid Hassan.

CHAPTER 20

CIA Headquarters, Langley, Virginia

Deputy Director Mark Byrnes spent the early part of his morning sifting through the available information on the shootings in NYC. As Craig Raabe predicted, the DD was less than pleased about having to come into the office at this hour to review a matter that would typically not even come across his desk. In this case, Byrnes realized the situation required his personal attention.

Not only had he heard from Raabe about the double homicide, but he also received a text about the incident from Beth Sharrow.

When Sandor was released from the hospital, Byrnes warned him not to become involved in anything resembling an investigation into the Hartford bombing. That done, Byrnes knew a simple admonition was not going to stop his best agent from looking into the death of his friend O'Hara—it was only a matter of time before Sandor began his own inquiry. Byrnes also knew the identity of Sandor's inner circle within the Agency, the trusted few he would go to for off-the-record assistance. That crew began with Craig Raabe at Langley, and included the talented analyst Beth Sharrow in New York. Rather than fight the inevitable, Byrnes instructed Raabe to let him know what, if anything, he heard from his friend, then reached out for Beth. He filled her in on Sandor's injuries and suggested that she was in a position to help.

"I know how you feel about him," Byrnes told her when they spoke the previous week. "I'm not asking you to betray him. I'm ordering you to help me protect him."

Beth said she understood, but informed the DD she had not heard from Sandor in some time.

"Don't worry," Byrnes told her. "After what happened in Hartford, you will."

The encounter with Sandor at the U.N. might have been happenstance, but his phone call to her in the middle of the night certainly was not. When she agreed to assist Sandor, she was ensuring they would remain in contact, just as Byrnes had asked. When Beth reminded Sandor to take his medications she was providing him a signal.

This morning Byrnes received word from Beth about running into Sandor, the subsequent phone call, and their arrangement to be in touch. She had reported back to the DD, just as he had directed.

Meanwhile, Byrnes learned from Craig Raabe that Sandor had reached out to Ferriello after the attack, and that Raabe had followed up by contacting the NYPD, requesting that they keep a lid on the investigation. The DD was shaking his head in disgust when his assistant knocked on his door and showed Gabe Somerset in.

"Sit down," Byrnes said, then handed part of the file across the desk. "Have a look."

"What's this about?"

"Two shooters found dead in New York City. Preliminaries on their fingerprints indicate they were connected to Ansar al-Thar."

Somerset gave the paperwork a quick read. "Who took them out?"

"Might have been one of our people," Byrnes said. For now he was gathering information, not sharing it. "The better question, it seems to me, is what were they after?"

Somerset nodded as he scanned the paperwork. "Who is this Howard Lerner, the man who rented the suite?"

"Some sort of international trader. American. Spends a lot of his time in the U.K."

"Where is he now?"

"Don't know."

"Report says no guns were recovered at the scene."

Byrnes nodded. "NYPD says the room was shot up in every direction. Whoever left the two bodies behind obviously removed their weapons."

Somerset continued to read, then said, "I have no idea what a splinter group operating out of North Africa has to do with a stock broker, or whatever he was, but I'll run it down."

"Please do."

"It would be helpful if we could speak with this Lerner."

Byrnes' secretary called on the intercom and announced that Jordan Sandor had arrived.

"Show him in," Byrnes said.

Somerset was already standing when Sandor walked in.

"Mr. Somerset."

Somerset held up the file Byrnes had given him. "Why do I have the feeling this is about you, Sandor?"

Sandor looked at the file and asked, "What might that be? A review of my record for a possible commendation."

Somerset responded with a grunt. "I'll be back to you ASAP," he said to Byrnes. Then he made his way out, shutting the door behind him.

"I don't think he likes me," Sandor said.

"Neither do I at the moment. Sit down."

"I got here as fast as I could. I'm not a well man you know."

"You're well enough to be violating federal law, my direct orders, and shooting up a midtown hotel room in New York."

Sandor took a seat but said nothing.

"I want you to give a full statement of everything that happened. I want to know what you've been up to, who Howard Lerner is, and what you were doing at the U.N. last night. Then I'm sending you to Walter Reed."

"I get points one and two. What's going on at Walter Reed?"

"I've arranged for a battery of tests. I want the current status of your recovery, especially after your escapades last night." Byrnes called in his assistant, Brandon Garinger, who switched on the digital recording device inside the cabinet beside the DD's conference table.

"Where do you want me to start?" Sandor asked.

"How about telling us who Howard Lerner is and why you were with him in the first place?"

The debriefing did not take long. Sandor explained that Lerner had served with him in the military under O'Hara, stayed in touch from time to time, looked him up when he was in town yesterday and invited him to the gala at the U.N. He said nothing about the reasons Lerner had sought him out, nor did he offer any theory on why two men had entered the hotel suite with guns drawn.

"Lucky thing I was there, don't you think?"

Byrnes frowned in response. "Where's Lerner now?"

"Don't know. We weren't waiting around to see if they had friends. We took off in separate directions."

Byrnes offered up one of his most skeptical looks. "You're telling me you have no idea where Lerner is?"

"As I said, sir, we went our separate ways."

"After removing the weapons and fleeing a crime scene without calling the authorities."

"I did make a call."

"Ah yes. Two hours after the shootings you called your accomplice Ferriello whom, I fear, will someday lose his pension just for the privilege of knowing you."

"Ferriello did nothing improper, as far as I'm aware. As for me, I took the safest course of action under the circumstances."

Byrnes stood, punched the STOP button on the recorder, rapped his knuckles on the table, and leaned forward. "That little fairy tale you just shared with us is about as sanitized as your State Department dossier."

Sandor responded with the blankest stare he could manage.

"Garinger," the DD said to his assistant, "get a car for Hans Christian Andersen here, have him taken over to Walter Reed. Right now."

Four hours later, Sandor was back in Byrnes office, this time with Craig Raabe present. They sat silently as the DD reviewed the results of the diagnostics that had just been emailed to him from the hospital.

The medical staff had given Sandor expedited treatment, performing an MRI on his leg and shoulder; a CT scan and EEG of his brain; a neurological evaluation; some general poking, prodding and reflex testing; and blood work for which the results would be coming tomorrow.

"Bottom line is that you've improved, but you're still not a hundred percent," Byrnes said as he removed his reading glasses and looked across the desk at his two agents. "Now, there's no recording device on and it's just the three of us here, so I want you to tell me what you're really up to."

Sandor was with two of the men he trusted more than any in the world, so he said, "Lerner's in trouble. I think it's fair to say the trouble is bigger than he realized, based on that attack last night. But since it's not Agency business and I was on leave, I was trading for my own account, just trying to help a pal."

"By shooting two men?"

"By defending myself against two hostiles. I promise you, they shot first."

"You said earlier that Lerner served with you under James O'Hara."

"True, but this has nothing to do with him or the bombing. At least not yet."

"What is that supposed to mean?"

Sandor looked at Raabe, then back at the DD. "I met a man named Hassan last night. Also injured in Hartford. He knew O'Hara, he was invited to the ceremony. Hassan is a Saudi, lives overseas, came to New York to be honored at the U.N., then he's leaving for Iraq on a humanitarian mission for the World Health Institute. Also has ties to the investment company Lerner works for." He smiled. "If there's one thing you and I agree about, sir, we don't like coincidences."

Byrnes nodded. "I'm still listening."

"What if the intended victim of the attack was not O'Hara? The FBI is proceeding on the assumption he was, but what if they're wrong?"

"I told you to stay away from the investigation," Byrnes reminded him, but this time there was not much conviction in his tone.

"I'm not investigating Hartford. But hours after I met Hassan, who just happened to be in Hartford two weeks ago, and just happens to be involved in business with my old Army pal from my days in Iraq, and just happened to know our C.O. from those same days, someone busts into a hotel room and tries to take Lerner, and shoot me in the process."

"You said Lerner was invited to Hartford but didn't attend the ceremony."

"That's correct, sir."

"What if Lerner was the target? What if they assumed he would be there but he didn't show?"

"Possible, I suppose. All I have so far are questions, certainly no conclusions, I'm just telling you what I know."

Byrnes thought it over. "What you're *not* telling me is anything about your friend's problems. You say he came to you for help."

"He did."

"And you think his issues may somehow be connected to Hartford. Or Hassan."

"You don't sound convinced."

"I'm not. But I am still determined to keep you away from an inquiry into a domestic terrorist attack. It is not within our jurisdiction and," he added as he pointed to his computer screen, "you're in no condition to be returned to active field duty even if it were."

"I feel I'm ready."

"I'll take that under advisement."

Sandor's cell phone buzzed and he had a look at the screen. "It's Ferriello."

"Put him on the speaker," the DD said.

Sandor did as he was ordered. "I'm here with my chief and Craig Raabe," he told the policeman.

"Good afternoon," Ferriello said, then gave his report.

The homicide team investigating the midtown shootings concluded that the rendition of events Sandor had provided Ferriello was consistent with the physical evidence at the scene. The pattern of the gunshots indicated the assailants entered the suite and fired in the direction of the chairs and couch. The responsive shots were initiated from the interior of the sitting room, aimed toward the area where the intruders had entered.

For now the NYPD was willing to keep a lid on making anything public, other than a bare bones statement about a hotel shooting where two men were found dead.

"Maybe you can claim the two of them shot each other," Sandor suggested helpfully. Byrnes responded with a disapproving look.

Ferriello said nothing about the discreet investigation he had ordered at Sandor's request into the break-in at the apartment. The police did a brief canvass of the building and the surrounding areas, but did not locate a single witness to any suspicious activity in or around the place. Sandor said he wanted that done on the down low, and the detective obliged. He would call him later and let him know. For now he said, "That's all I've got."

Byrnes thanked him and told him they would be in touch.

"If you don't mind me bringing this up Sandor, when are you going to drop by my place and do your civic duty?" Ferriello asked.

"I've already given a sworn statement to the Deputy Director here," Sandor told him. "He'll be getting you a copy of the portion relevant to the shootings." He looked to Byrnes, who nodded. "But don't worry," Sandor added, "I'll be by to see you soon in the flesh."

"I can hardly wait," the detective replied.

After they finished with Ferriello, Byrnes returned to the issue at hand.

"Your job right now is to finish rehab and follow orders. The notion that you can play detective for your old buddy is utter nonsense. You work for the federal government. If you get caught doing anything that embarrasses this Agency I'm not going to cover for you, and you certainly know the Director will not. You go off the reservation again, and I'll leave you there." Byrnes turned to Raabe. "That goes for you too. I find you passing information to your pal here, your ass'll be in the same sling."

They were all quiet, until Sandor said, "Since I'm apparently still the walking wounded, can Craig give me a lift to the airport?"

CHAPTER 21

New York City

Byrnes arranged a seat for Sandor on a company plane heading for White Plains. Sandor still had his go-bag, including weapons, and a commercial flight would have posed unnecessary complications. The DD also agreed Sandor should do his best to keep out of the public eye for the time being. A private flight and staying away from his apartment made for a good start.

En route to Westchester Airport Sandor telephoned Beth. First he apologized for having called her in the middle of the night, then he asked her to dinner.

"If this is your way of making up for ruining my beauty sleep, it better be a good restaurant."

"*Il Mulino?*"

"Sold."

"The ambassador won't mind?"

"Not if I don't tell him."

"That's not like you, Beth."

"I told you Jordan, he's my friend. And if *you* want to stay my friend you won't push it."

"I'm in the air, should be able to pick you up at eight."

"Don't bother, I know what it's like to wait around for you. I'll meet you there at eight-thirty," she told him, then hung up.

After he landed Sandor headed straight for *Il Mulino*, making sure to arrive early. He was greeted by the maitre 'd, Claudio, whom he had met the first time he stopped in for a lunch more than a decade before, the day it became his favorite restaurant in New York. The place was busy tonight, as it always was, but he found a seat at the small bar and ordered a drink. Then he pulled out the paperwork Raabe had slipped him. Among other things, it included a diagram of the blast patterns inside O'Hara's courtroom and the approximate positions of those present when the explosions went off. Since there was no seating plan for the ceremony, it would have been impossible for the saboteur to know where anyone would be at the moment the timing devices ignited the C-4. O'Hara might not have even been on the bench at that moment, he could have been mingling with guests anywhere in the room.

It doesn't make sense, Sandor told himself as he studied the other information.

"You look lost in thought," Beth said when she arrived a little while later. "I should add, 'as usual.'"

Sandor stood. "And you look lovely. I should also add, 'as usual.'"

Claudio came up and kissed Beth on both cheeks. "I'm so happy to see the two of you together again." Then he showed them to the corner table he was holding, where he took Beth's order for a glass of Sauvignon Blanc. Sandor had carried his own drink and his leather bag.

"*Il Mulino,*" she said as she gave the crowded room an appraising look. "Trying to dredge up some of our fond old memories, Sandor?"

"The thought never crossed my mind."

"But you knew I couldn't resist," she said with a smile.

"You mean you're only here because it's a great restaurant?"

"The point is, I'm here, so now you get to tell me what I can do for you."

"Do for me? Beth, I swear, this job is turning you into a cynic."

She was still smiling when she said, "Come on, you don't think I believe this is a social invitation, do you?"

Sandor allowed himself a short laugh. "If we're going to start that way, how about you explain your comment about my meds this morning."

"Please don't try to dignify your call in the middle of the night by characterizing it as *morning.*"

"Fair enough. Now, you going to tell me where you heard I'm supposed to be taking medication?"

"I'm an analyst, remember?" She had another look around the room, but this time it was with real purpose. Then she lowered her voice as she said, "I know you were in Hartford, and I know you were seriously hurt. Is that good enough?"

He stuck out his lower lip and thought it over. "Not bad, for an analyst."

"How do you feel? Truthfully."

"Truthfully? I'm about ninety percent. When the DD asks, I tell him I'm right as rain."

"But you're still on leave."

Sandor picked up his bourbon and had a sip. "That's true."

"So this midtown shooting I heard about today, and whatever else you're up to, is outside the authority of the agency."

"Right."

"Which is why you need my help."

"That's also true." He sat back. "You know, this honesty thing can become habitual."

"Not in your case," she told him.

A waiter brought Beth's glass of wine and they fell silent as it was placed on the table and they were handed menus.

When they were alone again, Sandor said, "You know about Hartford and you know about the shootings. What you may not know is that I was visited yesterday by a teammate from my service days in Iraq."

If she knew, she was not saying. "Go on."

"I will," he said. "Let's order first."

They signaled for the waiter to come back, listened to him recite an endless list of specials, made their selections, and Sandor chose a bottle of wine. When the man ambled away Sandor leaned forward and told her everything.

Sandor had figured that Beth would be one of the people Byrnes would call on to keep tabs on him. He also figured her comment on the meds was her way of letting him know that she was in the loop, without actually telling him outright. Now he needed to find out just how far Byrnes had authorized her to go.

When he finished describing what had happened in the past day and half, including a sanitized version of what Lerner told him, he said, "Now you're probably asking yourself what I intend to do next."

Beth smiled that impossibly warm smile of hers. "You're a mind reader."

"Bermuda," he said.

"I beg your pardon? I know this is only my first glass of wine, but I could have sworn you said Bermuda."

"My first stop is Hamilton, then on to London."

"I see. You're going to spend your rehab working on a British accent."

"First of all, the Brits don't have an accent. They invented the language, which means we're the ones with the accent. Second, I'm going to follow the trail of the two murders I just described, see if that tells me anything about what's happening at Lerner's company."

"Two accidental deaths, you mean."

"Not as far as I can tell. One was a drug overdose by a woman who doesn't do drugs, and the other was a hit-and-run with no viable witnesses."

Beth gave him a hard look. "What has all this to do with the bombing in Hartford?"

"There you go again, jumping to conclusions. Who said anything about a connection to Hartford? The DD told me to stay away from any investigation of O'Hara's death, and that's what I'm doing."

"Horsefeathers."

"Whoa, that's pretty strong language coming from a refined young woman like you."

"You're really going to Bermuda?"

They were brought the bottle of Brunello Sandor had ordered. After giving it a taste, Sandor nodded, their glasses were filled, and the waiter left them alone again. "Like I said, Bermuda and then London. Actually, I was hoping *we* were going."

"To Bermuda and London?"

"Is there an echo in here?" He held up his glass of wine. "*Cent anni*," he said.

She lifted her glass of the Italian red, touched it to his, and had a sip, never taking her eyes off him. "Convince me."

"Okay." He had a long swallow of the Brunello and placed his glass on the table. "I hear the pink sandy beaches of Bermuda are calling your name, followed by the excitement of Piccadilly . . ."

"Stop the nonsense. I want you to give me a real reason to go."

He leaned towards her. "Someone came after one of my best friends last night. They also shot at me. Add that to the fact that our former C.O. got blown to bits a couple of weeks ago, and I got pretty banged up that day myself. I think there may be a possible link, but even if there's not I've got some work to do and I want you with me."

Beth nodded slowly. "You've got my attention."

Sandor pulled out the chart of O'Hara's courtroom he had been studying when she arrived. "Have a look at this." As Beth examined the pattern of the explosions, Sandor said, "Don't try and tell me you haven't already been analyzing this attack."

She looked up at him. "When I heard you were involved, I admit I pulled the file."

Sandor smiled. "Always looking out for me."

"Old habits die hard," she told him, then began moving things around the table. The wine bottle, bread basket, salt and pepper shaker. "Here," she said, "let's say this is the judge's desk, these are the benches where people sit, and these are the counsel tables. Now look at where the explosives were set."

"I'm with you."

She sat back. "Maybe they simply chose the spots where they were least likely to be discovered."

"Possible."

Beth began moving their knives and forks around. "Assuming this is O'Hara, this is his law secretary, this is the state senator . . ."

"All of whom were killed in the blast, I know. But how could the bomber predict who would be standing or sitting where at the moment the timers ignited the explosives? Impossible. There were no assigned places."

"Except for the judge, who would be up there, at the front."

"But there was no way of knowing when. The report says he was mingling with his guests."

"Before he stepped behind the bench."

Sandor nodded.

"So you think this was a random attack?" she asked.

"No, that's the strange part. I think it was made to appear random, but I believe they had a specific target in mind."

At that moment two servers arrived with their appetizers. The waiters stared down with puzzled looks—the flatware, glasses and other items were scattered all over the table.

"You guys are about to disrupt a crime scene," Sandor said. Then he and Beth made room for the dishes. When the waiters left Sandor pointed to the chart she was still holding. "And why plant a charge in the back row? Presumably the least important people in the group would be seated there."

"You're right."

"So who were they after?" He didn't wait for an answer as he dug into his baked clams. He had eaten almost nothing all day and realized he was starving.

"Whoever it was, you think you'll find answers tracking down the two deaths your friend told you about?"

"Not necessarily, but it's a starting point that might help Lerner. And it keeps me out of the DD's hair. So what do you say? You in?"

Staring down at her plate, Beth said, "I've just been re-assigned, but I can probably get some time off."

Still concentrating on her salad she did not see him grin—first, because he had already heard about her new position in the Company and, second, because he assumed that Byrnes was the one behind that re-assignment and would be the one to approve her leave.

"Why is it important that I go with you?" she asked, finally looking up.

"Any number of reasons. It's better cover for me if we travel as a couple. You can also keep an eye on certain things when I'm otherwise occupied. And then there's the fact that you're the best analyst I know."

"You sure know how to sweet talk a girl, Sandor."

He gave her a stern look. "This may get nasty," he said. "You'll need to keep your distance and watch your back."

Beth smiled. "I'd have to be a contortionist to manage that maneuver."

"I'm not kidding," he warned her.

"I know the business we're in, Jordan. You worry about yourself, I'll take care of me."

"That's tough talk."

"Need I remind you of what I've been through?"

Sandor winced. "No, you don't," he said.

They finished their appetizers and returned to moving the salt and pepper shakers around.

Beth was once again focused on the position of the three improvised bombs. "These are not the sort of people who went to all this trouble to initiate an arbitrary attack. Who else was there that might have been of interest to them?"

"I have some questions about a Saudi named Hassan," Sandor said.

"I know who he is, I met him last night. You think he might have been the target?"

"Either that, or he was there to maneuver the target into position."

"He has impeccable credentials, Jordan."

"So did Edward Snowden," he said.

CHAPTER 22

New York City

Beth needed the following day to arrange permission for her leave from the office—which Byrnes promptly had the New York station chief grant—and to pack for their trip. Sandor was still traveling light and staying away from his apartment so, after seeing her safely home to her new place in Tribeca, he bid her good night and grabbed some much needed sleep at the Standard Hotel on the High Line off 10th Avenue. In the morning he bought some clothes and sundries, added them to his leather bag, then took a cab to the Bronx to visit Howard Lerner.

When he arrived at the safe house on City Island, he was informed that his friend was still in his room. There were two bodyguards on duty at the moment. Sandor knew Bob Kinnie, the head of the detail, very well. He had never met the other man, who called himself Bear.

After introductions were made, the three men sat in the small living room.

Kinnie gave the update, which was in essence a report that all was quiet. "I'll tell you though, the guy's a bit peculiar."

"Tell me something I don't know."

"Last night he wanted us to take him out to a strip club. I'm not joking," Kinnie added in response to Sandor's amused expression. "I mean, two guys almost offed him less than twenty four hours before, and he wants us to take him to some club he heard about near Yankee Stadium."

Now Sandor laughed. "I assume you explained the rules of the road."

"Oh yeah. We ordered pizza and dealt some poker. Jaeger was still here so we played four-handed. Your pal Lerner wiped us out. He some kind of cardsharp or what?"

"He's a financial wizard, Bobby, so I wouldn't be throwing my car keys in the pot if I were you." When Kinnie frowned, Sandor added, "Don't worry, he's very well heeled. You'll all have your losses covered when he pays the bill here."

"I hope so."

"How's his shoulder?"

"He's not complaining about it," Kinnie said.

The door to the far bedroom opened and Lerner joined them. He looked showered, shaved and ready for the day ahead. "Mr. Sandor," he said. "What a pleasant surprise."

"Sleeping in?"

"I was up late playing on my computer." He looked toward the kitchen. "I'm in desperate need of some joe."

As Lerner got himself a mug of black coffee, Sandor asked the two bodyguards to leave them alone, so they headed to another room.

Lerner sat across from his friend with his steaming cup of java.

"How are you doing?" Sandor asked.

"I'm sore, I'm cranky and I'm being bored to death."

"Not as bad as being shot to death."

"Don't be so sure. My choices are television or cards, and they can't play cards worth a damn."

"So I heard."

"You tell me I can't email or use the net, which means I can't trade. That's like cutting my head off."

"I also told you, if you need me to pass any instructions to your office, I'll take care of it."

Lerner stared at him as if he was speaking a foreign language. "It doesn't work that way Jordan. I have to make instantaneous decisions. I take a position, then sell it, then maybe buy it back. All in a matter of minutes."

"Then consider this a vacation from all that stress."

"If I want to take a vacation I'll go to Bali or the Caymans or just about anyplace but City Island."

"Hey," Sandor said, pointing to the window. "Look at that water view. What the hell do you have to complain about?"

"You want a complete list?"

"Enough," Sandor said. "You asked for my help. After the other night it's obvious that your concerns are real, and even more serious than you said. You want to head back to the city, it's okay with me, but then you're on your own. You want me to find out what's going on, I'll need you to hunker down for a few days."

Lerner actually appeared to be thinking it over.

"I'm heading for Bermuda on the late flight today," Sandor told him.

"Corinne?"

"Right. From there I'm flying to London. I want to meet with your boss again, one-on-one this time. Maybe the head of WHI too."

"Killian."

"I want to know what they have to say about what's going on."

Lerner leaned forward and placed the mug of coffee on the table. "You realize that what I do is highly sensitive. That the relationships I have are—how do I say this—they're a delicate balance of business, friendship and trust."

"I got all that."

"What I mean is, I can't have the cure be worse than the disease. You understand?"

Sandor looked at him for a moment without speaking. "Listen to me. At best, those two thugs at the hotel were trying to kidnap you. More likely they wanted information and, once they beat it out of you, they were going to bury you. Right now my main focus is keeping you alive." He held his hands out, palms up, as if prepared to weigh the options. "You tell me what you want me to do. If you like, I'll turn you over to the NYPD for questioning and head back to the gym where you found me. I'm overdue for my workout anyway. Otherwise you need to sit back and shut the hell up."

Lerner actually sat back. "I know you'll do what's best for me. Just tread lightly and keep me posted."

Sandor said nothing.

"A couple of days. I guess I can handle a couple of days here."

Sandor reached in his pocket and handed Lerner a sheet of paper. "It's everyone who attended the ceremony in Hartford. It indicates which of them were badly injured and those who were killed. Have a look and tell me any names you recognize."

Lerner scanned the list, then went over it a second time. "Good traders always double-check before sending out an order," he explained. After another moment he said, "You, Hassan, the Old Man and his wife. That's it." He paused. "Wait a minute. Rich Hogan. I know that name. Wasn't he an aide to O'Hara in Iraq?"

"At the end of our tour. He was injured in the blast, but survived."

Lerner nodded. "Nothing else looks familiar."

"Okay," Sandor said. "Keep that copy, see if you remember anyone else."

"I doubt I will."

Sandor nodded. "All right, then tell me anything you haven't told me yet about Charles Colville."

"Nothing I haven't already said."

"What about you?"

Lerner responded with a look of confusion.

"Come on, pal, you told me you missed the Old Man's ceremony because you were at that tech company in the south of France. What the hell were you doing there?"

"Corinne asked me to go. She was investing a lot of money in a company that was not very liquid. She asked me to check it out."

"What did you find?"

Lerner shrugged. "I met with the top executives, got a tour of the place. Let's face it, I know a lot more about investing in companies than understanding their technology. Looked like a solid operation."

"That what you told Corinne?"

"I did."

"Good. Now what else do you want to tell me about Corinne?"

"What do you want me to tell you about her?"

"Tell me whatever you've held back until now. I don't want to waste my time traveling to Bermuda without all the intel I can gather in advance. In case you hadn't noticed, you're my only source for information right now.

Lerner hesitated. "She was a helluva woman," he sighed.

"Great. How about something a bit more useful."

"Like what?"

"Like maybe some detail on the illegal trades she was working on." Lerner stared at him.

"Come on, I know I'm not a financial genius like you, but I didn't just fall off the potato truck. Those market patterns you explained don't mean a thing unless someone is using the information to make trades in advance. That's how you cash in, right?"

"Yes," he admitted, sounding more sad than guilty.

"Was she the conduit?"

"She was one of them."

"There were others?"

"Not that I dealt with."

Sandor nodded. "But she was handling some of these questionable trades. Is that why she was exiled to Bermuda?"

"In part. It was really a combination of things. There were rumors about her personal life, which was becoming an issue. When Freddie assigned her to Bermuda it got her out of sight, and therefore out of mind for a lot of the magpies. It was also a good spot for her to work from, setting up holding companies in other jurisdictions."

"Away from the normal scrutiny of headquarters."

"Something like that."

"What about your personal relationship with her?"

"What about it?"

"Create any problems for you within the firm?"

Lerner smiled, and for a moment he looked to Sandor like the younger man he had known as Joey Sax, up to his old tricks. "It didn't, and that was strictly because of her. I'm telling you, she was a special woman. Played the game like a man."

"What about the drugs they found in her place that supposedly caused the heart attack?"

Lerner sat up again. "I already told you, it's total bullshit. Not what she did, not her style. I'll bet my life on it."

Sandor gave him another serious look. "That may be precisely what you're doing."

CHAPTER 23

Bermuda

That evening, when Sandor and Beth arrived at the reception desk of the Princess Hotel in Bermuda, he produced his passport and credit card. "I made the reservation this morning," he told the young woman behind the counter.

"Yes Mr. Sandor, I have it right here. One of our deluxe rooms."

Beth took him by the arm and gently moved him off to the side. "One room?" she whispered in is ear.

"I'm not on the company's dime here."

Keeping her voice quiet, she said, "I can afford to pay for my own room."

He pulled away slightly and had a good look at her. "You can have the bed to yourself, no problem. I made sure there's a big couch."

Beth shook her head, but let it go.

A bellman escorted them to the room, where Beth confirmed there indeed was a long sofa. They dropped off their bags and headed back downstairs to dinner.

The balmy air was pleasant and they chose a table on the outdoor balcony overlooking the sea. Following the meal they had a walk along the shore and ended with a nightcap at a little bar on the beach. The time together gave them an opportunity to catch up on things, and to discuss something they had never fully addressed— the attack Beth had suffered, its aftermath, and the guilt Sandor still carried for all of it.

It occurred more than a year after their romantic relationship ended, when Sandor asked Beth to meet him for lunch in New York. As usual, he thought she might be able to help him on an assignment. They talked, she told him she would see what she could do, and they parted ways—neither of them aware they were being watched. An assassin had been dispatched to kill Sandor, but lost him in midtown. So he circled back, found Beth, and tried to force her to divulge Jordan's whereabouts.

In the ensuing confrontation, the assailant was killed by other agents, but not before Beth was made to endure a brutal beating. Her rehabilitation, both physical and psychological, had taken time, and more than one of the doctors involved suggested that Sandor stay away while she went through that process.

Sandor intended to defy that advice until Bill Sternlich convinced him to back off. Sternlich and his wife had become close with Beth, and he agreed with the professionals. Even since Beth returned to work, her contact with Sandor had been both sporadic and platonic.

"I don't think I ever properly said how sorry I am," he finally admitted.

"Yes you have," she told him. "Probably too many times. Best that we be done with all that, okay?"

"I just . . . ," he began again, but she cut him off.

"As *I've* said too many times, it was not your fault. We both need to move on."

Sandor waited a beat. "Does this mean I don't have to sleep on the couch?"

◉

Back in the room, Beth agreed it would be all right for him to share the king-sized bed.

"But understand, that's all we're sharing, got it?"

"Got it."

"Just to be clear, if you so much as roll onto my side of the mattress, even if you're sound asleep at the time, I'll find the Walther in that bag of yours and solve the problem."

"Wow, maybe I ought to give that sofa another look," he said. But he didn't. The mattress was very comfortable and he was confronted, again, with the realization that sleep had become more important than it used to be. He looked forward to the time when that would no longer be true.

◉

They passed a restful night and, in the morning, took turns in the bathroom preparing for the day ahead. Then they went downstairs for breakfast at the terrace restaurant.

After ordering, Beth said, "You were incredibly well behaved last night." The observation carried hints of both surprise and disappointment.

Sandor smiled. "As I recall, you threatened my life."

"That's interesting," Beth said. "As I recall, having your life threatened is what you live for."

Sandor nodded. After they finished their meal, they took a cab to police headquarters.

Before boarding the flight to Hamilton, Sandor determined which law enforcement agency in Hamilton conducted the inquiry into the death of Corinne Stansbury, then placed a call to their office. It entailed a few calls, actually, as he became entangled in the bureaucratic shuffle common to this sort of international inquiry. Using his State Department cover, he claimed that the death of Ms. Stansbury was of interest to his superiors, but was not at liberty to say why. As expected, the response in each instance was less than enthusiastic, which only confirmed his belief that nothing productive would be accomplished unless he made the trip and had an opportunity to question the investigators in person and review the evidence first-hand. He made the last of these calls from the airport, finally reaching the man in charge. When that officer made a final attempt to discourage Sandor from taking the trip, he responded by saying he was already boarding his flight and, when he arrived, he anticipated full cooperation in arranging for him to review the file, inspect the woman's apartment, and interview the coroner. Without promising any of the above, the officer gave him an address and set an appointment for the following morning.

The reception Sandor and Beth received at headquarters was only slightly chillier than the various phone conversations, although Captain Robison was polite enough, and did not lack for British civility. He appeared to be in his late fifties, tall, his posture ramrod stiff, and the mustache he sported was well groomed. Sandor figured him as ex-military, currently working on a second pension.

After Sandor displayed his credentials and introductions were made, Robison said, "I welcome the two of you to Bermuda. I would prefer, of course, if it were under different circumstances."

"We quite agree," Sandor replied.

The captain showed them into a small conference room. The walls were white and clean, the furnishings modern, and the view—

like almost every view on the island—was beautiful. The table was oblong shaped and their host sat at one end, in front of a manila file that had already been placed there.

"Please be seated," he said.

Sandor took a seat to Robison's right, Beth taking the chair to the captain's left. It was an old school maneuver, forcing their subject to constantly turn back and forth as he spoke, leveling the playing field on the comfort score.

Robison faced Sandor. "I understand that for reasons unknown or unspoken, you want to learn whatever there is to learn about Ms. Stansbury's death."

"That's correct."

"You already know, from our discussion yesterday, that this was not considered a criminal matter. It appears the young woman died of a coronary event induced by the use of amphetamines. There was no sign of foul play."

"My superiors have questions about the circumstances," Sandor explained. "Ms. Stansbury, as you say, was a young woman, with all indications from her colleagues that she enjoyed good health. A heart attack therefore seems highly unlikely. There is also considerable skepticism that she would be using the type of stimulants that would induce a coronary."

The captain reluctantly opened the slight file and thumbed through some pages. Finding what he was looking for, he said, "The drugs were by prescription. She apparently took too many of them, simple as that."

"May I have a look?" Beth asked.

Robison turned to her and handed her the page.

Beth studied the photograph, an enlarged view of a plastic vial of medication. "It appears this was prescribed by a doctor in London and filled in a pharmacy there."

"Yes, so we saw."

"Did anyone contact the physician to determine if Ms. Stansbury was his patient?" she asked. "Or if he prescribed these drugs?"

The captain swiveled his head from Beth to Sandor and then back to her. "Why, no. We didn't see the need."

Beth did not respond, leaving the next line to Sandor.

"You say she ingested enough of these pills to result in an overdose," he said. "Do we have that right?"

"Yes," the captain said.

"May I ask, what was that based on?"

Robison, whose demeanor was becoming a bit less assured, looked into the file again.

"Here it is. A blood sample was taken."

Sandor didn't bother to ask for the paper. He was staring at the policeman. "Was there an autopsy done after the blood sample was analyzed?"

"Not to my knowledge. We were told the blood test revealed enough amphetamines in her system to cause a heart attack in a much larger person. The matter seemed open and shut."

"Before we leap to any conclusions, I think it would be prudent to contact her doctor in London." Sandor made a show of looking at his watch. "Still business hours in the U.K." The captain's eyes narrowed for a moment, as if taking Sandor's measure.

"I see no reason not to. Excuse me for a moment." Taking back the photo of the prescription, Robison went to the door, recited the phone number on the bottle, and asked someone outside the room to phone the doctor. Then he returned to his seat. "If it turns out the doctor prescribed these pills, that would settle the matter, would it not?"

"Perhaps," Beth said. "I would be curious to hear what your coroner has to say about the timing of her death."

The captain lifted the first sheet in the file and read out loud the assumed time of death.

"Not what I meant," Beth said. "I want to know how soon after taking an overdose of these pills the coronary would occur. I want to know whether traces of the pills would have been in her stomach, or whether they would have been fully digested."

"I see," the policeman said as he went back to the file, uncomfortable that the issue might not have been addressed by his people.

The intercom rang and a voice told the captain that the doctor he had inquired about was not in the office, but his nurse was on the line. Robison took the call, placed it on speakerphone, identified himself and made the inquiry.

"I don't recognize the name," the voice of an English woman somewhere in London replied. "Give me a moment." A short time later she was back. "I believe I know all of the doctor's patients, but I wanted to be certain. I see no record of a Corinne Stansbury ever visiting our office. Does that answer your question?"

"Is it possible the doctor might have prescribed something for someone who was not formally a patient?" Sandor asked.

They could almost hear the nurse's back go up on the other side of the Atlantic. "You said this scrip was for amphetamines."

"That's right."

"It would be more than highly unusual, and I have been here over a dozen years."

"One more thing," Sandor interjected before the captain ended the call. He took the sheet of paper Robison was holding and read the nurse the name and address of the pharmacy on the bottle. "When your office calls in prescriptions, is this a pharmacy you would use?"

"No sir."

"You're certain?"

"That location is on the other side of town."

After thanking the woman for her assistance and ringing off, the three of them sat in silence until Sandor said, "It might be useful if you gave us a few minutes to read through the rest of the file. Then we should pay a visit to the coroner."

⊙

When they were done, Beth made a few comments about the information in the file, and it was evident Robison's initial resistance was turning to curiosity. He accompanied them to the coroner's office, which was located in the basement of the building. There, he introduced them to Dr. Jergen, an attractive woman in her forties. It was clear she had been forewarned about this visit and was even more defensive than the captain. After all, she was the last word on what had happened to Corinne Stansbury, and she was not pleased about being second-guessed.

In response to Beth's initial question, Dr. Jergen said, "There was enough of the substance in her bloodstream to induce a myocardial infarction in someone twice her size." She went on to explain that, once the blood test confirmed the presence of a large quantity of the amphetamines, there was no purpose in going further.

"A strange way to commit suicide," Beth said. "Don't you think? It must be extremely painful to have that sort of heart attack."

"Yes," the doctor agreed. "It would be."

"Statistically, sleeping pills are the drug of choice for women who kill themselves."

"As I recall," Robison intervened, "there is no evidence that she had any sleeping pills in her apartment."

Beth responded with one of her sweetest smiles. "But they're easy enough to obtain nowadays. Easier, say, than the meds that *were* found."

No one voiced any disagreement.

"It might not have been intentional," Dr. Jergen suggested. "She might have accidentally taken too many pills."

It was clear from another brief silence that no one was buying that, not even the medical examiner herself.

"I understand from the police file that Ms. Stansbury was cremated," Sandor said.

"Those were the instructions in her will," said Robison. "Her ashes were returned to her family in England."

Sandor turned back to the M.E. "Any photos taken during your examination?"

Dr. Jergen produced her file, which contained various shots of the woman. As Sandor looked through them, Beth posed the question about the ingestion of the pills and whether there would still have been evidence of them in her stomach.

"Impossible to know at this point," Dr. Jergen conceded.

"But something would have shown up, right?"

"It would depend entirely on how many she took and how quickly they entered her bloodstream."

"So, there's no way of knowing whether any of the drugs were in her stomach, since a full autopsy was not conducted."

The doctor glanced at the captain, then returned her attention to Beth. "That would be correct. Although I would expect that at least some traces would have been found."

Sandor, meanwhile, was studying one of the photographs. "You have a magnifying glass?"

"Of course," Dr. Jergen said, as he opened a drawer and handed it to him.

Sandor moved to the desk where he placed one of the photos under a lamp and had a closer look. It was a photo of Corinne's nude body, lying on the coroner's slab. Sandor was focusing on the woman's left thigh.

"Have a look at this," he said, handing the glass to Dr. Jergen. "What do you make of that mark?"

The doctor leaned over and took her time studying the photo, then stood up and said, "It could be anything. A bug bite. A blemish."

Sandor was staring at the doctor now. As he passed the magnifying glass to Beth, he asked, "Anything else come to mind?"

Dr. Jergen was blinking now, uncomfortable under the intensity of his gaze. "As I say, it could be almost anything."

Sandor let it go, turning instead to Robison. "I understand we have no official capacity here, nor do I pretend to be a homicide detective, but I think your people should look into the possibility that Ms. Stansbury might have had a visitor that night. Perhaps a neighbor saw something. Is there a doorman or parking attendant at her building? Are there surveillance cameras inside or outside her building?"

Robison responded with an icy stare. "As you say Mr. Sandor, you are neither a policeman nor an official of Her Majesty's government. I think I know my job, and so do my people."

"Not so far as I can tell," Sandor replied. Ignoring the coroner, he said to Robison, "I believe you and your people wrapped this up a bit too quickly and, respectfully Captain, I think you're beginning to reach the same conclusion."

Rather than respond, Robison turned to Dr. Jergen and thanked her for her time. Then, extending his arm, he indicated to his guests that it was time to go. "Unless there's something else I can do for you, in your unofficial capacity."

"In fact there is. Before we leave, we'd like to have a look at Ms. Stansbury's apartment, assuming it hasn't yet been cleared out."

"I'm afraid it has," he told them, the chill in his tone still hovering well below zero.

"Your file indicates a number of Ms. Stansbury's possessions were collected and held. I wonder if you still have them in storage."

"Was there something in particular that interested you?"

"Frankly, yes. Included in the list were her laptop and cell phone."

He and Beth exchanged a knowing look. Anyone wanting Corinne's death to appear a suicide could not risk taking either of those items, and there was no telling what answers they might find there.

"Those items were returned to her family in London."

Sandor frowned. "Captain, I don't believe for one moment anyone here intentionally screwed up this investigation, but I think it's clear to all of us that there's more here than a self-inflicted overdose of drugs. None of you were looking for anyone else who might have been involved. Time to check for that possibility, don't you think?"

"We learned she had dinner plans that night with a gentleman who had come to Bermuda on business. He called her office the next morning asking for her. Her body had already been discovered by then. When she failed to show up for work, her assistant phoned the building manager. In any case, we followed up with this man, had a discussion with him. He had gone to her apartment at the agreed time, claims there was no answer at the door, so he assumed he'd been stood up for one reason or another."

"I didn't see any of that in the file."

"We saw no purpose in embarrassing anyone."

"Let me guess. He's married."

Robison nodded. "We questioned him, but there was no reason to go any further given what we found."

"The pills."

"Yes."

"But there's something else."

Robison nodded again. "This individual mentioned that he saw two men leaving the building as he arrived. He thought it a bit odd that they seemed to be in something of a hurry once they saw him."

"Nothing more than that?"

"No."

"Did he give a description?"

"We asked, but it was dark, he said he would not be able to identify either man, just thought the way they reacted to him was peculiar. Frankly speaking, it didn't seem important at the time."

"The smallest details never do," Sandor said.

CHAPTER 24

At the airport in Mosul, Iraq

The humanitarian mission jointly organized by the United Nations and the World Health Institute was a carefully orchestrated event dubbed "FRIENDS OF PEACE." The stated purpose of the FOP program was to visit a refugee camp southeast of the border between Iraq and Syria, bringing food, water, medical supplies and—most prominently—media attention to a desperate situation. What had begun as a few hundred people running from the oppressive and lethal regime in Syria had now grown into a makeshift city in the desert, with an undocumented population growing into tens of thousands of suffering souls.

The provisions the FOP were delivering to these people were actually less important than the plan to raise international awareness of their plight—conditions at this camp had deteriorated, quickly going from bad to hazardous. These exiles were starving. There was not enough clean water to go around. Sewage and sanitation problems were rampant. The meager medical care on site could not keep up with the festering diseases that were spreading throughout the complex. Lately, renegade groups from Syria had begun a series of nighttime raids along the perimeters of the compound, murdering dozens while terrifying the rest.

The inhabitants, many of them adolescents and infants, were innocents. They had run for safety away from circumstances that promised almost certain death at the hands of a genocidal dictator, only to find themselves in the midst of a fetid nightmare.

After a third nocturnal assault by armed groups from the north, American troops were moved in to secure the amorphous borders of the growing colony. That done, there was a limit to the amount of water and foodstuffs that could be provided from within Iraq, especially given the inevitable geo-political conflicts. The camp was populated almost entirely by Syrians who had illegally crossed into Iraq. Syria's leader was characterizing these refugees as "war criminals" and demanding their return. Baghdad had enough of its own problems with ongoing insurgencies and ISIS attacks. They had no interest in creating another dispute with Damascus by providing aid to a group the Syrian leader was calling "fugitives from justice."

As the numbers inside the compound swelled, some help was provided, and a few makeshift buildings were erected at the center of the camp. These included a temporary infirmary and a large storage house—which stood virtually empty—crudely constructed of limestone blocks, corrugated aluminum and other available materials. These structures were surrounded by a seemingly endless sea of tents and lean-tos.

The FOP was on their way to this anarchic setting to lend their celebrity and assets to inspire, what they hoped would be, a flow of aid from other nations and charitable foundations. The entourage was guaranteed television and Internet coverage as it featured two of the world's most famous people and a supporting cast of dignitaries. They believed it was time these exiles received the attention and help they needed.

The mission was planned with great care, and the organizers of the FOP believed they had taken appropriate precautions for the safety of those making the trip. Both the United States and Iraq offered armed escorts, but the FOP had politely declined. They were loath to have their errand of mercy sullied by the involvement of any sort of military involvement.

"We are messengers of peace and love," Dedalus told the assembled journalists who saw them off at JFK airport in New York. "The world has had enough senseless killing. Our purpose is to spread the most important message in any religion—help your fellow man."

Nevertheless, the sponsors had yielded to the realities of the region, and arranged to have a small complement of armed escorts accompany the group.

The charter flight carrying all of the participants landed in Mosul just after daybreak. The two stars, actress Amanda Jensen and singer Dedalus, had slept on full fold-down seats in the first-class section of the plane. They were accompanied by their personal bodyguards and aides. Also up front were a handful of important emissaries, including Shahid Hassan.

Riding in the back were the men and women assigned to work on the delivery of goods, several doctors and nurses, a full media crew, and some random sycophants who never missed a chance to travel with Jensen or Dedalus.

When the plane landed in Mosul after the long flight, it taxied to the far end of the runway and made a wide turn inside a huge hangar where a collection of trucks, drivers, laborers—and another contingent of international journalists and photographers—awaited them.

It took some time, but when these travelers for peace finally began to disembark, they made sure Amanda Jensen was the first one off the jet. Dressed in olive drab, she was strikingly beautiful, even after a full night flying nearly halfway round the world. Whatever her makeup people had done on board before allowing her to make her appearance, she looked like the planet's most natural beauty, as if she had just arisen from a good night's sleep without the need for so much as a brush through her hair. In fact, every strand of her dark mane was in place, her complexion glowed, and those famous blue eyes were alight.

She stopped for a moment on the top of the rolling stairway that had been affixed to the open hatch, treating the crowd below to her dazzling smile and giving the photographers and cameramen a few moments. "Thank you so much for coming out to meet us," she said. "We are humbled by the experience." Then, her khakis doing nothing to disguise her voluptuous figure, she bounded down the steps, allowing Dedalus to emerge next.

The Irish rocker did not have his traveling companion's penchant for Hollywood entrances. He simply smiled and waved, then hurried down the staircase, followed by the others.

Now that the mission had reached Mosul, the reins of the security detail were in the hands of Thomas Orr, who would also be responsible for all of FOP's tactical decisions. A former Marine, he owned the company that was chosen to oversee safety and coordinate transportation. His first move on exiting the plane was to discreetly instruct the armed members of his team to take up positions at strategic points he chose for them both inside and outside the hangar. Then he took charge of the local ground crew, and the staff that had traveled from the States as part of the FOP, as they began working together to unload the cargo and transfer the heavy crates to the waiting trucks. The heat was stifling inside the metal hangar and the effort backbreaking, but everyone was anxious to get this done and be on their way.

As Orr had explained to everyone on the plane the night before, "The key for us is to hit the ground running. The roads will be rough, we can't be sure of the condition of the trucks, and we need to reach our destination long before nightfall." Everyone understood.

At the beginning of the transfer process, both Amanda and Dedalus pitched in, which created some wonderful photo ops, but it was clear their value was in talking to the media, not straining to lift large boxes of supplies. Amanda was endlessly charming and, as anyone who did not yet know would come to see, she was intelligent, resilient and genuinely committed to her charitable works. Dedalus was equally sincere in his humanitarian causes, an immensely quotable man who was far better educated than the vast majority of hip-hoppers and hard-rockers in his industry. He was also possessed of a wonderful combination of Irish charm and street sense.

The two stars answered all the questions posed by the crowd of interviewers, even the most inane. When inquiries were made about their careers, such as the next Amanda Jensen movie release or the next Dedalus album, they deflected attention to the plight of those they had come to help. It was an impressive performance all around, enough so that if Jordan Sandor had been there it might have been enough to force him to rethink his cynicism about celebrity do-gooders—but for one thing. In the end, he knew too well that the road to hell is paved with good intentions.

As it turned out, the road to the refugee camp had been constructed with that destination in mind.

CHAPTER 25

Outside Mosul, Iraq

The hardcore members of Ansar al-Thar in North Africa numbered well over a hundred. From those ranks their leader, Farashi, had selected thirty of his best fighters for this mission. As he and Gabir explained to their followers more than once, this was not going to be a crude, bomb-throwing attack. A measure of precision was required. They would likely meet with resistance, and the fighting might be fierce. Death in the name of Allah was a distinct possibility for many of them, but they had specific objectives that must be met.

Each of them said he understood.

Timing the attack was their first tactical issue. There was no way of knowing exactly when the plane would land in Mosul, but it was critical that Farashi time the attack properly, neither too close to Mosul nor to the camp. Surprise would be on his side, even if those defending this group of western intruders anticipated an assault.

There was simply no way they could guess how or when it would occur, nor how many of Farashi's men would come at them.

To that end, Farashi had insiders who would let him know when the trucks left the airport. Even more important, and unknown to Orr or any of the other people on the ground, two of the volunteer drivers in the convoy were armed members of Ansar al-Thar.

The route from Mosul to the refugee camp was comprised of two lanes of primitive, damaged road. It was a narrow thoroughfare, with desert rather than paved shoulders along much of either side of the road. Once the trucks were intercepted there would be no place for them to go. Any attempt at a U-turn would at best result in nothing but the slowest movement, and at worst would leave them literally spinning their wheels in the sand.

Farashi and his men were positioned approximately sixty miles from the airport, under a series of huge, temporary tents they had recently constructed less than a mile from the side of the road on which the mission would be traveling. Having now received word that the FOP vehicles were en route, Farashi told his men to make ready. The initial phase of the attack would be handled by all thirty of his chosen men in four trucks. They boarded the vehicles and waited for the signal to go.

When Orr had been given word that all fourteen trucks were fully loaded and ready to go, he called all his men back inside the hangar. In addition to the trucks and their drivers, there were two buses waiting to carry the key members of the mission and a few selected members of the media. It was now time to shepherd all of them on board. Orr had only been authorized to bring twelve armed men, including himself. He placed two on each of the buses, then told five others to ride shotgun in five of the trucks, including the first and the last in the convoy. Then he climbed into the Hummer that would lead the caravan, along with his remaining three armed operatives, and switched on his hand-held radio.

That was when he had given the order to move out.

Now, as they rolled along, Orr watched for activity in front of them and to the sides, also doing his best to scan the road ahead for signs of any I.E.D.'s. He realized that last effort was probably useless, since a well-positioned roadside bomb would not be evident unless you walked right up to it and bent down to look, but he remained alert nonetheless.

The driver of this Humvee was one of his most trusted men, as were the two seated in the back of the vehicle. All of them knew the importance of this assignment and its implications for the company, witnessed by the fact that Orr had decided to lead the team himself. He was comfortable with the men he brought with him, but was concerned about the situation on the ground.

When the sponsors of the trip had refused military aid, it spoke highly of their faith in Orr, but he felt it did not say not much for their grip on reality. If they would not hear of an army escort, Orr urged them to accept the offer of an escort from American choppers.

"Out of the question," one of the top people back in New York told him at their planning session. "You know how many cameramen are going to be there, shooting footage of everything we do? Just imagine what we'll look like when the video hits television and the Internet. We're going there to help people who are dying of thirst and hunger. In doing that, we don't want to look like a group of coddled elitists who need to be accompanied by Blackhawk helicopters as we carry out a mission in the name of peace."

Orr saw the woman's point, although he was tempted to challenge her repeated use of the word "we," since she wasn't going any further than First Avenue in Manhattan as part of the mission.

When he raised a question about how the local ground crew and drivers were going to be vetted, Orr's advice was again rejected. He was told that the workers in Mosul had volunteered for the task, and any sort of heavy-handed investigation into their backgrounds would be insulting.

The net result, as Orr understood far better than the organizers, was that the entire group under his protection would have to drive almost two hours through open desert in a region of the world replete with armed combatants of various religious, ethnic and political factions, while he and his men had only minimal firepower available to ensure their wellbeing.

Nearly an hour into the trip, Orr's driver said, "Dead ahead chief."

Farashi's trucks could be seen coming towards them in the distance, moving much faster than the FOP convoy. The terrorists' vehicles were not laden with water and foodstuffs, nor were they slowed by the pace of the buses that were right behind Orr's Humvee. As Farashi's group charged forward they kicked up a storm of dust and sand behind them.

Orr instinctively went to his radio, telling all the drivers to prepare to slow down, but whether they slowed or accelerated would not matter. In less than a minute, Farashi's trucks were only a few hundred yards away. The first stopped, and then the second. As they hit their brakes they turned so that they stopped cross-wise, blocking the lane in which the FOP was traveling. The other two trucks behind them also pulled to a stop so the entire road was barricaded.

"Halt, halt," Orr called over his radio to all the drivers behind him. Then, not taking his eyes from the blockade ahead of them, he told the man in back of him to get on his satellite phone and reach their liaison officer at the U.S. Army base back in Mosul.

Both buses screeched to a stop, followed by the string of heavy supply trucks behind them. Everything stopped and everything became quiet. There was less than fifty yards separating Orr's Humvee from the four trucks blocking the road ahead.

Then a series of actions occurred.

In the five FOP trucks where Orr had planted men in the passenger seats, each drew his weapon and opened the door to see what was happening. In two of them, however, the drivers were Farashi's plants. Each of those men pulled out his own automatic, leveled it at the back of the unsuspecting American's head and told him to drop his gun or be killed on the spot. In both instances the security guards were then subdued by a blow to the back of their skull delivered with the butt of the Arab's automatic.

No one in Orr's Humvee, or any of the other guards who had been riding shotgun, had any idea of the infiltration.

Meanwhile, there was a commotion inside the first bus, where Orr's men were doing their best to control a rapidly escalating sense of panic.

Orr was on his radio trying to get a sit-rep from the men in the vehicles behind him when he saw someone step out to the edge of the truck ahead of him, off to the left. The man was waving a white cloth.

Orr and his three men got out of the Hummer, each using his door as a shield. It was less than ideal cover, but it was something, and it was far better to be standing outside than trapped inside the vehicle once the shooting started. Seeing the symbol of truce, they waited.

"Come," Farashi called out to them in English, "we need to talk right now."

"You've got the flag," Orr hollered back. "Come over to us."

"No, American. You listen now because this will only be said once. If you cooperate, you may all live. If you resist, most of you will die. We are well armed. We have rocket launchers and RPG's. Very few of you will survive an attack. So," the voice paused, "I need to speak with the man in charge right now."

Orr was about to respond when he felt a hand on his shoulder. It was Reverend Kevin Moore, the man appointed by the sponsors as the nominal head of the mission. He had been quiet at the airport, respectfully allowing Orr to do his job. When the bus stopped he had climbed off to see what was happening. Hearing the threat that had been made, he said, "Thomas, I believe this is my role." Without awaiting a reply, Moore lifted his hands over his head and slowly walked out to the middle of the road.

"Are you the man in charge?" Farashi called out.

"I am."

"Good. You now have a choice. You must turn over all of your weapons and a small number of your people. I shall give you the names. The rest of you will then be allowed to turn your trucks around and return to Mosul."

After a brief silence, Moore said, "You told me I had a choice."

"I thought that was already obvious." Without another word, Farashi nodded to the man on his left, who immediately discharged a barrage of rapid-fire shots into Moore's torso and head. The missionary was dead before he hit the ground.

Many in the two buses began screaming, which was followed by the sound of gunshots from the rear of the FOP convoy. Orr's men had just seen what happened with the two drivers, provoking an exchange of shots that ended in the death of both Arabs and three men on Orr's team. The two who had been bludgeoned when stripped of their weapons, were on the ground in bad shape.

Meanwhile, the remaining truck drivers, who had nothing to do with Ansar al-Thar, abandoned their vehicles and began running back down the road from where they had come, away from the action. They had volunteered to drive supplies from Mosul to the refugees, not to be killed in a terrorist attack.

"So," Farashi yelled out amidst the increasing chaos, "who claims to be the second in command?"

"I am," Orr responded without hesitation.

"Good. I want to show you something, because we are short on both time and patience. I assume the truck at the end of your procession has been abandoned, since one of my men was the driver." He shrugged as if it was of no consequence one way or another. Then Farashi signaled to one of his men, off to his right, who stepped into the open, off to the side of the road where he had an angled line of sight on that last vehicle. The man hefted a rocket launcher on his shoulder and fired.

A *swoosh* filled the air as the missile streaked the length of the convoy, striking the last truck and exploding with a deafening roar, a ball of fire rising into the afternoon sky.

The screaming from within the buses became louder and more intense, along with audible shouts, such as "You were paid to protect us," and demands that someone should "Go out there and do something," but the pandemonium was being ignored by the two key actors in this drama, Orr and Farashi.

"What do you want?" Orr asked.

"I believe you mean, *who* do we want." Orr did not reply.

"Please, you are putting your people at risk. Do I need to provide a second demonstration by firing on one of your buses?"

Orr looked around at his three men, hissed, "Goddamnit," under his breath, then turned back to the Arab. "You have a list?"

"I do. I will send one of my men with it, but be assured, if he suffers so much as a scratch I will kill twenty of your people without hesitation or remorse. You believe me?"

"Yes," Orr said. "I believe you." He was tempted to add some appropriate epithets, but forced himself to remain calm as he waited for Farashi's emissary. A brazen young man of no more than twenty, with no trace of fear in his eyes, walked across the open area between them and handed Orr a hand-written list with four names on it. No sooner had Orr taken the paper in his hand than the voice from across the divide called out again.

"You have three minutes to gather these people together and bring them to me. There will be no exceptions and no delay. If you fail, we will open fire."

Orr stared at the list. Not surprisingly it started with Amanda Jensen and Dedalus. The others were a Saudi dignitary and a journalist to whom Orr had been introduced in the past thirty-six hours. He felt his heart rate quicken as the seconds ticked by.

The young messenger had not moved. "What shall I tell my leader?"

Orr stared at him without speaking. Then he turned, the list in hand, and headed for the first bus.

CHAPTER 26

London, England

Sandor and Beth had arrived in London, and this time she made no fuss about sharing a single room. They were both tired from the trans-Atlantic voyage, particularly because neither of them had gotten much sleep on the flight, having spent the time discussing what they had learned, what they thought it meant, and where that might lead them. Beth was grateful that Jordan had a friend at the Wellesley Hotel, who arranged for an early check-in so they could take a quick nap.

Using a diplomatic pass, Sandor was able to bring two automatics and ammunition into the country undetected. Now that they were alone in the room he felt he could relax for a while, prepare for his meetings, and continue to consider what he and Beth had learned thus far.

They had independently come to the same conclusions about Robison, Dr. Jergen, and the Bermuda police detectives who investigated the scene—there was no apparent intent on anyone's part to cover up what was likely a murder. The lot of them had all simply done a lousy job. When the easy solution presented itself, they accepted it and moved on.

No one could be sure that the mark on Corinne Stansbury's thigh was evidence she had been injected with a massive dose of amphetamines, not even Sandor. Still, their call to the U.K. had confirmed that the prescription was bogus. If Corinne had wanted the drugs through a falsified prescription she would certainly not have used her own name. The lack of a full autopsy meant there was no way to be sure how the amphetamines found their way into her bloodstream but, as Sandor reminded Robison, and the two detectives the captain brought into their meeting, there is more than one way to force drugs into someone's system. What troubled Sandor was the absence of any sign of a struggle in the few photographs they had seen of the woman's apartment, or the notations made by the officers. If one or more people had forced her to swallow a handful of pills, there should certainly have been something knocked over and broken in the process. Which led back to the injection theory.

Putting the details aside, it was evident to Sandor and Beth that Corinne had not committed suicide, or even accidentally swallowed an overdose. The woman was murdered by professionals, they were sure of that. The questions "Why?" and "By whom?" occupied a lot of their time during the flight.

They also reviewed the information Raabe had provided on the death of Charlie Colville. A hit-and-run with no useful witnesses. Colville had worked late, and his office was in a business neighborhood where pedestrian traffic all but disappeared after seven. His calendar showed a date with someone identified only by the initial "N" but there was no contact information in his book. His secretary was not sure who that might be, but given the hour and the use of the initial, she guessed it was one of his "lady friends."

Rumor had it that when Charlie went out with the ladies, he usually opted for an extravagant limousine. Yet there was no record of any reservation made for that night, nor had he called for a taxi.

No one made much of that, although his secretary admitted it was, "a tad odd." If a limo had been ordered, why was there no record of that?

All indications, then, were that he had simply walked outside the office building and stepped into the street, probably looking for a cab. According to the only two people who saw any of what occurred next, he was struck down by a sedan traveling at a high rate of speed which never braked, did not stop, and sped off before anyone could get the plate number or even identify the make of the car.

Sandor and Beth agreed on the obvious—this was no random accident, even if this were a crude attempt to do so. Charles Colville had been run down by people unknown for reasons yet to be ascertained.

Once Sandor and Beth were comfortably ensconced in their luxury room at the Wellesley, they returned to the riddle of Charles Colville's death.

"I don't know," Beth said as they lay back on the bed, side by side atop the duvet, still fully clothed. "You think that's as important as figuring out what's going on at RSL?"

Sandor sighed. "Two birds, one stone. We'll meet with Uncle Freddie. Without Lerner there to run interference it should be an excellent starting point for putting the pieces of this puzzle in place."

Before Beth could reply, Sandor's cell phone buzzed. He picked it up, saw the call was from Craig Raabe, and immediately answered. "Bubba's Barbecue."

"Wish I were hungry. You in a position to talk?"

"Does staring at the ceiling work?"

"You need to know something that'll be hitting the airwaves soon. That dinner you had at the U.N. the other night."

"I'm listening."

"The mission, called itself Friends of Peace."

Sandor turned to Beth as he listened. "What about it?"

"They were en route from Mosul to the refugee camp. You know what they're trying to do for these people?"

"Yes, I know. What happened?"

"They met with hostiles. We have satellite on it, but no boots on the ground. The WHI refused a military escort, so the C.O. at the Army base in Mosul is scrambling choppers."

"How bad?"

"No word yet. All we can see so far is that four trucks came from the northwest and brought the entire circus to a screaming halt. Some shooting, one truck destroyed, appears at least one of the people from the mission and a few others on the trucks were shot."

"Who?"

"Don't know yet."

"Bill Sternlich's on that trip."

"Sorry Jordan, this doesn't look good."

For a moment Sandor felt a sense of light-headedness that was becoming all too familiar. With Beth beside him, he said nothing about it. He took a deep breath and told Raabe, "I appreciate the heads up. You going to keep me posted?"

"Will do."

When Sandor ended the call he turned to meet Beth's anxious gaze. "Our new pals at Friends of Peace are in trouble."

CHAPTER 27

Outside Mosul, Iraq

"They'll kill us all if we don't go with them," Thomas Orr explained to the group gathered around him on the first bus. "You've seen what they did when Reverend Moore just asked a question they didn't like. And time is running out." He looked at Amanda Jensen and Dedalus as he said, "It's your call. We have to make a decision now."

"What do you mean 'we'?" Amanda's husky bodyguard asked. "I don't see your name on that list."

"I'm going to insist that I be part of the hostage group," Orr explained as calmly as if he were inviting himself to a garden party.

Dedalus spoke up. "These are terrorists, Mr. Orr. They gave you this list, and your name is not on it. You insist on accompanying us, they may shoot you like they did Moore." The group around them could not bear to look at Orr now, but Dedalus was staring square into his eyes.

Orr had already judged the rock star a solid citizen. "That's a risk I am willing to take, if the four of you on this list are willing to go with them."

"Not much choice, as you say." Dedalus turned to those standing behind him. "They take the people they've named or they kill the lot of us." The chill in the air was palpable.

"Let me explain a few things," Orr said. "You all know we have no military escort, but satellites are monitoring our position. These terrorists are undoubtedly aware of that, and realize they have very little time to get this done. If we stall, they have the capability of blowing us to kingdom come. That was the point of their demonstration."

Dedalus nodded. "I understand."

"My men and I were only allowed handguns. We try and shoot it out with them, to buy some time, none of us will have a chance."

"So then," Dedalus said, "time to make a decision."

"Very much so," Orr agreed. Then he looked to Amanda Jensen. "This is not going to be easy."

"How soon do you think help can get here?" she asked.

"We've already placed calls to the base in Mosul and, as I say, they've seen what's happened on satellite. My guess is not soon enough. These murderers know what they're about, this attack has been well-planned. They infiltrated our ground crew and had their own men driving at least two of our trucks. That gave them our timing and our route. They're not waiting to see if the cavalry rescues us."

With that, a prolonged burst of gun fire from outside was followed by Farashi calling out, "Your time is up."

Orr looked at the group. "You need to tell me what it's going to be."

When no one else answered, Dedalus said, "Make the deal. As my grandfather said, it's always best to live so you can fight another day."

When the journalist nodded in agreement, everyone turned to Amanda Jensen.

Staring at Orr, she said, "You're telling us we have no choice." It was not a question, it was a statement, and no one disagreed. "All right," she told him, "we can't put everyone at risk. Let's do it."

Orr climbed off the bus and walked towards the Humvee. This time, however, he did not make any show of standing behind the open door of his vehicle. He stood out in the open as he spoke. "We are prepared to meet your demand provided that I can accompany the group. They're my responsibility, and whatever fate you intend for them I should be made to share."

Farashi made a show of taking a couple of steps forward. "You will relinquish your weapon of course."

"Understood."

"If you so much as hint at an intention of becoming a hero, you will be summarily shot. You understand this?"

"I do, just as I am sure you understand it is my obligation to stay with these people."

Farashi smiled. "You are a brave man. Do not allow that instinct to overtake your reason." He nodded. "All right," he said. "Bring them out."

The terrorists' plan was elegant in its simplicity. They only wanted four hostages. With Orr they had five. After they herded their prisoners onto the truck with Farashi they collected all of the weapons from Orr's surviving men. They removed the ignition keys from all of the trucks, the two buses and the Humvee, leaving the balance of the FOP retinue stranded until help arrived. Some of the terrorists climbed back into their own trucks and maneuvered U-turns, while others commandeered four of the trucks from the FOP convoy. Then the eight vehicles headed north toward the tents Farashi's men had constructed.

When they reached the tented area, in less than ten minutes, all eight trucks disappeared from satellite or drone view under the cover of the white overhangs. There they transferred their five hostages into one of the FOP trucks. Next, in a coordinated move, all eight trucks emerged from beneath the tents and sped off. As soon as they reached the first crossroad, one of the trucks turned left and the other right. This was repeated at the next three intersections until, in just a few minutes, the eight vehicles were headed in eight different directions. All of this was executed according to their master plan.

PART TWO

CHAPTER 28

CIA Headquarters, Langley, Virginia

Not since 9/11 had a terrorist attack received such immediate and intense international attention. Acts of violence, such as the shootings in the Kenyan shopping mall, the explosions in the hotel in Mumbai, and ISIS beheadings, did not carry with them the sensational headline being played and replayed today—Islamic radicals had kidnapped two of the most famous people on the planet, Amanda Jensen and Dedalus.

The back story, however, was even more compelling.

In a world plagued by this sort of wanton violence and amoral villainy, there were certain lines that were rarely crossed. The mission organized for the Friends of Peace was a humanitarian venture, and an assault on them was unconscionable by any standard. Early reports confirmed that the assassination of their leader, the Reverend Kevin Moore, was completely unprovoked.

Satellite images showed him standing helplessly, hands raised above his head, when he was gunned down. There were additional scenes revealing the murder of several others among the retinue, some armed, some not. The incident, still in its earliest stages, was already being condemned by leaders around the globe.

Thus far no group was taking responsibility, but there was a general supposition that Assad loyalists had conducted the raid, intended to teach the refugees—and their intended champions—a cruel and violent lesson.

That view, however, was not shared by the analysts at the CIA.

The brains in I & A at Langley theorized that if this had been orchestrated by a group of Syrian loyalists, they would have attempted to make their way back across their own border to safety. Instead, the trucks scattered to all points on the compass, only one of them traveling in the general direction of Syria. As it turned out, that vehicle was actually heading for the refugee camp.

As Deputy Director Mark Byrnes sifted through the data that poured in, he found himself concurring with the opinions of the people downstairs. The attack was an ISIS undertaking, possibly orchestrated by the same group believed responsible for the Hartford explosions, Ansar al-Thar. There were various factors pointing to that conclusion, one of which was the pattern of the routes followed by the eight trucks after they emerged from beneath the tented area.

Other than the truck driving straight for the refugee camp, each of the seven others quickly found indoor destinations less than thirty miles from the attack—garages, warehouses or empty buildings. Since the activities within those structures could not be seen from above, there was no way to tell where the hostages were being taken, and whether they had been split up or not. Matters only became more complicated when a series of smaller vehicles exited from those locations, each going its own way.

Tracking any or all of them from the sky was difficult enough, but chasing them on the ground was becoming a practical impossibility.

Meanwhile, the truck heading toward the refugee camp was the only one that did not make a secondary stop. In less than half an hour it was barreling toward the makeshift entrance to the primitive colony. There was a small complement of U.S. soldiers out front, but they had already been alerted to the situation and ordered to stand down. It was impossible to determine if any or all of the hostages were on board, and they could not risk a gun battle in an attempt to intercept the vehicle.

The frustration on the faces of the soldiers could be seen on the video taken as the truck barely slowed, kicking up dirt and sand and debris as it barreled into the complex and sped straight for the empty storage buildings in the center, the driver obviously familiar with the layout of the camp and his ultimate destination. The truck finally braked to a halt and two men jumped out and opened the large overhead door to the warehouse, allowing the truck to enter, then closed it behind them once they were inside.

Byrnes shook his head as he, Craig Raabe, and several others on his staff studied the video in real time. "I know it seems too obvious," he said, "but it appears that's where they took the hostages."

His assistant, Brandon Garinger, disagreed. "I realize that's the only remaining vehicle in play that would be large enough to hold them all, but what if they were split up right from the beginning, when they had them under that first group of tents? When those trucks scattered, it would have been easy for them to take five people in five different directions."

"True."

"My point is, their leverage will be much greater if rescue operations are required for one hostage at a time, especially since we don't know which of the prisoners has been taken where. Then there's the obvious question—of all places why take them to the refugee camp? Wouldn't they be most vulnerable there, especially since they have to know we have satellite feeds? Some of the analysts down in I & A think this may be an elaborate decoy."

Gabe Somerset joined the meeting, handing Byrnes a folded slip of paper. "Your receptionist wanted me to give this to you," he explained, then he voiced his agreement with Garinger even before he sat down. "The reason they would drive a truck into the compound is to force our hand. We mount a rescue operation and they murder hundreds, maybe even thousands of the refugees. No telling how much firepower they have with them. Then, as Brandon suggests, there's the possibility none of the hostages are there."

Byrnes nodded as he opened the note and read it.

"Far as we can tell," Somerset went on, "this is the work of Ansar al-Thar. They've become more aggressive, and recent chatter monitored in the area indicates their intent to follow up on the Hartford attack."

"You think the two are related?" the DD asked, sounding a bit distracted.

"You mean beyond the fact that it may be the same group? It's really too early to tell."

"The chatter you mention, did we have any of that intel before the Hartford assault?"

Somerset shook his head. "Not that I'm aware of."

Byrnes said, "Until three weeks ago I knew less about this Ansar al-Thar group than I did about cold fusion. You just got back from North Africa. Didn't you have any inclination this was an active cell?"

Craig Raabe sat up a little straighter in his seat. It was not like the DD to challenge anyone so highly placed in the Company while other personnel were present, but it was evident his appetite for surprises was running out.

Somerset also stiffened a bit. "As you know, there are any number of ISIS and al Qaeda splinter groups. Some are merely aspirational, others are operative. We had no indication Ansar al-Thar was this well-organized. As I've reported to you, one man is clearly in charge, a Syrian namd Nizan Farashi. Distantly related to a family of well-regarded clerics, although they disavow the connection."

"You've already told us about Farashi," Byrnes said. "I want to know why the hell we're playing from behind on this."

"Director Walsh and I had just been discussing what steps need to be taken," Somerset replied. He took any opportunity he had to lob in a reference to his close relationship with the CIA Director, but Byrnes was not impressed.

"My agents are already tracking the information we have," he said. "But we're not getting ahead of the curve on this. I want you to find out everything you can about Farashi and his group. I'll deliver whatever report we need to share with Director Walsh."

"As you say," Somerset said.

Byrnes was silent for a moment, staring down at the note Somerset had passed him. Then he looked up at Raabe. "They've confirmed the names of the five hostages," he said. "The workers from the mission who were left behind, they identified the people that were taken."

He held out the paper to Raabe, who took it, saw the names, and said, "This is not good news."

"No it's not," Byrnes agreed. "I'll need to speak with Sandor."

CHAPTER 29

London, England

Sandor had traveled to London to investigate the death of Charles Colville and to learn whatever else he could about the inner workings of Randolph Securities. News of the attack on the FOP delegation outside Mosul changed his agenda. Whatever Lerner's suspicions about his company and its dealings, matters had become more urgent, especially given the thickly tangled connections between RSL and the World Health Institute.

He also wanted to know if Bill Sternlich was all right. He had already called Sternlich's wife to assure her that everything possible was being done to ensure his safety. He only wished he were that confident of the situation himself.

Lerner arranged for Sandor to meet with Freddie Colville, but the head of RSL was now trying to put it off through a phone call from his assistant. As the young woman explained, "Mr. Colville apologizes, but believes the reasons are obvious."

Sandor did not agree. "Tell Mr. Colville that my position in the United States government will likely prove a helpful conduit for him at a troubling time such as this." When she began to fumble for a response, Sandor added, "You can also tell him that I'm already in London, so I'll be on time for our appointment."

The allusion to his government role—a vaguely defined assignment with the State Department—was double-edged. On the one side of the blade, Sandor might indeed be useful to Colville in furnishing or facilitating back channel information. On the other, it was never a good idea for a company trading international funds to irritate someone playing on Uncle Sam's team, regardless of how marginal the role.

After being put on hold for a few moments, the assistant returned and told Sandor that Mr. Colville would be meeting him after all.

A couple of hours later, after Sandor and Beth were shown inside Colville's office and the appropriate pleasantries were exchanged, the tall Englishman attempted another end-run before they even sat down. "I realize you've come a long way, so it would not do for me to peremptorily cancel our meeting. As you are well aware, however, we are dealing with extremely difficult circumstances. In fact, I have been asked to meet with WHI as soon as possible."

"I understand," Sandor said, although his tone made it clear he was not in any rush, and he was not going anywhere. Not yet. He waited until Colville pointed them toward his conference table.

When the three of them were seated, their host said, "So, the other night Howard was telling us how far back the two of you go."

"Army mates, it creates a special sort of bond."

"As he mentioned." When Sandor did not respond, Colville said, "I must admit, I am not really sure why you've come to see me, Howard did not make that clear." Making a show of checking his expensive gold watch, he said, "Perhaps, if I'm not being too indelicate, we can get right to it?"

Beth had agreed that Sandor would do most of the talking, leaving her to do what she did best—observe and analyze. "Your nephew's death," Sandor said, making it sound like a question.

When nothing more was forthcoming, Colville was forced to inquire. "Yes?"

"I'm sure it was extremely upsetting to you. I know it had a profound effect on Lerner."

"And everyone else here," Colville assured him. "A tragic loss."

"As well as the death of Corinne Stansbury."

"Also devastating to the RSL family. So young to have suffered a coronary. Unspeakable."

"So is murder."

Colville responded with a single blink. "I beg your pardon."

"We've just come from Bermuda. Met with the authorities there. Reviewed the case file and the available evidence. We believe Ms. Stansbury's death was a homicide."

If Freddie Colville was acting, he was very good. His expression was a display of pure shock. "What are you saying?"

"I understand Ms. Stansbury worked here for the past few years."

"Quite right."

"Did you ever know her to take any sort of recreational drugs? Cocaine? Uppers? Speed?"

"Of course not."

"To your knowledge was she upset, depressed, even suicidal?"

"She was not."

Sandor nodded. "Are you familiar with the results of the investigation the authorities did in Hamilton?"

"I believe I am," Colville replied.

"Then you know the cardiac episode you referred to was drug-induced."

"I, uh, yes, although I may not be clear on all the details."

"Let me fill you in, then. She had a toxic amount of amphetamines in her bloodstream. The same medication was found in her apartment, apparently prescribed by a physician here in London. When we checked with the doctor's office we learned that he had never written the prescription; that he did not use the pharmacy that filled the order; and that Ms. Stansbury was not even his patient." Colville stared at him in silence. "As her boss and someone who knew her well, you've just confirmed that she was not a user of this sort of drug, not for medication or recreation. I have that right?"

"Yes you do."

"The obvious conclusion, therefore, is that she was forced to swallow these drugs, or she unknowingly took them, or they found their way into her system through some other means. The point is, Ms. Stansbury was unlikely to voluntarily take a lethal dose of those pills. The bottle found in her apartment was probably placed there after she was poisoned."

"My God."

"Lerner has been concerned about the circumstances of her death, as well as the death of your nephew Charles. I understand in his case it was a hit-and-run."

"Yes, that's correct."

"A car, moving at a high rate of speed, struck your nephew, never stopped, and it happened so quickly that no license plate information was obtained by either of the only two witnesses who admit to seeing it happen." Colville began nodding slowly.

"Now Mr. Colville, it must have occurred to you that your nephew's death might not have been an accident."

The Englishman was still nodding. "Scotland Yard suggested that possibility."

"We'll be speaking with them too, I assure you."

"They asked about a possible motive, but I have no idea why, or who—"

Sandor stopped him. "Right now I have no idea either, and no sense of where this will lead. I also have no way of knowing whether these two deaths were connected, but by now you must have heard that an attempt was made on Lerner's life, after we left you the other night at the U. N."

Once again, the man was either a wonderful thespian or far less informed about the comings and goings of his people than he should have been. He displayed a look of utter confusion and said, "What?"

In response, Sandor told him what happened at the St. Regis in New York.

"You say Howard is all right?"

"He is."

Colville took a deep breath, then exhaled it all in one blow as he sat back in his chair.

"I realize you've got to deal with WHI regarding the attack in Mosul, but Lerner felt you were entitled to know everything that we've learned."

Trying to pull himself together, Colville did his best to adopt a knowing look. "Are you here in an official capacity or as Howard's friend?"

"Both," Sandor lied.

"Then your candor is appreciated, but I'm not sure what I can do for you."

"You can help by instructing your people to provide me access to information I may need about dealings in which your nephew, Ms. Stansbury, and Lerner may have been involved."

As if on cue, Colville sat up again, his spine stiffening as he said, "I'm afraid that would be impossible. We have client confidences to protect. I cannot possibly offer you carte blanche to rummage through our records." He paused. "What I *can* do is entertain any specific requests you have and see what information I can share if it will assist you in your, uh, investigation."

"That would be helpful," Sandor said, then stood. "I know you've got to meet with your clients at WHI, we won't take any more of your time now. We'll be back in touch when we identify something specific we want to review."

Colville and Beth also got up, but no one was leaving, at least not yet.

"Since you've raised the issue," Colville said, "can you provide me any insight as to what your State Department is doing about this horror in Iraq?"

"The situation is in flux at the moment," Sandor told him. "The problem, as always in these situations, is that we are not dealing with a foreign government. We are dealing with renegades, and it's impossible to judge the situation until they show themselves, identify their leader, and indicate what they're after."

"Of course."

"I will do my best to keep you up to date on developments as they occur on the diplomatic front."

Colville thanked him. "I understand you also have a meeting set with Mark Killian."

"I do. Later this afternoon."

Colville did not shuffle his feet in the dirt, exactly, but he came as close to that as a proper Englishman could. "You understand that WHI is our largest client."

"Lerner has made that clear. We will be extremely discreet."

Colville thanked them again, bid them goodbye and had his secretary show them to the lift.

On the way down, Sandor turned to Beth and asked in a voice that was barely a whisper, "What do you think?"

In a voice equally quiet, she said, "He's not going to give us access to anything we need."

Sandor nodded and, in his best Knightsbridge accent, said, "Quite right, quite right."

CHAPTER 30

Refugee Camp, south of the Syrian border

Amanda Jensen was terrified.

When the convoy was first intercepted, she felt the danger was surreal, as if it were happening to someone else. She remained calm as events unfolded, shielded by the illusion of safety that lasted as long as she and the others remained on the bus with their armed escorts. Even when the terrorists launched the rocket that sent one of the FOP trucks exploding into the afternoon sky, it seemed no more threatening to her than something from one of her action movies.

It was only when they saw Kevin Moore shot down in the middle of the dusty road that she was truly confronted with the brutal reality of their situation.

A short time later, when the four of them were led off the bus by Thomas Orr, she felt as exposed as if she had been stripped naked.

A group of armed killers stood by, gawking at her as she trudged slowly ahead under the glare of the blazing sun. She became numb, her eyes cast down while she and the others walked toward the waiting truck. Once they climbed aboard, two of the Arabs roughly yanked dark hoods over their heads, bound their hands behind their backs with plastic strips, and shoved them to the floor.

Amanda Jensen, one of the most influential women in the world, felt powerless and alone.

At first she could hear Orr's voice through the thick fabric as he told them all to remain calm and do as their captors told them. His tone was firm and reassuring, but he was promptly told to "Shut your mouth or you will be shot."

As she sat in the dark, absorbing every bump of these primitive roads without the ability to place her hands out to brace herself, she was left to face an unimaginably harsh truth—they were at the mercy of terrorists who had just murdered an innocent man and were clearly prepared to kill any or all of them. And help was nowhere near.

She heard another man begin to speak, the journalist from *The Times*, but that was promptly followed by a *thump* that sounded like a blow to his head, then a groan, then a *thud* as he toppled onto his side.

"Silence!" a voice called out, and then there was only the roar of the truck's engine and the rattling of the vehicle as it made its way across the desert. The ride seemed endless as they were jostled and tossed on the hard metal floor.

Amanda tried to compose herself, wondering where they were being taken and what would be done with them. She tried to take solace in what Orr had told them before they left the bus—"If they wanted to kill us, they could have done that already."

It wasn't much to hold onto, but it was something, and she struggled to avoid thinking about the other possibilities that might await them. Interrogation. Torture. Rape. Disfigurement. She was painfully aware of what men like these were capable of. The best possible scenario was that her group was being kidnapped for ransom, in which event their captors might resist the impulse to harm them.

If that was so, she knew her studio would pay anything to ensure her safe return.

This last notion almost made her laugh. Amanda was no cynic, but she was a realist, and it occurred to her that the entire adventure would be a box-office bonanza. Imagine the media coverage. The hero's return. What if she were rescued rather than ransomed? That would be even more dramatic, and one of the biggest stories in the history of Hollywood, she told herself.

All she had to do was stay alive.

As she wrestled with that macabre thought she felt the truck slow and then come to a stop. They remained there for what seemed a long time, no one speaking inside her truck, although noises and discussions were audible from outside. Suddenly they started moving again, suffering a second long ride until she felt them again come to a halt.

"Up," someone hollered this time, but before she could move she felt a strong grip take hold of her beneath the arm and yank her to her feet. She was dragged forward until what felt like two or three men lifting her off the truck and depositing her in a heap on the ground below.

"Up," she was ordered again, but this time no one was helping.

Amanda managed to get her balance, her hands still bound behind her, and stood.

Someone came up from behind and pulled off her hood.

As her eyes struggle to adjust to the light she could see that she was still with the others, standing in the middle of what appeared to be some sort of warehouse. She shook her head back and forth, her lush, dark hair swirling about her as she tried to get her bearings.

She exchanged an anxious look with Dedalus, but neither of them said anything.

The man who had led the attack on their convoy, stepped forward. "I am Farashi, and I now hold your fate in my hands. If you want to stay alive you will do everything you are told. This is not a democracy," he said with a sneer that allowed him to spit out that last word. "You are our prisoners and you will depend entirely on us for your survival."

Amanda was still blinking as she demanded, "Where are we?"

Farashi gave her an appraising look, impressed that it was the only woman in the group who had the nerve to speak up. "You are where you were meant to be," he said, staring at her. "That is all any of you need to know for now."

CHAPTER 31

London, England

Back at their hotel, Beth fired up her computer as Sandor used his backup cell phone to call Bob Kinnie in New York. He was still cautious about what he said and how he said it, conveying only a small part of what had just occurred.

"Bottom line," he told the man in charge of Lerner's detail, "My connection to your package is now known way outside our small circle."

"What do you want us to do?"

"The plan has changed," Sandor told him, his message clear—Kinnie needed to make an immediate move from the current safe house to another location. "It's also possible there's a party line in play," he said, meaning that some or all of his discussions with Lerner—and possibly with his bodyguards—may be compromised.

"Roger that, we'll tighten the net."

"Do that. Now let me speak with him, and explain the ground rules."

Kinnie turned to Lerner and began to describe how he should handle the call, reminding him that he should avoid mentioning names or giving locations.

Lerner responded with an impatient look. "When Sandor and I were in Iraq we invented our own language," Lerner told him, "but I don't think we need to go that far today." Then he held out his hand and Kinnie passed him the phone.

"Joey Sax here. I understand you don't think I can speak English."

"Just wanted to be sure we're on the same page. How's your vacation?" Sandor asked.

"A little claustrophobic. I could use a vacation from this vacation. How's yours?"

"Not the warmest reception. My guess is you're having a better time than I am."

"How's that?"

"All the people we need to see are distracted at the moment."

"Roger that. Things heated up at the beach."

"Yes they did."

"You on top of that?" Lerner asked.

"On the sidelines so far. I take it you believe all these events are part of the same play."

"*Como no?*"

"I'll keep that in mind," Sandor told him. "Meanwhile, there are a lot of dots to connect here."

"My specialty. Where do you want to start?"

"How about the bromance between the big boys? Real love or not?"

Lerner thought it over. "Let's say it's a marriage of convenience."

"Understood. Meanwhile, my take on Mata Hari is that you were right."

"It doesn't change anything for her, of course, but it does for me," Lerner said.

"That would be affirmative. I have less information on Fredo at this point, but my conclusion is the same."

"As I told you."

"Incidentally," Sandor said, "I haven't witnessed a lot of tears for either of them around here."

"You may be surprised. Not a group given to big displays of emotion, if you catch my drift."

"I'll say I do. Meanwhile, once I get past all the polite behavior, I don't see much chance of getting the paperwork I need."

"I'll do what I can from my end."

"Stay off the grid for now."

"Understood."

"I'm off to see the other guy."

"You getting resistance?"

"As you said, recent events give him a pretty solid excuse to avoid me."

"You don't want me to do anything to straighten that out?"

"I want you radio silent."

"Got it."

Sandor gave him an oblique summary of what Beth had found as she continued to review connections between the suspicious trades Lerner had witnessed and terrorist activities. She had several questions, but he wasn't ready to discuss any specifics on the phone.

"How do you want me to respond, then?" Lerner asked.

Sandor thought it over. "I'm not sure," he said.

Beth had taken the available data and brought it to the next level, incorporating various terrorist threats that had been prevented, then plugging them into Lerner's matrix. These were the type of activities not in the public domain but monitored by the CIA, and the supposition was that Lerner and his fellow traders could not have known of or anticipated them. Once the market trends were compared to those chronologies, they would see if those events also dovetailed with the trading parameters Lerner already had in place.

If they did, the implications were much wider than mere insider trading. It meant that the people placing the orders to buy or sell currencies and securities had access to highly classified information about upcoming terrorist attacks that would create the market shifts they were betting on.

Or worse, they were directly connected to those creating the havoc intended to affect currencies and stocks.

"Can you get the data to me?" Lerner asked.

"I'll arrange a secure route. Once you have it, though, I need you to make sense of it as quickly as possible."

"You know me."

"I do," he said. "Now, from this point forward you have to assume that none of your communications are secure. Incoming or outgoing. You copy?"

"Got it."

"You cannot possibly be too careful," Sandor warned him. When he hung up he saw that Beth was staring at him, looking even more upset than when they had first gotten back to the room. "What is it?" he asked her.

She had taken a call while he was speaking with Lerner. She handed him her cell phone. "Byrnes."

Sandor took the phone. "Sir."

"We have the names of the five hostages that were taken north of Mosul," the DD said.

"Let me guess. Jensen and Dedalus lead the parade."

"Yes. They also took Shahid Hassan, and the head of the private security detail, Thomas Orr, volunteered to go."

When Byrnes paused, Sandor prompted him. "You said there were five."

"They wanted a journalist in the group." He hesitated again. "They took Bill Sternlich."

CHAPTER 32

Refugee Camp near the Syrian border

When Thomas Orr volunteered to accompany the hostages, he saw himself as responsible for their safety. Since they reached the warehouse, however, the man who had become the *de facto* leader of this small group was Shahid Hassan. From the outset, the terrorists were intent on instilling a sense of mortal fear in their captives. Nevertheless, it was evident to everyone that Hassan was being treated differently. He was handled with an unmistakable deference that set him apart.

Hassan was the only Arab among the five.

The other three men were slapped and shoved, spit on and cursed at—Sternlich had a nasty bruise on the side of his head from the blow they hit him with when he tried to speak up on the truck, but he was not complaining, and they were not providing any medical care.

Other than Hassan, only Amanda Jensen was spared physical abuse. The presumption, whispered among the hostages, was that their captors were determined not to maim or disfigure her. A sign, Hassan assured them as best he could in hushed tones, that the terrorists were going to seek an exchange of the prisoners for ransom and did not want the actress injured.

When any of the hostages asked their guards a question, even something as simple as a request to visit the primitive lavatory, they were shouted down, told to remain silent, even struck. Hassan became their spokesman, asking for bathroom breaks, or water, or an opportunity for them to stand and stretch. Rarely were the requests granted, but he was never punished for speaking up.

The five hostages were being held in an overheated room on the second floor of the warehouse. They were seated on the floor, their hands still bound, their backs to the outside wall of the building. The room had only two small ventilation windows, without glass, near the ceiling. They were kept here in the sweltering heat, shut away from the outside, watched at all times by two armed guards who sat on chairs facing them.

The leader, Farashi, had come up several times to look them over. From comments he made to them in English it was apparent he was well aware of who Dedalus and Amanda were. There was something else in his manner that suggested he and Hassan knew each other.

If it was true, neither man was saying so.

On the ground level of the building was another small room. It was intended to serve as an office to keep track of incoming goods and to monitor their distribution. Thus far, no shipments had reached this storehouse. Every time a truck entered the main gate of the complex, it would immediately be overtaken and emptied by a swarm of starving men, weeping mothers and desperate children.

Ironically, the largest delivery of provisions to make it inside the warehouse had been brought in by the terrorists. In addition to their prisoners, they had carried enough food and water to remain self-sufficient for several days. They had also brought the necessary electronic equipment, batteries and a generator, to keep them in touch with the outside world.

Farashi was in the office, seated behind the desk, his chief lieutenant Gabir in a chair to his right. They had already powered up three laptops and two cell phones. Several of their men, all carrying weapons, stood around as Farashi took a moment to explain the present situation. "We are doing our best to monitor the pursuit of our other trucks. As you saw, the soldiers made no effort to impede our entrance here. They had no way of knowing if we were carrying their precious celebrities and would not take the risk." He scanned the room, then said, "Rock musicians and movie stars," which elicited a round of bitter laughter. He became serious again as he reminded them, "Our comrades are not likely to be so fortunate. They have all moved to smaller vehicles and are doubtless being hunted. Some will be captured. Hopefully most will escape."

The others voiced their support.

"The Americans are establishing a perimeter around this building as we speak. They are keeping their distance and will not make a move on us, not yet. But you will continue to work in shifts, two men on the roof and four men covering corners of this building. We cannot afford any surprises."

His men told them they understood. Then one asked, "You have plans in place for our escape?" It was posed less as a question than as a request for some form of assurance.

"We are just about to communicate our ransom demand. Once the next phase of our operation is put into place you will understand that there are no concerns about our safe passage." Farashi paused. He had only entrusted a few of his closest men with details of his scheme. In the event anyone was captured he could not risk having the operation compromised. "If it is not obvious to them already, the capture of our other men will lead them to the conclusion that all of the hostages are here. Although we have made efforts to disguise the location of the transmission we are about to make, it will ultimately be tracked and they will know we are headquartered here. Their efforts will intensify quickly at that point." He shook his head as if dismissing a bad thought. "It will not matter. We have made appropriate arrangements for our own safety." He smiled. "Can you imagine how they must be wondering why we came to this camp?" The others relaxed again. A few even laughed as Farashi turned to Gabir. "Are we ready?"

"We are," the younger man told him.

"All right then. Send the demand."

Gabir went to work at the keyboard, sending an email through a circuitous path of interconnected sites, ultimately to addresses at the United Nations and the World Health Institute.

Once the transmission was confirmed, Farashi went upstairs to the room where the captives were being held. It was only their second day of confinement, but they already looked drawn and exhausted. Fear is an enervating emotion, which Farashi knew only too well as he stared down at his prisoners.

"I bring you good news," he told them. "The council has decided you shall be permitted to live."

As the others stared up at him without speaking, Hassan asked, "What council is that? What governing body do you claim has the right to hold us like this?"

"The council of the true believers of Allah."

"Nonsense," Hassan replied. "I know of no such savagery that Allah would have ever permitted."

Farashi smiled. "You are as defiant as you are misguided, Hassan," he said, for the first time addressing him by name. "We all serve Allah for his greater glory, and for the defeat of the infidels. That is the only permission we need."

"You murdered a man for no reason. You have taken us hostage, tied us up and now treat us like animals. Is that for the greater glory of Allah?"

"It is merely one step in a long journey, my friend." He then made a grandiose gesture toward the others, spreading his arms as if welcoming them all to his home. "Please, do not think of yourselves as my prisoners, think of yourselves as my guests." Then he returned his attention to Hassan. "We have offered all of you safe return in exchange for payment of one hundred million dollars. We considered making our demand in Euros, but felt this was more appropriate since we assume Ms. Jensen's friends will finance a large portion of the total."

"A hundred million?" Orr blurted out. "Are you insane?"

One of the guards charged forward and cracked the barrel of his rifle across the top of Orr's head.

Farashi reached out, grabbed his man's arm and spun him around. He yelled at him, with no translation required for the hostages to understand what had just occurred. When Farashi was done dressing him down, the guard hung his head and returned to his post.

"Mr. Orr," Farashi said calmly as Orr lay on his side, blood oozing out of the fresh gash at the edge of his scalp, "I apologize for my colleague's overzealous reaction, but I don't recall inviting you into this discussion. Am I mistaken?" He held up his hand. "No need to reply." Turning once again to Hassan, he said, "These people have no idea who I am or what I am capable of, but you do. I suggest they look to you for guidance."

With that, he turned and was gone.

CHAPTER 33

London, England

Other than the few field agents he worked with, Jordan Sandor had no closer friend, nor anyone he trusted more, than Bill Sternlich. The fact that Sternlich was one of the group taken hostage was a total game-changer for him, as well as for Beth.

Their phone call with Byrnes was brief. The DD told them that Sternlich was on the list of four people Farashi demanded to take with him. There was no news beyond that.

"What's being done?" Sandor asked, knowing it was a foolish question, something asked by a friend rather than a professional.

"Everything possible," Byrnes replied, told them he would pass on any new information, then signed off.

The first order of business was for Sandor to convince Beth she should wait at their hotel while he visited the headquarters of the World Health Institute. He explained that Lerner made this appointment for one, not two, and the arrival of a second person might be all the excuse Mark Killian needed to cancel the meeting. "Things are hectic enough for them without adding any complications," he said.

What Sandor did not say was that Sternlich's abduction raised an entirely new series of questions about everything that had occurred over the past two weeks, causing him to replay those incidents, revising some of the assumptions he had been making up to now.

What if he was the target in Hartford, or at least one of them? Why was he followed back to his apartment after his meeting at the King Cole? Later that night in the hotel, were the shooters really after him and not Lerner? And now, it could not be mere happenstance that his best friend was one of the hostages taken in Iraq.

If there were people out there who intended to make another run at him, he liked his chances much better if he was on his own, without bringing Beth in the line of fire.

He removed the PPK from his bag and tucked it inside the waistband holster at the small of his back. Then he dug into a side pocket of the case and pulled out the thumb drive Lerner had given him. He held it out to Beth.

"What's this?"

"I don't know," he admitted, "but Lerner thinks it's important. I'm hoping it gives you more data to play with while I'm gone."

"When were you going to tell me about this little item?"

"Right now," he said.

Beth could not hide the look of concern that darkened her lovely features.

"Worried about me?"

"You?" she said, forcing a smile. "Hardly ever."

"Bill," Sandor said simply.

"I'm frightened for him, Jordan."

"Me too," he admitted. "Now lock up behind me, I'll be back before you know it."

⊙

The building that housed the headquarters of WHI was a glass and steel monolith located on Broadgate Circle in Bishopsgate, a contemporary design with corresponding interior furnishings. Sandor was greeted at a hi-tech security checkpoint just inside the front entrance, where he was made to relinquish his weapon despite a display of his State Department credentials, a routine that was beginning to wear awfully thin for him. He was then passed through a scanner worthy of an Israeli airport.

From there he was escorted into a lobby fitted out with post-modern furniture and artwork. The receptionist told him he would be announced and should have a seat while he awaited the arrival of Mr. Killian's assistant. Sandor politely declined the offer to sit, choosing instead to have a look at the various paintings that adorned the walls, and the sculptures that were placed around the spacious atrium.

Killian's assistant took her time getting there, but when she arrived Sandor figured it was worth the wait. She appeared to be about thirty, with light blue eyes, angular features and full lips decorated in a becoming shade of pink. Her hair was light brown and worn short, just like her skirt. The outfit was finished off with a blouse and jacket that just barely qualified as reasonable business attire.

"Mr. Sandor?"

After completing the once-over, he said, "Very attractive."

"Excuse me?"

"The artwork," he replied evenly, not taking his eyes off her. "Rather an extravagant display for a charitable foundation."

It wasn't a question, but he waited her out all the same. She finally said, "We have very generous donors. Most of these are on loan to WHI."

"Ah, that explains it then. I was curious if you ever considered auctioning them off for the greater good."

She gave him a look that said she didn't much care for his American sense of humor, assuming he meant it as a joke. "Please follow me."

She treated Sandor to a silent elevator ride to the top floor of the building, where she ushered him into Killian's private office. The head of WHI was seated behind his desk, wearing an expression that made it clear how he felt about having been cajoled into this meeting. Like Colville, Mark Killian had reluctantly agreed to Lerner's request that he see Sandor and, like Colville, he tried to beg off when all hell broke loose in Iraq. Once again, however, Sandor had effectively waved the American flag and his diplomatic credentials, and so the appointment was kept.

After a moment's hesitation Killian lifted his large frame out of the chair and stepped forward.

"Good to see you again, Sandor," he said without enthusiasm.

"I appreciate you making the time for me, under the circumstances."

Killian nodded, said to the woman, "That'll be all Lucy," and pointed his guest to one of the leather and chrome chairs facing his desk.

When Lucy left, it was clear Sandor was not going to be offered coffee or tea or anything that might prolong this discussion. He waited as Killian resumed his seat of power. "Spoke with Freddie. Said you two already spoke this morning."

"Yes," Sandor said, "we did."

Sandor decided he would take a different approach here than he had with Freddie Colville. Charles Colville was obviously not Killian's nephew, nor was Corinne Stansbury his employee. Although Killian knew them both, the same level of delicacy was therefore not required. He also had the sense that Killian was the type who would want to get right down to cases. If the man had information Colville was not willing to share, Killian might be the person to provide some insight.

Given that strategy, Sandor had to grade the earliest part of their discussion a failure. If Killian knew anything helpful, the burly man who ran WHI was not saying. He was even less forthcoming than Colville, prompting Sandor to change course and come at him from different directions. Each time, however, the result was the same. As he approached any topic that might be useful, Killian made an effective feint, claiming he was distracted by the current problem and his need to deal with the kidnappings. He couldn't focus on matters he characterized as "ministerial."

Sandor finally allowed himself a grin, and said, "I can see your mind really is elsewhere. Perhaps there's someone else in your organization who might be able to help me."

Killian responded with a wary look. "I'm still not clear what you're after, Mr. Sandor. What sort of help are you looking for exactly?"

"Information that might bear on the murders of Charles Colville and Corinne Stansbury, for starters."

Killian did not flinch, and made no disingenuous protest that their deaths had been accidental. It was evident his discussion with Colville involved more than a mere confirmation of this appointment. "Our liaison with RSL is Eduardo Cristo," Killian replied. "Shahid Hassan also has dealings with them, but . . ."

"He's one of the hostages."

"Sadly, yes."

"Would you arrange a meeting for me with Mr. Cristo?"

"Dr. Cristo," Killian corrected him, then hesitated. "As a charitable foundation the finances of WHI are effectively an open book. Our records are regularly audited. I'm sure you understand how critical it is that our donors feel confident their contributions are being invested properly and used wisely. We pride ourselves on transparency, as well as our ability to keep operating expenses to a minimum."

Sandor had a quick look around the office and smiled.

"Everything is relative," Killian said in response to the unspoken criticism. "We raise large amounts of money and distribute large amounts to those in need. It is a major undertaking on every level."

"I realize that. I have no interest in disrupting your operation or causing any trouble. There are, however, certain transactions about which I have specific questions."

"I see," Killian said, taking a moment to think it over. Then he picked up the phone and punched in a few numbers. "Eddie, there's someone I'd like you to meet." Hanging up, he turned back to Sandor. "He will give you his cooperation, with the following understanding. Should you uncover anything improper tied to the actions of RSL, you must report that directly to me. I have nothing but the greatest respect for Freddie Colville and the people at Randolph, but my loyalty is to the work we do here at the Institute."

"I don't expect to find anything that would compromise your relationship with RSL, but if I do, I can promise you'll be the first to know."

CHAPTER 34

London

While Sandor was being escorted by Killian's assistant down the hall to Eduardo Cristo's office, Beth was in their hotel room on her cell, again calling Mark Byrnes at Langley. The DD and his team were working on the kidnappings in Iraq. He took a break to receive Beth's report on the progress she and Sandor were making.

"Doesn't sound like much," Byrnes observed when she concluded her debriefing.

"I wouldn't say that, sir. We've determined the woman in Bermuda was probably murdered."

"You discussed that with Colville?"

"We did, may have ruffled some feathers."

"Tell me something I wouldn't expect from Sandor."

"He may learn more from his meeting this afternoon at WHI."

"Perhaps. What about this Lerner character?"

Beth described the thumb drive and the additional data Lerner had provided.

"Lerner is essentially saying that people are betting on market shifts being caused by terrorist attacks they know about beforehand. Do I have this right?"

"Yes," she said.

"Where is Lerner now?"

"I don't know."

Byrnes paused. "Is that true, Beth?"

"It is. You're familiar with how Jordan operates, sir. I'm on a need-to-know basis."

"All right. Just keep in mind that Sandor is on a frolic of his own here, this is not company business."

"I'm not so sure."

"Come again?"

"Too many paths are crossing here, sir."

Byrnes shared Sandor's respect for Beth's abilities as an analyst. "I'm listening," he told her.

"Lerner keeps talking to Jordan about connecting the dots, and that's what I've been trying to do. Take the Hartford bombing. Shahid Hassan was there."

"Among many others."

"But none of the others are now being held hostage by Ansar al-Thar, which is the same group we believe to be responsible for the attack in O'Hara's courtroom."

"Point taken."

"Corinne Stansbury and Charles Colville were both murdered. Let's accept that as a predicate for now. We know they both worked for Randolph Securities, where Hassan also has a significant position. The other night, Lerner was at the U.N. with Hassan and the heads of Randolph and WHI. Later, two shooters attacked him in his hotel room."

"Preliminary data indicates they were also related to Ansar al-Thar."

"My next point."

"All right, I'll grant you there are a lot of interconnected elements here. Where do you believe they lead?"

"I'm not sure, but it's difficult for me to believe they're not related to these kidnappings in Iraq."

Byrnes took some time to piece it all together. "That conclusion does not bear your usual syllogistic construction."

"No," she admitted, "it doesn't. But now that Bill Sternlich turns up as one of the hostages, this becomes more than just a hunch. These lines intersect in too many places not to be part of a larger piece."

"I can't disagree. Incidentally, how's Sandor taking the news about Sternlich?"

"He's better at compartmentalizing than anyone I've ever known."

"One of the reasons he's so good at what he does," the DD agreed.

"But as soon as we're done here, you know where his focus will be."

"Yes I do." Byrnes grunted, then said, "I have some new information that's about to become public knowledge." Beth waited. "The terrorists have made a ransom demand. One hundred million dollars, payable through banks in countries sympathetic to the jihadist cause, such as Yemen and Syria."

"A hundred million dollars?"

"They're demanding it be paid in gold. More details to follow. They obviously know a normal transfer will be traceable. On the other hand, they must realize that acquiring and moving that much bullion is impossible."

"Unless they actually expect some central banking system to cooperate."

"Utter nonsense."

"I agree sir. I'll tell Jordan."

"All right," Byrnes said.

"Sir, there's something I have to ask."

"Go ahead."

"Since this man Lerner turned up, Sandor has been in the middle of several close calls."

"It has not escaped our notice."

"Then, of all the journalists on that mission, they chose Bill Sternlich as a hostage."

"He's well-known, writes in-depth pieces about the Middle East for *The Times*."

"Respectfully, sir, you don't believe that's why he was named, do you?"

Byrnes sighed. "No, I don't."

"Jordan hasn't said anything to me about it, but it's written all over his face. He believes Bill was taken because of their relationship. Crazy, I know, but something else to consider."

The DD let that go, at least for now. "Whatever Sandor may think, his recent medical tests indicate he is not fully recovered. What's your take on his condition, from what you've seen up close?"

"I admit he's not a hundred percent, although he's doing his best to hide that from me. But when the time comes and he needs to act, he'll be fine. He has better instincts than any agent I've ever seen."

"Well, let him know I need to speak with him as soon as he gets back," he said. "As usual, I can only hope his expectations don't exceed his capabilities."

"Will do."

"What are you up to now?"

"I'm heading to our field office here in London. Need to run some things on an agency computer. My laptop isn't going to get it done, there's just too much information to filter."

"Keep in touch," Byrnes told her, then he rung off.

Beth packed her computer and phone, slung the bag over her shoulder, and made her way downstairs. The quickest route to the office was through Hyde Park, directly across from the hotel, so she crossed South Carriage Drive, entered the park, and headed on foot toward South Audley Street.

A few moments later, a man came up beside her from the right and said, "I wonder if you could help me with directions."

She turned to him but, before she could respond, a second man approached from the left, slid his arm under hers, and said, "That is the barrel of a pistol you feel in the side of your ribs, Ms. Sharrow. You can either live or die, the decision is yours. I believe you would be well advised to keep walking and do as we say."

"Who are you?" she asked, turning from one to the other.

Neither man answered as they propelled her forward to a van that was waiting on Park Lane, the engine running, a driver behind the wheel.

Once they forced her in the back of the vehicle, the man holding the gun said, "You have a nice little nap, now." Then his companion struck Beth across the back of the head with a hard rubber blackjack, knocking her unconscious.

CHAPTER 35

Port Chester, New York

Howard Lerner was taken to the new location Bob Kinnie and his men arranged, and it was even less to his liking than City Island. They traveled farther away from the city, up Interstate 95, to a small house in Port Chester, a working-class town in Westchester County.

"I didn't think it could get any worse. At least in the Bronx we had a water view," he grumbled.

"We won't be here long," Kinnie assured him. "Sandor promised to get back here in three days, four at the most. Then you'll be his headache again."

Lerner set up his laptop in the living room shortly after they arrived and began monitoring international markets. He was most curious to see which currencies were moving, if any, in the wake of the abductions in Iraq. As he worked, he was careful not to let his escorts see what he was doing.

Kinnie snapped on the television, flipping from one news channel to the next. Each program featured the latest details of the kidnapping of Amanda Jensen and Dedalus. It seemed they could not run enough photos of the two celebrities, particularly the curvaceous movie star.

One of Kinnie's men, known as Butch, came by his nickname honestly. He was over six-three, broad and muscular. "I think I'd grab her if I had the chance," he said as he flopped into an easy chair to have a look at a montage of her starring roles.

"There's a thought," Kinnie said, although his gaze was also fixed on the screen. "She ever make a movie where she's fully clothed?"

"Sure, as long as the outfit is skin tight. How about that string of action flicks she made? The female Indiana Jones."

"I saw them all," Kinnie admitted. "What kind of archeologist runs around in a friggin' leotard?"

Without looking up from his computer, Lerner said, "One with a perfect body."

A few moments later, the newscaster announced that there was a breaking development in the story. Credible sources were reporting the terrorists had demanded ransom of one hundred million dollars, payable in gold.

"Wow," Butch said. "How many truckloads would that take?"

Lerner was about to make a quick mental calculation, then thought better of it, more interested in seeing how the ransom demand was affecting the markets. A hundred million was certainly not enough to move currencies, but it was having an impact on several publicly traded movie studios. Then, of course, there was the intangible impact of a new terrorist initiative.

"They can't afford to let her die," Lerner said to no one in particular.

"How's that?" Butch asked.

They turned out to be his last words.

The front door came crashing open, followed by the sound of the kitchen door in the rear being kicked in. The first shots, from the man who burst in the front, were sent through a suppressor. They spit through the extended barrel of his automatic rifle and drilled Butch several times in the chest. Butch was dead before he could draw his weapon.

Kinnie was already on his feet, gun in hand. Without a silencer, the sound of his shots reverberated through the small house like a violent thunderstorm. He took the first intruder down, his face a bloody mess as he hit the floor.

Meanwhile, a second man was coming in right behind him, and he opened fire.

Kinnie dove for cover behind the door to the nearest bedroom, then scrambled to his feet beside a large chest of drawers. Lerner had already leapt over the back of the couch where he had been sitting.

"Stay down," Kinnie hollered, but from his vantage point he couldn't see that Lerner had chosen the wrong place for cover. The intruder who had charged in through the back door was now rushing toward him from behind.

Kinnie's other man, Swenson, had been in the bathroom, and he now burst into the living room, his gun leveled and ready for action. Just as the rear-flank attacker was about to get to Lerner, Swenson took him out with two rounds to the body and a third that struck him in the center of his forehead. Swenson then spun toward the second man who had come through the front door, but he was too late. Swenson took a hit in the left thigh and another bullet in his right side. He fell to the floor in a heap as the shooter advanced toward the couch Lerner was still using for cover.

Kinnie had dropped to his knees near the doorjamb. He had a better line of sight now, but before he could squeeze off a shot the intruder also went into a crouch, hiding behind a chair, then using the other furniture in the room for cover as he circled around towards Lerner.

Kinnie opened fire and a furious exchange ensued until Kinnie caught the man with a shot to his shoulder. It provided just enough force to spin the man into view. Kinnie stood and fired at his head. Two more rounds were all he needed.

The earsplitting sound of gunfire came to an abrupt end, the sudden silence almost as unsettling as the noise of the battle.

"Don't move," Kinnie yelled at Lerner. "Not sure if they have friends outside. Sven, you okay?"

Swenson moaned, then managed to say, "Losing blood."

"Damn," Kinnie said. He slowly edged his way to the side of the living room window and checked out front. The only car in the driveway was his, which made sense. The hitters would have parked down the street and approached the house on foot.

Kinnie moved cautiously, staying close to the wall as he looked out the other windows. There was no sign of anyone else, at least not yet.

Kinnie turned to survey the carnage in the small room. Butch was dead, still in the easy chair, slumped to the side and covered in blood. Swenson was on the ground where Kinnie ran to him and knelt down to have a quick look. The shot to Swenson's side was not bad, but the bullet in his leg had hit an artery.

"Tourniquet, man," Swenson gasped.

Lerner, who come from behind the sofa and was crouched beside them, already had his belt off. He'd seen enough action in Iraq to know what to do, wrapping it around Swenson's thigh, and cinching it up tight. The bleeding was cut off, at least for now.

Kinnie nodded at him, then said, "We still can't be sure there won't be a second wave.

They've got to have a driver out there someplace." He grabbed the Colt M1911 that was still in Butch's waistband, and handed it to Lerner. "I assume you can you handle this."

Lerner checked to see a round was already chambered. "Got it."

"Okay, help me move him."

Together they dragged Swenson into the bathroom. Kinnie put some towels under his head, then handed him his own automatic. "Try to stay awake Sven, will you please? I'll get some help pronto, but you need to keep alert."

Swenson nodded. "Hurts too much to take a nap, buddy."

Kinnie turned to Lerner. "Crawl out there and take a safe position with a view of the front," he told him. "I'll check the back door." As they left Swenson, Kinnie pulled out his cell and began punching in numbers.

The first call was to 9-1-1. Kinnie didn't like the idea of bringing in the local authorities, but Swenson was in bad shape. They couldn't risk lifting him into the car and racing to a hospital, especially if hostiles were still lurking outside.

The next call was the overseas number Sandor had given him. When there was no answer he used the emergency number in Washington. Craig Raabe answered on the third ring.

"Craig, it's Bob Kinnie. We have a situation."

In less than five minutes a police cruiser arrived, followed close behind by an ambulance, both of them with sirens blaring. The 9-1-1 call said a man was down, injured badly as a result of gunshots, so the two uniformed officers approached the house first. With guns drawn they climbed the few stairs and entered the house, cautiously. Then, when they walked into the living room, one of them said, "Holy shit," and called out for the EMT. The medics were right behind them, bringing a stretcher to the bloody scene.

"My God, it looks like a war zone," one of the cops said as he surveyed the scene. The room was splattered with blood, furniture was overturned and shot to pieces, and there were four dead bodies. "Anybody still alive?"

"In here," a weak voice called out from the bathroom.

The officers went first. One pulled the door open as his partner trained his weapon on Swenson.

"What the hell?" the second cop said.

"Anyone else in the house?" the first officer asked.

Swenson, who was barely conscious, said, "Not that I know of. Can someone get me to a hospital please?"

Kinnie and Lerner were already gone and on the move.

CHAPTER 36

London

Dr. Eduardo Cristo had a large office on the top floor of the WHI building and, if it was not as grand as the accommodations enjoyed by Colville or Killian, the room was nevertheless a dazzling display of technology, where form followed function. The credenza behind Cristo's desk held three computer monitors, while the wall off to his right featured two large-screen displays. All manner of international markets were being tracked in real time, with Cristo in position to keep an eye on all of it, clearly comfortable in his surroundings. There was also a balcony, which provided an impressive view of London.

Sandor had run a background check on Cristo, learning that the man had arrived at his present position via an unlikely path. Lebanese by birth, Cristo was moved during his infancy to South America—his parents were determined to raise their only child away from their war-torn home. They settled in Colombia, where Cristo was schooled by the Jesuits. A bright student, he won a scholarship to the university in Bogota, where he earned his undergraduate degree. From there he went to medical school in Miami, completed his internship at the state hospital, and finished training in New York City. After a stint in the oncology research department of Albert Einstein, he held various positions in biotechnology companies, ascending the ladder of influence as he demonstrated an uncanny knack for blending finance, fund raising and medicine. Killian had several dealings with him, recognized his talents, and convinced him to join WHI and run its investment department.

As Sandor was shown in, Cristo stood and, as the two men shook hands, he said, "I see you are admiring my terrace view."

"Impressive," Sandor replied.

"I have a difficult time living and working in a metropolitan setting. A bit claustrophobic for me," he explained, displaying a warm smile. "Standing outside from time to time is my salvation."

Cristo spoke English fluently, albeit with a slight Spanish accent. He was bald, with a thick neck, large head, dark complexion and Semitic nose, his Middle Eastern roots evident.

He showed Sandor to a chair and returned to his own seat.

"I have heard a bit about you from both Mark and Freddie. How can I help?" His manner was surprisingly unhurried. He was clearly accustomed to these displays of endlessly flashing and mutating financial data and, coupled now with the crisis in Iraq, it was remarkable how relaxed the man seemed.

Sandor said, "Howard Lerner and I are old friends. He has some concerns he wanted me to look into."

Cristo waved that preamble away with a quick chop of his muscular arm. "I'm aware of all that. Corinne. Charlie. Terrible tragedies, don't you think?"

"I never met either of them."

Cristo reacted with a curious look. "Certainly anyone dying young is a tragedy, don't you think?"

"No, I don't. I think it depends on who's doing the dying and what the circumstances are."

"I see," Cristo said, showing off his disarming smile again. "A fascinating, if morbid, perspective."

"We all die Dr. Cristo. I believe the how, when and why are relevant to whether the death is tragic or not."

"Please, my friends call me Eddie."

The completion of his westernization, Sandor thought. He said, "Lerner believes that Corinne and Charles were both involved in certain trades that might have had something to do with their deaths. Both Colville and Killian thought you might be able to shed some light on those transactions."

"Sounds melodramatic."

"Investments in the French company Fronique, for instance."

Cristo sat back. "Ah yes, Fronique. An interesting little think tank, of sorts."

"Think tank?"

"Yes, it specializes in advanced technologies. Research and development, rather than actual production."

"I assume they manufacture prototypes."

"Of course."

"Anything they're doing that might be of a sensitive nature?"

"Sensitive how?"

"Military-grade weapons or surveillance equipment, for example. Things that might be interesting to more than one potential buyer."

"Technology that might inspire a bidding war?"

"That would be a start."

"I would have to take a careful look into that before I could say."

"Since WHI has a position in the company, I assume you're already familiar with the sort of work they do there."

"What makes you think WHI has an interest in Fronique?"

Sandor pointed at the screen on the wall to his left. "I see the symbol up there. Why would you be tracking it unless you have an interest, of one kind or another?"

Cristo uttered a throaty laugh. "Well done."

Sandor waited.

"I know they are engaged in certain cutting-edge technology." Cristo's phone rang, but he ignored it. "I could check into the status of their programs if you like."

"That might be helpful."

A second call came in, but again Cristo did not so much as glance in the direction of the phone. "I must admit, I fail to see how work being done at Fronique would bear on your investigation into these two unfortunate deaths."

"Nor do I," Sandor said. "I'm just following the leads that present themselves."

"What other leads do you have?"

"Ms. Stansbury had been transferred to Bermuda a few months ago. After she arrived she established a number of shell companies in various jurisdictions around the world. She then opened accounts for them at Randolph Securities. Fronique was one of the investments made on their behalf."

"Interesting."

"The more interesting moment will come when we identify the beneficial owner or owners of those accounts."

"I see. And was Charles part of this, uh, scheme?"

"Not that I'm aware of. It seems he was tracking the purchase and sale moves as they were being made, then trading for his own account. Outside RSL."

"The look on your face tells me you already knew what Charles Colville was up to." The toothy smile reappeared. "Freddie was very fond of his nephew. Frankly, so was I. Charles saw himself as something of a playboy. Beautiful young women. High stakes card games. Drinking, and the other recreational activities that go along with that territory. The trading was a mistake, particularly when he began bragging about it."

"I assume he didn't risk talking about it in the office. I'm going to guess he would show off for the beautiful young women he liked to play with."

"You are an astute man."

"Other than Fronique, are you aware of any other transactions either of these people were involved in that were, shall we say, of a sensitive nature?"

Cristo took a moment before answering. "That's a complicated question. Typically, the only sensitivity relates to whether a particular investment gains or loses money, regardless of the nature of the company. Your inquiry is somewhat open-ended, however, since it relates to the identity of an undisclosed client as well as your suspicion that there may have been a peculiar sort of danger in the nature of the project being funded."

Sandor nodded. "How about adding into the equation the fact that two men tried to murder Howard Lerner the other night? I'm sure you heard about that from Colville or Killian."

"Freddie called to tell us, after your meeting with him. Most disturbing."

Sandor ignored the understatement, figuring Cristo had been spending too much time in London. Instead he said, "That certainly raises the bar another notch on the danger issue."

"Assuming these events are related."

Sandor nodded. "You're obviously a man comfortable with numbers and the calculus of things. You now have not two, but three intersecting lines representing three traders. Two of them are dead, Lerner almost met the same fate. When you chart their recent activities, do you see a pattern? Do you see where all three of those lines converge at a single point?"

Cristo made another show of thinking things over, then began slowly shaking his head. "I do not, but now that you have raised this with me I shall certainly give the matter my most serious consideration."

"I would appreciate that."

Cristo began to stand up.

"Are we done?" Sandor asked.

"Aren't we?" Cristo had already gotten to his feet.

Sandor remained seated. "I told Freddie Colville, your boss Killian, and now I'm telling you, I have no interest in creating any sort of tension or disruption between Randolph and this Institute. My concern is simple. Howard Lerner has been my friend a long time. He came to me with certain concerns, and that very night two shooters tried to kill him. I intend to find out why, and to do whatever I can to protect him."

Cristo nodded. "You must have an unusual assignment at the State Department, to be allowed to engage in this sort of work."

Now Sandor stood. "Let's just say I'm not considered as diplomatic as most of my colleagues."

Cristo showed him the smile one more time, then led him to the door.

As Beth had said, Sandor was capable of putting even the most urgent issues aside to deal with the matter at hand. Now however, as he rode down on the elevator, he thought of his two friends, Howard Lerner and Bill Sternlich, realizing how powerless he was at the moment to help either one. Trying to shake off that uncomfortable sense of vulnerability, Sandor stepped out on the ground floor and approached the security desk to retrieve his gun.

The receptionist called to him. "Mr. Sandor?"

"Yes."

"I have a call for you."

"For me?

"Yes. We have a booth over there, I'll transfer it in."

Sandor closed himself in the small room, sat down and waited for the call to ring through.

He picked up the phone and said, "Sandor."

"You need to listen very carefully," an unfamiliar voice told him.

"Who is this?"

The question was ignored. "We have Ms. Sharrow with us, and that is all you need to know."

"Listen to me—"

"Please, Mr. Sandor, dispense with any histrionics and allow me to get to the point. Do I have your attention?"

"Let me speak with her."

There was some background noise, then the sound of Beth's voice. "I'm sorry Jordan," she said, then he could hear the phone being pulled away from her.

"Are you listening now?" the man asked.

"I'm listening."

"You have your cell phone with you?"

"I do."

"Give me the number." Sandor did.

"In five minutes you will receive a call telling you where to meet us. For now, you should spend the time getting as close as you can to Canary Wharf. Meanwhile, if you fail to take the call, miss the meeting, or show up with anyone else, Ms. Sharrow will be delivered back to your hotel in pieces. Am I clear?"

"You are."

With that, the line went dead.

CHAPTER 37

London

Sandor hurried out of the booth and approached the receptionist. "The call you just took for me, was there an I.D.?"

The woman checked her digital switchboard. "Sorry sir, the source was blocked."

"Naturally," Sandor said as he rushed out of the lobby, hailed a cab, and got on his phone to Langley.

"Craig, it's me. I've got an urgent problem."

"I'll say you do. Your safe house in New York was hit. Two men down."

"What the— "

"Heard from Kinnie, he and Lerner are okay, but one of Kinnie's men is dead, the other shot up pretty bad. They're on the move, gone radio silent for now. Kinnie figures someone tracked them to the second house through Lerner's computer hookup."

"Put that problem on hold for a minute. Someone over here has Beth."

It was Raabe's turn to listen.

"Just finished my meetings at WHI," Sandor said, then described the call he received as he was leaving the building. "In less than four minutes I'm going to get another call, telling me where to meet them. Someplace near the Canary Wharf. I have to assume they intend to kill us both."

"Based on what you've described, I think that's a fair assumption."

"I'm not even certain this phone is secure anymore, since I had to give them the number, but we'll have to take the chance it is."

"Not much choice."

"Tap into my line, I want you to hear everything I hear in real time when they call me back."

"Done."

"Now, who've we got in London who can react quickly enough to help me?"

Raabe made two calls, then ran the length of corridor to Byrnes' office and gave his chief the bad news.

"I just spoke with Beth an hour ago," the DD said.

"They took her from the hotel after that, while Sandor was at WHI headquarters."

Byrnes shook his head. "Two men dead in a New York hotel, four bodies in Port Chester, his friend Lerner on the run, Sternlich a hostage, and now *this*? The man is supposed to be on R & R, for chrissake."

"Time is tight, sir. I've called in a favor from an old friend at MI6 and rallied some men from our London office. Meanwhile, Sandor has no choice but to go wherever these people tell him to go."

"They're obviously going to kill him. They're going to kill them both."

"Yes sir, but Sandor's not going to abandon Beth."

"Understood. All right, hook us up to our station chief in the U.K. We have access to choppers over there, let's get one in the air right now so we can monitor this from above, see if we can pull his ass out of the fire."

Sandor was still in the cab when the call came through.

"I'm listening," he said.

"Good. I assume by now you've called everyone you know, including your famous U. S. cavalry," the voice said.

"Horses would be a mess in downtown traffic at this hour."

The man recited an address near Lyle Park in East London.

"Got it," Sandor said.

"You have ten minutes to get there, not a second more."

"Impossible. I'll never get there in ten minutes."

"Then your friend will die," the man said, and ended the call.

Sandor leaned forward and gave the driver the new address. Then he phoned Langley. "You get all that?"

"I did," Raabe told him. "I'm in the DD's office, and you're on speaker."

"Hello sir."

"You armed?" the DD asked.

"One automatic."

"Which they will doubtless take as soon as you arrive."

"That's my assumption."

"You have a plan?"

"Not yet. A lot depends on the resources we can line up in the next few minutes."

Byrnes looked to Raabe who provided Sandor the sit-rep. MI6 had two men in the area on their way, the local Agency office had scrambled two agents of its own who hoped to get there in time, and air reconnaissance would try to monitor the action and track any movement if Beth and Sandor were taken to another location.

"Much appreciated, I'll do what I can on my end," Sandor said. "Just one thing. Please give everyone a heads up that our primary objective is to get Beth out unharmed. As for me, *que sera, sera.*"

◉

Sandor had gotten a good jump on his ride to the Canary Wharf. Now that he had the actual address and was pushing the driver to hurry, he was confident he would arrive ahead of the deadline. He knew the area, and realized the location they gave him was along the river, not far from the City Airport. Sandor figured the noise being generated from the docks and the airplane traffic would provide excellent cover if someone meant to fire weapons or otherwise raise havoc.

Not necessarily a good thing.

On the other hand, it might give him an opportunity to get close without being heard. All he had to do now was get there early and avoid being seen.

When the cab approached their destination, Sandor told the driver, "Don't stop, just keep going." He had him make a right turn at the next corner, past the target address, then told him to continue to the end of the dead-end street where they came to a stop facing the Thames River.

If the driver overheard any of Sandor's telephone discussions he wasn't saying so, but as soon as he was paid and Sandor got out the back of the car, the cabbie engineered a fast U-turn and sped away.

By then, Sandor was already walking briskly to his right. He made his way along the wharf, circling back to the side street that ran along the building where they told him Beth was being held. He stopped behind a stone wall to have a quick look around, but there was no one in sight. Sandor assumed they had sentries in place, so he removed the Walther from the holster, pulled back the slide to send a round into position, then held the gun under his jacket and resumed walking.

There was an abandoned warehouse to his left, which sat directly on the edge of the river behind him. It was separated from the building ahead by a narrow alley and, if there was a way to enter from the back of that building, he figured that would be preferable to strolling through the front door directly into a firing squad.

He stayed close to the age-old brick wall on his left, repeatedly checking over his shoulder and looking above him as he hurried forward to have a quick look down the narrow alley.

No one was there, at least no one he could see.

There were also no doors, and the windows were far above street level. There was a fire escape, but it was too high for him to reach. The rusting metal ladder attached to its side appeared to be hinged on a lever that could only be released from above, presumably by someone making their way down. Shoving his automatic back in the holster, Sandor got a grip on a couple of protruding bricks and started to scale the wall. All he needed was to reach the ladder's lowest rung.

As soon as he began his climb he felt a burning sensation in his left leg, the one that had been injured in the Hartford blast. He ignored the pain as he clung tightly, moving slowly, slipping once, then again, but ultimately getting close enough to reach out. The bottom of the ladder was just inches away now, and he strained to grab it, his left foot almost losing its hold as he made a second attempt that also failed. For the moment he gave up his effort to stretch above him, instead securing his tenuous grip as he hugged the wall. He was some eight feet off the ground.

When he felt more stable, he drew a deep breath and placed his right foot on a brick that was several inches higher. The ancient piece of stone stuck out enough to give him a solid position, and he hoisted himself up, reaching out again from this new angle.

This time he managed to take hold of the metal strut.

He swung free, letting go with everything but his right hand, then grabbing the rung with his left. He was still not that far off the ground, but if his grip gave out and he fell he would not only be out of time, he would also be vulnerable to an attack from anyone checking the perimeter of this ancient building.

Pulling himself up, he managed to climb the ladder, hand over hand, until he could get a foot on the bottom rung and clamber onto the fire escape. As Sandor anticipated, the noise from the airport and the river covered the creaking of the old metal.

Drawing his Walther, he crouched down and had a look through the window.

The glass was so dirty he could barely make out anything inside. It appeared to be a large open space with some rooms off to the side. He did not see anyone or anything moving, but he took no comfort in that. They were probably in one of the offices on the main floor, or in some dark corner. Checking his watch, he saw he had reached the ten minute deadline they had given.

He pulled out his phone and put it on mute just before it began to vibrate.

They were calling back. He was out of time.

Looking up and down the street he saw no sign of anyone, not from his support team nor any hostiles. He looked above him. The building was only three stories high and he had already confirmed there was no rear entrance. As he saw it, he had only one option left, only one way inside.

The DD had asked him if he had a plan. Now he did.

Moving as quickly and quietly as he could, Sandor climbed the fire escape. When he reached the top level he stopped and peered above the stone parapet. There was only one man stationed on the roof, and if he had heard anything he was giving no indication. The lookout's back was to him, his attention on the front of the building, awaiting Sandor's arrival.

From this distance, Sandor knew he could take him out with a single round, but even one shot would be one too many. The welcoming party inside would certainly hear that, regardless of the noise from the airport and docks, and there was no telling what they would do to Beth. Instead, Sandor used the butt of his gun, scraping the metal railing three times. Then he shoved the automatic in his waistband, braced himself against the metalwork of the fire escape, and waited.

The sentry came straight toward the sound, his weapon drawn. There was no way for him to know what had caused the noise without looking over the edge of the roof, and that was all Sandor needed. As soon as the man came into view with his gun hand extended, Sandor took his wrist and twisted it, then grabbed a fistful of the man's hair. The guard was already leaning forward so, using the fire escape for leverage, Sandor jerked him over his shoulder and tossed him past the railing.

Uttering only one astonished yelp, the man fell through the air and hit the pavement in the alley below with a sickening *thud*.

Sandor did not bother to look to see if the man had survived the fall. He hoisted himself onto the roof and ran toward the door at the center of the tar covered surface that led inside the building. As he opened it, the hinges made a raspy noise, but otherwise all was quiet. Stepping onto the landing he waited. Still there was no sound.

His automatic in hand, Sandor moved silently down a darkened flight of stairs, then a second. Here he stopped. The stairwell opened up, giving him a clear view of the building's ground floor and interior. Kneeling down he surveyed the place. Numerous large crates were stacked near the center of the open area. On the far side there were doors that led to offices. At the front entrance he could make out one man, standing in the shadows, holding a submachine gun.

Sandor knew he could not risk a run down this last set of stairs. The metal steps would be too noisy, and a shootout with his handgun against a fusillade from the man's MAC 10 was not a good strategy. Now that he was inside, however, he decided that firing a shot *before* he headed downstairs was the right play. He took aim and squeezed off two rounds.

He only needed the first, which hit the lookout in the back and dropped him to his knees. The second hit the wall just above him.

As soon as he had squeezed off the second round, Sandor charged down the stairs, using the handrails to slide as if he were descending a ship's ladder. He hit the ground just as a door across the way flew open and two men, holding automatic rifles, emerged from the room closest to the front of the warehouse. Sandor had already taken cover behind a stack of the wooden containers, off to his left, when they began calling out.

"Rahmad," a voice hollered, but there was no response. That short silence was followed by a string of Arabic profanity as one of them spotted the body of their fallen comrade.

Sandor stayed out of sight as he listened to a lot of frantic movement and discussion across the way. Then a voice, that was becoming all too recognizable, called out.

"Mr. Sandor, you have just made a tragic mistake. You may have just cost the life of this young woman, which we were willing to spare in exchange for yours. If you do not surrender yourself immediately we will have no choice but to kill you both, beginning with Ms. Sharrow."

Sandor assessed the risks. There was no percentage in them killing Beth, not yet. If they did, Sandor would have no reason to remain there, and at the moment they had no idea where he was, what angle his shots had been fired from, or if even he had come alone. He looked to his left and saw that the configuration of crates gave him an opportunity to circle around to the back of the warehouse undetected.

For the moment he stayed where he was and remained silent.

"Mr. Sandor, you are trying my patience."

Lowering himself to the floor, Sandor peered around the edge of the containers on his right. He had no line of sight on any of them, nor to the room where they were apparently holding Beth. However, one of the armed men now came into view. He was moving warily, his head swiveling back and forth. He was inching forward, toward the sentry Sandor had shot.

Sandor took aim and fired two more rounds, hitting him twice in the back. The man, mortally wounded, cried out, followed by yelling from the others who were still somewhere on the far side of the warehouse. Without hesitating, Sandor pulled back and raced around the stacks of boxes to his left. When he reached the rear of the building, he climbed atop one of the stacks, and began crawling forward over the tops of the wooden crates.

He stopped short of the edge, where he could now see an armed man standing just inside an open doorway to one of the rooms on the left. Before Sandor could react he felt the vibrator on his cell again. Retreating slightly, he pulled out the phone and saw it was a text from the support team sent by MI6. They advised that they were just down the street and wanted instructions.

Sandor texted back, *Approach with caution. Three men down but girl still being held. No headcount on hostiles. Do not to advance into warehouse without my signal.* After he put the phone away and moved forward again, the guard was no longer in view, but the door to the room was still open.

"You have twenty seconds to show yourself," the voice called from inside, "or I will shoot Ms. Sharrow and leave your fate to another time and place."

Turning onto his back and cupping his hands to holler upward, so the source of his voice would be difficult to ascertain, Sandor shouted toward the rafters, "This place is surrounded. Time to give it up."

Turning back on his chest he saw that his reply had brought one of the guards back to the edge of the doorway, less than thirty feet away. Sandor fired just once, hitting the man in the forehead, then he scampered backward and lowered himself down to the floor. Back on the ground he took a position at the far left-end of the containers, along the side of the warehouse where the offices were located.

Four men were down, counting the sentry on the roof. Sandor figured it was unlikely there were many others. "Bring her out," he hollered. "Then we'll deal."

Everything was quiet for a few moments, then Beth was shoved into the open doorway. Sandor could see that someone was standing behind her, one hand clutching her hair, the other holding a gun to her temple.

"Drop your weapon and show yourself," the voice demanded.

"Your men are all gone," Sandor said. "This is about *your* survival now, not mine or hers. I have agents positioned front and back, there is no way you walk out of here alive unless you let her go."

"Please Mr. Sandor," the voice responded, "enough of your theatrics."

Sandor drew back behind the crates, pulled out his cell, hit the number he had just used to exchange texts, and said in a loud voice, "Move to the entrance. He has the girl, but he's alone."

However, Sandor's guess had been wrong. The man holding Beth was not alone.

The noise behind him was a barely audible scrape, but instinct caused him to spin around. A tall man, coming out from behind the corner of the crates, was holding a short-barreled submachine gun, about to open fire.

Sandor dove to his right and came up firing, missing with the first shot but scoring with the second, striking him in the abdomen.

As the man stumbled backward, Sandor sprang to his feet. He had no time to replace the magazine and needed the man's weapon. Lunging ahead, Sandor drove his knee hard into the man's groin, using all of his weight to knock him backward onto the concrete floor, smashing his head with a dull *thump*. Sandor retrieved the man's MAC 10 and rose onto one knee.

Beth was standing in the open now, her captor using her as a shield. The man was holding her tight and the automatic was pressed hard against her head.

"Time for heroics is over," the man said. "Drop your weapon."

From his crouch, Sandor was barely able to see the man's eyes and, with Beth in the way, he had no clear shot at him. Even so, Sandor did his best to point the barrel of the weapon in the direction of the man's head as he said, "I took out your man on the roof and your crew down here. Unless you have any more surprises, you shouldn't do anything foolish."

"You're the one acting the fool, Mr. Sandor."

Sandor shook his head. "Don't move, just listen." He stood, still holding the submachine gun, and called out, "You, at the front. This is Sandor. Fire one shot in the air so he knows you're here."

In the ensuing silence, the Syrian holding Beth stared at Sandor with a look of utter contempt.

Then they heard the loud report of a shot fired into the roof.

"Now," Sandor said to the man, the automatic rifle still leveled at his eyes, "we have no reason to kill you if you let her go. The choice is yours. Live or die."

ROGUE MISSION

CHAPTER 38

London

Contrary to contemporary mythology, not every Islamic is a sociopath, and not every Islamic sociopath is suicidal. It took the man only a few seconds to assess the situation, release his grip on Beth's hair and drop his gun to the floor.

"On the ground," Sandor barked while Beth hurried away from him and stood beside Sandor. "Face down."

The man did as he was told.

"You all right?" Sandor asked Beth.

"They hit me in the back of the head. Still a bit groggy," she said.

"You'll be okay."

"When they first came at me, Sandor," she began, and for the first time he could see the fear in her eyes. "When they came at me all I could think about was . . ."

"Corinne Stansbury."

She nodded.

"You're with me now," he said as he gently felt the bump on her scalp. "We'll have a doctor look at you." Turning toward the front of the warehouse he called out, "You guys, it's Sandor. Come on back here."

The two men from MI6 approached with caution, followed shortly thereafter by the American agents dispatched at Byrnes' order.

"We have any idea who he is?" one of the Brits asked as he bent down and bound the Syrian's hands behind his back with a plastic restraint.

"I'll leave that part of the puzzle to you," Sandor told him.

It only took a couple of minutes for them to review the situation. There was a man in the back alley, confirmed dead, victim of a fall from the roof. There were four more corpses in the warehouse, all gunshot victims, including the last attacker who had bled out after Sandor shot him in the stomach and knocked him to the ground.

There was only the one survivor, who was not giving his name and had begun insisting that his rights be recognized. "I want to be taken to the Syrian embassy," he began repeating.

Sandor finally tired of him intoning the same demand over and over. He nudged the Arab in the side with the toe of his shoe, and said, "Hey pal, you know the expression 'eat shit and die'?"

The Syrian, who was still lying on the floor face down, looked up and began blinking.

When he started to repeat his request, Sandor cut him off with a hard kick to the ribs.

"Shut the hell up," Sandor told him as the man tried to catch his breath. Then he turned to the other agents. "I need to get Beth out of here."

The other four men looked at each other, none of them wanting to be left cleaning up this mess.

The senior man from the Agency asked, "Could you at least tell us what this is about?"

"I don't know for sure," Sandor admitted, "but I have some guesses I'll run past Langley."

The agent nodded in the direction of the two operatives from MI6. "We're old friends, we'll figure out a way to sort things out between us."

Sandor stared at him, realizing the man must spend most of his time riding a desk. "I'm sure you will. Right now I'm going to need some help. First, call a doctor, have him meet us at the hotel, I want him to have a look at Beth. Then I want secure phones for Beth and me, and I need to be re-armed."

"Got all that covered," the younger American agent told him. "We have a van parked a block away, fully stocked. I'll call the office now, get a doctor on the way."

"Good," Sandor said. "We can also use a ride, and some protection while we grab our things from the hotel."

"Done."

Sandor looked to the Brits. "You guys okay if we leave you with this mess for now."

"We taking custody of him?" one of them asked as he gestured toward the Syrian who was still lying on the ground.

"Your town, your jurisdiction."

"All right then."

Sandor looked down at their prisoner, who had resumed muttering his demands, then took a few steps away. Speaking quietly, he said, "Whoever this group is, I'm guessing he's not very high on the food chain. We need to determine who they report to. Have your tech people check out his cell phone, see who he called and who called him. Seems he was the host of this little party, must have had contact with someone above him." Addressing himself to the two agents from the CIA, he added, "Whatever you find, get it to Deputy Director

Byrnes. The important thing is to get this cleaned up and keep it quiet as long as possible. I need to buy some time before the man pulling their strings discovers they screwed up."

The younger agent smiled. "From the look of things, you helped them screw up big time."

⊙

Beth seemed remarkably calm during the ride back to their hotel.

Sandor had his arm around her shoulder in the back of the van, but she wasn't trembling or weeping or even complaining. "You getting used to the action?"

She looked up and gave him a disapproving frown. "Being knocked out probably slowed me down a bit."

"You'll be fine."

"We have a lot of blanks we need to fill in," she said.

"Agreed. Let's get back and call the DD."

By the time they returned to the hotel, a doctor was waiting. They left the two agents with the van and went up to their room. After a quick examination, the physician told Beth she was fine.

"I'm giving you some painkillers, that's a nasty bump, but I don't want you sleeping, not just yet."

"Concussion?" Sandor asked.

"I don't think so, but give it an hour, let her get some rest. Just keep an eye on her. You know what to look for."

Once the doctor left, Sandor and Beth cleaned up, and then called Langley, placing the call on speaker. Byrnes told them he had already received a summary from the men at the scene.

"Efficient," Sandor said.

"Disciplined," the DD replied, the hint of rebuke unmistakable. He was in his office with Brandon Garinger and Craig Raabe on the call.

"Discipline may not be my long suit," Sandor replied. "I admit that, but I did manage to take out five men before backup arrived, then handed over the leader of the group. And he was still breathing."

"Not really your style, is it?"

"Thought it might be worth asking him a question or two."

"So, how are you feeling?"

"My leg hurts, I have a headache, and I'm hungry. Thanks for asking."

"I was asking Beth," the DD said.

"I'm all right, sir," she said. "Just seem to have caught Jordan's headache."

"Interesting," Byrnes said. "He's the only human being I've ever met whose headaches are contagious."

"I'll be fine," Beth said.

"So, getting back to you Sandor, it appears your performance exceeded expectations."

"They were holding Beth, sir, I had motivation."

"I suppose your latest medical reports didn't take motivation into account."

"I suppose not."

Byrnes said, "I'm reinstating you to active status."

"Thank you."

"Understand something, Sandor, I haven't made this decision because your friend Sternlich is one of the hostages. It's because I need you in the field as a professional, not a vigilante."

"I admit I'm worried about Bill," Sandor said, "but I have no plans to launch a one man rescue."

"Not yet, you mean."

Sandor had the good sense not to reply.

Byrnes turned it over to Raabe. "Fill him in."

Raabe recounted what most of the world now knew, since the situation in Iraq was now the headline for every news outlet in the world. Not only were two celebrities being held, but the story was further sensationalized by the terrorists' demand—a ransom of $100,000,000 payable in gold. The bullion was to be transferred into accounts in countries believed to be sympathetic to their jihadist cause, primarily Yemen and Syria.

The media, supported by a number of celebrities, were mobilizing support for the hostages. They were planning events in New York and Los Angeles to raise awareness, as well as funds to pay the ransom, and proposing a concert in Algeria to support their efforts in a locale closer to the action.

Byrnes, who typically kept his political philosophy to himself, interrupted with a few choice words about the unwanted interference of left-wing extremists who did not understand the most basic concepts of modern geopolitics. "It gets worse by the minute," he went on. "Amanda Jensen's movie studio and Dedalus' recording company have gotten involved, warning our government that it cannot allow these beloved artists to be murdered."

"Maybe they're going to start negotiating with the terrorists themselves," Sandor suggested.

"Hell no," the DD replied testily. "They just want to incite their fan base, cash in on the publicity, then dump the whole thing in our lap."

"The boys at Foggy Bottom must be hating this."

"All the way up to the White House. So, what do you have for us that might be relevant?"

Sandor reported on his discussions with Colville, Killian and Cristo. He voiced his suspicions about their investments in the French company, Fronique.

"I need a little more than the *Reader's Digest* version on your friend Lerner. He's already been at the scene of two multiple homicides."

Reluctantly, Sandor explained why Lerner had reached out to him. Then he described what he and Beth had learned about Corinne

Stansbury and Charles Colville. "There's also the matter of Shahid Hassan," Sandor said.

"What about him?"

"I'm not sure, but he's becoming a bit like *Zelig*, don't you think? He was at O'Hara's ceremony, at the U.N., he's part of the Saudi royal family, he's connected to the WHI . . ."

"And now he's a hostage in Iraq."

At that point, Gabe Somerset joined the meeting in Byrnes' office.

"Glad you came in, Sandor and Beth Sharrow are on the line," the DD said. Returning to the call, he said, "Sandor, we'll get back to that issue later. I want Gabe to fill you in on a scientist by the name of Remmell. Heard of him?"

"Don't think so."

Somerset gave a brief but thorough description of Harry "Doc" Remmell, an American expert in drone technology, based in California. There were rumors he was currently working at the Fronique plant north of the French Riviera.

"Fronique," Sandor said. "There's a name that keeps popping up. Any reason to think this is connected to the kidnappings in Iraq?"

"There may be," Byrnes said, "but not enough to discuss now. I'm organizing a plane for Raabe and Garinger. They'll meet you in France tomorrow. I want you on the next train from London to Paris. We'll work on the hostage crisis, you find Dr. Remmell."

"Find him and take him?"

"Just find him, then report in."

"What about Beth?" Sandor asked as he looked over at his sleepy-eyed accomplice.

"What about her?"

"I don't want to leave her on her own, and I think she could be helpful."

"Fine," the DD said. "The two of you should get going then."

"One thing," Sandor said. "I may know someone who could be helpful with the Remmell issue."

"I'm listening."

"Haven't seen him him for a long time, but we keep in touch. Served with me under O'Hara. Lerner knows him too. Actually wondered if I might run into him at the Old Man's ceremony. Name is John Coman."

"How would he be helpful?"

"Last I heard he was working for military intelligence, involved with drone technology. Part of the team that built the new drone base in North Africa. One of the smartest gadget guys I've ever known."

"Gadget guys?" Somerset repeated derisively.

Sandor let it go. "He's more than likely to know Remmell. Could be useful. Maybe Craig could track him down before he leaves, find out where he is?" Byrnes asked Somerset if he knew of Coman.

"Yes, solid citizen, met him at the base in Niger."

"All right," Byrnes said, "we'll get on it."

As soon as Sandor hung up, Beth said, "I need a nap. Need to sleep off whatever they gave me."

"You can nap on the train," he told her as he got up and began collecting their things. "We shouldn't stay here a minute longer than we have to."

⊙

Back at Langley, Byrnes was ticking off several instructions to Raabe and Garinger, then told them to be on their way.

As soon as they were gone, Somerset voiced his concerns about Sandor. "We can't have him running wild, not if anything he's involved in might be related to this abduction. The lives of those hostages are at stake."

Byrnes fixed Somerset with a cold look. "Of all the things you need to worry about, Jordan Sandor is not one of them. Get in touch with our London office and see what they've found out. I want to know everything about the people who took Beth Sharrow, and I want to know why they took her. Whatever Sandor is up to, he's obviously getting under someone's skin."

CHAPTER 39

London and Paris

Sandor got on the hotel phone and arranged two first class seats on the next EuroTrain from London to Paris. Then he used his cell to call the agents waiting in the van outside to say they needed a ride to St. Pancras station.

All the while, he did his best to keep Beth talking, keeping her awake as the doctor had ordered. He would let her enjoy a peaceful rest on the train, but he didn't want to have to carry her on board.

He packed their bags, took her by the arm and led her downstairs to the waiting panel truck. On the short ride to Euston Road, the senior agent provided details on how the Agency and MI6 were handling the cleanup of that afternoon's events. Sandor did his best to appear interested, but he was not. Like his superior officer, the main thing he wanted to know was what they had learned about the identity of the men who abducted Beth.

"That part is still in the works," the agent admitted. "As you guessed, the surviving member of their group appears to have been their leader. He's a Syrian national on the watch list here and at home, but we're still trying to sort out what group he's connected to."

"I'll tell you what I'd like to connect him to," Sandor responded.

They reached St. Pancras station and, after saying their goodbyes, the younger agent took Sandor aside. "I have to admit, I know who you are. By reputation, I mean."

Sandor nodded. "Not all bad, I hope."

The man smiled. "Just wanted to say, it was a privilege to be able to help you today. Wish we could have done more."

"You did plenty," Sandor told him. "Now find out who that sonuvabitch is working for. For what it's worth, you may want to start by checking out Ansar al-Thar."

Sandor held Beth as they made their way through the terminal and into the First Class compartment of the high-speed Chunnel train. He got her comfortably settled in her seat and asked if she wanted anything. "Other than rest, I mean."

Beth managed a weak smile. "You mean you're finally going to let me sleep?"

Sandor reached for her wrist, felt for her pulse and waited a few seconds. Then he had a good look at her eyes.

"So doctor," she asked, "what's the diagnosis?"

"I recommend a nice two hour snooze now, followed by another few hours in a comfortable hotel bed."

"I get to nap there too?"

"Naturally." He surveyed the compartment. "I'm going to organize some sandwiches and a cocktail or two." He smiled at her. "The drinks are for me, my guess is you don't need one."

She shook her head. Then, as he was standing up, she put her hand on his forearm.

"Before I pass out here, I need to tell you something."

Sandor sat back down. "I'm listening."

"When we had dinner the other night in New York. At *Il Mulino*."

He waited.

"Byrnes knew I was meeting you."

"I know."

She looked a bit puzzled, but went on. "I called him after I saw you that night at the U. N. I was worried about you."

"Thanks mom."

"Don't be a jerk, Sandor, I'm trying to tell you something." She sighed. "I'm trying to tell you that Byrnes asked me to keep an eye on you, so I've been letting him know what we've been doing."

"I know that too."

She shook her head, looking as if she might be too exhausted to go on. "You knew?"

"I work for a clandestine unit, Beth. I wouldn't be very good at my job if I can't figure out what my closest friends are up to."

"I guess I can accept that. What troubles me is that I told him what I knew about Lerner, and I keep thinking that the protection detail you set up for your friend might have been compromised because of something I said on the phone."

Sandor took both of her hands in his. "Please don't give that another thought. In case you forgot, I never told you the location of Lerner's safe house." He waited for that to register. "I realize you're tired and confused and this has been a horrible day, but you had nothing to do with the attack on Lerner. I'm fairly sure that team was compromised because my old friend got on his computer, hooked up to a wireless signal, and their location was tracked when he started trading his accounts."

"Really?"

Sandor nodded. "That's my best guess, and I'll be sure to have him answer for that later. For now, I want you to remember what Sternlich always says."

"Guilt is the most useless emotion known to man," she recited with a wan smile.

"Correct."

She was about to close her eyes when she said, "I recognize that look, Sandor. Something else is bothering you."

"More than one thing," he admitted, "but you're tired, we'll talk later."

"It's Bill, isn't it?"

"Of course. It's also this Remmell thing," he said. "And how I keep ending up in someone's crosshairs."

She fixed him with a look that said she was summoning all the energy she had left. "You taking all of this personally? Not like you."

He leaned forward, held her face in his hands and kissed her on the mouth. "Get some sleep," he said. "I'm going to search for some bourbon and ice."

◉

A couple of hours later, a Mercedes sedan picked them up outside the Gare du Nord. Beth was still groggy, but seemed much better for having slept. Jordan also managed to doze after two short whiskies, and felt refreshed.

"Paris," he said. "I feel rejuvenated just being here."

Beth looked out the car window at the famous skyline. "Where are we staying?"

The chauffeur, not Sandor, replied. "Why, the *George Cinq* madam."

"The *George Cinq*?" she repeated, her mind clear enough to realize what that meant.

"Hey, I'm on the company's dime again," Sandor told her.

"I'm not sure that entitles us to a five star hotel."

"If not us, who?"

"Does that mean I get my own room this time?"

"Hell no. I want you close by, where I can protect you."

"Need I remind you, that hasn't worked out very well up to now."

"Ouch."

"You asked for it."

"Maybe we weren't close enough."

"How close do we need to be?"

Sandor smiled. "Close enough so you feel safe."

"I'm afraid there may be a point of diminishing returns somewhere in that calculation."

"I guess we'll find out," he said.

Christophe, one of the managers at this famous Parisian hotel, was someone for whom Sandor had done a favor a few years back, without asking anything in return. It was a policy he found often paid dividends when least expected, and when most needed. After a quick exchange of emails initiated from the train, Christophe arranged for the driver and a room. When the car pulled up to the entrance of the hotel, the handsome young Frenchman was waiting for them.

"Jordan," he said as he embraced his guest, "so good to see you my friend."

"The pleasure is all mine Christophe."

"I must say, an unexpected pleasure," the manager whispered. "I think we had to turn out a viscount from some lesser country to make room for you."

"At least it was a lesser country," Sandor said. Then he stepped back. "Please say hello to Beth Sharrow."

Christophe kissed her hand, welcomed her to the *George V* and said, "Let us not delay any further, I am certain you want to freshen up. Let us show you to your room."

Accompanied by an attractive young woman he identified as an assistant manager, as well as a housemaid and a bellman, Christophe led the entourage through the lobby restaurant, to the lift, and up to the suite that had been made ready for them.

They were treated to a tour of the bedroom, sitting room and lavish bath. The obligatory bottle of Veuve Cliquot was on ice, and a platter of strawberries recently dipped in dark chocolate was on display.

Christophe insisted that they come down later to see him, then, with *savoir faire* only the French can muster, he and his aides seemed to disappear rather than depart, leaving Sandor and Beth alone.

"That was impressive," Beth said. "He owe you money or something?"

"Let's just say I once did him a good turn, and he's not the type to forget. A story for another day."

Beth had a look around. "Well, I'll have to admit it, Sandor, every now and then you really can sweep a girl off her feet."

"Apparently not," he said.

"I'm sorry?"

"First, you never call me Sandor when romance is on the menu. Second, if I really swept you off your feet, you would already be undressed and in bed." He waited a beat before adding, "I mean that in the most innocent way possible."

"Aren't you going to mention a third item? You like to list things in threes."

"I'll reserve that for later."

She stood, hands on hips, staring at him. "Then let me tell you something, *Jordan.* 'Innocent' is not part of your repertoire."

They looked at each other for what seemed a long time. Then he stepped forward, took her in his arms and kissed her. "I want to make love with you," he whispered in her ear.

"It's been a long time."

"Too long."

Beth smiled. "That was the right answer."

"Can I carry you inside?"

"Byrnes says you're ready for active duty."

He reached down, lifted her in the air and brought her into the bedroom where he deposited her gently on the lavishly appointed king-size bed.

"Be gentle with me," she said. "I have a tender heart."

"Sure you're not still too tired?"

"If I fall asleep while you're making love to me, then Byrnes was obviously wrong about reinstating you."

They kissed again, the shared familiarity of scents and tastes overtaking them both, physical passion blending with emotional tenderness. He undressed her, pulled off his shirt and pants, then together they climbed beneath the soft sheets and fluffy duvet.

"I've been looking forward to this," he said.

"So have I," she admitted.

◉

The hotel phone woke them a few hours later. Sandor answered.

"You turn your cell off?" the familiar voice asked.

"Yeah. We both needed a little rest."

Craig Raabe chuckled. "Well, I hope you both got what you needed. You have some time for me now?"

"Where are you?"

"In the lobby."

"Give me twenty minutes."

"I'll be in the bar."

Sandor told Beth to take her time getting up. Then he took a quick shower and dressed.

As he tucked in his shirt he said, "Whenever you're ready we'll be waiting downstairs."

"Last time you left me alone in a hotel room . . ."

"Don't worry," he said as he leaned over and kissed her. "This time I've got you covered."

⊙

The opulent barroom was situated just off the hotel lobby, a spectacle of glass, brass, and polished wood, with a high ceiling, museum-quality tables and comfortable chairs. The room managed to be both impressive and warm.

Sandor found his colleagues seated at a table for four in the far corner.

"Good evening gents. You certainly got here in a hurry."

"The DD sent us in style," Raabe said. "We took one of the company jets, and it's ready to take us to Nice first thing tomorrow. After we see Remmell we'll get orders for the next move."

"Glad to see Byrnes is feeling generous."

"Time is tight on all fronts," Raabe said. "Although he wasn't too thrilled when he found out you were staying at one of the most expensive hotels in Paris."

"It's okay, I'm getting the family discount."

"Can't wait to see how you sell that story to the bean counters at Langley."

"Let me worry about that. What've you got that's new?"

"For starters, I heard from Kinnie again. He and Lerner are safe. He's awaiting your instructions."

"My first instruction would be to toss Lerner's computer and phone into the Hudson River."

"Already done. He's none too pleased about losing Butch."

Sandor nodded. "How's Swenson?"

"Lost a lot of blood, it was bad for a while, he'll be okay."

"What about the shooters?"

"One was a Syrian. Sad to say the other three were American citizens, born and bred, all from Arab backgrounds."

"Seems that ISIS recruiting terrorists in our own country is becoming a cottage industry."

"Yes it does."

"Have we connected them to a group?"

Garinger spoke up now. "We're working on it. The obvious presumption is that they were working for Ansar al-Thar, since that's the name that keeps popping up. No confirmation yet."

"I'd like to know."

"As for their cabal in the Middle East," Raabe went on, "there are teams tracking the vehicles that scattered after the abduction in Iraq. We may be close to taking one of them."

"Good."

"Analysts from the various agencies are pretty much in agreement that the hostages are being held in a warehouse inside the refugee camp."

"Bizarre place to take them, no?"

"It certainly is," Raabe said. "Why bring them there? More important, what's their escape plan?"

"Those are my questions too," Sandor agreed, then thought it over for a moment. "Any plans being made for a rescue operation?"

"Not so much made as discussed. The safety of the hostages has to be considered, of course, but there are thousands of refugees in that camp we have to think of too. Once the shooting starts it'll be a blood bath."

Sandor thought that over. "Yes it will," he agreed. "But I have a special concern."

"We all know you're worried about Sternlich."

"It's more than just worry," Sandor said. "It's the fact that Sternlich is involved at all. I mean, what are the odds that my friend was taken, especially after what happened in New York and then London?"

Raabe and Garinger waited until Sandor shook his head, as if dismissing the topic.

"Never mind that for now," Sandor told them. "Solving that mess is not our assignment at the moment. Our job is to find the infamous Doc Remmell."

"Agreed," Raabe said.

"What's the presumed tie-in between Remmell and this terrorist group?"

"Don't know. Don't know if there is one."

Sandor thought it over. "Seems odd the DD would be sending us after him at a time like this, unless there's an important connection."

"For the moment we're on a need-to-know basis."

Sandor looked to Garinger. "Don't you just hate that?"

Garinger laughed. "We have some more background information on Remmell and Fronique, I'll fill you in. We leave at dawn, have a car lined up for us when we land."

"We also have a lead on your friend Coman," Raabe said.

"As you said," Garinger jumped in, "he did some work on our drone base in Niger. Presently in Germany, being flown out tonight, he'll be meeting us tomorrow morning at the airport in Nice."

"That's good work Garinger."

"Thank you, sir."

Sandor grinned. "Garinger, we'll get along a lot better if you don't call me 'sir.' 'Sandor' is fine. 'Hey you' is okay. I can even live with 'Your Excellency.' Save the 'sir' for Byrnes."

Garinger smiled. "Got it."

"So," Sandor said as he looked at his watch, "as soon as Beth comes down I'll take you around the corner to *Chez Andre*, where I'll buy you the best escargot and steak tartare you've ever tasted."

"I hope so," Raabe said. "Because every drink in this place costs as much as a prime rib."

"And worth every Euro," Sandor said. "So, who's treating me to one?"

CHAPTER 40

Iraq

As Sandor was drinking his bourbon at the *George V*, a special unit of United States Army Rangers finally located the small truck it had been tracking the past two days. The hunt began via satellite, was augmented by the use of surveillance drones, then proceeded on the ground. The advance team now had the vehicle in sight through their binoculars. After meandering back and forth across various sections of northwestern Iraq, the truck entered a small building less than a hundred yards away.

The driver and two passengers had switched vehicles three times over the past two days, using garages, warehouses and a covered marketplace to disguise their movements, frustrating efforts to track them from overhead. Despite those shell-game maneuvers and their crisscrossing route, the Rangers were convinced they had now cornered three of the terrorists involved in the kidnappings that occurred north of Mosul.

Brian Kahler, the lieutenant in charge of the detail, reminded his men that they wanted to take their targets alive. "Keep in mind, they may be willing to die if they can take one or more of us with them, and that is simply unacceptable."

In the darkness, the two Army Humvees were hidden behind a two story dwelling.

Nevertheless, given the network of insurgency that existed in Iraq, the Americans believed the terrorists already had word that the Rangers were in close pursuit.

"We cannot rely on the element of surprise," Kahler told his men. "Assume they know we're here and that we're coming for them."

Every man in the unit nodded his understanding.

Kahler had phoned his position into the base, first to confirm that he had a green light to take the men, second to have backup ready as needed. He was promptly given the "go" order, and he opted for a three-pronged attack. The first four men would have the furthest distance to negotiate, making their way behind the buildings to the right and circling around to the far side of their target. A second group would head out to the left and provide a flank across the street from the garage the truck had entered. Kahler and two men would "Stroll right up Broadway," as he told them. He would be the first to engage the enemy.

All of his men were fitted with PNVG night vision goggles, which they now lowered in place. They also checked the microphones and headset assemblies inside their helmets. Each of them was fully armed with automatic rifles and side-arms, conventional grenades and stun grenades, and additional ammunition. Two men carried shoulder-mounted rocket launchers.

All of the Rangers were well trained, among the elite of American servicemen. They understood their assignments and knew their jobs.

At Kahler's signal they moved out in radio silence. Until instructed otherwise, the only voice they would hear would be the lieutenant's.

After giving the men to his right and left sufficient lead time, Kahler started off. He kept close to the buildings, where a couple of curious onlookers stuck their heads out of windows to see who was on the street. At the sight of the armed soldiers, they immediately drew back and pulled their curtains closed.

Kahler was soon directly across from what appeared to be a one story repair shop. The only windows were small and well above eye level, designed for ventilation rather than viewing.

Kahler looked to his men across the unpaved street to his left. He gave a signal, two fingers to his eyes, but the leader's response was negative. They could not see anything more than he could.

The front of the building was on the far side, across from which his Alpha team had already taken its position. Kahler pointed to the two men behind him, sending them to the rear of the structure, off to the right, to see if there was another way in.

As soon as the two soldiers stepped out to cross the street, the first gun shots rang out.

Both Rangers managed to leap back to safety.

"Anybody see where that came from?" Kahler demanded.

"Shooter on the roof," came the reply from his Beta team leader, off to the left.

Before the Rangers made another move, a grenade landed with a thud in the middle of the street, followed by a second. All of the Americans were out of harm's way when the two blasts went off.

After Kahler confirmed no one was hurt, he called out the name of the team leader now on the far side of the building. "Froman, give me a sit-rep."

"Two doors, one normal, the other a large metal garage roll-up. Both closed. Two windows, street level on either side of the doors. Also closed, and covered from the inside. The shots came from the roof, but we have no line on the sniper."

"Is your team visible to them?"

"Negative. None of us is exposed."

"Use the rocket launcher to take out the big door. Aim high."

His order was followed without hesitation as one of the men on Alpha team dropped to his knee. The night was suddenly filled with the roar of a loud explosion, then a second. The large metal door was torn from its upper hinges and the pieces that were not obliterated fell to the ground.

The sniper on the roof began firing wildly in the direction of the Alpha team, and Froman immediately saw why—the shooter was giving cover to the men inside. Although the garage door was gone and replaced by a gaping hole, the small truck inside appeared to be intact. One of the hostiles had started it and was about to drive it out of the building.

Froman reported to Kahler and then, without awaiting instructions, had his men commence firing at the tires and engine of the vehicle. The truck did not even make it to the street before it collapsed in a dead stop.

Two men emerged and took cover behind the truck. Froman hollered out in Arabic, telling them to drop their weapons and place their hands on their heads.

No one moved, and for a moment the firing stopped.

Froman reported to Kahler, who made a strategic decision. The only danger to his men was the man on the roof, and taking two prisoners rather than three was preferable to risking any casualties. Speaking into his microphone, he said, "First man to get a bead on the sniper, take him out."

Since the shooting had stopped, the sniper approached the edge of the rooftop to see what had happened to his comrades below. The Ranger standing across the way from Kahler had a line of sight. His shots rang out, and the terrorist was hit twice, the first twisting him to the side, the second doubling him over as he tumbled to the sidewalk below.

Froman resumed yelling at the remaining two terrorists as they crouched behind their truck. An exchange of gunfire ensued, but the Americans had the advantage. They all held safe positions, while the hostiles were trapped.

"This is your last chance," Froman hollered. "We will blow you to hell and back if you don't show yourselves right now."

After a few moments of eerie silence the driver threw down his rifle, stepped out into the open and placed his hands in the air. The second man did the same.

The Rangers approached with caution, remaining behind cover and not moving too close. They had all been in the region long enough to remain wary of suicide vests, grenades and I.E.D.'s that would take them out along with their prey who sought entry into *Jannah*.

"Strip down," Froman ordered.

When the men refused, Froman fired several rounds into the sandy earth in front of them.

"You want to die, you die without getting near any of us. Now strip."

They relented and began disrobing.

Kahler, not sure of who else might be inside or near the building, ordered the two men in the rear of the building and some of the Bravo team to secure the area. Others were sent to bring up the Humvees. By the time their vehicles roared up to the front of the garage, Froman's men had finished binding the prisoners' hands and feet with plastic restraints.

They dragged the two men through the street, tossed them into the Humvees, then they all piled into their Humvees and took off.

CHAPTER 41

Sophia Antipolis, France

Early the next morning, Raabe and Garinger picked up Sandor and Beth at the hotel and drove to the private hanger at Le Bourget. The foursome boarded the Gulfstream 550 Byrnes had arranged for them, landing in Nice little more than an hour later. A Mercedes sedan was waiting at the terminal, and from there they made the drive north.

Sophia Antipolis is France's answer to Silicon Valley. Northwest of Antibes, it is home to numerous firms specializing in software, hardware, electronics, engineering and biotechnology. Among this large complex of such companies, located just on the edge of the village, Fronique maintained its corporate headquarters. The facility included its research and development department where Doc Remmell—one of the world's foremost experts on drone technology, who had recently disappeared from his lab in California—was believed to be visiting for reasons as yet unknown.

Byrnes instructed his agents to locate the scientist but not take him, so the team opted for a direct approach. While en route north, Sandor placed a call, confirming that Dr. Remmell was in but unavailable. When they reached Sophia Antipolis, Sandor dropped Raabe and Garinger at a café in the center of town, had Beth sit in the back of the car, and played the part of chauffeur.

He followed the navigation system, heading for the industrial park.

Byrnes had approved Beth's involvement as part of this team, permitting her to make the dangerous transition from analyst to operative. It was not an easy decision, given the DD's affection for her, not to mention her relationship with Sandor, but they all saw value in having a woman involved, and there was no time to bring anyone else into the action. On arrival, their plan was simple. Beth would enter on her own and ask to see Doc Remmell, claiming to be a colleague from back home. They would see how far that got them.

The Fronique building was a contemporary design, constructed of architectural precast concrete and very little in the way of glass. Whatever they were doing inside, they were not eager to have it on display from the outside.

As Beth got out of the car, Sandor reminded her, "Keep it simple." He was still facing forward, a good and discreet driver, watching out of the corner of his eye as she walked toward the entrance. Then he spun the vehicle around and found a spot in the visitors' parking lot where he had a view of the entrance and could engage in the pastime he liked least—waiting.

Beth entered an enclosed area where she pressed the button on an intercom and stated her interest in seeing Dr. Remmell. She spoke

French, which was always a plus in a country that cherished its own language as much as the Gauls did. She was buzzed in and found her way to the front desk where she was asked for identification. She displayed her passport and repeated the reason for her visit.

"You don't have an appointment," the woman at the desk said, making it sound like an accusation.

"No. I'm in France on holiday and decided to look him up."

The woman stared at Beth as if this might be the strangest thing she had ever heard. "Have a seat and I'll see if he's available."

Beth found her way to one of the sleek, leather Barcelona chairs off to the side of the lobby and waited. She watched patiently as the receptionist took and received several calls until, five minutes later, she raised her hand in summons. Beth returned to the desk.

"I'm sorry, Dr. Remmell has no time to see you."

Beth did her best to appear shocked. "Really?" Then she stood there, unwilling to move unless a further explanation was provided.

The receptionist leaned forward as if to prove, despite their differences in nationality and her inherently sour attitude, she was still one of the Band of Sisters. "He actually said he didn't recognize your name. I sent him a photo," she added, pointing to a device on her switchboard. "He doesn't know you."

"What about John?"

The receptionist sat back and blinked. "John?"

"Oh my goodness. John Coman. Didn't I give you his name? He's the one who asked me to stop by."

The receptionist's reaction reverted to her default mode of petulance and, if she did not convey an odor of downright suspicion, there was certainly an aroma of skepticism. "No, you did not mention another name."

Beth said, "My fault, I'm so sorry." But she still wasn't moving.

The receptionist nodded. "Have a seat, I will try him again."

After another wait, Beth was called back to the desk and told, "Dr. Remmell will be down to see you."

It was not long before Harry Remmell stepped off the elevator, an aide right behind him. The scientist was tall and lanky, his hair a clichéd mess. As he strode toward Beth his weathered features were a map of distraction.

Beth stood, but, before she could greet him, he said, "I don't know you, Ms. Sharrow. What is this nonsense about Coman?"

Now that the two men were standing right in front of her, it was clear Remmell's companion was more bodyguard than assistant. He appeared to be of Arab descent, bald with a thick neck and menacing demeanor.

"You and I have never met, it's true, but we have a friend in common," she said, flashing her most charming smile.

"Who told you Coman was my friend? *He* certainly didn't."

"Actually, no. I was told by another friend of mine. She suggested I look you up since she knew I was coming to France."

Annoyance turned to distrust as he asked, "And who might this other individual be?"

"Corinne Stansbury," she told him.

If the name registered with him he was an even better poker player than he was an engineer. "Who?"

She repeated the name, then added, "With Randolph Securities."

That drew another blank look from Remmell, but not the henchman with him.

"We've got things to do, Doc," he said, tugging on the sleeve of Remmell's lab coat.

Remmell backed up a step and gave Beth an appraising look from bottom to top. "I don't know who you are, why you're here, or who sent you Ms. Sharrow, but you best be on your way." Then he turned and, without another word, headed to the bank of elevators and disappeared. He did not even bother to look back, but his Arab escort did, and the message in his eyes was unmistakable.

As Beth turned to go the receptionist gazed up at her.

"Scientists," Beth said with a shrug. "More temperamental than artists."

As soon as she stepped outside, Sandor pulled the Mercedes to the front door. She climbed in the back and they took off.

"From the way they run things, I think they'll have us on digital video," she said. "Inside and outside."

Sandor nodded. "I assumed as much. What happened?"

Beth filled him in as they sped past several other buildings, exited the industrial park and made their way back toward the center of town. She turned around and had a look behind them.

"No sign we're being followed."

"Not yet," he said. "Time to check in with the chief."

After picking up Raabe and Garinger, Sandor suggested they head out of Sophia Antipolis. "At least for now. No telling who they might send to have a look at us. I know a place just south of here with outstanding *soup du poisson*."

Garinger started to laugh. "You ever give up espionage, I'll bet you'd make one hell of a tour guide."

Sandor glanced at the rear-view mirror. "Not a bad thought," he said.

They arrived at the restaurant, pulled into the parking lot and remained in the car as they checked in with Byrnes. Sandor put him on speakerphone.

"Go ahead," the DD said.

Beth gave the report in her customary fashion. Succinct, accurate and efficient. Then she offered her analysis. "He's under some sort of protection, that was evident. There was no indication he was being held against his will. In my brief discussion it did not appear Remmell recognized either name, Corinne Stansbury or Randolph

Securities, but his bodyguard certainly did. As for John Coman, let's just say Remmell does not count him among his close friends."

Byrnes listened patiently and, when she was finished, said, "The question we need an answer to is, what is he doing there?"

"There are really two questions," Sandor suggested. "First we need to know why he came here, of all places. Then, as you say, we need to find out what he's doing while he's here."

"Agreed," Byrnes said. "Any thoughts on how we might get that information?"

Garinger spoke up. "Only two possibilities come to mind sir."

"Go on."

"Either we find a way to get inside Fronique and see what he's up to, or we take Remmell when he's away from the building and grill him."

Sandor smiled at the young man. "I like that. Take him and grill him."

"From Beth's description," Byrnes said, "it sounds as if it'll be difficult to gain entrance to their facility."

"Yes sir," Beth agreed.

"Given the limited time and resources," Sandor said, "I think we have to go with Plan B."

There was a long silence before Byrnes spoke up again. "Can this be accomplished without creating an international incident?"

"Can't say," Sandor responded with characteristic bluntness. "We don't know his hours there, where he's living, or how much protection he's given once he leaves the building. If we're going to take him, as Garinger says, it'll have to be off the premises, and we'll have to set up surveillance for that right away."

Byrnes let out an audible sigh. "All right. Let me tell you what's going on in Iraq." He gave a brief description of how the U.S. Army Rangers had captured two members of Ansar al-Thar. "They're being held in an undisclosed location and interrogated as we speak."

"Successfully?" Sandor asked.

"Somewhat. We have new information that heightens my interest in Remmell."

The four agents exchanged looks as Sandor said, "We're all ears."

"To start with," Byrnes said, "they've confirmed that all of the hostages are being held in the refugee camp. As you know, that was the supposition we've been working from."

"I take it you believe this intel is credible," Raabe said.

"Quite." The DD paused. "We have also intercepted some chatter that becomes relevant to our interest in Remmell."

"Sir?"

"It seems part of their overall scheme involves the use of drones."

"An attack?"

"We don't know."

"These two men gave you information on that?"

"No, our agents in Iraq don't believe these detainees are privy to any such plan. But they do claim to have heard something about drones."

"The terrorists are certainly not going to call a strike on themselves," Sandor said. "Not while they're still in the middle of that camp."

"I agree it would not make sense, but there are too many related activities to suit me."

"Including Remmell's move from California to France?"

"Correct. The Remmell piece may amount to nothing, but he's said and written quite a bit in the past year about his disenchantment with how the United States has corrupted the use of drone technology. As for the communications we've intercepted, those leads may not be reliable. They may even be disinformation. The leaders of the group may have lied to their own people in the expectation some of them would be captured."

"I have the same thought," Sandor agreed.

"But part of the chatter has to do with work on a device to intercept or sabotage our drones." Byrnes hesitated again. "And there is one more piece that might tie it all together. One of these prisoners heard something about people connected to his group making a visit to the south of France. Our people never mentioned France, which lends some credibility to the intel."

None of the four agents in the car spoke.

"Now you know everything I know," Byrnes said. "We have no intel on timing, but it should be obvious they can't hold the hostages much longer. Private groups keep making noises about paying the ransom, State is working the back channels, and the military is doing what it can to secure the perimeter of the compound without causing a panic inside. Time is short to say the least."

"Got it," Sandor said. "So our orders regarding Remmell have changed."

"They have. We need to question him, and it seems obvious that's not going to happen inside Fronique's offices."

"Understood, sir."

"The possibility of Remmell's involvement has taken on a new urgency. I hope I'm clear about that."

"You are. We'll be back to you as soon as we have a plan in place."

They signed off and the car fell silent again.

"What next?" Beth finally asked.

"Well, for starters we're going to miss a great lunch," Sandor said.

CHAPTER 42

Sophia Antipolis, France

There was no way to predict when Remmell would emerge from Fronique headquarters.

He might head out for the very sort of lunch Sandor's team was missing. Or go home early. Or work well into the night. They debated what approach would be most effective in catching up with him, and concluded there were only two viable alternatives. The first was to stake out the Fronique facility. The second was to find out where he was staying and wait there.

Sandor decided to do both.

Even if they saw him leaving the building there was no telling who might be with him or what opportunity they would have to take him. Finding his current residence would make it easier to confront him and would provide a venue more conducive to the discussion they wanted to have. Since Remmell had already seen Beth, Sandor took Raabe and Garinger to rent a second car and sent them to watch the corporate headquarters. He and Beth then went about determining where Doc was spending his nights.

As it turned out, one call to Langley was all they needed. It did not take long before the analysts in the Office of Information Technology came up with the recent charges on Remmell's American Express card. He was staying at the *Mercure Antibes*, less than half a mile from the center of Sophia Antipolis. Sandor and Beth headed there and checked in.

Sandor decided it would be easier for them to move about the hotel, and to determine which room Remmell occupied, if they became guests themselves. After dropping their bags off to make the stay appear legitimate, they did a quick reconnaissance of the hotel and its well-tended grounds. Beth's French, along with a hundred Euro note, inspired a maid to tell them where her old friend, Doc Remmell, was staying. The woman didn't recognize the name, but as soon as Beth described him it was clear who she meant. As she tucked the money inside her apron she gave the room number, then expressed surprise that a pleasant young woman would be friendly with such a grumpy old slob.

"We used to work together," Beth explained with a slight smile.

The woman shrugged, as if to say she would never solve the endless mystery of American taste, and moved on. Sandor and Beth headed outside where they found a couple of seats in a quiet area by the pool. Sandor phoned Raabe. "Anything?"

"Not that we can see," Raabe told him. "We took a ride around the entire complex when we got here. There's an exit in the rear of their building, but that's a loading dock. There's a ramp to an underground garage. Otherwise everyone seems to move in and out through the front door. We're positioned in a lot where we have a view of both the entrance and the garage."

"Any curiosity seekers?" "Nobody's bothered us so far."

"Good. We're at his hotel."

"Nice work."

"You can thank the boys in I.T."

"Should we pull back then?"

"No, for now just keep me posted on anything you see, but don't move on him. Our best shot is to get him alone in his room."

"Roger that," Raabe said. "We've got eyes on the situation."

CHAPTER 43

Refugee Camp, south of the Syrian border

Dedalus was born Peter Richard Dawson in Dublin, Ireland. His parents were poor and uneducated, and the various websites and magazines that reported on his life often described his upbringing as "hardscrabble," adding a touch of pathos to the story of his glamorous rise to stardom. The truth, however, is that his working-class mother and father realized early on that their only child was an extremely gifted musician and student, and did their best to provide him an opportunity to explore his talents and rise above the low station where he began.

On the other hand, the man who eventually took his stage name from Joyce's *Portrait of the Artist as a Young Man*, was not a product of any sort of hothouse conservatory training. He grew up on the streets where he learned to be tough both physically and mentally, and his musical training was balanced with strict religious teachings and a Jesuit education. It was a childhood that served him well in contending with the vagaries of a difficult world, never more so than when he had to deal with the death of his mother while still a teenager.

Now, as a hostage with his life at stake, he had time to contemplate how far he had traveled, who he had become, and how he would survive the ordeal. Sitting on the floor of a bare room in the middle of nowhere, his hands bound behind him, and his group ordered to remain silent, the anger within him grew. He had volunteered to be part of this humanitarian mission so they could bring food, water, and medical supplies to people desperately in need of help. Their captors had not only taken them prisoner, but they had murdered the leader of this expedition for no reason other than a show of force, and deprived the refugees of the cargo that had been had hauled so far on this errand of mercy.

The five hostages were lined up with their backs to the wall, two guards in chairs facing them, with weapons across their laps, keeping watch. Dedalus spoke to the terrorist closest to him.

"Hey asshole."

The Arab started as if he had been slapped.

"Yeah, I figured you spoke English. That's why you were chosen to sit here, right? In case we said something interesting, you could report back to the asshole-in-chief."

"Silence!" came the response.

"Go screw your mother," Dedalus said.

The Syrian stood and walked towards him. "Shut your mouth, American pig."

Dedalus forced a dry laugh. "I'm Irish, you moron, and what are you going to do if I keep talking? Beat me? I don't think so."

The terrorist stared down at him, blinking, but the other guard told him to return to his chair.

"You better listen to the other camel-humper over there. He knows you aren't going to mess me up, not yet anyway."

The Arab remained standing over him, quivering with rage. He finally spat at Dedalus, then backed off and resumed his seat. The Kalashnikov he had been holding on his lap was now pointed at the Irishman.

Dedalus turned to the others. "Well, we now know two things about these jerkoffs," he said.

"Silence!" the other guard hollered.

Orr looked down the row at Dedalus and nodded. They had indeed learned two things.

First, the guards spoke English, which meant the group had to be careful about what they said.

Second, the guard had displayed unexpected restraint after Dedalus intentionally provoked him. After Farashi's angry tirade at one of the other guards the day before, when Orr was struck, it was evident they were under strict orders not to harm any of the hostages. As Hassan had whispered to them before, this likely meant the terrorists were demanding ransom for their safe return, which meant there was still hope.

◉

Downstairs, Farashi was seated behind the desk in the office, Gabir beside him. They were speaking to two of the younger men in the group, who were standing before them.

"So, you understand what you need to do?" The two young men nodded.

"Mingle among these people, see what they're saying, what they've heard about us and what they've heard about the actions being taken by the Americans outside the compound."

"Understood," one of them said.

"Good. You will leave here tonight, after dark. We are being watched from the ground and from above, but Gabir will help you make an escape. Getting back inside will be more difficult."

"I will give you a signal to use tomorrow night," Gabir said, and the two young men nodded again. "If you are identified and caught, you tell them nothing."

"Of course."

"Nothing," the other said.

"No matter what they ask, no matter how innocent the information they may be seeking. How are the hostages? Are they all alive? Are any of them harmed? How many men do we have here? Tell them nothing," Farashi said. Then he turned to Gabir. "Go over the details again," he said, then stood, wished the two young men good luck, and left the room.

Farashi realized there was no chance either of these young men would make it back inside. He also knew, once they were captured, they had no real information about his plans, but would be forced to divulge the lies Gabir was now going to impart to them, having them believe they were being taken into the strictest confidence. They would ultimately share that disinformation with the Americans, which could only help Farashi's cause. Whatever happened to these two believers afterward was of no consequence.

CHAPTER 44

Sophia Antipolis, France

It was a simple matter for Sandor to open the door to Remmell's hotel room. In an area renowned for high-tech research and innovative companies, this lock was one of the standard mechanisms for which guests received plastic key cards. Sandor manipulated the magnetic receptor using a device Raabe brought from Langley and let himself in. Sandor and Beth were already waiting inside when they got the call.

"He's on the move," Raabe said.

"Good," Sandor replied. "Don't let them spot you but stay on his tail in case he's not coming directly here. Use text, I want to go silent."

"Got it," Raabe said and signed off.

Fronique was not far from the hotel, so Sandor straightened out the bedspread where he'd been sitting. Beth returned the chair she'd occupied to its position at the writing table, closed the drapes across the large picture windows, and the two of them headed into the bathroom. They had already retrieved their bags and placed them there—they did not expect to be visiting their own room again.

Just a few minutes later Sandor received a text that said, "Hotel." Sandor withdrew the Walther that Raabe had provided him and chambered a round. It was not long before they heard the door to the room open. Two men were speaking in the hallway.

"Maybe later," one of them said.

"All right," the second replied. "You know where to find me."

Then they heard someone come into the room and close the door behind him.

Sandor stepped out of the bathroom, Beth right behind him. He had a quick look into the small foyer, confirmed the man was alone. "Doctor Remmell."

There was a mixture of confusion and concern in the man's craggy features as he tried to make sense of this intrusion. Then, recognizing Beth, he said, "Ms. Sharrow. You are a persistent woman." Turning to Sandor, he asked, "And who might you be?"

"Her persistent friend," Sandor replied, raising his hand and displaying his weapon for the first time. "Have a seat there, at the desk, and keep your hands where I can see them."

"How melodramatic," Remmell said, his gaze moving from the cold steel of the automatic to the cold look in Sandor's eyes. "As you wish," he replied in a tone of mock surrender. He walked around the bed, pulled out the chair, and lowered his lanky frame into the seat. "So, what is all this about?"

"That's what I'm here to ask you."

"How's that?"

"You're a principal in a respected company in Silicon Valley. You have an international reputation in advanced engineering including, among other things, drone technology."

"You flatter me."

"Now you're here, living under the protection of bodyguards, involved in some sort of undisclosed work with a French company."

"I don't hear a question."

"I thought the question was obvious. What are you doing for Fronique?"

"Nothing. In fact, I'm learning a great deal from them."

Sandor responded with a skeptical look.

Remmell regarded Sandor curiously. "No one from my company sent you. They can be a bit heavy-handed at times, but I cannot imagine them dispatching an armed man to break into my hotel room and point a gun at me. Yet Ms. Sharrow mentioned John Coman earlier today. Where would that come from? Only one place I can think of—the beloved United States government. So, who are you with? NSA? Military Intelligence? Wait, don't tell me. CIA."

"In case you missed the point Doc, I'll be the one asking the questions."

Remmell smiled. "Or what? You going to shoot me?" He shook his head. "Having that gun is only meaningful if there's a real threat of using it, and I'm guessing you have neither the intent nor the authority. Not because you're a nice person, mind you, but because you came here for information, not to end my life."

Beth said, "Don't be so sure. You don't know him the way I do."

Sandor sat on the edge of the bed facing Remmell. "At one time you were instrumental in taking drone technology to a new level. Lately you've been criticizing the use of drones as tactical weapons. You've gone so far as to suggest you might be willing to develop methods to reverse the advances you helped create."

"Am I really thought to be that clever?"

"Yes," Sandor said, staring at the man. "You understand how they operate as well as anyone in the world."

"Better."

"Point made."

"What about John Coman?" Remmell asked with a smirk.

"What about him?"

"He certainly has a high opinion of his role in the evolution of drones."

"Let's put Coman aside for the moment, and you tell me why you've come to Fronique?"

Remmell looked him squarely in the eyes. "I'm not at liberty to say."

"I'm afraid that's not an acceptable answer."

Remmell waited.

"You know Doc, if you believe I'm not prepared to harm you, you're dead wrong."

"Then it appears we are both mistaken on some level. You see, you are proceeding on the assumption that the two men assigned to follow me here are safe, when they are most decidedly not. That creates something of a stalemate, I believe."

Sandor said nothing.

"Security at Fronique is tight. Your friends were spotted in the parking lot when they followed me here, so they in turn have been followed. At this very moment they are in an extremely vulnerable position."

Sandor glanced at Beth, who was standing off to the side. She looked at her cell and the latest text exchange she had shared with Raabe. She shook her head.

Remmell said, "In the interest of everyone's welfare, I think it best if you leave my room and go on your way, don't you agree?"

"I do not," Sandor told him. "My friends know how to take care of themselves. If there really is a threat to them, that only means that our time together has become limited." With that, he reached into his pocket with his left hand, removed a silencer and screwed it tight to the barrel of his .380. "I came here for answers and I am going to get them, one way or another."

For the first time, Remmell tensed. It was a subtle, involuntary reaction, but it was the only tell Sandor needed. He stood and moved next to the scientist.

"If you're not going to tell me what you're doing at Fronique, you're better off dead to me than alive." He aimed the gun at Remmell's face now. "As a talented man of science, I'm sure you can see the logic in that."

As Remmell appeared to be considering his options, they all heard a *click*, as someone opened the lock to the front door and entered the room.

The first man appeared to be French, and he was holding an automatic pistol. The second was the Arab bodyguard Beth had seen with Remmell earlier that day. He was carrying an H&K MP5 submachine gun, which he immediately trained on her.

Sandor moved behind Remmell, squatting low with the barrel of his gun pressed to the back of the scientist's head. "Everyone stop where you are," he warned them.

The first man froze, had a look around the room, then said in English with a French accent, "Before anyone does anything foolish, let me explain the situation."

"Have at it," Sandor told him.

"Despite the threat you made before we entered, I am certain you would prefer Dr. Remmell alive. If that were not the case you could have killed him already."

"You've been eavesdropping on our little chat? How rude."

"We heard everything," the Frenchman said as he pointed to his earpiece, "and felt it was time to step in."

"Well," Sandor replied, "If you believe I care whether Remmell lives or dies, you've misjudged my plans for the good doctor."

"Possibly," the man allowed, "which is why I have an insurance policy in place."

"You mean the gun trained on my partner there?"

"No, I refer to your two colleagues in the car out front. As Dr. Remmell already advised, they are unaware that they are in the crosshairs of my associates, who are listening to this exchange and are therefore apprised of what happens and what action they should take."

"I see."

"I hope you do. As I said at the outset, no one should do anything foolish."

"You obviously want Remmell to survive this event. If anyone pulls a trigger here or outside, I assure you he'll be the first to go. So, what do you suggest?"

"I will call off my snipers if you agree to let us take Dr. Remmell with us. No shots fired, no harm done, as you Americans like to say."

"How do I know you won't ambush us when we leave here?"

"For that you will have to take my word."

Sandor shook his head. "Can't put much faith in the word of a Frenchman who eavesdrops on other people's conversations. What do you think, Beth?"

Beth looked at each of the four men in turn, beginning with Remmell and finishing with the man standing right in front of her. "They want Remmell alive but, as you say, we don't care one way or another. If it comes down to it, I think you can take out Remmell and the man in front of you before you get hit. This one here may or may not make it, although I'll be shot in the exchange. My money is on you."

"Thank you."

"The wild card," she said, "is the situation out front, and whether they're really in danger or this is just a bluff."

"Well done," Sandor said, his gaze having remained on the two intruders. "She's an excellent analyst, don't you think?"

The Arab holding the submachine gun on Beth turned his head and eyes ever so slightly towards Sandor in response to the question.

It was only an instant, but in Sandor's world, an instant is far longer then it may seem to people who do not dwell in the midst of ever-present danger. Sometimes, an instant is all that is needed.

Without hesitation, and with only the slightest flex of his wrist, Sandor yanked the elongated barrel of his Walther away from Remmell's temple and fired, hitting the Arab gunman twice in the chest.

The move was so sudden that the Frenchman reflexively turned in the direction of his companion, stunned to see him slump to the floor. Again, Sandor's reaction time prevailed. He fired three shots, knocking the Frenchman backward, dead before he collapsed against the wall. It all happened so quickly that no one had a chance to utter a sound. Sandor's suppressor had rendered his deadly shots virtually silent to anyone listening through the Frenchman's earpiece. Not chancing that Remmell might try to cry out, he clamped his hand over the scientist's mouth.

He nodded to Beth, who picked up the MP5 that had fallen to the carpet and went for the mechanism through which the Frenchman had been communicating with his people outside.

Sandor mouthed the words "sink" and then "bags." She understood, taking the two-way device into the bathroom, turning on the water and placing it under the faucet. When she came out she had their bags slung over her shoulder.

Sandor, who was still behind Remmell, whispered into the ear of the now terrified scientist, "You make one sound and you die." Sandor then yanked the tall man up from his chair, his hand still over Remmell's mouth, and nodded to Beth.

Again she understood, walking past Sandor and opening the sliders behind them that led to a small patio outside. They would not be leaving through the front door.

CHAPTER 45

Sophia Antipolis, France

There was no way to know whether anyone was actually outside the hotel with Raabe and Garinger in their sights, but Sandor was not taking any chances. If shooters were in position, they might react once they lost radio contact with their compatriots in Remmell's room. Sandor took his phone back from Beth as the three of them moved out. They were outside now, hurrying along the rear of the building as Sandor punched in the speed dial number.

"Raabe," his friend answered.

"Do not make any sudden moves," Sandor told him, "just listen. Two armed men came to Remmell's room, claimed you're being watched. I took care of them, but any hostiles tracking you will know something went wrong since they've gone radio silent. Beth and I are heading around back, toward the parking lot. If they have a bead on you, I should be able to get behind them, but I have no idea what the timing is and you need to know you may be vulnerable."

"Roger that," Raabe said. "Let's keep this line open."

"Good idea," Sandor agreed, and handed the phone back to Beth. "Keep him on speaker," he told her.

Meanwhile Remmell, who seemed more confused than afraid, said, "You need to let me go."

Sandor grabbed him by the arm and pulled him along as he said, "The best thing you can do right now, is shut the hell up until we're all out of danger."

"I demand to know what this is all about!"

Sandor gave him a quick, disapproving glance. "That's precisely what you're going to tell us, once we have time to resume our little chat."

The threesome reached the end of the building where Sandor brought them to a stop and had a look around the corner. From where he stood he could not see Raabe's rental car, which was parked near the front entrance. What he could see, however, was a car off to the right, the engine running, with two men sitting in the front.

"Here's the drill," he told Beth, with Raabe listening in. "You stay here with Remmell.

He gives you any trouble whatever, if he so much as utters a word, you shoot him in the knees. Just cripple him. We'll worry about carrying him out of here later."

The scientist's eyes widened, but for the first time he demonstrated the good sense not to speak.

"I see two men in a dark red sedan," he reported to Raabe. "First parking lane, car looks to be running. I'm going to circle around and see if I can get the drop on them. Keep an eye in your rear-view mirror. If you see them move, assume they're hostile and act accordingly."

"Roger that."

"I'll have the phone, but I'm shutting off the speaker."

Sandor pulled a full magazine from his leather bag, snapped it into his Walther, then backtracked to where he could get behind a hedgerow that ran along the property's perimeter. Staying low he moved quickly to the far end of the parking area, using the vegetation for cover, coming out behind the back row of cars where he began moving forward, still in a crouch.

His gun drawn, he held the phone in his left hand and whispered, "You see any movement?"

"I think I see the car you're talking about in the corner of my side-view mirror. Don't want to adjust anything until you're in position."

"Good. Not sure how they might come at you, not even sure it's only these two. Sit tight and give me a minute."

Sandor raced forward again, stopping when he was just a row away from the front line of cars. He could see two men inside a sedan engaged in an animated discussion. Their communication with the Frenchman inside the hotel had ended a couple of minutes ago, and Sandor guessed they were unsure of what action to take without receiving instructions. He considered several options for how he should approach the situation, then said to Raabe, "I want you and Brandon to open your car doors and make a move like you're pulling some things together, preparing to get out. Do not get out though, I don't want you giving them a line of fire."

Raabe and Garinger did what he asked, opening their doors and making it appear they were about to climb out of the car. Almost at once, both front doors to the sedan in front of Sandor also swung open, and the two men stepped out.

Sandor stood, held out his automatic and said, "Either of you take another step and I'll shoot you both."

Neither man waited to see what might happen next. As if on cue, both spun around, their weapons drawn and ready, but Sandor was already firing as he moved forward, his silencer spitting out a series of shots that tore into them. They each managed to squeeze off a couple of loud, misplaced rounds, but it was over before it began.

"Nice work," Raabe said. He had raced toward the scene as soon as Sandor fired the first shot. He bent down and checked the driver. "Dead," he reported.

Sandor had a look at the second man. "Finished," he said.

Garinger had stayed with their car. He fired up the ignition and quickly brought it around.

Beth raced toward them with Dr. Remmell in tow. The scientist was looking paler by the moment.

"My god," Remmell said. "Who are you people?"

"Shut up," Sandor told him.

At the sound of the gunshots, people had already gathered at the hotel entrance and were peering outside.

"What now?" asked Raabe.

Sandor reached down for one of the guns on the ground and fired several loud shots in the air, sending the curious onlookers scurrying back inside.

"I think it's time for us to get the hell out of France."

They shoved Remmell into the back of the sedan, Sandor and Beth climbed in behind him, and with Raabe riding shotgun, Garinger drove to the spot where they had parked the Mercedes sedan. They switched cars there, then raced south from Sophia Antipolis toward the private airfield outside Nice. As Sandor had said, they needed to get the hell out of the country, and fast.

The police were likely at the hotel already, looking for someone who could explain the dead bodies in the parking lot, and the two they would find inside Remmell's room. Even more dangerous at the moment, were the people those corpses had worked for, and what they might do about their deaths and the disappearance of the scientist they had been assigned to protect.

As Garinger drove, Sandor phoned ahead to the flight crew and told them to be ready for an immediate takeoff. He was assured everything would be ready to go.

"You need to be prepared for the fact that the local authorities might be unhappy with us," Sandor warned them. "We left a mess behind, and even though I don't see them tracing it to us that quickly, you should be ready for anything."

The pilot said he understood. Then he said that there was someone waiting for Sandor at the private terminal. "Name is John Coman."

"Good," Sandor said. "That's very good." Then he turned to Remmell who was seated in the back of the car, between Raabe and Beth. "Seems you're about to have a reunion with an old friend."

CHAPTER 46

En route from Nice, France to Niamey, Niger

As it turned out, the reunion with John Coman actually belonged to Jordan Sandor. They had served together under James O'Hara in Iraq and, although they stayed in touch from time to time, they had not seen each other for years.

Coman was a tall, stoop-shouldered man, with a wide mouth, large nose and straight hair that was perpetually unkempt and prematurely gray. His posture only accentuated his flabby middle and lack of muscle tone. Only a couple of years Sandor's senior, he looked more than a decade older.

After they exchanged a warm greeting, Sandor hustled the group from the tarmac of the private airfield onto the plane where he told the pilot and co-pilot to take off as soon as they could get clearance. Thus far there was no sign they were being pursued, but someone had surely taken down the license plate of the car Garinger was driving when they left the hotel, and their exchange of vehicles could not be counted on to buy too much time.

They only relaxed after air traffic control gave them the go ahead and they were airborne. Once they took off, Sandor changed seats and sat opposite his old comrade. "You look like a rumpled old chemistry professor," he said with a laugh as he slapped Coman on the knee.

"You look like you're still in basic training," Coman replied. "Too much exercise can kill you."

"It's not the exercise I'm worried about, pal."

Coman responded with a knowing look, then pushed his wire-rimmed glasses up the bridge of his nose. "I heard about the Old Man."

"Awful."

"Yes it was. O'Hara was one of the good ones."

"The best," Sandor agreed. He introduced Coman to Beth, Raabe and Garinger.

"I take it you and Dr. Remmell are old friends."

Coman uttered a throaty chuckle. "Describing us as friends is a stretch." He turned to the sullen looking man seated across the aisle from him. "Hello Doc."

Remmell responded with a curt nod. "Maybe *you* can tell me what this is all about."

"I'm not sure myself. Just got orders to get my ass here, so I did."

"Orders," Remmell repeated, making it sound like a profanity.

Sandor said, "I suppose I should provide some information. For starters, we're heading to Niamey."

"What are you talking about?" asked Remmell.

Sandor ignored him, addressing himself to Coman. "It seems Doc, as you call him, recently had a change of heart about drone technology."

"So I've read."

"Not too fond of the military using unmanned aircraft to carry out missions."

"Assassinations," Remmell interrupted.

Sandor continued to disregard the interruptions. "He left his company in California after being invited to France to work with a company there."

"Fronique," Coman said.

"That's the one."

"They're doing some cutting-edge work."

"So I'm told," Sandor said. "I want to know what aspect of that work Dr. Remmell has been helping them with."

Everyone turned to the renegade scientist now. He looked away without speaking.

"Let me be blunt," Sandor said to Remmell. "You've seen four armed men die this afternoon. It must be obvious to you that those deaths were the direct result of your presence in France. It should also be clear that I will do whatever it takes to convince you to tell us what you were doing at Fronique."

The scientist winced.

"If you doubt my resolve, even after seeing those four men die, just ask Coman about me. You two have worked together, you know that John is a plain talker."

"Coman is a hack," Remmell said.

Coman laughed. "Doc doesn't believe in sharing credit for anything," he explained. "We did work together for a while, but he doesn't feel there's any spotlight bright enough for two, not when he's involved."

Sandor nodded, then turned back to Remmell. "Who contacted you and suggested you come to France?"

Remmell blinked several times. "I met a young engineer in San Francisco," he began. Then he described the evolution of that relationship, his meeting with other like-minded scientists who had come to believe that drones should be regulated and not used for illegal invasions of privacy or, far worse, lethal attacks.

"As I understand it, Fronique is working on refinements that will make drones even more effective," Sandor said. "How did you figure working with them would advance your goals?"

Remmell averted Sandor's determined look, looking around at the others until his gaze fell on Coman. "The more we refine the technology of a device, the more we know about how to re-engineer it."

"You're talking sabotage," Coman said.

"Sabotage is only a word," Remmell replied. "The meaning depends on which side of the argument you stand."

Sandor was not about to host a political debate. "Tell me what sort of sabotage."

Remmell leaned back in his seat. "Interception. Destruction. Replacing targets. Rerouting flight patterns."

Sandor looked to Coman. "How difficult would any of that be?"

"It depends on where you're sitting, and I mean that quite literally. Drones have become the ultimate video game. They're operated remotely, of course, and the person at the controls can do pretty much whatever he or she wants."

Sandor shook his head. "I don't think he's talking about a rogue technician. I think he's talking about interfering with the device from off-site. Can that be done?"

"Assuming we're talking about military grade drones, UAV's that are armed with weapons, it becomes extremely complicated. Fact is, I've never heard of anyone trying. It simply has never been done."

"But that doesn't mean it's impossible," Sandor said.

Coman shook his head. "Nothing's impossible."

"Aren't there safeguards? Redundancies?"

"Of course. It all depends on how sophisticated the disruption is and what they see as their ultimate goal."

"Which is why they brought in Remmell."

"I suppose so," Coman agreed. "Intercepting and destroying a drone would be the easiest means of sabotage, but even that would be difficult. People seem to think we have the capability to locate a cell phone in the middle of the ocean. Not true. Look at the trouble they had with the Malaysian jet that disappeared. Finding something as small as a drone in the middle of the sky is almost impossible. At the very least you would need information on the point of embarkation, the flight path, or the target."

Sandor returned his attention to Remmell. "What about it, Doc?"

"It pains me to agree with my former colleague, but he's right."

"So what about the other things you mentioned? Re-routing a drone, or changing the target?"

"That's where true genius is required," Coman said.

"A genius such as you," Sandor said, looking at Remmell.

Remmell smiled.

"So you and your supposed peacenik pals were working on ways to re-route military drones to have them fall harmlessly to earth, is that the concept?"

"Is there something wrong with saving lives?"

"It depends whether or not those people deserve to die."

"It's not for me to make those moral judgments. Nor for you."

Sandor responded with an icy stare. "Don't be so sure about me."

Remmell flinched.

"What if you gave this information to the wrong people? What if you showed terrorists how to redirect a weapons grade drone and have it strike innocent people? Did you consider that, Einstein?"

The color drained from Remmell's face as he stammered, "Sheer nonsense."

"Really? Who the hell do you think those gunmen were, the ones supposed to be protecting you? They didn't look like pacifists to me."

Remmell responded with a blank stare.

Coman leaned across the aisle. "Doc, tell us the truth. How much of the research did you give them about the remote digital signals we were working on last year?"

Dr. Harry Remmell did not speak, but the look on his face told them everything they needed to know.

Sandor turned to Raabe. "Get Byrnes on the line."

CHAPTER 47

CIA Headquarters, Langley, Virginia

While his team of agents was making its way out of France, Deputy Director Mark Byrnes was working tirelessly on the hostage crisis in Iraq. He was becoming increasingly frustrated with the interference of politicians, pressure from the media and the meddling contingent from Hollywood. He did his best to ignore all of them as he and his opposite numbers in various governmental agencies worked on a viable rescue plan.

Pressure was mounting from the White House, the media, and from within the various agencies involved in dealing with this crisis. The latest development was the issuance by the terrorists of a deadline for the payment of the ransom, giving two days to arrange the transfer of gold that had been demanded.

Why two days? Byrnes wondered. It seemed an inordinately long time, given that the hostages had been held that long already.

He knew these terrorists were not going to allow so much as an extra minute for a rescue mission to be launched. The only logical conclusion was that Farashi and his men had something else planned that would take that long—elements of their scheme that were not yet in place. The only logical conclusion, Byrnes knew, was that Farashi needed more time.

But for what?

In response to the new deadline, executives from the movie and music businesses formally announced they had created a steering committee to arrange funding of the ransom.

Byrnes read the press release. "Just what we need," he said aloud to no one as his intercom rang.

"Mr. Bebon of the FBI," the receptionist told him.

Byrnes hit the speaker button. "Hey, Dick."

"I assume you've heard."

"The deadline?"

"That, and the lame-brained announcement from Hollywood."

"Got them both," Byrnes told him. "Any reaction from the White House?"

"Not yet, but I can hardly wait. Meantime, I'd like to know what's happening on the ground. Knew you were the one person who'd give me the straight dope."

Byrnes took a deep breath. "You're aware of the latest intel, confirming all five hostages are being held in the middle of that refugee camp?"

"I heard."

"Seems to be true. The Iraqis won't lift a finger, afraid of getting into it with the Syrians. The Syrians don't give a damn about the hostages, they're focused on the refugees, claim they're enemies of the state. They want them all returned to Damascus as political prisoners."

"Fat chance."

"The Pentagon has every available platoon on high alert, local battalion in Mosul has men surrounding the compound, but so far no one is making a move. The White House renewed its demand that the hostages be released."

"I had most of that already. Now tell me what's really going down."

"Exactly what I was trying to figure out when you called," Byrnes admitted. "Why give us two more days to pay the ransom? Why hold these people in the midst of twenty thousand Syrian refugees? What could their escape plan possibly be?"

"You have any ideas?"

"I have one. Got a team working on it now."

"In Iraq?"

"In France."

"France?"

"Teleconference in ten, I'll fill you in."

That was when he got the call from Sandor.

CHAPTER 48

New York City

Bob Kinnie and Howard Lerner were staying in an apartment on the Upper East Side of Manhattan. It was a CIA safe house, and Sandor had arranged through Byrnes to let them use it for a couple of days.

After his experiences at the past two locations, Kinnie was not sure what 'safe' meant anymore.

As promised, he had taken away Lerner's phone and computer and trashed them. Their only means of communication with the outside world was a burner phone Kinnie had. All they could do now was wait. They were sitting in the living room staring at the television, but neither of them had much interest in the Knicks game, so Lerner changed to FOX Business.

"For a guy supposed to be as smart as Sandor says you are, you are one stupid bastard." It was at least the twentieth time Kinnie had offered that opinion since yesterday.

"I already said I'm sorry about your friends. How many times am I supposed to say it?"

"That's it? You're sorry?" Kinnie blew out a noisy lungful of air. "Bear was a professional. He knew the risks. Same with Sven. They also knew how to prepare for danger. But they didn't expect some asshole to be running computer programs using wifi access. That was the only way those shooters could have tracked us." He glared at Lerner. "That was a dumbass move. Lucky we all weren't killed."

Lerner was staring at the screen now. He waited for Kinnie to take a few more deep breaths. "I need to speak with Sandor."

"I'll bet you do."

"I'm serious. I just realized something that might be helpful."

Kinnie shook his head. "You have any idea what sort of trouble you've made for him since you rolled into town?"

"I wasn't the one who started this trouble, in case you forgot. I nearly got my head shot off twice."

"How about Sandor? What do you think he's up against right now?"

"I'm not sure. That's why I need to talk with him."

They sat there, staring at each other in silence. Then Kinnie said, "Tell me what you've got."

Lerner nodded, realizing that Kinnie was all that stood between him and the next attempt on his life. "Sandor was checking out a company in France."

"He told me."

"It may not mean anything at this point, but inside RSL only Corinne and Charlie and I knew about that investment. Freddie Colville doesn't involve himself in the day-to-day operations."

"I'm listening."

"Hassan works with WHI. For obvious reasons his most valuable contacts are in the Middle East and Asia, but he gets around."

"You think he might know about this company?"

"Not sure, but it's possible."

"So why would Hassan end up a hostage in Iraq?"

"I wish I had an answer."

"I'm still listening."

"When the kidnapping was announced, a lot of the related entertainment stocks took a hit."

"For obvious reasons."

"Right. Normally that would be followed by a correction, especially after they announced the ransom is being raised."

"Makes sense."

"When I was tracking things on the computer, it was clear a lot of those companies were still being shorted. You know what that means, shorting a stock?"

Kinnie responded with a frown. "People are betting the prices on those stocks are going to drop."

"Exactly. Normally, I'd just say there's always a bearish element in the market and leave it at that. But the entire matrix I asked Sandor to investigate has to do with trends that occurred immediately prior to terrorist attacks."

Kinnie sat up. "You believe someone already knows this swap of the hostages for the ransom isn't going to happen."

"Maybe even worse than that. Look at the screen." Lerner reeled off the names of several media stocks, pointing out their movement to Kinnie. "It's more than a belief. I'm saying the people shorting these stocks could be the same people calling the shots on the hostages."

Kinnie picked up the disposable cell. "I'll make the call."

CHAPTER 49

Outside Niamey, Niger

Niger is one of the poorest countries in the world. Two-thirds of its land is desert, the rest is dominated by stony basins and an unfriendly mountain chain that stretches across the north. Niamey is the capital, situated in the southwest, where the only major area of arable land is along the river from which this nation takes its name.

With Algeria and Libya to the north and Chad to the east, Niger provided an ideal location for the installation of the newest American base for monitoring activities in North Africa, including surveillance and an advanced drone program. International cynics criticized the choice, claiming the United States was taking advantage of an impoverished nation, buying them off so it could establish yet another foreign military stronghold. Advocates of the plan back home argued that national security dictated the need for a presence in an area of the world rife with terrorist camps, insurgencies and armed buildups.

The scope of the debate was quite limited by Washington standards, and most people were unaware of the issue, or even realized the facility was being constructed.

John Coman was involved in the design of the technology as well as the installation of the systems at the base. His role was well known to Remmell, part of the reason the older man had come to disdain his former colleague. Since Remmell experienced his change of heart about the use of drones, he saw every scientist on the other side of the argument as his enemy. As a consequence, the two engineers did not have much good to say about, or to, each other on the remainder of the flight to Diori Hamani International Airport in Niamey.

When they landed, two black SUV's were waiting on the tarmac to escort the six passengers directly to the base. The facility was cut into the side of a large hill northeast of the city, a natural fortress guarded by American sentries. After security clearances, they were all shown into a conference room where Col. Roger Brighton was waiting.

Brighton was in his late fifties, his crisply pressed uniform, closely-cropped gray hair and stern demeanor announcing that he was a no-nonsense career soldier. He greeted Coman, then responded formally as he was introduced to the others in his group.

"The infamous Doc Remmell," the colonel said, refusing to shake the scientist's hand as he turned back to Coman. "What the hell is he doing here?"

Sandor spoke up. "That remains to be seen, sir. Perhaps you, John, and I can speak alone for a few minutes."

Brighton led them to an office down the hall and pulled the door closed behind them.

Sandor told the colonel what he knew and what he suspected about Remmell's recent activities.

"Let's bottom line this," Brighton said. "The concern is that Remmell has been working on technology that could remotely interfere with, or even reprogram, a drone already in flight."

"Perhaps even before the drone is launched," Sandor said. "We have to consider that possibility too."

The colonel looked to Coman. "Is that right? Is this really possible?"

"It may be, sir. I only joined this party this morning, but that would be consistent with the intel Sandor has developed."

"Okay, any idea how far along he's gotten?"

"No," Sandor admitted. "And he's not talking."

"First he helps us develop the program, then he attacks everything we do. The lefties on Capitol Hill want to make him the poster boy for America's conscience, but none of them have a friggin' clue what we're up against in this part of the world. They think CNN gives them the real picture, but they have no idea."

Sandor nodded. "I'm up to speed on Doc Remmell, believe me."

"So what the hell did you bring him here for, of all places?"

"Can I speak freely sir?"

"As a bird."

"I want him incommunicado, and I want the opportunity to interrogate him."

When Brighton and Sandor locked eyes, there was no mistaking what the unspoken issue would be. "I run this base, and I have to account for everything that happens here. My desk is where the buck stops, so to speak."

"Understood, sir. I would never do anything to compromise you or the uniform you wear."

Brighton studied Sandor for a moment, then turned to Coman. "You vouch for him?"

"I do, sir."

"All right, let's find out what this sonuvabitch has been up to."

ROGUE MISSION

⊙

Brighton escorted Coman, Raabe, Garinger, and Beth through the facility, giving Coman an opportunity to show off the remote avionics he helped create in the large control room at the center of the base. It had high ceilings and was filled with multi-colored monitors variously flashing numbers, signals, and flight patterns. A series of control panels were attended to by a couple of dozen operators.

Raabe laughed. "This place looks like the sports betting parlor at Caesar's Palace."

"Not all wrong," Coman agreed with a grin, "but the stakes are much higher here."

While Coman described how remote UAV operations worked, two of Brighton's men were leading Sandor and Remmell down a flight of stairs to the basement. They were taken to a small room with a low ceiling, overhead fluorescent lighting, concrete walls, a metal table, and two metal chairs. Sandor forced Remmell to sit, then took the chair facing him. Their two-man escort left them alone, slamming the door shut. The sound of a lock being turned outside was unmistakable.

Sandor stared at Remmel without speaking.

"You think you're going to scare me?"

"No," Sandor said. "If you don't give me your immediate cooperation, what I'm going to do is inflict such intense pain that fear will not even enter into the equation. You will tell me everything and anything I want to know, without condition or reservation." Then he grinned. "Just think about it, Doc, you can tell all your friends about your first-hand experience with enhanced interrogation techniques. Assuming, of course, you survive the event."

Remmell blinked.

"You're a scientist, not a warrior. Given your background and physical condition, your level of resistance is not likely to be great.

What I'm saying is, don't bother trying to play the hero, you'll just make it worse for yourself."

Remmell responded with a blank stare.

"You've been a complete jackass, you must see that. It's incredible to me you could be such a dupe."

"So you say."

"You're the victim of a scam," Sandor told him, his voice rising in anger. "Are you really so vain you can't admit that to yourself?"

"You mean those men, back in France?"

"Is the light finally dawning?" Sandor got up, stepped around the table and bent down, so he was in Remmell's face. "However you got to Fronique, and suddenly you had guards all around you." Sandor grasped a handful of Remmell's collar, yanking the man out of his seat and forcing him to look him in the eyes. "Didn't the alarm go off in your over-sized cranium, you stupid prick?"

"Fronique is a secure facility," he said defiantly. "Think tanks like that need protection."

"Sure they do. But you had to realize there was something wrong when your armed babysitters were watching over you full-time. You had to know you'd actually become their prisoner."

"I don't believe you," he said, but there was no conviction in his tone.

"And I don't care what you believe, and I don't give a damn about you. As it happens, however, there are people with their lives on the line I *do* care about." Sandor released the grip on Remmell's jacket and let him fall back into his chair. "I want you to tell me what happened. Let's start with how you ended up at Fronique."

Remmell took a deep breath. "All right."

Sandor walked back around the table and sat down.

"I already told you, I met a young engineer, back in San Francisco, who said he was taken with my recent blogs about the evils of the unrestrained use of drones. We began discussing UAV engineering, a general conversation at first, but eventually he started talking about this idea he had—what if a series of armed drone strikes went amuck? Imagine the outcry. How would the world react? Safeguards would be demanded. Restrictions would be put in place."

"This was just a theoretical discussion?"

Remmell nodded. "At first, but I have to admit, I found the concept intriguing. As drone technology becomes more widely available, sabotaging just a few of the most lethal devices would make the point."

"So then what?"

"He told me about Fronique, the work they were doing there, said I should really visit the place. Before I knew it, he was making the introduction and I was making plans to visit the south of France. When I arrived, their team showed me what they were doing, conducting experiments in corrupting guidance systems and re-directing drones."

Sandor shook his head. "After a short honeymoon with your new peace-loving friends, didn't you realize what they were up to? They weren't planning to force a UAV to crash harmlessly into a mountain or into the sea. They wanted to know how it could be diverted from its target and aimed somewhere else. They want to intercept an armed drone sent to attack a terrorist camp, then re-route it to hit a shopping bazaar in Tel Aviv. Or a government building in New York. Or a grade school filled with children in Baghdad. Then they could blame the United States for the attack, claim we lost control of our own weapons. Am I getting through to you?" Remmell began nodding his head slowly up and down.

"The U.N. mission in Iraq? They ever say anything about that to you?"

"Never."

"Never mentioned the refugee camp north of Mosul?"

"No."

Sandor stared at him. "I am only going to say this once. I therefore suggest you pay close attention. You with me?"

Remmell nodded.

"Those people conned you, you realize that by now, whether you're willing to admit it to me or not. They weren't interested in learning how to disarm drones. They wanted you to show them how they could remotely reprogram them. So here's what I need to know, and I need to know right now. Tell me whether or not you actually created that program. Tell me how effective it is, how much of the technology you gave them, and how much they can actually use. Then I need you to explain all of it in detail to John Coman, so we can figure out how to undo the damage you've already done."

CHAPTER 50

London

Eduardo Cristo was in his office when Freddie Randolph walked in unannounced. It was something he did from time to time, but today Cristo did not welcome the intrusion.

"Came over to have a chat with Mark," the head of RSL explained as he lowered himself into one of the armchairs. "Difficult times."

"They certainly are," Cristo agreed as he continued to gather together the reports and account statements he had been assembling.

"Getting ready to go, I see."

Cristo looked up. "Flight's in a couple of hours."

Randolph nodded. "You make any progress with the group from California?"

"They appear serious about raising money for the ransom. Two of their biggest celebrities are being held, so they need to do something. I'll meet with them when I get there. They say they're bringing representatives from their banks, they obviously mean business."

"Paying a ransom like this won't make the American State Department happy."

"No, it won't. I'll be careful to walk the line on this one."

"Good idea," Colville replied absently. "Anything new about the situation there?"

"Nothing I've heard that isn't being reported in the media."

"No word through our back channels?"

Cristo shook his head. "That's why I'm leaving today," he reminded his guest, then resumed pulling together the last of the files and shoved them in his bag.

"This is awful, just awful," Randolph said.

Cristo closed his leather case and placed it on the floor. Then he leaned back against the edge of the desk and faced Colville. "Yes," Cristo agreed, "it is."

Colville hesitated, then said, "I find the timing of all these things extremely odd, don't you?"

"I'm not sure what you mean."

Colville stood and began pacing the room, looking as if he was finally ready to have a discussion he had been struggling to avoid. "Corinne and Charles die. Howard Lerner goes to New York and becomes involved in some frightful business, involving who knows what. His friend comes here asking us scads of questions that make it clear he is more likely an intelligence officer than the mid-level diplomat he claims to be. Then, in the middle of all that, the mission is attacked, Reverend Moore is murdered, people kidnapped, Hassan taken. I mean, what is going on here?"

"I wish I knew. That's why I need to be there in person."

"I'm not just talking about the abductions, Eduardo. I'm talking about all these other events as well."

Cristo waited.

"The discussion I had with that Sandor fellow," Colville went on. "He doesn't believe the hit and run that killed Charles was an accident. He also made the case that Corinne was murdered." He stopped moving and turned to face Cristo. "Can you imagine any of this?"

"He made similar comments to me."

Colville nodded. "I have no idea whether he's right or wrong, but it gives one pause, considering all that's happened. I feel as though we've become tangled up in some bizarre nightmare."

"I obviously share your concerns. I'm going to stop in Riyadh first, to meet with Hassan's people. Then I'll get to Mosul to do everything possible to help sort this out. We'll make sense of it, believe me."

"Of course, of course. Don't mean to hold you up." He paused again. "It's just something that fellow Sandor said the other day that keeps nagging at me." Colville shook his head. "He said he didn't believe in coincidences even in the most innocent circumstances, but when a series of them run together in a situation like this there simply must be something that ties them together."

"He's not wrong about that."

"No, he's not. As Mark and I were just saying, you need to be very careful what you say and who you trust."

Cristo responded with a warm smile and held out his hand. "You can count on me not to take any unnecessary risks," he said.

CHAPTER 51

Outside Niamey, Niger

When Sandor finished with Remmell, he left him alone in the small, dimly lit room to contemplate his own gullibility, then went to find Colonel Brighton. The C.O. was with the other three agents and John Coman, waiting in a secure conference room at the center of the facility. They phoned Deputy Director Byrnes, brought him up on the video monitor, and Sandor provided a report on his discussion with Remmell.

When he was done, Byrnes asked, "You believe he really gets it now?"

"I do," Sandor said. "But that doesn't mean I trust him. Good news is we don't have to. Coman here is our fail-safe mechanism. I didn't ask Remmell to get into any of the technical details, it'd be too easy for him to feed me a lot of scientific double-talk. He won't be able to fool John."

"Understood," Byrnes said. "Did you get any sense of how far he got with this program?"

"From his reaction, once he realized what these people are really up to, I would guess that he's gone too far. I'm afraid he's given them enough information about our applications to attempt the sabotage of one or more of our armed drones."

"When you say 'given them information' . . ."

"John Coman, sir," the scientist introduced himself. "Sandor and I were just discussing this, and I think it's safe to say that they were less interested in Remmell creating new computer pathways than in divulging existing systems."

"Explain, please."

"Remmell might have been convinced they wanted his input on their technology, but it's more likely they wanted him to provide classified data on our existing hardware and software."

"What do you base that on?"

"Experience, sir. Programming drones is what we do here, and we do it using highly sophisticated equipment and techniques. The more insight into our applications they acquire, the easier it becomes to re-engineer one of our guidance systems. Doc was involved in the work that led to the construction of this base, as well as other bases the Air Force maintains at home and overseas."

"You're saying he may have given them the ability to interfere with our drones by giving them information about our software?"

"It's more complicated than that, but you have the gist. Our ability to remotely operate the drones is based on programming the devices, then having the compatible software and encrypted passwords to ensure the UAV recognizes the instructions we send."

"So," Byrnes said, "if someone has the ability to speak to one of our drones, the drone will listen."

Coman allowed himself an indulgent smile. "Yes sir, in a most rudimentary manner of describing the process, that's correct."

"It's worse than that," Sandor interrupted. "If they can divert American UAV's, the world will think our drone program is out of control."

"Right," Byrnes said. "If they have the ability to pick their targets, just think of the damage they could do."

Colonel Brighton spoke up. "Attacks in Pakistan. Saudi Arabia. The Ukraine."

"The political fallout would be immeasurable," Byrnes agreed, "not to mention the obvious problem, the loss of lives."

No one disagreed.

"All right," Byrnes said, "it appears you're in capable hands with Colonel Brighton, and you know what to do with Remmell. I realize what I am about to say is obvious, but the key is to stop this before it happens."

Again, no one disagreed.

"Please keep me in the loop, Colonel."

"Will do," Brighton said.

"Would you mind if I spoke privately with my agents now?"

"Not at all," Brighton said. He and Coman left the room, shutting the door behind them.

"I need a straight answer," Byrnes said to Sandor.

"I'm listening, sir."

"Do you need to stay around there to be sure that Remmell cooperates?"

Sandor never tired of his boss's euphemisms. "Are you asking me if I've instilled enough fear in him to be certain he won't have second thoughts about telling Coman what he knows?"

"Something like that."

"I actually believe he sees the realities of his mistakes. Besides, there's no reason for Brighton to tell him I'm gone. Coman will convince him I'm standing just outside his door, and that should be enough."

"I hope you're right, Sandor."

"Sir, I request that I be allowed to head to Mosul, ASAP."

"That's exactly where I'm sending the three of you."

"Three of us?"

"Beth can remain at the base and help coordinate things."

Beth was not about to be left behind, and said so. "I've been kidnapped, knocked unconscious and shot at, sir. I know you think of me as an analyst, but I've had field training and I believe I've earned the right to see this mission through."

"I appreciate both your courage and your tenacity, but you'll be heading into what is likely to become a war zone. Not only that, but these hostiles have a rather archaic view of women."

"I'm an American, sir, not an Iraqi or a Syrian or any sort of Muslim that would disqualify me from doing my duty. I also think these three men will attest to the fact that I've been a valuable asset."

All of them spoke up at once, confirming that she was right.

"Sandor," Byrnes said, "you're the lead agent here. The decision is yours."

Sandor did not hesitate. "She's on the team, sir."

PART THREE

CHAPTER 52

Refugee Camp near the Syrian border

As dawn broke over the refugee camp, Farashi gathered his men in the office on the main floor of the warehouse. He sent two of them to the roof to relieve the scouts that had been posted there the past few hours. Two others were dispatched to replace the guards keeping watch over the hostages.

"Tell us," Farashi said, as the men who had been stationed on the roof joined them, "any movement?"

The older of the two sentries, Talal, spoke up. "There has been quite a bit of activity since yesterday. In the distance we can see the Americans bringing in troops and equipment."

"From which direction?"

"All around the camp," Talal reported. "The soldiers and vehicles at the front gate have been reinforced. Now there are tanks and personnel carriers on every side of the compound."

"What about the traitors living in this pigsty?"

"They can also see the buildup of American and Iraqi troops outside the fence, but they have no way of knowing if it's for their defense or an assault on us that will catch them in the crossfire. It is obvious they are becoming nervous."

"You can tell that from the rooftop?"

"We see them moving around, talking. They are agitated, much more so than when we arrived. People point to this building, but they stay away. Those who had tents nearest to us have moved back."

Farashi nodded. Then he mentioned the names of the two young men who left the building the night before, under the cover of darkness. "Have they been seen?"

The two who had acted as sentries at ground level shook their heads.

"They have not given the signal they are ready to return?" "No," they replied.

"Any sign of them from your view on the roof?"

"None," Talal responded. Then he began to say something else, but stopped.

"What is it?" Farashi asked.

Talal looked around at the others, then asked, "May I speak freely?"

"You may."

"Some of us have been wondering about our ultimate objective here. We are running low on food and water. We have been here longer than any of us anticipated." He hesitated again. "You said I may speak freely, and so I will. You are a great leader Farashi, and we support whatever you have planned, but you have not seen fit to share the details of the next phase with us. We are aware you have demanded a large ransom, and we understand such arrangements take time. But we have no idea how you propose for us to leave this place. We are surrounded by a growing number of soldiers, Americans and Iraqi, and their weapons are being placed on all sides of this camp, as I have described. I think it is fair for us to have some idea of how we will make our escape, and when that time will come."

The reaction from the other men made it clear they also shared these concerns.

"You have raised serious questions," Farashi responded, "and I believe you are entitled to answers. I hope you all understand that I have been silent on these matters until now for security purposes. The fewer of us who were informed, the less danger there was of someone being taken prisoner and being forced to divulge what he knew."

"We would never—"

Farashi held up his hand. "Talal, I am well aware of the bravery and sacrifice each of you displays every day. Some things are beyond the control of man, however, and only Allah can intervene."

A round of *Allahu Akbar* chants ensued, then Farashi brought them back to order.

"You are correct, our supplies are diminishing, and our risks are increasing as the hours drag on. But take heart my friends. We will not be here much longer." With that, he picked up the phone he had dedicated for use with the Americans.

When Farashi entered the number he had been given yesterday, the call was picked up after the second ring. "Frank Wilson here."

"We are tired of waiting," Farashi announced in his heavily accented English.

"Again please?"

"I said, we are tired of waiting for your answer," Farashi repeated with obvious annoyance.

"We are still working on it. You gave a deadline that has not passed."

"Deadlines can be changed. We need assurances *today* that the ransom will be paid."

"I will speak with my people."

"You do that. You tell your people our patience is at an end and I no longer wish to speak with you. You are nothing more than an errand boy."

Wilson began to object, but Farashi cut him off.

"Do you think we are fools, Mr. Wilson? Do you think we do not understand your government is never going to pay the ransom? From this point forward I will speak only with someone who has authority to actually pay us."

"I will pass that on."

"You do that, because there is something else I need to tell you. I will behead one of the hostages at sundown today, unless I receive satisfactory answers when I speak with the person in charge of the ransom payment. The death will be broadcast live, for all the world to see, with the blame to be laid at your feet."

"Please repeat."

"Bah. Don't play those games with me, American. You heard what I said. Everyone listening on your line heard it. In case you missed something, you can play back the recording you make of our calls." Farashi let a silent moment pass, for effect. "To be clear, if I do not receive proper assurances, by sundown today, that arrangements are being made for the payment of the ransom, then one of the five hostages dies tonight. I will call back in four hours to judge your intentions." With that, Farashi cut off the connection and looked up at his men.

"You appear pleased," he said with a smile. "I told you, we will not be here much longer."

CHAPTER 53

U.S. Army Camp, Mosul

As soon as the call with Farashi ended, a secure email with a transcript of the conversation was sent to the designated members of the task force in Washington that were dealing with the crisis. As Farashi had correctly noted, there were a number of operatives listening in, and a recording of the call was also being circulated.

Now all Wilson could do was sit in the makeshift office he had been assigned at the Mosul army camp and consider the implications of Farashi's new threat. He was lost in thought when the sergeant designated to assist him knocked on the door and announced they had visitors, reading the names off a slip of paper.

Frank Wilson was with the State Department, had been stationed in Mosul when the abductions occurred, and was now assigned to coordinate local efforts on the civilian side. He was also designated to communicate with the terrorists. Wilson served three tours with the Marines before taking a position with State twenty years ago. He was a man of few words, well respected, and known by his colleagues to be all business. Even so, he had to smile when he read the last name on the list.

"Show them in," Wilson said, then stood. When the foursome entered he said, "Damnit Sandor, can't you ever find a normal place for us to meet?"

"Don't I wish, you old jarhead," Sandor replied as they shook hands. When he turned to the others, he responded to their puzzled looks. "A story for another time. First let me make the introductions."

When that was done, Wilson asked if Sandor had heard the latest.

"Just landed and came straight here. Our DD told us you were the man in charge."

"In charge? I don't know what that means right now." Wilson paused. "Can we have a moment alone?"

"We can if you like, but if you're concerned about clearance levels, I assure you we're all good to go."

"Sorry," Wilson said to the others. "Things are pretty tense around here."

"No offense taken," Raabe told him.

Wilson invited them all to sit, then described his call with Farashi and the threatened execution.

"I thought the latest demand gave two days for the ransom to be raised," Sandor said.

"So did I," Wilson agreed.

"What do you make of it?"

"Not sure."

"Maybe they're getting nervous," Garinger suggested.

"Maybe," Sandor replied, "but I don't buy that."

Wilson agreed with Sandor. "People willing to blow themselves up to take out their enemies don't tend to get nervous."

"You're right," Beth agreed. "I see two scenarios that are far more likely."

Sandor smiled. "Beth is the best analyst in the agency."

"One of the best," she demurred.

"Either way, we're listening," Wilson told her.

"First, they may never have believed they were going to receive the ransom, and they figure it's time to ratchet up the level of brutality. A hundred million in gold bullion is an unrealistic demand, especially when they knew from the outset our government will never pay it. How could private citizens, or even corporations, commandeer that much gold?"

The man from State nodded. "And your other thought?"

"They might still hope to be paid something, even if it's not in gold, and they feel the need to create some urgency by killing one of the hostages. ISIS loves to videotape a beheading, then air it all over the world. It will certainly provoke some action."

"Both of those make sense," Wilson agreed, "since they come from the same root motivation. As you say, Ms. Sharrow, they need to increase the immediacy of their demand, and a beheading will certainly do that."

"What's next?" Sandor asked.

"A contingent has arrived from Hollywood," Wilson told them, making the last word sound like a cause for indigestion.

"Pushing their plan to pay the ransom?"

"That would be affirmative. The U.N. also has reps on the ground, and we hear the WHI is sending someone later today."

"You have a name?"

Wilson looked down at his desk. "Eduardo Cristo. Heard of him?"

"Met him," Sandor said as he glanced at Beth.

"I'm told he'll be authorized to negotiate directly with Farashi," Wilson said.

"I thought that was your role."

"On behalf of the government it is, but the mission was a WHI and U.N. show. At this point Farashi says he doesn't want to speak with me anymore."

"You hurt his feelings Frank?"

"I'd like to hurt more than that, but no, it's just as Ms. Sharrow said. He knows the U.S. government isn't going to pay him. Going forward he only wants to speak with people who control the ransom payment."

"So Cristo is being advertised as the money man for WHI?"

"He is."

Sandor nodded. "Only Cristo? What about someone from the U.N.?"

"Word is that the U.N. does not want to violate the policy a lot of its members have against negotiating with terrorists."

"Especially the U.S."

"Right. The Secretary General is usually happy to see us get slapped around by third world countries, but not with these lives at stake. They're getting past it by handing the ball to WHI."

"Understood."

"They tapped Cristo because he has a relationship with someone in WHI who would normally handle issues in this region. Unfortunately, he was one of the people taken by the terrorists."

"Shahid Hassan."

"So you *are* up to speed," Wilson said.

"I'm sure Farashi and the rest of his thugs in Ansar al-Thar are too. They have to know who Hassan is, that he's a member of the Saudi royal family."

"Which is why Cristo has not arrived here yet," Wilson explained. "He's making a stop this morning in Riyadh."

"To ask for money?"

"Presumably."

The sergeant knocked, then opened the door. "Sir, there's an Alan Goldberg here with a number of other people. He says you're expecting them, and they're asking to see you."

The pain in Wilson's eyes was evident. "How many of them?"

"I counted eight, sir."

"All right. Show them into the briefing room, I'll be there directly."

They all stood as the sergeant closed the door. Wilson turned to Sandor.

"You might as well come with me. No reason I should have to suffer through this alone."

"Only if you insist," Sandor replied. "Play your cards right and they may put you in the next Amanda Jensen movie."

"If I don't play my cards right," Wilson replied, "there won't be another Amanda Jensen movie."

Sandor took hold of Wilson's arm. "It cuts a little deeper than that for me, Frank. One of the hostages is a close friend. Bill Sternlich."

"Editor with *The Times*?"

Sandor nodded.

"All right, let me check in with the task force, then we'll head over there."

Before Wilson initiated the videoconference, his assistant called over the intercom.

"There's a call for Mr. Sandor," the sergeant said. "Robert Kinnie."

CHAPTER 54

Riyadh, Saudi Arabia

Eduardo Cristo flew to Riyadh on the WHI private jet. He was met at the private terminal, led to a stretch Bentley limousine, and driven to the Palace of Yamamah, where an audience had been arranged with key members of the royal family. On his arrival he was shown into an ornate conference room that could have comfortably held a hundred people. He was left alone to admire the opulent surroundings for almost an hour.

Finally, more than twenty men filed in. Most were members of Hassan's extended family, a few of whom Cristo had met before. Prince Azziz was the last to enter, and he took his place at the head of the long table, signaling that Cristo should sit to his left. After an exchange of formalities they got down to business.

The prince acknowledged his family's understanding of the current crisis, and added with no hint of irony, "We realize time is precious."

Cristo wondered where that realization had been for the past hour.

"So," the prince went on, "there is no reason to discuss the obvious."

"Thank you, your Highness."

"We know you have been in transit. Have you been advised of the kidnappers' latest threat?"

"I have."

"If they intend to carry out this beheading tonight, there is no telling how the Americans will react. There is also no indication which of the hostages they are planning to execute."

"Understood," Cristo said. "We only have a few hours to coordinate our response."

"Which is why you have come here."

"Yes."

"We appreciate the respect you have shown by presenting yourself in person. We also realize that when you began your journey you had no way of knowing the terrorists would foreshorten the timeline in this manner."

"I did not."

"So, let us not mince words, Dr. Cristo. You have come here to ask us our position on payment of the ransom being demanded."

Cristo bowed his head in acknowledgment.

"You are aware of the position the United States takes in such matters."

"I am, of course."

"They are our most important ally, but Hassan is a member of our family."

Cristo lowered his head again.

"We are informed that there are private interests prepared to fund some of the payment for the safe return of the hostages, particularly the two, uh, entertainers being held."

"I have the same information, your Highness."

"Have you any indication how much they have raised?"

"Only through third party sources. They advise they have commitments, but no amount has been discussed yet. It is one of the reasons I am en route to Mosul."

The Prince took a moment. "These terrorists are not to be trifled with. They have already murdered the clergyman who was leading the mission, as well as several of the armed personnel assigned to protect the group. They now threaten to take the life of another this evening. What is your view of this negotiation?"

"I have not yet had any discussion with them. I am authorized to contact them as soon as I arrive."

"We know that. I am asking for your impressions to date."

"Without any direct communication to base my opinions on, it is obviously difficult. However, as you have said, their conduct speaks volumes about their commitment to this undertaking. I have grave doubts they will agree to compromise."

The Prince agreed. "These groups tend to be absolutists. They not only advocate extreme views of our religion, but they are also unwavering in their convictions. I share your pessimism."

Cristo waited.

"I have no idea what the Americans will do, being faced with this new deadline. It may provoke them to act. If they choose to wait, calling their bluff as the expression goes, I fear the worst. These are not people who bluff." The prince paused again. "What perplexes our council— and we have discussed this at length this morning— is why they would have given an ultimatum that payment must be arranged by tomorrow, and then announce their intention to murder one of the hostages tonight."

"It is indeed perplexing, Excellency. As I say, I have no means of assessing their motives, or what change in circumstances has led them to this more aggressive posture."

The prince looked to his advisors, then faced Cristo, and spoke again. "You have come here for an answer, and I shall give it. Neither the Saudi government nor the royal family can be part of any direct effort to negotiate with terrorists or to pay a ransom. The political fallout would be immeasurable, and the damage to our relationship with the United State too great. On the other hand, we know you are a man of great discretion, and I say this to you based on that reliance. In the event a ransom payment is arranged, and funding becomes an issue, be assured that Hassan has a loyal and loving family." The Prince then stood, and everyone else, including Cristo, scrambled to their feet. "We wish you a safe and speedy journey. Please keep my people informed."

CHAPTER 55

U.S. Army Camp, Mosul

After Sandor and his team were shown to a room where they could take the call from Bob Kinnie, Wilson tied into the videoconference in Washington.

The task force in D.C. was receiving information in real time from assorted military and administration sources. Now they wanted to hear directly from Mosul about the latest developments—the threatened beheading of one the hostages, and the arrival of the Hollywood contingent.

Wilson began by reporting his belief that the warning needed to be taken literally.

"Farashi murdered several innocent people when he intercepted the mission. There's no reason to think he won't offer further proof that he's serious."

"He hasn't said which of the hostages is going to be executed."

"No," Wilson replied. "He did not."

"What's your advice?"

"The representative from WHI is on his way here. Farashi made it clear he only wants to speak with someone authorized to discuss payment of the ransom. When he calls back I'll explain that he will be hearing from that person later this afternoon."

"Will that buy enough time?"

"I hope so," Wilson said.

There was a debate about whether the time for military action had arrived, but Forelli put that off for now. "What's going on with the group from California?"

Wilson advised that they had arrived at the base and were demanding a meeting. Since he was nominally the chief negotiator with the terrorists, everyone on the call agreed he was going to have to deal with them as well.

"You have my condolences," Bebon from the FBI told him.

The senior officer on the call from State told Wilson the Secretary wanted him to make it clear to this ad hoc delegation that he was only seeing them as a courtesy. "Remind them of our policy in these matters, then show them the door as quickly and politely as you can."

Wilson said he understood, and requested the attendance of Sandor at the meeting.

CIA Director Walsh, who was on the video conference, turned to Byrnes and said, "Your call, Mark, we have no time for any drama here."

Wilson interrupted, telling the group that he had known Sandor for years and would regard his presence as an asset.

Byrnes approved the request, at which point Walsh said, "Better make sure he goes in unarmed."

Given the gravity of the situation, not to mention Walsh's notorious lack of anything resembling a sense of humor, no one on the call laughed.

When the conference call ended, Byrnes immediately phoned Sandor. "Your man Kinnie was trying to locate you. We provided a link, did he find you?"

"Just reached me. I also spoke with Lerner."

"I'm listening."

"We weren't sure the line was secure, had to be careful about what we said, but Lerner made a couple of key points."

"Such as?"

"Beth reviewed some of his data when we were still in the U.K. She ran some numbers on the grids Lerner created, matching market and currency trends with terrorist attacks and related world events. She managed to create a matrix containing all of the information, then compared it to trades made by Corinne Stansbury for her shell companies. The results were pretty clear. Either the woman had a crystal ball or someone was telling her what was coming before it happened."

"I assume we can rule out the crystal ball."

"We believe someone with better connections than she had was providing the leads, she filled out the order forms from Bermuda."

"You have a guess who her source might have been?"

"Not sure, neither is Lerner, but we we're working on it."

"Got it," Byrnes said, not asking for names over an open line. "Anything else?"

"Lerner says a lot of media stocks are being shorted right now."

"When you say media stocks . . ."

"Companies related to the motion pictures of Amanda Jensen and the music of Dedalus."

"So if the pattern holds, something bad is about to happen to those firms."

"That would be consistent with everything Lerner and Beth have charted."

"Meaning what?"

"Meaning someone is betting the hostages will not survive this event."

"A terrifying sort of insider trading."

"Yes sir, it certainly is."

Wilson knocked on the door and stuck his head in. "Time to meet with Hollywood," he said. "Sandor, you're with me."

The briefing room in the Army compound was a bare-bones space with dozens of folding chairs, a number of easels holding various charts and maps, and a table at the front with a large television monitor behind it. The crowd in attendance included a collection of executives and financial types from the movie and music industries; a couple of staff from the State Department to give Wilson moral support; and a few military officers who had been instructed to attend as observers. Frank Wilson walked to the head of the room where he stood behind the table, Sandor right beside him.

"Please be seated," he said. He remained standing, introduced himself, then told the group, "Time is short. For those of you who are not aware, the terrorists have threatened to murder one of the hostages at sundown today unless they receive assurances that their ransom demand will be met."

There was a general uproar, as everyone in the audience began speaking at the same time. Wilson held up his hand until order was restored. He was a tall, imposing figure, and the look on his face told them he was in charge. "This is not a town hall meeting, and I have neither the time nor patience to put up with any outbursts. I understand you have designated Alan Goldberg as spokesman for your group. Would you please identify yourself?"

Goldberg, who was in the first row, stood.

"In the interests of moving this discussion along, Mr. Goldberg will be the only one authorized to speak on your behalf at this time. You have the floor sir."

Goldberg nodded. "They have not told you which of the hostages will be murdered."

The statement sent a chill through the room.

"That is correct."

"It could be Amanda. Dedalus. Any of them."

Wilson did not argue the point.

"You know why we're here," Goldberg said. "We all want the safe return of these five people. Our first question is whether there is a viable plan in place to rescue them."

"The appropriate personnel are working on that right now."

"The news you just shared creates incredible urgency."

"What is your question sir?"

"Will a rescue attempt be made before this threat is carried out tonight?"

"That would be classified."

Goldberg, who had been facing Wilson, took a moment to look toward the others in the room. Then, returning his attention to Wilson, he said, "What sort of assurances do these terrorists want?"

"They were not specific."

"Then what sort of guarantee can anyone give?"

Wilson took a moment before responding. "As you are all well aware, the United States will not pay them a ransom."

"We know that, but we come here as private citizens, not as representatives of our government. If you have no means of freeing these people, we are prepared to enter negotiations on our own behalf, and to arrange payment for their release."

"I have been directed to tell you, if that is your intention, the United States government will not assist you."

"Which means you will not put us in touch with the terrorists."

"I didn't say that. However, we will not support any independent attempts to pay the ransom."

"You understand that we are working hard to put together the funds for that purpose."

"I do."

"The World Health Institute has also pledged a substantial contribution. We are informed that their representative will be arriving shortly in the hope of persuading you to allow us to pursue this course of action."

"We are aware WHI has dispatched someone, yes, but that does not alter the situation."

The sergeant who had been acting as Wilson's adjutant came into the room, hurried to the front and spoke quietly to him.

Wilson nodded, then turned back to the group. "The sergeant tells me there is something we should see. Go ahead," he told his assistant.

The sergeant picked up the remote control for the monitor, turned it on, and a broadcast by Al Jazeera appeared on the screen with English subtitles. The image was a video of five people, each wearing a hood. It scanned the group as they sat against a wall without speaking or moving. Then the image changed. This time the recording was of a single hostage, still wearing a hood and covered in what appeared to be a burlap sack. There was no way to determine if it was one of the four men or Amanda Jensen. This lone hostage was seated on a chair, hands out of view, apparently still bound behind the back. A voice could be heard, in Arabic, followed by a close-captioned translation:

"This is evidence of our resolve. Preparations are being made for the fate of this infidel if our demands are not met."

There was silence, then a second figure appeared. He was wearing a mask and holding a large saber. The voice resumed with the translation crawling across the bottom of the monitor:

"There will be no clemency. There will be no delay. We have waited long enough. The blood shall be on your hands if you do not comply with our instructions."

The scene was replaced by a newscaster who explained they had just received a remote transmission of this video with a message insisting that the world be shown what was about to happen. Failure to broadcast the video would result in the immediate beheading of the hostage.

Wilson, who had been facing the screen, turned back to the group. In an even tone he said, "As you can see, we have work to do here. Are there any other questions?"

Goldberg appeared dumbstruck. The immediacy of the situation and the ruthlessness of the terrorists was no longer a theoretical issue. One of the five hostages was facing a gruesome and imminent death, and no one knew which of them it was. "My God," he said. "You must help us to do something to save these people. Surely you can see that."

"Mr. Goldberg, no one is more painfully aware of the exigencies of this crisis than I," Wilson told him. "Yet even if we were to put aside our stated policy for the sake of this exchange, you must understand what is obvious to those of us who deal with these dangers every day. First, payment of a ransom will not ensure the safe return of these people. These terrorists are coldblooded killers, and their word is worthless. Second, payment of one hundred million dollars in gold is a practical impossibility, which is well known to these people. Third, even if they were to agree to a ransom payment in currency, think about how that money will be used. The tragedy we are confronting will pale in comparison to what comes next. Perhaps most important of all, what message would it send if we capitulate? What dignitary, celebrity or statesman would be safe?"

Goldberg had no answers.

"Ladies and gentlemen," Wilson said, "please excuse us but, as I said, we have work to do."

Sandor stood and followed him out of the room, which had fallen into a deathly silence.

⊙

While Wilson's adjutant was politely ushering the Hollywood group to another building, Sandor went off to gather his team. They met Wilson back in the briefing room, this time to hear from the Army Rangers who were charged with devising a scheme to enter the refugee camp and take out the terrorists.

Brigadier General Johnson Randall, leader of the Ranger platoon, reviewed the key obstacles they faced. The building where the hostages were being held was in the middle of the compound, surrounded by thousands of Syrian exiles. Any attempt to clear so many refugees out of the camp would create panic, and likely cause the terrorists to fire into the crowd. If the Rangers opted instead to initiate a frontal attack on the warehouse, the collateral damage in the ensuing fight could not be contained. And then there was the underlying problem—since they had no intel on where the hostages were being held inside the building they could not be sure how to direct the assault. Added to that was the probability that the men guarding the hostages had been given instructions to kill them all in the event any shooting started.

Various approaches were discussed and dismissed. Now that the terrorists had threatened an execution at sundown, the Rangers could not even wait for the cover of nightfall to launch a recovery mission. Someone raised the prospect of an attack by air, but it carried the same risks as a ground offensive—the hostages would likely die in the process, along with hundreds or even thousands of Syrian refugees. They discussed using helicopters to carry snipers who might take out the men on the roof of the warehouse, but they would still have no line of sight on the hostiles inside the building, which was essentially windowless. Once again, the commencement of the assault would almost certainly seal the fate of the hostages.

"Sir, may I say something?" Sandor asked.

"Who are you?" General Randall asked.

"Sandor, Central Intelligence."

Wilson had vouched for Sandor's team when the meeting began, but no one had wasted time on introductions.

"You have an idea, we're all ears," the general said.

"WHI has someone showing up here, may have arrived already. He's going to ask to speak with the terrorists."

"That's what we've been told," the general confirmed.

"He's not an American and he's not representing any government," Sandor said. "Whether we like it or not, he's probably going to assure Farashi he'll get him the ransom money, even if it's just to buy some time."

"What's your point Sandor?"

"We all saw the video of five people with hoods on, but we're not even sure they were pictures of the hostages. For that matter, they didn't seem to be moving. Some or all of them may already be dead. I met the man WHI is sending. His name is Eduardo Cristo. He was trained as a physician, highly intelligent, probably coachable. Before you set up his call with Farashi, tell him to demand a doctor be allowed to enter the building to confirm the hostages are still breathing and in good health. Have him tell Farashi he needs this before he can commit to any arrangements for payment. Then I'll go in there as the doctor."

The general thought it over. "What if they offer to send us another video? Hoods off, showing something that proves it's taken today?"

"Tell Cristo to anticipate that, to say it's not good enough. They can photoshop a video in no time, or send us something they took hours ago, or even yesterday. For a hundred million dollars Cristo should say he needs on-site confirmation these people are alive and well."

"What if they balk?"

Sandor shook his head. "Why should they? Your sources estimate they've got as many as a dozen armed men in there. They'll obviously search me when I arrive. What threat does an unarmed doctor pose?"

"All right, tell me what you're going to do when you get in there."

"I can get you a sit-rep. A more accurate count of the hostiles. A reading on their weapons. I can eyeball how they've laid things out and, most important of all, I'll find out where they're holding the hostages. I can also pick up any other nuances a real doctor won't notice."

"You'll be able to convince them you're a physician?"

Sandor grinned. "Served here under Jim O'Hara, was in and out of the Baghdad infirmary too many times to count. Since then I've been getting knocked around for the Agency, seen the inside of so many hospitals I could get board certified."

Randall nodded. "Let's say we can make this happen, you going in alone?"

"Two would be better than one, but I don't want to push it. I'll leave that decision up to you."

"Anybody have an objection to the idea?" Randall asked. His bearing made it clear he wasn't opening the matter for a vote, he was just curious.

The others thought it made sense, especially since it might also buy some additional time.

"Let's see what we can do," the general finally said.

As the meeting broke up, Sandor took Randall and Wilson off to the side. "If we can make this work, sir, I do have one request."

Randall managed a smile. "Only one?"

"No one outside this room is to know we're not sending a real doctor, especially Cristo. Since he's about to take over the negotiations with Farashi, it might compromise his credibility if he has any idea what we're planning."

"I understand," Randall said. "We don't want Cristo slipping up in any way."

"Precisely. If he believes we're really sending in a doctor, it'll be easier for him to sell it. As a doctor, the request should make sense to him."

"It also makes sense to me."

"I've met Cristo, so he shouldn't even see me, shouldn't know I'm here."

"Uh huh." The general called out to one of his men. "Find out if Dr. Cristo has arrived."

He turned to Wilson. "You brought Sandor to the party. What do you think of this idea?"

"Just to be clear," Wilson said, "the task force has authorized the involvement of Sandor and his team, so his invitation to this party comes from the top, not from me. As for his idea, I think it works on two levels. If this guy Cristo plays it right, the medical examination may buy us time. As for Sandor, I can assure you if there's something important to see in there, he'll see it."

"That assumes they let him out. Once he's inside, they may tell him to make his report by phone so they can listen in. Then they might hold him with the hostages."

Before Wilson could reply, Sandor said, "If they hold me that would be even better, sir. Believe me."

CHAPTER 56

U.S. Army Camp, Mosul

As if Frank Wilson did not have enough on his plate, he had also become unofficial ringmaster of the inevitable media circus attending the crisis.

The video of the unidentified hostage had been aired numerous times on Al Jazeera, and virtually every other network around the world. That image, and the accompanying threat of a beheading, had fueled the latest international firestorm over the kidnappings. The cries for action depended on the country of origin and the position of the broadcaster on the political spectrum.

One reaction, however, was fairly universal: Most of the world thought the United States had the responsibility to make this right.

Many called for the Americans to take military action, some believed the ransom should be paid, while others insisted the government stand its ground and not negotiate with terrorists. In between those extremes, there were an assortment of demands and opinions being voiced from every conceivable quarter. There was the typical condemnation of Islamic extremists and the splinter group, Ansar al-Thar, but somehow the crux of their culpability was getting lost in all the ambient noise. In the end, all eyes were on Washington to see what the administration would do.

Meanwhile, Wilson and his staff had their hands full with emails, texts and phone calls from every news agency on the planet.

Members of the media in and around the army installation were obviously hungry for updates. An experienced group, most of them understood there was little Wilson or anyone else in Mosul from the State Department could or would say for now. Several spent their time chatting up anyone who would speak with them, from enlisted men to private contractors, eager for any shred of information that might pass for a story. Others traveled to the refugee camp and were parked outside in their vans—as Wilson described it, biding their time until the shooting started.

Alan Goldberg's group had recovered from the stark reality the video had injected into the process. Instead of backing off and allowing the authorities to do their jobs, they were becoming more vocal than ever. They were demanding to see Wilson again, but the former Marine had neither the time nor the inclination, so he decided to outflank them.

After receiving the reluctant approval of the group in Washington—many of whom were career politicians mindful of the importance of keeping the money people in Hollywood happy— Wilson had General Randall declare a state of emergency on the base, and Goldberg and his associates were placed under guard in a storage building. They were told they were being held for their own safety and, in the worst indignity of all, were stripped of their cell phones, computers and tablets—for this group, an action akin to a mass amputation. They protested and made various threats of legal action, to which Randall responded personally, sending a warning that this was a matter of national security and, if they had any idea what was good for them, they would behave themselves for a few hours or face charges that would include treason.

With that troupe temporarily under wraps, Randall and Wilson provided yet another status report to the task force. The leaders in Washington obviously wanted specifics on the action being planned since time was counting down to the threatened execution, but Randall explained it would be best for now only to say that various approaches were being explored.

Although the video link to Washington was a secure connection, they were taking no chances.

Sandor's offer was not even mentioned.

"By my calculation you have a little more than five hours until sundown," Peter Forelli from the White House, reminded him. "That means you've got less time than that to advise us of any strategy you develop. I'll need to advise the President of any proposed action, and he'll want an opportunity to review the plans. If you have no plan, we'll need to know why, and we'll need to know what's going to be done about the threat."

No one had to ask what 'the threat' meant. Everyone was painfully aware that sand was running through the hourglass.

"Loud and clear," Randall replied.

Wilson said, "Farashi is supposed to be calling me back in less than thirty minutes."

Forelli and Wilson had history together in government service, most of it good. The man from the White House leaned toward the camera and said, "Frank, you up to this or do you need some sort of help?"

"I've got it," Wilson assured him. "No time to go to the bullpen now. Let me meet with Cristo. I've just been told he arrived. After I speak with him I'll put him in touch with Farashi, then I'll report back."

When the screen went black, Wilson sat back in his chair and took a deep breath.

"This isn't going to get any easier," Randall told him.

"I know," Wilson said.

Randall stood. "I'll get out of your way. Probably makes sense for you to meet with him one-on-one to start with." The general went to the door, ordered the sergeant to bring Cristo in, then left Wilson on his own.

A few moments later the man from WHI was shown into the makeshift office. He was elegantly attired, had an easy smile, and his English was spoken with an accent that was—given his Middle Eastern features—surprisingly Spanish, not Arabic. Perhaps the most remarkable aspect of his appearance was how fresh he looked after two flights and the burden of what he had come here to accomplish.

Wilson stood and they shook hands. "You don't look any the worse for wear."

Cristo shrugged. "I'm accustomed to traveling the world on short notice."

Wilson nodded and asked him to have a seat. "You're here to speak with the terrorists on behalf of WHI."

"That's correct. As your State Department has been informed, I met with members of the House of Saud in Riyadh before coming here. WHI believed it would be best if I came here to handle the negotiations. No telling how things will proceed, and calling these people from an office in London did not seem appropriate."

"I can assure you we'll provide our full cooperation in arranging the call."

"That will be very much appreciated."

"But nothing more," Wilson said.

"Understood."

They discussed the video, the threatened execution, and the deadline they were facing. Then Wilson told Cristo that they wanted him to demand a doctor be allowed to examine the hostages.

Cristo was in complete agreement with the suggestion. "Trained as a physician myself," he said. "But of course, you knew that already." He realized Wilson would have reviewed his background before he arrived. "An examination of the hostages makes sense. Can't be too careful in such difficult times," he added with a warm smile.

"No," Wilson said, "we can't."

"I'm sorry I didn't think of it myself. I could have brought one of our people."

"The terrorists are already holding enough of your people. We intend to send one of our own."

Cristo seemed to be thinking that over. "You have someone in mind?"

"We do. Obviously, we first need you to persuade them to allow it."

"Of course."

"We prefer to send in two people, but I leave that to your negotiating skills."

"I will do my best."

Wilson waited.

"All of us at WHI feel responsible for the hostages. They would not be in harm's way had it not been for our supporting this mission."

"Understood," Wilson said.

"We want to see them returned safely, but I will be forced to advise their captors that we have no means of complying with a demand for a hundred million dollars in gold. It is simply impossible. We are prepared, however, to propose alternative means of payment."

"Unless they're fools, which they do not seem to be, they'll know that currency transfers of this magnitude will be easy to track."

"Indeed. I assume that is why, from their first communication, they stipulated the gold was to be transferred to banks in Syria and Yemen. I will attempt to convince them that currency transfers to banks in those countries will be equally safe. Once the deposits are made it will be impossible for us to retrieve the funds. Those governments can be remarkably uncooperative when being asked to assist the west."

"I know that only too well," Wilson said as he nodded in agreement. "I need to raise a somewhat delicate issue."

"Go right ahead."

"WHI is a charitable organization. It raises money for humanitarian causes, such as the provision of medical care, services and supplies to the needy. Contributors give their money to WHI believing the funds will be used for those purposes."

"Yes, quite an ethical dilemma. Using the funds for ransom rather than to minister to the sick and needy poses a problem."

"A large problem as we see it, given the amount involved."

Cristo responded with a concerned look that said he had already wrestled with the issue and had come to terms with its implications. "As you know, there are companies with a substantial interest in the fate of the two celebrities, Ms. Jensen and Mr. Dedalus. They are prepared to contribute to the payment. Part of my task is to maximize their involvement."

"Their representatives are already here."

"So I have been told. We have been in contact since yesterday, and I will meet with them after we place this call."

"Understood."

"So, time is short."

"Yes it is," Wilson agreed, then explained that several people would be present for the discussion with Farashi. "I'll speak first, then turn the call over to you." Without awaiting a reply, Wilson said, "I'll bring everyone in now."

CHAPTER 57

U.S. Army Camp, Mosul

As Wilson was meeting with Cristo, Jordan Sandor and his team were in an office located in a far corner of the base where they were making arrangements of their own.

Their first call was to Mark Byrnes.

"Wilson already gave us the party line," the DD told them. "Give me the back story."

"Is this line being scrambled?" Sandor asked. "Wilson told me he was concerned about security on the videoconference. Not sure why."

"We're good on this call."

Sandor described the various tactical challenges that were discussed, then explained his plan to enter the compound posing as an Army doctor. "Get us some much needed intel, and maybe buy us some time."

"You think Cristo can get it done?"

"I do."

"Based on what?"

"Can we just say my instincts tell me he can?"

"Under other circumstances I might say yes, but I've got too many agencies and other countries involved. I'm afraid I can't ask them all to rely on your instincts."

"I've met the man. He's a smooth operator. He's also Lebanese by birth, literally speaks their language."

"That it?"

"So far."

There was silence, followed by one of Byrnes' patented sighs. "All right, let's see how Cristo plays this out when he speaks with Farashi."

"That's precisely my thinking," Sandor said. "Wilson is about to connect us so we can also listen in."

"They told us it'll be five minutes or so. What's going on with Remmell and Coman? I got word they reached out to you from Niamey."

"My next call," Sandor said, then signed off and phoned the drone base in Niger.

"We're on a tight timeline," Sandor told Coman. "What've you got?"

"Remmell was instrumental in developing the guidance systems we use, it was not a stretch for him to develop ways to interfere with them."

"We understand that already. Can it be done remotely?"

"Nowadays almost anything can be done remotely, Sandor. We fly these craft from a video screen. Interfering with the flight pattern is definitely possible. The more difficult part would be re-routing the drone to a new location, rather than simply jamming the signal or causing it to explode."

"Go on."

"There are two parts to the process. The first, obviously, is to change the drone's target. I'll put aside the techno-babble because I know you hate it and won't understand it anyway."

"Bless you."

"Point is, Remmell was working on ways to decode the imprints on the microchips that regulate both the flight path and the operation of the devices."

"When you say 'operation,' that includes the firing of weapons."

"When they're armed, yes. Most of them just provide aerial surveillance."

"Okay. Assuming he can accomplish that, you said there's a second part."

"It's actually the first part, if you will, which is tracking down the UAV and taking control. Once the drones are launched, we don't just wait to find out if they achieve their objective. Regardless of whether the device is being used for surveillance or attack we monitor each one, much like air traffic control keeps watch over flight patterns. That means, even if the planned route for the drone can be remotely altered, the technician in charge of the device would immediately see the change in its direction. If a drone began to veer off course there are fail-safe mechanisms."

"Meaning what, that you can remotely destroy the device yourself?"

"Correct."

"Which means a saboteur who wants to be sure he succeeds in sending a drone on a completely new path would also have to corrupt the tracking system."

"Ideally. There are some variations on that theme."

"For instance?"

"The smaller the delta between the original target and the revised destination, the less obvious the tampering would be to the operator at the base, especially if the terrorists only have the drone wander off its course at the very end."

"Makes sense."

"Then there's a good old fashioned blackout."

"Explain that please."

"Remmell says that manipulating the equipment at the base is far more complicated than just sending signals jamming the drone's flight pattern."

"So you said."

"A better solution would be to have the UAV stay on course as long as possible, then do something to cause a short-term blackout at the base itself. All they would need is enough time to prevent the operators from seeing the drone's final deviation from the intended route. When the base came back on line it might be too late to make a correction or even destroy the UAV."

"Doesn't the base have redundant power sources?"

"Of course, but nothing is perfect. Take EMP's, for instance."

"Electromagnetic bombs."

"Correct. They create huge impulses that could knock our systems sideways, just long enough for their purposes."

"And this stupid bastard has been working with them to set this up?"

"Yes," Coman said. "For what it's worth, Remmell insists he was helping them find a way to intercept armed drones and redirect them so they would land harmlessly, rather than killing people."

"So he explained to me. Do you believe him?"

"I do. I don't like the guy, but I think his intentions started off that way, and they did one helluva job of manipulating him."

"Big ego, easy target."

"Exactly."

"All right, so how much of this capability do they actually have?"

"Too much," Coman replied.

CHAPTER 58

U.S. Army Camp, Mosul

Wilson's office was being used for the phone call from Eduardo Cristo to Farashi. The room was crowded with several key players in attendance—General Randall, other officers from the Army and Air Force, Wilson and his assistant, and a woman from the State Department attached to the Iraq detail. There were also three technicians monitoring the call and tying it into the task force in D.C., as well as the office where Sandor, Raabe, Garinger and Beth were listening in.

Wilson began the discussion by warning Farashi that, should harm come to any of the hostages, the United States government would be left no option but to retaliate with military force.

"You are not making the rules, Mr. Wilson, we are. I have already told you I want to speak with someone who has real authority."

Wilson resisted his Marine instincts in offering a response, instead introduced Cristo, and turned the call over to him.

Cristo began by greeting Farashi in his native tongue. Then he suggested they conduct their discussion in English.

"So all of your American friends who are listening in will not need a translator?" the Syrian asked.

"No," Cristo explained in an apologetic tone, "because my Arabic is a bit rusty."

"So be it," Farashi said.

"As you have been told, my name is Eduardo Cristo. I have been empowered by the United Nations and the World Health Institute to discuss this situation with you. I do not represent the United States, the Iraqi government, or any other nation. I have no authority to speak or act on their behalf."

"Then you are a fortunate man."

"We have several issues we must address. You have made demands and I am prepared to discuss them, but only if you are also prepared to discuss them."

"Meaning what?" Farashi asked.

"First, as a show of good faith, you must rescind your threat to murder one of the hostages at sundown today."

"You are direct, Cristo, and I am equally blunt. There shall be no clemency unless I am satisfied you are a serious man."

"I believe you will see that I am very serious. "

"Good. Then tell me about the ransom."

"We are working to put the funds in place. There are private concerns willing to join with us to trade for the hostages. But, as I have said, there are issues."

Farashi was silent.

"We cannot make payment in gold," Cristo told him. "There are several problems, the most prominent being the impossibility of private citizens amassing that amount of bullion. Even if we could, obstacles in timing and transport render it impossible."

"How do you propose to pay us?"

"In Euros."

"Marked and traceable, no doubt. You must think me an idiot, Cristo."

"Not at all. You had already named banks to handle the transfer of gold. We will wire the funds into those institutions, to whatever accounts you designate."

"I see." There was some background chatter, as if Farashi was discussing this with others. Then he came back on the line. "You said there are other issues."

"We need confirmation the hostages are alive and uninjured."

Farashi forced a bitter laugh. "What if some of them are not? Will you abandon the survivors? If some of them have been hurt are you going to leave them behind?"

"Of course not."

"We all know the identity of each of these five people," Farashi told him. "Some are more expendable than others, are they not?"

"No," Cristo replied firmly. "Each is a human life."

Farashi uttered a bitter laugh. "Still, by hiding the identities in the video we have made your life more complicated, have we not?"

"You asked if I was a serious man, and I am. Your video did not show anything to identify any of the prisoners. All I ask is that you allow medical personnel to examine them before we arrange for this payment."

"Medical personnel? What does that mean, Cristo, how many people do you expect me to allow in here?"

"Just two physicians, to briefly visit with the hostages."

Farashi had another side discussion with his people before coming back on the line. "No," he said. "We will arrange to send you a video showing all of our guests are alive and well."

Cristo had been prepped by Wilson, and did not hesitate. "That is not acceptable. You realize, for many reasons, a video will not be as reliable as a face-to-face examination."

"Are you suggesting I would falsify the video?"

"I am not. I am merely telling you that under the circumstances we require an examination of the hostages."

"So then, you believe in the value of meeting face to face."

"It is always worthwhile to stare into the eyes of those you are dealing with."

"I very much agree. I therefore think you and I should also have that privilege, if you expect me to rely on your word when so much is at stake."

For the first time, Cristo looked to the others in the room. Wilson whispered, "Ask him what he has in mind."

Cristo did.

"You ask that your doctors have access to the hostages," Farashi replied. "You ask me to delay the execution I have already scheduled for sundown today. These are major concessions. If I am to grant them I need to sit with you and, as you say, look into your eyes."

"How do you propose we arrange that?"

"You must provide safe passage for me and one of my men. We will meet you, and you alone, outside this camp. I will give you the details of where and what time today this will take place. Our movements will be monitored from here. Any effort to harm us or take us prisoner will result in the immediate execution of all five hostages."

"I am informed there is a military presence surrounding the camp, as you undoubtedly know. I cannot speak for them, nor can I personally guarantee your safe passage outside the camp and back in."

"Of course you can. To use your word, their leaders are *undoubtedly* standing beside you as we speak."

Cristo did not respond immediately. Then he said, "What about rescinding your threat to execute one of the hostages?"

"When we meet, that decision will be based on your ability to convince me that you are indeed a man of honor, and that you have the means to satisfy our demands."

"And the examination of the hostages?"

"I agree to this, subject to certain conditions."

"Go ahead."

"Two doctors, both of whom will be searched."

"Of course."

"No supplies. No needles, medication, not so much as a bandage, nothing."

"Agreed."

"All right. Give me a phone number that will reach you directly."

Cristo did not hesitate. He recited the number for his personal cell phone.

"Good," Farashi said. "I will call you in fifteen minutes."

CHAPTER 59

U.S. Army Camp, Mosul

When the call ended, Craig Raabe turned to Sandor. "What do you make of it?"

"We'll see. Whatever comes next between Cristo and Farashi, we still have the same problem."

"Finding a way to get the hostages out without causing a slaughter in the camp," Raabe said.

"Precisely. So we start with what we've been given. I'm going to see the hostages and find out what I can about the situation inside that building."

"Cristo told them he wanted to send in two doctors," Beth reminded him. "What if I go with you?"

"Brave girl," Sandor said with an admiring smile. "Couple of wrinkles in that idea. First, you're a woman. We'll have enough trouble without bringing a female physician to face a gang of Muslim misogynists. Second, you're not trained for field work."

"Neither would a real doctor be, right?" she challenged him.

"Right, except I'm not risking the life of a real doctor, and I'm not risking yours."

Beth forced a smile. "It's nice to know you care."

Sandor fixed her with a serious look. "If I thought your being there would help the mission, I would make that call. Luckily, having you there is not our best play." Then he turned to Garinger. "You up for this?"

Garinger stood and said, "If you think I can help, I'm in."

"Got to earn your merit badge some time. We need Craig and Beth to run ops from outside the fence."

"We have your back, brother," Raabe told him.

"Good. Let's gather up some gear and go play doctor."

⊙

With the help of General Randall's medics, Sandor and Garinger dressed for their roles as they conducted a short meeting with Frank Wilson. When they were ready, the two CIA agents, General Randall, and a Ranger escort boarded an Army helicopter and headed toward the refugee camp.

During the flight they phoned Byrnes, who wanted an update on Coman and Remmell.

Sandor described the damage that had been done. "Coman is doing his best to unravel the mess, but Remmell created a serious problem."

"Do I need to move directly on Fronique? Have State get in touch with Paris and try and shut them down? Maybe we can contain some of the information."

"Too late for that. Anyway, from what Coman can figure, the company was an unwitting accomplice. They thought they were hosting a brilliant scientist. It doesn't appear Remmell's playmates were good sharers."

"Meaning what?" Byrnes asked impatiently.

"Meaning the technology Remmell developed has already been passed on by the people we ran into there."

"You took those people down," the DD said.

"Just the locals. The data was already in the pipeline."

"That *is* a problem," Byrnes agreed. "Does Remmell know when and where they intend to try to intercept the drones?"

"He claims not to have a clue," Sandor told him. "Coman says he swears they never discussed anything like that with him. But I have an idea."

⊙

Ten minutes after Cristo's call with Farashi, Wilson received a text message with a video attached. Everyone, with the exception of Randall, was still in his office.

Wilson handed the phone to one of his aides, who transferred the video to the monitor on the wall. It showed Amanda Jensen and Dedalus, each on their knees, bound with their hands behind their backs to separate stakes, which were set a couple of feet apart. They appeared to be on the ground floor of the warehouse.

The actress appeared haggard and frightened. The Irish rock singer had the fire of defiance in his eyes.

Someone could be heard, prodding them to say something. Amanda had her head down, while Dedalus was staring angrily at the camera, neither of them speaking. An off-camera voice, in heavily accented English, began taunting him.

"Sing something, sing something for them."

Dedalus turned his head to the right and said, "Go fuck yourself."

A slight commotion could be heard in the background, then Amanda Jensen finally looked up at the camera. "They want us to tell you to do whatever they ask."

Suddenly, her beautiful face seemed to come to life as she started to say something else, but the screen went black.

Before any of them could speak, Cristo's cell phone rang. It was Farashi.

Cristo leaned toward the phone, which was sitting on the desk, and initiated the speaker function. "Cristo here," he said.

"You received the new video?"

"We did."

"I hope I have your attention then," Farashi said. "I will now tell you the terms of our meeting."

CHAPTER 60

Refugee Camp near the Syrian border

By the time Sandor's chopper landed, just a hundred yards from the main gate of the complex, the men on board had word of Farashi's call and the arrangements that had been made for the examination of the hostages. Everyone quickly disembarked and trotted toward the entrance. Along the way, Randall took hold of Sandor's arm.

"Going in there, you might want to try to look a bit more like a nerdy medic and not so much like a Green Beret."

"Good advice."

"You should appear nervous and scared and anxious to get the hell out as soon as you can."

Garinger, who overheard the general, forced a smile. "That'll be no problem for me."

At the gate Randall exchanged greetings with Major Bretter, the officer in charge of the operation on the ground. The general introduced him to the two agents who were going to pose as doctors and examine the hostages. Then he asked for the sit-rep.

"Two interesting developments. First, video surveillance from the ground and in the air shows that things have quieted down. Not much movement at the perimeter of the warehouse where we've occasionally seen sentries, but there are still two men on the roof. Second, and more important, we've taken two of their men."

"When the hell did that happen?"

"Five minutes ago, sir."

"Let's have it."

"Two young Syrians. We thought we saw some movement last night at the edge of the building, but weren't sure, tried to follow the satellite images, not much luck. This morning some of the refugees in the compound became anxious." He turned to Sandor and Garinger and explained, "We have people inside, working undercover. They heard about two men moving around during the night, didn't seem to fit in, acting suspicious, that sort of thing. They picked up on it and grabbed these two just a few minutes ago. Odd thing is they both seemed as if they expected to be taken."

"Expected to be taken or wanted to be taken?" Sandor asked.

"You might say both."

"How young?"

"I just saw them for a few seconds," Bretter said, "but I would guess late teens."

Sandor looked from Garinger to Randall. "Why would Farashi set two men loose in the middle of the camp?"

"Gathering information?" suggested Garinger.

Sandor shook his head. "More likely spreading disinformation."

Randall nodded. "Farashi might send them out to feed us false leads, but it's a risky ploy to entrust to a couple of teenagers."

"Not really," Sandor said. "There are members of ISIS who've been murdering people for years by the time they reach eighteen. The point is, whatever stories these two tell us are probably fabrications planted by Farashi."

"Lies they really believe," Randall agreed.

"Absolutely. They'll fight the interrogation, tell us they would face torture, and even death, rather than divulge any of these secrets to us."

"Not realizing the information has no value and is merely intended to mislead."

"That's my guess."

"I'll arrange the interrogation with Raabe," Randall assured him. "But it's time for you to move out."

"You're right," Sandor agreed. "Let's go find out what they're up to."

The soldiers that accompanied them in the helicopter now escorted Sandor and Garinger through the front gate of the compound, providing a phalanx as they headed for the warehouse. Looking around, Sandor realized how difficult it was to fully comprehend the desperate situation faced by these refugees until you walked among them—the filth, the sewage, the crowds, the ragged tents that did little to protect them from the desert heat. The ground was a dusty haze of sand and dirt and, all around him, people were dying of starvation, thirst and disease.

As the group hustled forward, little children, emaciated and hopeless, began running towards them. The Rangers fended them off as they trotted ahead until they reached the front of the warehouse. Once there, Sandor turned to the lieutenant who was leading the detail. "You guys should back off now."

The six soldiers stepped away, remaining close enough to act quickly if things went sideways. In a few moments the front door of the building swung open and a young man carrying an AK-47 stepped out into the late afternoon sun.

"I am Gabir," he said. "I speak English and I will tell you how this will be done. You," he said as he pointed to the six men in uniform, now just ten paces away, "you will give my emir and me safe haven out the front of the compound. You will provide us a vehicle and driver, which we will take to meet with this man Cristo at a location we will designate once we are outside the camp. It shall be a spot not far from here. The driver must not be military. You two," he went on, now directing himself to Sandor and Garinger. "You will be thoroughly searched. Only then you will be allowed access to our guests. You will conduct a brief examination of each. When you are done you will be held here until my emir and I are safely returned."

"Excuse me," Sandor interrupted before the Syrian could continue. "We have been told that we may not bring any supplies or medications with us, and we have complied with that demand. Once we have completed our exam, however, we have been asked to communicate with our superiors to advise them of the condition of the hostages."

"Yes," Gabir replied. "A call will be arranged to your Mr. Wilson. That will be the only communication you will be permitted."

Sandor nodded. "Thank you," he said.

"Now, unless there are other questions, I will bring these two inside and we can proceed."

The lieutenant in charge of the detail spoke up. "Is it your intention to remain armed?"

Gabir responded with a sullen look. "You are all armed, are you not? This is war, is it not?"

"If this is war, I don't recognize your uniform," Sandor said.

Rage instantly replaced insolence as Gabir turned to Sandor. "I wear the uniform of Allah!" he shouted. "Who are you to dare question my allegiance?"

Sandor stared into Gabir's angry eyes, his gaze unblinking. "Shall we get started?" Sandor said.

Gabir held out his arm, pointing him and Garinger toward the door.

As they stepped toward the entrance into God only knew what was to come, Sandor whispered to his fellow agent, "Sorry, sometimes I just can't help myself."

Without looking at him, Garinger said, "So I've heard."

CHAPTER 61

Inside the warehouse of the Refugee Camp near the Syrian border

Once they were inside the warehouse, Sandor was immediately struck by the utter barrenness of the place. A building designed to store dry goods, bottled water, and medical supplies was empty, bereft of any sense of purpose, any sign of utility, any hint of the most important thing it was intended to convey to the wretched people outside—hope. Instead of the provisions it was constructed to hold, the building had instead become shelter to a collection of grimy nomads, dressed in tattered clothing, holding automatic weapons, who were presently staring at their two visitors with looks that were less than welcoming.

From behind this lineup stepped a man who, although attired in similar garb, was better groomed and had a more intelligent look in his eyes. "I am Nizan Farashi," he announced in clear but accented English. "What are your names?"

"Sandor."

"Garinger."

Farashi gave the younger man an appraising look. "Jew?"

Garinger did not flinch. "Lutheran, if that matters. What about you?"

Farashi smiled, but did not take the bait. Instead he turned to Sandor. "Have we met?"

"I don't believe so, but it's possible. Ever play golf at Winged Foot?"

"No," Farashi replied evenly. Then he asked, "Ever go scuba diving near Ras Mohammed in the Red Sea?"

In that moment it was as if all of the cylinders of a lock clicked into place and a door of understanding swung open. Sandor's gaze held Farashi's as he said, "Can't say I have. Scuba diving is not my thing."

The two men stared at each other in silence until Farashi turned away and began pacing slowly back and forth in front of them. "You will be permitted to examine each of our five guests," he said. "There will be a minimum of discussion. There is nothing wrong with any of them, and no treatment of any kind will be allowed. You are here only to confirm that they are alive and healthy, and to report that information to Mr. Wilson. You will be given use of a phone in that room." He pointed to the office behind him, not taking his eyes off the two men. "Then you will remain there until Gabir and I have been safely returned from our meeting outside." He did not wait for a response. He had another long look at Sandor, then turned to his men.

"Search them."

With that, Farashi and Gabir strolled out the front door, appearing as relaxed as if they were heading someplace to take afternoon tea—

except that Gabir still brandished his assault rifle and Farashi had a 9 mm pistol in his sash.

Sandor would not want to hazard a guess as to how many times he had been searched over the years, but he would have to admit he had rarely been treated as roughly or examined so thoroughly as he was here. As he often noted, the least trustworthy people in life are invariably the least trusting.

When Farashi's men were done with their poking and prodding, one of them said, "I am Elazar. You will follow me."

Sandor and Garinger fell in behind Elazar as he led them toward a staircase in the far right corner of the building. They were being trailed by three armed henchmen, apparently in case the two doctors had any ideas about grabbing Elazar from behind.

At the top of the steps they reached a landing that opened directly into the area where the hostages were being held. The four men and Amanda Jensen were sitting off to Sandor's left, backs against the exterior wall of the building, hands bound behind them. It was apparent they had not been prepared for this visit, as their faces registered a variety of expressions, ranging from surprise to relief to hope.

Two armed guards were seated in chairs to the right. Sandor had counted six men downstairs, not including Farashi and Gabir, who were now gone. Counting these guards and the two men that Capt. Bretter indicated were still on the roof, the total number of armed combatants on hand was now ten. Certainly a manageable number if this standoff ended in a firefight—provided no one was concerned with the survival of the hostages or the fate of the refugees surrounding the building.

The room was intensely hot and humid, with virtually no ventilation but the two small windows above. All the hostages appeared to be suffering from heat exhaustion.

Sandor took a few steps toward the prisoners. "We are medics attached to the United States Army base in Mosul. We are here to conduct a brief examination to ensure that each of you is healthy and not suffering any abuse."

Sandor was barely able to finish his simple introduction before Elazar drove the butt of his automatic rifle into Sandor's shoulder, hollering, "Shut up, American. You were told there would be no talking."

Sandor did not rub his shoulder. He would not give Elazar that satisfaction. Instead he glared at the Syrian. "That is not what Farashi told us. We were told to keep discussion to a minimum. I had to inform these people why we have come."

Elazar said, "I will tell them what they need to know. You are only to do what you have come to do."

Sandor turned away and began walking the length of the room slowly, having a good look at each of the five hostages in turn.

The first man he passed was Shahid Hassan. As Sandor knew, the Saudi represented the one unpredictable element in this plan. Given the intrigue Sandor had uncovered in the halls of RSL and WHI, there remained a remote possibility that Hassan was somehow in league with Farashi. If Hassan had been taken hostage as part of some larger ruse that Byrnes' team had not yet divined, Hassan would identify Sandor immediately upon seeing him.

On the other hand, Sandor had the chance to meet Hassan and form a judgment about the man. Coupled with the fact that he was a friend of O'Hara's, Sandor judged it a risk he was willing to take.

When their eyes met there was an unspoken acknowledgment by Hassan that he understood why Sandor had come. But he said nothing. To the contrary he did his best to look away as if he were an unconcerned witness to events that did not involve him.

Sandor moved slowly to Amanda Jensen who was looking tired and angry and confused.

She was seated beside Hassan and, as Sandor looked down at her, she began to speak.

"Who are you? Are we going to be released?"

When she began to ask a third question, Sandor held up his hand to quiet her. "These men have made it clear they will not tolerate a dialogue between us. We are here only to assess your medical condition and report back. You will not be helping yourselves by engaging in unauthorized conversation with us." Sandor had a look at Elazar. "I am correct in telling them that, am I not?"

This time the Syrian only nodded, satisfied that he had made his point.

But the presence of these two Americans seemed to rally the actress. She said, "I'd like to get up and rip my clothes off for your examination, see these bastards run for cover." Then she stared up at Elazar, her eyes filled with pent-up fury. "That's what you'd have to do, right? Couldn't bear the sight of a naked woman?"

Elazar came forward, but Sandor turned and faced him. "Enough," he told the Syrian. Then he turned back to the actress. "Silence please, Ms. Jensen. You're not making things any easier for yourself with that sort of outburst." Then, before turning away, he winked at her.

The next man in the row had obviously been struck in the side of the head. From the look of the wound it probably happened a day or two ago. There was a nasty gash, dried blood, and no evidence that anyone had tended to the wound. "You all right?" Sandor asked.

"Tom Orr," the man said, then gave a brief nod. "This cut isn't going to kill me, if that's what you're asking."

Sandor recognized the name, head of the security detail that had been outmanned and outgunned. Members of the mission, who were left behind after the hostages were taken, described Orr's bravery. They told of how he insisted he accompany the prisoners, even though he was not on the terrorists' list. Sandor said, "My colleague will have a look at that for you. We're not allowed to administer any treatment, but we'll want to confirm there's no infection."

Orr nodded again, but said nothing.

The next man was Dedalus, as immediately recognizable as Amanda Jensen, a face that seemed as familiar as an old friend's. He gave Sandor a look that revealed plenty about the man—he wanted it known there was still a tough guy from the streets of Dublin lurking behind the veneer of music magic.

"We'll have a look at you," Sandor said, then moved on to the last man. He stood there, gazing down at his friend, Bill Sternlich.

Looking up, the journalist blinked several times. "Bill Sternlich, from *The Times*."

"You all right?" Sandor asked, noticing the bruise on the side of his head.

"I've been better," he admitted.

"And so you will be again," Sandor told him. He turned to Garinger. "All right, we'll begin here."

The two of them bent down and started to perform a cursory exam, Sandor using a stethoscope, while Garinger took Sternlich's temperature with a digital-touch thermometer. Each of them had a small pad in which they scribbled some notes. That was the extent of the medical paraphernalia they were allowed to bring, but for Sandor's purposes it was enough for them to be able to play their roles.

Sandor spoke in a normal conversational tone, asking about symptoms, having Sternlich breathe deeply and then cough, trying to sound as much like a physician as possible. Elazar and his men were standing back, near the guards, giving Sandor the opportunity to speak in a quiet voice, telling his friend, "Hang in there Bill. I'm going to get you out of here."

Sternlich tried not to smile as he asked, "Really? And who the hell is going to get *you* out of here?"

"Funny," Sandor said, then stood. Looking at the Syrians, he told them, "This man appears to be suffering from dehydration. Are these prisoners getting enough water?"

Elazar glared at him in response. "You are here to examine them, not make demands."

Sandor made a show of writing something in his notepad, then moved to Dedalus. As soon as he knelt beside him, the Irishman whispered, "Always two guards up here. Armed, sitting in those chairs. Best I can estimate they run in shifts of three or four hours. Rest of these towel-heads stay downstairs."

Garinger provided cover for their discussion, making as much noise as possible as he tended to Dedalus.

Sandor plugged the stethoscope into his ears and pretended to be listening to the man's chest. "They ever fall asleep?"

"Sometimes, but never both at the same time."

"They ever leave you alone?"

"Never," Dedalus told him. "Sometimes they pull hoods over our heads. Intimidation I guess. Maybe just for fun. Real assholes."

"You all have your hands tied. They ever bind your ankles?"

"No."

Sandor pulled off the stethoscope. "Good. So if you all needed to make a run for it . . ."

"We'll be ready."

Elazar stepped forward now. "Enough discussion," he growled. "Move on."

In response, Sandor stood and announced, "This man is suffering from acute bronchitis. He needs antibiotics."

"Move on," the Syrian repeated.

The next man was Orr. Sandor bent down, did a quick examination of his wound, then looked up at Elazar who was hovering over them now, struggling to overhear their brief conversations.

Sandor looked up at him. "I know we cannot treat them, but could I at least get a clean cloth and water to clean this wound?"

"No," came the immediate response.

Sandor continued to stare up at him. "You're enjoying having this power, with Farashi gone, eh?" He smiled. "Don't you know that great power carries with it great responsibility?"

Elazar appeared to be considering the notion when Amanda Jensen burst out laughing.

"You're kidding, right? You're quoting *Spiderman*?"

"Silence!" Elazar shouted at the group, then glowered at Sandor and Garinger. "Get done with this," he told them.

Once again, Garinger engaged in as much chatter as he could conducting the exam as Sandor turned back to Orr and apologized. "Sorry pal, thought I might be able to clean this up for you. Looks okay though. Like you said, I'm not going to convince anyone this is life-threatening."

Orr looked directly into Sandor's eyes as he whispered, "You're also not going to convince *me* you're a doctor."

Sandor smiled. "Hope I'm fooling our hosts."

"You're doing all right," Orr replied. "I actually recognized you from the event at the U.N. the other night."

Sandor nodded. "It was a big crowd. You're obviously good at your job."

"Not good enough, apparently."

Sandor let that go.

"You have a plan?" Orr asked.

"Working on it," Sandor said. "Just be ready to get this group moving when the time comes."

Sandor felt the heel of Elazar's boot in the small of his back. He spun around.

"Too much talk. You are done with this one now."

"He needs his gash treated. It's becoming infected."

"*Bah*! Move on."

Sandor and Garinger did as they were told, tending next to Amanda Jensen.

"You all right?" Sandor asked her.

She replied with a theatrical look that told him it might be the dumbest question she had ever heard in a career of fielding stupid questions. "What do you think?"

"What I mean is, have they harmed you in any way?"

"Not really. Shoved around. Starved. Not enough water. But no physical attacks."

"Mind if I listen to your chest for a moment?"

This time her look was more amused than annoyed. She owned what might be the most famous chest in the world. All she said was, "Do what you have to do."

With appropriate delicacy, Sandor undid the two top buttons of her cotton blouse, applied the metal bell of the stethoscope above her left breast, and asked her to take a few deep breaths. Then he moved behind her and reached under her shirt to have another listen. When he was done he came back around to face her. "You're a tough lady."

"You mean because my lungs are clear?"

Sandor smiled.

"Despair gave way to fatalism in the past day or so," she admitted. "Now that you're here we have hope." When he didn't reply, she said, "Why would they allow us to be examined if they weren't getting ready to exchange us for money, or terrorists in Guantanamo, or something else?"

"Tough, and smart too," he said.

She managed her own little smile. It wasn't much, but it was dazzling.

"Stay with hope rather than fatalism," he told her.

"That doesn't sound like run-of-the-mill medical advice, doctor."

Sandor began to stand, then leaned forward. "It's not, but I'm not your run-of-the-mill doctor."

CHAPTER 62

Outside the Refugee Camp near
the Syrian border

Farashi was specific about the arrangements for his face-to-face discussion with Dr. Eduardo Cristo.

They would meet inside the mosque located in the center of Sinjar, a small town less than ten miles west of the refugee camp, in the foothills of an arid mountain range between Iraq and Syria. Farashi and Gabir were to be taken there in a vehicle driven by an unarmed civilian. There would be no military escort. They would be allowed to speak with Cristo in absolute privacy, the conversation to last no more than one hour. When they concluded their negotiation, Farashi and Gabir would be returned to the warehouse. At that time, after they had safely rejoined their men, Farashi would call Wilson and advise him of the results of Cristo's efforts and their intentions regarding the ransom and the hostages. Then he would release the two doctors and arrangements would be made to exchange the hostages for the ransom.

If any of these terms was violated, or the negotiation with Cristo found to be unsatisfactory, the beheading would proceed that night.

Needless to say, neither the bureaucrats in Washington nor the military personnel in and around the camp were comfortable with the demands. After a brief debate, however, they were forced to concede it was worth the effort. At the very least it would buy time, and would give Cristo an opportunity to persuade Farashi not to murder any of the five people being held. Alan Goldberg and his contingent were furious when informed of the arrangements. They were prepared to contribute a substantial portion of the ransom money. They felt it was their right to have a representative at the meeting, to judge the situation first-hand. Moreover, as Goldberg pointed out, they were from Hollywood. They negotiated for a living, all day, every day. They could certainly cut a better deal than this doctor from London.

Wilson did his best to explain the circumstances. First, Farashi made it clear he would only meet with one representative. Second, this was a mission organized by the U.N. and WHI, but the U.N. would not participate directly in the process, as a result of which Cristo became the lead spokesman by default. Finally, after Wilson apologized for his lack of tact, he added, "You're a Jew, Mr. Goldberg, and these are Arab terrorists. Need I say more?"

Goldberg was indeed Jewish. He was also wealthy and powerful, and yet he was now left to do nothing more than shake his head, feeling utterly frustrated. "Unbelievable, isn't it? I mean, we're in the twenty-first century and these morons still think we're the devil incarnate. Haven't they noticed that Arabs kill more Arabs than anyone else? What the hell does being Jewish have to do with any of this?"

Frank Wilson had no answer for him. "We're doing the best we can," was all he could think of to say.

⊙

As Goldberg left Wilson's office to deliver the bad news to his group, and Sandor and Garinger pretended to be doctors while trying to collect scraps of information from the five hostages, Farashi and Gabir sat in the back of a Humvee being chauffeured by an Arab-American soldier, dressed in civvies, en route to the meeting site.

"You are from here?" Farashi asked in the language of the region.

The driver responded that he was—what he did not reveal was that he had been selected for this task because of his knowledge of the area, his facility with various dialects, and his fearless loathing of Farashi and all those of his ilk who were perverting the message of Islam and the reputation of his people.

"Good," Farashi replied, then glanced over at Gabir. Now that they knew the man spoke the language, they would not risk any discussion during the ride, not even in Syriac.

⊙

At the same time, Cristo was being delivered to Sinjar by helicopter. Despite Farashi's insistence that there be no military presence, the chopper and its full contingent of Rangers were going to stay right where they landed, on an open patch of ground a couple of hundred yards from the mosque.

Prior to embarking on the excursion, General Randall and his men had suggested that Cristo wear full body armor. He objected, reminding them, "This is a negotiation, gentlemen, not hand-to-hand combat. A little trust must be displayed." Randall was insistent that some precaution be taken and so they reached a compromise. A staff sergeant fitted Cristo with a Kevlar vest, then Randall saw him on his way.

Now, as the chopper settled on the ground and the rotors quieted, the lead officer tapped Cristo on the shoulder.

"You sure you're okay going in alone?"

"What choice do we have?" Cristo replied. Then he climbed out of the Blackhawk.

⊙

A few moments later, as Cristo crossed the square in front of the mosque, he saw a Humvee pull up just across from him. He watched as Farashi and Gabir got out and entered the ancient temple, after which the driver did as he had been instructed, pulling away and parking fifty yards or so down the road.

Cristo did not break stride as he followed the two men inside.

The two Syrians had removed their shoes and Cristo now did the same. The mosque was empty, which had been arranged in advance, with no windows through which the three men could be viewed from outside. None of them spoke until they gathered at the *mihrab*, a small semicircular niche in the far wall.

On the floor was a portable music player that one of Farashi's people had placed there the night before. Gabir bent down, switched it on, and instantly the recorded sounds of Islamic prayer resonated around them.

"Cannot be too careful with the soldiers outside eavesdropping on our discussion," Farashi said in a quiet voice. Then he and Cristo embraced like long-lost brothers.

"So good to see you my friend," Cristo said, also keeping his voice low.

Farashi said. "This young man is Bassel Gabir. He can be trusted with our lives."

"*Allahu akbar*," Cristo said, and the other two men repeated the refrain.

"So, things are all in place?" Farashi asked.

Cristo responded with a look that made it clear not all things were as they should be.

"The scientist has been taken by the Americans."

Farashi had not heard, and the news was not welcome. "When?"

"Two days ago. In France. The entire matter has been kept from the media, but my sources have confirmed it."

"Had he completed his work for us?"

"I am told he had. I have obviously needed to exercise great care in my communications. We are all being closely watched at the Institute, especially me. I am, after all, the chief negotiator," he reminded them with a flash of his gleaming smile.

"Understood. Do you have any information on the progress of the assault?"

"I do not. I expect to receive word when I return to the base. Ironically the Americans may be the ones to tell me."

Farashi responded with a grim look. He did not like the idea of relying on the Americans for anything. "What of the money?"

"Right now I am convincing you to reduce your demand."

"You are very persuasive."

"The insistence on gold has also worked as I predicted. Once I tell them you have agreed to accept currency, they will be eager to make the deal."

"You are a sage man, my friend."

"Let's hope so. The American government obviously objects to paying a ransom of any kind, but the Jews in Hollywood are acting just as we expected they would."

"They will fund the entire payment?"

"No, no, WHI will be contributing a substantial portion."

Farashi nodded. "Let's discuss timing."

For the next several minutes they reviewed their plans, then addressed the difficulty they would face in retrieving the funds once the deposits were made.

Farashi made it clear he remained more than a little skeptical on that point. He warned Cristo, "These banks and their governments will be under intense pressure to return the ransom, once our work here is done."

"Of course, of course," Cristo agreed. "But they are still the enemies of our enemies. Do you really think they will give the money back?"

Farashi's look made it clear he regarded that as a distinct possibility.

"Leave the finances to me," Cristo said as he treated the two Syrians to another confident grin. "The banks will do with the funds as I tell them, don't you see? They will never capitulate to the Americans, but there is more to it than that. My involvement on behalf of WHI provides them the perfect excuse. They will not be criticized for abetting terrorism, they are cooperating with WHI to save lives."

"You are sure we will be able to gain control of the money after that?"

"Very sure."

Farashi appeared unconvinced. "Once we have accomplished our goals, won't there be demands from various nations to return the money to the WHI? And to the others who contributed to the ransom?"

Cristo laughed. "Trust me. I have made all of the necessary arrangements. As soon as this money is deposited, it will disappear in an untraceable series of transfers." Cristo pulled a sheet of paper from his pocket. "This is the list you just gave me containing the banks and account numbers to which you want the funds to be wired. Believe me, I have friends in many places."

Farashi finally appeared to relax. "All right."

Cristo handed him the page. "I need your fingerprints on the paper."

"You never fail to surprise me."

"One cannot be too careful."

"So true," Farashi said as he scanned the bank names. "I assume you have a copy of this for me."

Cristo reached into his jacket, took out a copy and exchanged it with Farashi.

"Excellent," the Syrian said.

"Now perhaps you should move along, yes?"

"We are well short of the allotted hour."

Cristo looked at his watch. "Another fifteen minutes or so, make it appear we're each driving a hard bargain with the other."

Farashi nodded. "And so we are," he said. "But now it is time for us to part."

CHAPTER 63

Outside Niamey, Niger

Harry Remmell was seated in Col. Brighton's office, elbows on the desk, head in his hands. John Coman was standing above him.

"Doc, there's no sense in going over all of that again. If they're going to use your work to launch an attack anytime soon, our job is to stop them, not to worry about how they arranged for it to happen."

"How could I have been such a jackass? I just don't understand."

Brighton and Coman exchanged a quick glance—it was a question to which they would also be interested in hearing an answer. For now that would have to wait, as the colonel said, "Coman is right. Everything you've told us, about their timing and the way they pushed you, suggests they mean to take action soon. This is not the time to discuss blame, this is the time for action."

Remmell looked up. "You think I don't know that? Problem is, I was never privy to any discussions about how they meant to use the technology. We talked about disabling or destroying armed drones. If they intend to re-engineer armed UAV's to hit alternate targets, I don't know when or where they intend to make it happen." He turned his doleful gaze from Brighton to Coman. "If I had any sense they were using me to arrange their own attacks, you think I would've continued helping them?"

"You never heard a single conversation involving targets of any kind?" Coman asked.

"How many times can you ask me the same question? Never. Not once."

Coman turned to the colonel. "I know this will probably sound ridiculous, but what sort of logistics would be involved in grounding the UAV's presently in the air?"

"You know the answer to that," Brighton replied. "You might as well ask me to stop our military satellites from circling the globe."

"I don't mean every drone," Coman said. "Just the armed devices in this region."

"It would still be a tactical nightmare on many levels. First, the logistics, as you call it, would be extremely complicated. No one knows that better than the two of you. Then there's the public relations disaster Washington would have to deal with. Do you think we want our enemies, or even our allies, knowing how many armed UAV's we have floating in the sky at any given moment?"

Coman nodded glumly.

"We realize the whole world watches this area," Brighton said, "and we're accustomed to being under close scrutiny. But at the moment the attention is over the top, right now they're shining a klieg light on us. We start calling in every armed drone and it'll look like we were gearing up to start a world war."

For the first time in hours, Doc Remmell perked up. "You see, that's exactly what I thought I was fighting against. Big Brother in the sky, raining death and destruction on an unsuspecting public."

Coman glared down at the senior engineer. "You know I am not normally a violent man, Doc, but in your case I am willing to make an exception. One more political rant from you and I swear, I will punch you senseless."

Remmell's eyes widened and he drew back slightly. "When you said you were old friends with that assassin Sandor, I didn't see any basis for the connection, not until just now. Your true colors finally come out."

"Trust me, Doc, Sandor takes my colors to a whole new level."

Col. Brighton interrupted them. "Doctor Remmell, I strongly suggest you confine anything you have to say to solving this problem."

After a moment's pause, Remmell nodded. "I may actually have an idea."

"We're listening," Brighton replied.

"When I arrived in France I got a sense how far along they were with this concept, and I obviously know what I told them once I was there. What if I work with Coman and a couple of your key operatives to see if I can reverse what I did? Maybe I can cut off any signal they send before it results in an interception."

"Not a bad approach," Coman admitted, "with a couple of basic flaws. We have no idea how much time we have left to get this done, and unless we know which of our UAV's they targeted, how can we be effective in stopping it?"

"None of us knows the answer to that first issue," the colonel admitted, "but the second may be easy. I'm obviously not the scientist the two of you are, but it seems to me that we'll know which of our drones is being manipulated as soon as one of them goes off course. Then Remmell might be able to undo the damage."

"Provided there's enough time," Coman reminded them.

The three men began to debate the approach, including whether or not they had sufficient reason to trust Remmell enough, at this point, to allow him inside their computers, when they were interrupted by a knock at the door. Brighton's adjutant charged in and handed his superior officer a slip of paper. From the look of concern in the young soldier's eyes, no one needed to inquire if he was bringing them good news.

Brighton read the note quickly and looked up. "Gentlemen, I think it's fair to say that the timetable has been moved up. According to our command center, in the past few minutes we lost control of four heavily armed UAV's. They were flying routes proximate to the areas around Mosul, the refugee camp, and the Syrian border. Now each of them appears to be veering off course."

CHAPTER 64

Inside the warehouse of the Refugee Camp near the Syrian border

The last hostage Sandor examined was Shahid Hassan. He was worried the guards might be most interested in any exchanges he might have with the Saudi so, when he first kneeled beside him, he said nothing. With Garinger standing behind him, Sandor put on the stethoscope and reached inside Hassan's shirt. "Take a deep breath through your mouth and exhale slowly."

Hassan obliged, not betraying his amusement at Sandor's attempt to appear every bit the medical professional.

As his patient breathed in and out, Sandor whispered, "Just one question. Is Cristo involved?"

Hassan nodded slowly. "I could not bring myself to believe it, but it must be so."

Sandor directed him to lift his shirt. Then he looked up at Elazar. "Heard something in his lungs, I want to have a listen at his back."

"Hurry up," the Syrian scowled.

As Sandor moved behind Hassan, he quietly asked, "Have you actually heard any of these men mention his name?"

"No," Hassan admitted. "But recently I have had my doubts. With this unexpected time to consider everything, I can see his hand in all of this."

"Do you think Cristo knows you suspected him?"

"I do."

"Which is why they came after you in Hartford."

"A clumsy attempt that took the lives of good people for no purpose."

Sandor nodded as he thought of Jim O'Hara. "That's also why you were one of the people taken hostage."

"And that is the reason I don't believe any of us are meant to survive."

"A lot of trouble to eliminate one man."

"There is much more to this than Farashi's revenge on the House of Saud."

Sandor recalled Farashi's comment to him about scuba diving near Sharm el-Sheikh. "I believe you're right," he said.

They were not certain how much Elazar heard, but the Syrian came forward and shouted, "Enough talk. You are done."

Sandor began to object. "This man is not well—" he started, but for the first time the Syrian lifted his weapon and aimed it directly at him.

"I told you, you are done. You two will come with us now."

When Sandor stood he paused to exchange another look with Hassan.

"Come," Elazar growled.

Sandor and Garinger followed the Syrian to the landing and headed down the stairs, the other armed escorts right behind them.

When they reached ground level they were shoved forward toward the office. Inside, Sandor told them he was ready to contact the base, as arranged.

Elazar was in no rush for them to make the call. "What will you tell them?" he asked.

Sandor smiled. "What would you like me to tell them?"

"You will tell them the truth. These people are healthy. They are fed and they are given water to drink."

Sandor nodded. "You forgot to mention that one of them was also given a gash on the side of his head. Another of them has a bad bruise. A few of them have respiratory issues, and they are all dehydrated."

The latter statement evoked a confused look.

"Breathing problems," Sandor said, demonstrating by drawing a deep breath and then coughing it out.

"Bah," Elazar responded. He pointed Sandor to a chair. "Sit. We will make the call." He picked up a cell phone on the desk and punched in some numbers. When Frank Wilson answered almost immediately, Elazar hit the speaker button and held out the phone to Sandor. The malicious look he gave made it clear he was not going to brook any unauthorized discussion. "The medical report," he snarled. "Nothing more."

Before he left the base, Sandor had outlined a simple code to Wilson and Byrnes, key words to convey the data he accumulated, none of which would have anything to do with medical diagnoses. With the phone on speaker mode, and Elazar listening, he said, "Mr. Wilson? Dr. Sandor here."

"Yes doctor."

"We have seen all five hostages. They are all alive and in reasonable physical and mental condition. Mr. Orr was struck on the side of his head. From the wound it appears this occurred two or three days ago. The injury was not treated and I estimate ten stitches will be required to properly close it and avoid infection. If the infection returns, count on two more."

"Go on."

"Ms. Jensen has an upper respiratory issue in her right lung."

"Upper you say?"

"Correct. With two spots discernible upon stethoscopic examination."

"Are the hostages being fed, do they have water?"

"Minimally so. They are confined to a single room, so sanitation is an issue. The best solution here will be immediate treatment for all concerned. This is the kind of infection that is so contagious it can become an epidemic, with inevitable fatalities."

Elazar suddenly pulled the phone back and said, "That is enough. You told them the hostages are alive. You are done." He cut off the speaker function, held the phone to his ear and said to Wilson, "We await the return of Farashi." Then he hung up.

No one in the room had any idea of what that wait was about to entail.

CHAPTER 65

U.S. Army Camp, Mosul

When the call with Sandor was abruptly ended, Wilson turned to the group assembled in his office. Based on the rudimentary code Sandor had arranged with them, they now knew the following:

The hostages were being held in one room.

The room was upstairs to the right of the building as you face the front.

They were being guarded by two men.

There were ten hostiles in total, not counting Farashi and Gabir who had gone to meet Cristo.

Sandor felt action was required sooner rather than later.

His assessment was that some or all of the hostages were going to be killed regardless of what arrangements were made to pay ransom.

It was that last piece of the message that was the most alarming.

Wilson immediately set up a videoconference with Washington and imparted the information Sandor had gathered.

Peter Forelli, at the White House, was the first to respond. "You're sure you're reading him right?"

"As sure as we can be under the circumstances," Wilson reported. "He was on a speaker and it sounded like Farashi's men were standing right beside him."

"He said fatalities were inevitable?"

"He was clear about that," Wilson said. "Based on the key words Sandor told us he would use, I feel certain we're interpreting him correctly."

"I believe you are, particularly about the likelihood of fatalities," Deputy Director Byrnes weighed in from Langley. "We've just had an update from our base in Niamey. It appears they've lost control of four armed UAV's."

"Lost control?" Dick Bebon asked. "What the hell does that mean?"

"CO there says four drones have veered off course. Each of them was patrolling areas within striking distance of Mosul and the refugee camp. The technicians at our base have lost the ability to remotely operate them. Someone else is manipulating their flight patterns."

"We just received the same alert," Forelli said. "Any word yet on what they're doing about it?"

"The engineers in Niamey are trying to reverse whatever codes caused the interceptions," Byrnes replied. "But thus far they've had no success."

Everyone on the call began speaking at once until Wilson managed to restore order. "This is obviously a game changer," he said. "I have no idea what capabilities they have in Niger to handle the situation, but I think we should have General Randall join this call. He's stationed outside the refugee camp and he's in charge of the troops on the ground there and at this base."

The others agreed, and Wilson's assistant added another line.

Randall was in a tent outside the refugee complex. He was with Major Bretter, Craig Raabe and Beth Sharrow. After Wilson was done explaining the situation, Randall said, "Well it just keeps getting worse."

"This is Byrnes at Central Intelligence, General. You saying you have something else for us?"

"We do. I'm assuming my line is secure?"

"It's encrypted."

"All right," the general said. He placed the satellite phone on the small folding table and put it on speaker mode. "First you need to hear from Craig Raabe."

"Go ahead," the DD told him.

Raabe said, "Before Sandor entered the camp, he confided to the general and me that he has doubts about Dr. Cristo."

"What doubts?" Forelli asked.

"Sandor believes Cristo might be working with Farashi," Raabe told them.

After a brief uproar on the call, Forelli told everyone to be quiet so Raabe could continue.

"When Cristo met Farashi at the mosque we intended to use remote eavesdropping devices to listen to their conversation, but they covered it up with some sort of recorded chanting."

"Recorded chanting?"

"Yes sir. We know the mosque was empty, the general's men had a quick look before Farashi arrived. Someone must have left a device to play a recording, so we couldn't listen to them from the outside."

"Go ahead," Forelli told him.

"Before the chopper took Cristo to the meeting, we convinced him to wear a Kevlar vest for his protection. He didn't know that Sandor had us imbed a microphone in the chest pad."

"Did that work?"

"The chanting was a problem on that transmission too, but they were obviously up close as they spoke, which helped. We've managed to cut out a lot of the ambient noise from the recording we made. Sandor was right. Cristo is in this up to his eyeballs."

Once again, a number of participants on the call began speaking at the same time, but this time it was General Randall who interrupted.

"Simmer down everyone, we've got other issues," he said.

"Such as?"

"Sandor doesn't believe the hostages are ever going to be released," Randall told them. "He thinks they're going to be victims of a much larger attack. His last comment to Wilson a few minutes ago, about a fatal epidemic, confirms it. That was one of the key phrases we agreed on."

"He thinks the sabotage of our drones is related to the kidnapping of these people?" Forelli asked.

"Raabe here."

"Go ahead," the man from the White House told him.

"Sandor is convinced there's a connection. Some of the comments Farashi made in his discussion with Cristo are consistent with that."

"Did he actually mention a drone attack?"

"Not directly," Raabe admitted, "but there is enough at this point to put it together that way."

Forelli told him to spell it out.

"Holding their hostages in the middle of the refugee camp. The timing of this sabotage of our drones. And the general just received word of another development."

"As I said when we tied into the call, it keeps getting worse," Randall told them.

"We're listening," Forelli said.

"Dr. Cristo left his meeting at the mosque in Sinjar less than half an hour ago, and the chopper returned him to our base in Mosul."

"Yes," Wilson confirmed, "Cristo just arrived back here at the Army base."

Randall went on. "We had a driver assigned to bring Farashi and his aide back here at the refugee camp. The driver is one of ours, and waited in the Humvee after Cristo left. When the other two didn't come out, he figured they were praying, so he radioed in the situation. I checked with the Rangers I had stationed around the perimeter of the mosque. They confirmed they had a line of sight on all four sides. No one was coming or going without them having eyes on the situation. We waited a while, then a few minutes ago I made the decision to send a team inside to bring them out." He paused. "They're gone."

"What do you mean gone?" Forelli asked.

"I mean the mosque is empty. Farashi and Gabir have disappeared."

The town of Sinjar was chosen with purpose by Nizar Farashi as the place for his meeting with Cristo. Close to the border between Iraq and Syria, it had witnessed centuries of fighting, its temples having provided solace to the families of countless victims. Only recently, however, had ISIS sympathizers thought to use one of those mosques as a path to physical safety as well spiritual guidance.

Inside the temple, off to the left of the main hall, one of the prayer rugs concealed a trap door that led to steps below. That stairway led to a tunnel beneath the street, extending to a nearby building, some fifty yards away. Before Cristo departed, the two Syrians lifted the rug-covered panel, climbed down, pulled the door closed behind them, and made their escape. Cristo made sure the rug was in place, then waited ten minutes before stepping out into the late afternoon sun and strolling toward his waiting helicopter.

During those ten minutes, Farashi and Gabir hurried through the length of tunnel, and used a wooden ladder to climb up into a small, windowless storage room on the ground floor of the structure across from the mosque. There, they changed into clothes that had been left for them—Farashi dressing in the native garb of an old man, the younger Gabir covering up in a burka, looking every bit the elder's wife. They then exited the utility room and walked down a corridor to a makeshift garage where they climbed into a small sedan that was facing out the rear of the building. With Farashi at the wheel, they began the drive heading northwest, toward the Syrian border.

In this town of more than twenty thousand people, their departure was not unusual and drew no curious looks. The far side of the building through which they made their escape was behind the cordon of soldiers who were positioned around the area. All eyes were on the mosque, with curious locals as well as the American soldiers waiting on the results of this conference between the two terrorists and the representative from WHI. No one bothered about an old couple leaving a building behind them, making their way out of town.

Now, however, their disappearance had been discovered, and it was clear they had a lead of as much as thirty minutes or more.

Farashi and Gabir could be almost anywhere.

CHAPTER 66

Inside the warehouse of the Refugee Camp near the Syrian border

Earlier, when Sandor watched Farashi and Gabir leave the warehouse for their meeting in Sinjar, he knew they were never coming back. The feeling was nothing he could easily define; it was just something about their demeanor, and the look in their eyes.

Byrnes would chastise him for relying too heavily on his instincts, without supporting evidence to back him up, but there was also the comment Farashi made about having met Sandor before, followed by his mention of the Red Sea. Sandor was certain he had never laid eyes on the man until that moment, but Farashi was sending a clear message—he knew what happened when Sandor's life was threatened near Ras Mohammed, and he was obviously aware of what Sandor had done—and the people he had killed—in order to survive.

When Farashi made that reference to the action outside Sharm al-Sheikh, that was the instant when Sandor began to make sense of things. O'Hara. Lerner. Sternlich. The incidents at the St. Regis and in London. He had been struggling to find a common thread and, if all of these events were not connected, he finally understood some of them were indeed tied together—and he was the common link.

As he began to make sense of this puzzle, Sandor felt increasingly helpless, unable to act since he had volunteered to walk into this prison from which he now believed no one was intended to escape.

It had been more than two hours since he arrived, far more than enough time for Farashi to meet with Cristo and return. But they had not come back. Sandor and Garinger were being held in the office used as Farashi's communications center, and there had not been any contact by phone. Not only did that confirm Sandor's suspicion that the leaders of this cabal had abandoned his men, it also put his greatest fears about this crisis front and center. It was increasingly apparent what they intended for the hostages, the thousands in this refugee camp, and now Garinger and him, all of whom would share the same fate.

Sandor already understood that the plan to intercept drones—aided by the egomaniacal Harry Remmell—was not intended to simply disable the UAV's or even send their missiles on random courses of destruction. That became apparent when they met with Remmell's handlers back in Sophia Antipolis. These men were engaged in a more purposeful, sinister scheme, and now their intentions were clear.

Those UAV's were being aimed right here, right now.

Clever boys, he told himself. Farashi and Gabir had created a house of death, then worked with Cristo to create a ruse for leaving the place by demanding a face-to-face negotiation. Wherever they were at the moment, they would not be at ground zero when the attack came.

The same, however, could not be said of their brothers-in-arms, who had been left behind to die with all the others.

Sandor turned his focus on two of those men, the guards who had been ordered by Elazar to remain in the office and keep watch over the American doctors. Sandor guessed they were beginning to have similar questions and concerns about the whereabouts of their leader. He doubted they knew a drone attack was part of the plan.

The two had barely exchanged a word for a very long time and, as the minutes ticked by, the anxious look in their eyes and the way they fidgeted in their seats told Sandor all he had to know.

A nervous opponent is a vulnerable opponent.

He and Garinger were seated on the floor against the outside wall, much like the hostages upstairs, except their hands were not bound. There was no way of knowing where Elazar and the other armed men were positioned or what, if anything, was going on outside the building. None of that mattered now. Given all he had concluded, waiting any longer was simply not in Sandor's DNA.

"You guys speak English?" he asked the guards.

"Silence," the man to his right snapped.

"Simple question, no?"

"I told you, shut your filthy mouth."

"You see, you do speak English. I thought you might. That's why they picked you to watch us, so you could tell them if we said anything, am I right? You guys are very smart."

"Silence," the guard repeated with growing anger.

Sandor shook his head, as if he were incapable of obeying the order. "Farashi is never coming back, you know that don't you?"

The Syrian responded with a fierce stare. "If they are not returning it is because the Americans are lying infidels."

Sandor pursed his lips and nodded, appearing to be giving the notion some thought. "Or—and I'm just tossing this out as a possibility—maybe it's because Farashi is the one who's a lying infidel, am I right?"

The guard did not hesitate. He propelled himself out of his chair and lunged at Sandor.

That was his first mistake.

Sandor was already rising. He fended off the attack with a sharp elbow into the man's side and a leg sweep that took out his feet. The guard's momentum sent him falling directly into Garinger, who had already gotten up and managed to deftly wrap his right arm tightly around the man's throat as the guard stumbled toward him. The Syrian instinctively reached up to free himself from the chokehold. That was his second mistake.

With a quick twist of his arm and a driving move with his legs, Garinger took the guard down, smashing his face into the hard floor, using the force of all of his weight to knock him senseless.

Sandor's next play had been to get to the second man before a shot could be fired. That was critical to their survival. They needed to be both fast and quiet in subduing their captors. Unfortunately, the second guard was not as reckless as the first. Instead of moving forward, he got out of his chair and took a step backward as he raised the barrel of his AK-47. But the action had begun too quickly and, even with the exercise of such caution, he did not properly judge Sandor's speed or agility.

He had no way of knowing that the man racing toward him was no doctor.

Sandor had already launched himself into the air, a human projectile that drove the Arab backward against the wall before he could fire a shot. The blow knocked the wind out him, but Sandor needed to end this quickly. Using his left hand to grab the man's right wrist—keeping his finger away from the trigger of the automatic— Sandor tensed the knuckles of his right hand and repeatedly hit the Syrian in the throat until he shattered his windpipe. Then he spun the guard around with a forceful counter-action, jammed a knee into his back and, using both hands, broke the man's neck.

Sandor let the man fall to the floor and turned to Garinger, who gave him the thumbs up. The guard beneath Garinger was a lifeless mass and the young agent was already taking the man's UZI and two extra magazines of ammunition. He moved close to Sandor, and they spoke in hushed tones.

"I always said Byrnes knows how to pick 'em."

Garinger nodded his appreciation. "Next time, though, you might want to give me a little advance notice."

"Wasn't really an option, was it?"

Sandor reached down and picked up the AK-47 that was lying on the ground beside the second guard and grabbed the extra magazine inside the dead man's sash. Now they were both armed and ready.

They moved to the door.

"Two must still be upstairs with the hostages," Sandor said. "Two presumably still on the roof, and these two here."

"Leaving four armed hostiles."

Sandor nodded. "But where?"

Garinger pointed to the desk. "Time to call for help?"

Sandor went over and picked up the cell phone. "Not sure what kind of help we want," he said. "Once the shooting starts those people upstairs are done."

"It's at least worth letting them know our situation."

"I guess that's the playbook move." Sandor hit the 'redial' function. "Let's do it."

CHAPTER 67

Outside the Refugee Camp near the Syrian border

Wilson was stunned to hear Sandor's voice on the cell line that had been dedicated for use with Farashi. He promptly patched in Randall.

"We're listening," the general said.

Sandor provided a brief sit-rep and confirmed the information he had previously conveyed in code during the call to Wilson. "No telling how soon the others will be in here to check on us." He was speaking in a whisper. "I'm concerned that if a shot is fired down here the guards upstairs are going to take out the hostages."

"Maybe not," Wilson said. "Cristo is back here at the base, claims he made a deal with Farashi. Got them to accept currency and reduce the number to fifty million Euros in exchange for safe return of all the hostages."

"And Cristo claims to have the money in place?"

"Between London and Hollywood, he says they have it covered."

"I assume he's making the arrangements for the payment as we speak."

"He's lining that up right now."

"Naturally," Sandor said. "So I suppose the good news is that Garinger and I are the only ones they'll want to kill."

Raabe, who was still with the general, said, "I'm getting the DD on this call. You need to be brought up to speed."

As Byrnes was patched in, Raabe told Sandor he was right about Cristo. He described their conversation in the mosque, then told him that Farashi and Gabir had vanished.

"What about the threatened beheading at sundown tonight?" Sandor asked.

"Cristo claims he got Farashi to agree to call it off, based on their ransom deal. Part of their play-acting."

"How do we know his people here got that message? How do we know they won't go through with it anyway?"

"We don't," Byrnes admitted.

"It's been two hours, and I'm almost certain there's been no contact here from Farashi," Raabe said. "You should also know that four armed drones controlled by the base in Niamey have gone rogue."

Sandor drew a deep breath to calm himself. This was time for clear-headed action, not rage. "This all fits with our suspicions about the work Remmell was doing. Farashi is not coming back because he's arranged to kill everyone he left behind. The hostages, his own men, and as many people in this refugee camp as he can take out. Remember this, he sees everyone in this compound as a traitor, and killing them serves his purpose of spreading terror and sending his bloody message."

"Then why even bother to have Cristo negotiate the ransom terms?" Randall asked.

"That's easy," Sandor said. "First, it gave Farashi a means of escape. Second, they probably think Cristo can orchestrate the transfer of funds before the drones hit. This way Farashi gets to keep the money *and* score a huge victory in the name of Allah."

Craig Raabe said, "Sandor is right. At this point, there's no chance they intend to let anyone go." Returning his attention to his fellow agent, he said, "Jordan, you said the hostages are upstairs, backs to the outside wall. Small windows above them, two guards facing those windows. That right?"

"Correct," Sandor said.

"What if we bring in snipers on a couple of Apaches, take the guys out on the roof and see if we can get a clean shot at the two guards through the windows upstairs?"

"That could work. Once we hear the choppers coming, Garinger and I can bust out of here, remove the hostiles on the ground level, then head upstairs for the hostages. Problem is the position of the ventilation windows up there. They don't give our snipers a line of sight inside the room, and I have no doubt those guards have orders to shoot the hostages at the first sign of trouble."

Given those risks, no one was prepared to approve that plan of attack, at least not yet.

Sandor asked, "How long do we have until the drones get close enough to fire?"

"Not sure," Raabe answered. "Best guess is less than twenty minutes before the missiles are in range."

"Then the clock is running out," Sandor told them. "And it won't be long till the guy Farashi left in charge comes in to check on us."

"What about lobbing in tear gas," Raabe suggested.

"Won't work fast enough to prevent the guards upstairs from firing," Sandor said. "But gas is not a bad idea. General, what if your men can get close enough to pump nerve gas into the building? Knock everyone out before they know what hit them?"

"Getting a truck close enough will be difficult," Randall told them. "They still have two lookouts on the roof."

"Take out the damn sentries," Sandor said. "Use a chopper from long range, take them out with a couple of head shots using suppressors. No one inside will hear it or know what happened, at least not soon enough to act. Their Achilles' heel is the lack of windows on the ground floor of this warehouse. They rely on the men upstairs for their intel. Take those two out, then approach from the rear, it could give you enough time to start pumping a non-lethal gas like fentanyl into the building."

"It's a big building, and we'd need time to get everything in position," Randall said. "Not even sure what sort of chemical agents we have that wouldn't kill everyone inside. Including you."

"The general is right," Raabe pointed out. "Gases like fentanyl are not an exact science. Too much of it could kill everyone in the building."

Byrnes said, "Look we all agree time is tight on every level. Give us a couple of minutes Sandor. Will you be able to call back?"

"Only if I'm still breathing. What's being done about the drones?"

"We're working on it," the DD said. "Meanwhile, if you can't get back to us, you and Garinger listen for choppers. If they come, you take appropriate action. If you're engaged by hostiles in the meantime, do whatever you need to do to protect yourselves and the hostages. Everyone understands your position."

"Roger that," Sandor said, then hung up and turned to Garinger. "Something about this feels wrong. I've been played from start to finish." He paused. "Assuming we're near the finish."

"You mean Cristo?"

"Cristo for sure. But there have to be others. Hassan told me they're not going to let him leave here alive. The question is who is 'they'?"

"Maybe he just meant Cristo and Farashi?"

"Maybe. But there seem to be more moving parts to it than that. My friend Lerner tracks me down in New York and two different hit teams come at him. The woman in Bermuda and Colville's nephew are murdered. Those men in London take Beth."

Garinger responded with a nervous look. "I realize you want to figure all of that out, sir, but I think our problems here are a bit more immediate."

Sandor nodded, then had a look at the two bodies on the floor. "Drag those two behind the desk where they can't be seen when someone opens the door. See if they're carrying knives. Might be useful. And Garinger, I already told you to stop calling me 'sir.' You do it again, you won't have to worry about Farashi's men shooting you."

CHAPTER 68

U.S. Army Camp, Mosul

While events accelerated inside and outside the refugee camp, Eduardo Cristo was seated at the front table in the briefing room at the Army base in Mosul. He had completed an interview with Wilson and his staff, professing astonishment at the apparent disappearance of Farashi and Gabir and expressing his belief that the two leaders of the terrorist group would soon be located. Now he was leading a discussion with Alan Goldberg of Freshwood Studios, together with the others who had come bearing pledges to help save Amanda Jensen, Dedalus and—only because the terrorists had taken them along for the ride—the other hostages.

Cristo presented his sanitized version of his meeting at the mosque and was instantly hailed a hero. Not only had he persuaded the terrorists to forego their impossible demand that the ransom be paid in gold, but he had reduced the amount from one hundred million dollars to fifty million Euros.

Regardless of the ethical and geopolitical issues, money was money, and this was all good news.

"One of the key parameters," Cristo told them, "is that we must move with dispatch. Who among you has the ability to order the wiring of the funds you have accumulated?"

Their lead financial agent, Greg Kearney, was introduced. He was a handsome man of around forty with a California tan and movie-star looks, not at all the traditional bookish type Cristo expected from central casting, and certainly not of the ethnicity he anticipated.

"We have the funds in several different accounts," Kearney explained. "As I'm sure you can understand, none of the contributors is releasing their money until we're sure a deal is in place."

Cristo did not hide his look of concern. "You all must understand the importance of timing here."

"We do," Kearney assured him. "The transfer of funds can be initiated from each of the trustee accounts." Then he turned to Goldberg. "But there is an overriding issue."

"Yes," Goldberg said, taking the cue and standing to face the assembled group. "Dr. Cristo has explained the circumstances, and the commitment of WHI to fund fifteen million Euros. Our group is prepared to provide the balance, which we will pay in dollars equal to the thirty-five million Euros. We assume that will be satisfactory."

"Yes," Cristo said. "I discussed that detail with them."

"Then the matter before us is how we ensure the safe return of the hostages in exchange for these payments."

Everyone turned to the front of the room to face Cristo. He remained seated as he said, "Of course, of course. That is the most important thing."

"So what arrangements were made?" Goldberg asked.

"As soon as the funds have been transferred to the specified accounts," Cristo said as he held up the sheet of paper he claimed Farashi had given him, "the hostages will be released."

The uproar among the various participants was immediate. These were Hollywood people, and they were only too familiar with deals that had a string of green lights all the way to the sound stage before falling apart.

Goldberg held up a hand and quieted them. "Dr. Cristo, these men are terrorists. They murdered the leader of this mission in cold blood, along with several others. They then kidnapped five people and just today threatened to behead one of them. Forgive me if I have no confidence in their assurances that the hostages will be released *after* the ransom is paid."

Cristo allowed himself a slight smile. "Naturally I understand your concerns. However, there are still ten or so men inside that building. Their safe passage out of the camp will be the *quid pro quo* for the return of the hostages."

Goldberg shook his head. "Suicide is regarded as an act of valor by these lunatics. What if we wire the funds and then they shoot the hostages and engage in a standoff with the troops at the camp?"

"Why would they have negotiated for the payment of the ransom if they are not going to survive to use the money?" Cristo asked.

Goldberg fixed him with a look that said he did not believe Cristo could possibly be that naïve. "You say there are only ten or so in the building. All reports indicate there were more than thirty involved in the kidnapping. God only knows how many more of their ilk are hiding out there in the desert. Now we've been told the men you met with have vanished. Believe me, the survivors will find enough evil uses for our money once this is over. Our own government is determined that we not make the payment for that very reason. Compounding the mistake by paying the ransom and not recovering the hostages would be an unmitigated disaster." He shook his head. "No. We are men of honor. We are not murderers or kidnappers or suicide bombers.

We are a group of businessmen willing to pay an outrageous sum to save these lives. We are prepared to prove the funds are available. We are even willing to agree upon the appointment of an objective third party to hold the money. However, we are not willing to trust these people to keep their word." The others, seated behind Goldberg, voiced their support. "You must contact this leader Farashi and tell him the hostages must be released before he receives the payment."

"Impossible," Cristo said.

This was clearly not the response Goldberg expected. "Impossible? It seems to me, if they really want to exchange the hostages for the ransom, they will be receptive to a further discussion about the details."

"Ladies and gentlemen, don't you think I went through all of this with Farashi when we met? He was intractable in his demand. He conceded a substantial portion of the ransom and agreed to accept currency. I have taken this as far as I can."

"Very well," Goldberg said. "Since I represent the group funding seventy percent of the ransom, we will have to speak with him."

"I think you're making a huge mistake," Cristo warned. "We are at a very delicate point in this process. Need I remind you that my meeting with him narrowly averted his threat to murder one of the hostages at sundown today?"

"You are to be commended for that and for everything else you have done. But we need to know the hostages are free before we fund, and I am prepared to tell him that."

"Forgive my bluntness, Mr. Goldberg, but an American Jew is the last person with whom Farashi will negotiate."

"Your bluntness is forgiven. That's why we'll have Kearney speak with him." Cristo did not reply, suddenly understanding that the choice of their financial spokesman was no accident.

The two men stared at each other until Goldberg said, "I believe we've accomplished all we can here. It's time to bring Mr. Wilson back into the conversation."

CHAPTER 69

Outside Niamey, Niger

Sandor had asked what was being done about the drones, and Deputy Director Byrnes had the same question. As soon their call with Sandor ended, Randall set off to put the pieces in place for a military rescue, as and when that was authorized. At the same time, the task force in D.C. reconnected with the base in Niamey where Col. Brighton, Remmell and Coman were gathered for the videoconference.

"Report," Forelli ordered from the White House.

"We have lost control of three UAV's," Brighton replied. "We managed to scramble a signal on the fourth, engineered a forced crash in the desert. We have Blackhawks en route now to recover the remnants and weapons."

"What's being done about the other three?"

"Our technicians have been working with Coman and Remmell, trying to regain control. It appears whoever has taken over the remote piloting of these drones has successfully infiltrated our system, identified our codes and overridden the failsafe mechanisms."

"Failsafe?" Forelli barked. "I hope you're joking, using that term, colonel."

"We're doing all we can on this end, sir."

Bebon from the FBI asked, "We must have satellites tracking them, right? Why can't we just shoot them down, use ground to air missiles?"

Brighton turned to Coman for help. "These UAV's are very small devices," the engineer explained. "And they're programmed to evade attack. Our ground to air missiles operate either on radar coordinates or heat-seeking sensors. The drones are small, fast, agile and generate very little heat."

"You're telling me we can't shoot the goddamned things out of the sky?" Bebon demanded.

"We can, but we need to get close enough to hit them with short range anti-aircraft technology."

"Is that it?" Bebon demanded. "We have to wait until they're close enough to launch a strike?"

"Not necessarily, but we have to get close enough to them to be effective."

"There are other options," Brighton jumped back in. "We've alerted the Air Force and they've scrambled F-16's to see if they can track and shoot down the drones."

Forelli was not pleased. "The intel you provided us earlier is that these rogue drones appear to be circling toward the refugee camp northeast of Mosul, that right?"

"Yes sir, that's still our best guess."

"You're telling us that armed, United States Air Force fighter jets are going to be flying along the border of Syria, possibly entering Syrian airspace."

"That may be necessary if they're going to chase down these UAV's."

"Perfect," Forelli said, practically falling back in his chair. "You know what the Syrians are going to say and do about that, Colonel? They're going to accuse us of violating their airspace with military aircraft. Then we're going to have to claim that we're making an effort to possibly—and I emphasize possibly—prevent an attack on a group of refugees by parties unknown. Then they're going to say those refugees have already been declared enemies of their state."

No one spoke for a moment, until Byrnes said, "We all recognize that there are serious political implications to this crisis, but we need to remain focused on our principal goal here. We have five hostages and two of my agents in that warehouse, which is surrounded by thousands of individuals about whom I make no judgment with regard to national loyalties. All I know is that we need to do everything possible to prevent a catastrophic attack on the site."

"Damn right," Molly Stroup from NSA chimed in. "Someone give us our best options. Any chance we can clear out the target area before a strike?"

Major Bretter, who was sitting in for Randall, spoke up. "Evacuating the camp is not practical. Not only would it take too long, but these refugees have seen the military buildup around the complex. Anything we do to alarm them further would result in utter chaos. You agree Frank?"

"I do," Wilson said.

Bretter explained, "If we make such an attempt we'd still be left with the problem of what the hostiles will do to the hostages and your two agents inside the warehouse, once they see a mass evacuation taking place."

"All right," Byrnes said, returning his attention to Brighton and the two engineers.

"You're the experts. As Molly said, give us our best options."

"The jets are the first line of defense," Brighton said. "We're doing all we can to track the altered flight paths of the three drones, try to take them out with Sidewinder air-to-air strikes. I would also recommend that we surround the camp with assault helicopters, Apaches, Super Cobras, whatever General Randall has at his disposal. Create a perimeter with infrared missiles at the ready. Hopefully take the UAV's down before they can fire. I assume you already have ground to air capabilities in place. If the weapons are launched, we might still be able to shoot the missiles themselves out of the sky."

Frank Wilson was worried about that approach, and he said so. "Once we make a lot of noise mobilizing choppers and hardware, there's no telling what the terrorists inside the warehouse might do."

"If you want to stop the attack, I don't think you have a choice," Brighton said.

Peter Forelli agreed. "Let's prepare to throw everything we can at this, just as Colonel Brighton suggests, but hold off moving too close until we have no other option. Now that Farashi has disappeared, whatever he planned cannot be good. The last possible result we want is for these people to be blown to pieces by one of our own weapons."

CHAPTER 70

Inside the warehouse of the Refugee
Camp near the Syrian border

Sandor figured he and Garinger were out of time. "Any second Elazar or one of the other goons is going to walk through that door to check on us," he said. "We need to control the how and when."

"You have an idea?"

"I do."

Garinger had retrieved the knives the guards had been carrying. Sandor chose the karambit, with its curved blade, while Garinger held onto a hefty, straight-edged model that resembled a Ka-Bar.

Sandor held his up and tested the sharpness of the point with his thumb. "You need to go back and sit on the floor where you were," he told Garinger. "Keep the knife, the automatic, and your hands behind your back. I'll stand behind the door. The first man through is mine.

No telling how many will come, but my guess is more than one. We've got to take out as many as we can before any shots are fired."

Garinger looked at him with obvious skepticism. "I'll be a sitting duck, there on the floor. What if they haven't gotten the memo about not firing weapons?"

"Surprise is the key. They'll walk in and only see you, no one else. That'll give us the edge. As soon as I move, you're on your feet."

Garinger nodded very slowly.

"Your idea about knockout gas, what about that?"

"You heard Randall. We'll all be dead before they can organize it."

Garinger's head was still moving slowly up and down.

"Trust me," Sandor said.

"You told Byrnes you'd call back."

Sandor glanced at the door. "No time left, I can just feel it. We have to act now."

"How are you going to draw them in?"

"Easy," Sandor said, then pointed to the desk.

As Garinger took his spot on the floor, Sandor picked up one of the phones, turned up the volume, and downloaded its number. Then he punched that number into the second phone and placed it back on the desk. By the time the first cell began to ring he had already opened the door halfway and was standing behind it, waiting.

By the fourth ring they could hear the footsteps coming their way.

As Sandor predicted, Elazar was the first to respond, but he was not alone. He pushed his way into the office followed by two of the others.

Elazar entered, grumbling something in his native tongue that Sandor assumed was a complaint about the guards not answering the call. Then he stopped in his tracks.

The bodies of the two sentries were out of view, hidden behind the desk. One of the two Americans was gone. The only person in the office was the second American, still seated on the floor. Garinger smiled up at him and, for an instant, all three Arabs seemed frozen in place.

Sandor moved swiftly, coming out from behind the door, knife raised, and in a single motion spun the tall Syrian to the side and, with a vicious lateral movement, slashed his throat from ear to ear with the sharp, semi-circular blade. Elazar clutched at the lethal gash as blood began spurting out, but Sandor pushed him to the floor as he went for the second man. Using all of his strength, Sandor shoved the tip of the karambit into the center of the man's chest, driving it deep and then jerking it upward, ripping through his lungs and heart. The dying man let go of the automatic that was slung across his shoulder, reaching up with both hands as if he might somehow hold together the gaping wound through which the last few moments of his life now flowed.

Meanwhile, as Sandor was ripping Elazar's throat open, Garinger sprang to his feet and raced forward, driving the long, serrated knife into the neck of the third man. In less than forty seconds, all three terrorists were on the ground, dead or dying, and Sandor had closed the door.

"Check to be sure none of them has a finger anywhere near a trigger," Sandor said, then went to the desk and turned off the cell phone.

"All clear," Garinger said.

Sandor came over and looked down at the three bodies. "Nice work."

"You think the others heard anything?"

"No way of knowing, depends where they are. Down here, checking the perimeter, upstairs with the two goons watching the hostages, who knows? Hopefully there are still two on the roof." He looked at Garinger. "You speak some Arabic."

"I do."

"In a minute you're going to call out to them. First let's take the weapons from these three and move the bodies away from the door."

Just then they heard a noise from outside and, even through the walls of the warehouse, the sound was unmistakable.

"Choppers in the distance," Garinger said.

"Time to make that call."

Again using the phone Farashi used to contact Wilson, Sandor hit the recall number.

"Wilson," the man from State said after one ring.

"Sandor. Situation here has changed, I need to report in."

CHAPTER 71

Outside the Refugee Camp
near the Syrian border

General Randall had two Apache helicopters positioned less than a mile from the refugee camp, which he ordered airborne. He began arranging additional support, working from his field tent, when the phone rang and Frank Wilson tied him in to the call with the D.C. task force and Sandor.

CIA Director Walsh told Sandor to make his report, and he did.

"So," Byrnes said when his agent was finished, "you believe there are still five hostiles in and around the building?"

"Affirmative. If I can get a confirmation from General Randall's people in the sky that two are still on the roof, Garinger and I can take a run at the remaining three and try and cut the hostages loose. Right now I can't be certain of the position of the other three inside the building." He shot a look at Garinger, who was standing by the door, listening for any activity.

Garinger shook his head.

"Randall here. I have visual confirmation two lookouts are still on the roof, but when the Apaches flew into view they started to move around."

"General, it might be helpful if the choppers pulled back for now," Sandor said. "We need those two men to keep their positions on the roof so we can make our play inside."

"Roger that, calling it in now."

Almost immediately the sound of the helicopters began to recede.

"Where are we on the drones?" Sandor asked.

"We've been playing hide and seek with them," Byrnes told him. "Right now they're over Syria heading southeast."

"Towards us," Sandor said.

"Yes, you were correct," Byrnes said. "We believe your location *is* the target."

"I'm signing off," Sandor said. "We've got work to do." He hung up and turned to Garinger. "Open the door a crack and say something that'll bring him in," he said.

Garinger opened the door and, in as deep a voice as he could muster called out in Arabic, "Come here."

CHAPTER 72

U.S. Army Camp, Mosul

Frank Wilson was doing his best to juggle his frequent communications with the task force, assisting with the operational issues being spearheaded by General Randall outside the refugee camp, and managing the ransom negotiations between Eduardo Cristo and the group from Hollywood.

That last element was the most frustrating.

After their meeting with Cristo, Goldberg and his colleagues insisted on getting Wilson involved. When the latest call with D.C. ended, Wilson agreed to have a brief discussion, provided it was limited to the two principals—he was not about to confront the entire cast of characters when time was so precious.

Goldberg and Cristo were shown into his office, but before they could even be seated Wilson said, "Let me make this clear one more time." He gestured to his assistant, who was about to leave the room. "I want you to remain here to witness this conversation," he told the sergeant. Turning back to his guests, he said, "The United States does not pay ransom money to terrorists. We disapprove of what you are doing, but will not interfere. If the two of you have differences on how to handle this situation, I will not act as your referee."

Cristo displayed his most charming smile as he took his seat. "Then please consider this an opportunity for us to apprise you of the situation."

Wilson nodded, then listened impatiently as Cristo explained that the funds were in place, the banks designated for receipt of the funds had been identified, and he was ready to initiate the wire transfers. When he held up the paper listing the accounts, Wilson took it from him and asked his aide to make a copy on the machine in the corner of the room.

"The problem," Goldberg interrupted, "is that we will not release our share of the money unless and until the hostages have been released."

Wilson waited.

Cristo said, "Farashi was quite specific about this. He does not trust us to deliver the money once these people have been set free. We have no reason to think he will not free them once he is paid."

Wilson had to be careful about what he said next. He knew the truth about Cristo, and while the status of the crisis was changing moment-to-moment, he had to work at keeping his very best poker face. "Dr. Cristo, I respectfully disagree. There is every reason to doubt these terrorists will keep their word. They have proved themselves to be kidnappers and cold-blooded murderers. As recently as just a few hours ago, they threatened to behead one of the hostages, in case anyone has forgotten that detail."

"Which I averted by dealing with their leader."

"For which you are owed a debt of gratitude by all involved. Nevertheless, while I am not authorized to take an official position on your disagreement, in my personal opinion it would seem unwise for the ransom to be paid until the safe return of the hostages has been guaranteed. As I say, that decision is yours and I will have no part in it."

This time Cristo did not bother to hide his frustration. "You are aware, I take it, that any delay will be putting the lives of every hostage at risk."

"Their lives are at risk because they were kidnapped by a band of terrorists. My role is to do what I can to help bring them home. Now, if there's nothing else, events are occurring in real time and I am extremely busy."

Goldberg suddenly appeared even more anxious than Cristo. "Are you saying circumstances have changed?"

"I have said no such thing."

"If the level of danger has increased, I think we have a right to know."

Wilson did not hide his surprise. "What right is that, Mr. Goldberg? You come here, brandishing your checkbook, disregarding United States policy, and now you're asserting some unspecified right to be informed of our efforts to resolve this crisis in spite of your interference." He stood. "Gentlemen, this meeting is over."

Outside, as they made their way back to the briefing room, Cristo said, "You had better talk with your people. Mr. Wilson is covering his ass and protecting the policy of his State Department. He is telling us nothing, just trying to scare us off. You and I came here to pay for the release of these people, and that is what I mean to do."

Goldberg nodded. "Give me a few minutes. Let me talk to the group."

Cristo patted Goldberg on the back. "Time is short, but I trust you will come to the right decision. I'll wait in the commissary." Then Cristo walked off, leaving Goldberg to do what he must. As Cristo knew better than anyone, time was short. He had already secured the fifteen million Euros from WHI. He was not about to give up on the thirty five million Euros from the Jews in Hollywood.

CHAPTER 73

Inside the warehouse of the Refugee Camp near the Syrian border

As they waited inside the room, Sandor had taken the same position behind the door, but this time Garinger was not sitting on the floor. He stood with his back pressed against the wall, just to the other side of the entrance. Once again, they were preparing for close-order combat.

The man coming through the door had his weapon at the ready. The command to "Come here," had not been given by a familiar voice, and he was prepared for action. Even so, the sight of his three fallen comrades, lying dead on the floor in a growing pool of blood, brought him up short.

Garinger did not wait for him to react, lashing out across his right wrist with the large knife, causing the Syrian to let go of the automatic. The man managed a short, guttural scream before Sandor silenced him as he had Elazar, with a lethal slash across his throat, dropping him to the ground with the others.

"Let's go," Sandor said.

They had their automatics in hand, with safeties off and extra magazines at the ready, as they charged into the open area of the warehouse.

It was empty, but the man's shout must have been heard upstairs—they heard the sound of chair legs scraping on the floor above them, followed by a discussion between the two guards.

Sandor whispered, "No reason to be quiet going up, but we don't want to spook them by running. Let's walk as if we're two of their own." Then he led the way to the staircase and up.

Just before they reached the top, one of the guards stepped onto the landing. His expression was a mixture of surprise and confusion, but Sandor was not waiting for him to sort things out. He hit him in the chest with a spray from the AK-47, then raced up the last few stairs two at a time, Garinger right behind him.

The remaining guard was standing in front of the terrified hostages, waving his weapon in their direction. He was saying something in Arabic, which Sandor guessed was along the lines of, "Stop or I'll shoot them all," but Sandor was not there to negotiate, nor was he about to wait for Garinger to translate. He fired at the man's head, ripping his skull to shreds.

Unfortunately, as the guard fell to the ground he managed to get off a series of shots, hitting two of the hostages—Dedalus and Orr.

"Goddamnit," Sandor cursed through gritted teeth.

At the sound of the shooting, the men on the roof could be heard moving, likely getting ready to make their way down.

Garinger said, "We've got company."

Sandor turned to Sternlich. "How do they get up there?"

Pointing to the end of the long room, Sternlich said, "That hatch there." Just beneath the opening were rungs set against the wall.

"Get everyone downstairs," Sandor told Garinger. "I'll wait for our friends to show up." He then moved toward the far end of the room, his gaze and gun trained on the trap door.

"Let's go, let's go," Garinger urged the hostages, and they began to scramble to their feet. Their hands were still bound, and he used the large combat knife to cut each of them free, then had a look at the two wounded men. Dedalus had taken a bullet to his left shoulder, but it did not appear to have hit any major artery. Although he was already pale and shaken, he managed to stand on his own. Orr had fared worse, and blood was already spreading across his chest.

Garinger looked to Hassan. "Help me get him out of here," he said.

They lifted the injured man, each supporting him under an arm, and headed for the staircase.

Sandor heard the roof hatch open. One of the snipers had decided to stick his head out to see if it was safe to come down.

It was not.

All of the hostages spun around when Sandor opened fire, hitting the man in the face with several shots. They then watched as the sentry fell through the opening and landed on the floor. Sandor did not wait to see what the next shooter might do. He moved just below the hatch and fired upward through the flimsy roof, aiming at the areas all around the opening until he heard a man scream out in pain. He continued firing at that spot until his magazine was empty, then replaced it and handed the weapon to Sternlich.

"Billy, you cover us, just in case that other sonuvabitch up there isn't dead."

Sternlich stared at his friend as if he had just been asked to climb Mt. Everest in flip-flops. "Are you kidding?"

Sandor turned Sternlich so his back was to the wall, then aimed the muzzle of the automatic the newspaperman was holding so it was pointed directly at the hatch. "You see anything, you just squeeze this trigger."

Sternlich pushed his glasses up the bridge of his nose with his left hand, then nodded without speaking.

As Sandor pulled out the .45 he had taken from one of the men downstairs, he noticed Amanda Jensen. She was at the landing, watching him.

"Get down the stairs," he shouted at her, but she paused for another moment.

Staring into his eyes, she mouthed the words, "Thank you," then turned and followed the others down.

Sandor smiled. She had not screamed or carried on, not when bullets were flying or blood was being spilled. *Might have to change my mind about actresses*, he thought. *Or at least about her.* Then, holding the automatic pistol at the ready to back up Sternlich, he pulled the cell phone from his pocket with his other hand and called Wilson.

CHAPTER 74

Outside the Refugee Camp
near the Syrian border

Until a few minutes ago, when he decided to make a move on the guards, Sandor felt things had been moving at a glacial pace, which was not at all his style. Now events were unfolding at warp speed, a pace which he not only preferred, but at which he excelled.

The gunfire had been heard outside the warehouse, in the neighboring area of the camp, and panic was quickly spreading. Ironically, those closest to the warehouse seemed the least concerned. They could tell that the shooting had occurred inside the building, the battle had been extremely brief, and it now appeared to be over. The further from the action people were, it seemed the wilder the stories were and the more frightened the refugees became. Chaos began to reign.

When Wilson received Sandor's call, he connected Randall, and the two men listened to a quick summary of what had just occurred. Randall dispatched two U.S. Army personnel carriers and an ambulance, and the three vehicles were soon speeding through the frenzied scene inside the refugee camp until they reached the front of the warehouse.

Sandor was still upstairs with Sternlich when the trucks arrived. He took the automatic rifle from his friend and emptied the magazine through the roof near the hatch.

"If he wasn't dead before," he said, "he is now. Let's go."

Downstairs, Sandor ordered the two overhead garage doors raised so the rescue vehicles could enter. Once they were inside, the doors were pulled shut again, keeping everyone out of view from the refugees and anyone else in or around the camp. Medics tended to Dedalus and Orr, then placed them on stretchers while soldiers helped the others board the two trucks. The doors were raised, allowing the ambulance and first truck to take off. The second personnel carrier pulled outside, where Sandor jumped down and pulled the door to the warehouse shut.

Then his vehicle also sped away, all three now heading for the base at Mosul.

In the truck with Sandor were Garinger and Sternlich.

Turning to his friend, Sandor had a look at the bruise on the side of his head. "You all right?" he asked.

"Whole lot better than I was," Sternlich said.

Sandor nodded, then had a look through the canvas cover at the back of the truck. "We're going to have to do something about getting these people under control," he said, although, for his purposes, he didn't want that to happen just yet.

As the truck raced ahead, Sandor got back on the phone and was promptly tied in to the task force. The first thing he did was deflect any congratulations. "This mission is far from over," he told them. Then he asked about the UAV's.

Craig Raabe was also on the call, and his update was less than optimistic.

Peter Forelli added, "It sounds like we're almost out of time on the drones."

General Randall said, "The good news is, now that Sandor cleared out the hostages, we can throw everything we have into counter-measures. No need to tip-toe around anymore."

The others voiced their agreement.

"Where's Cristo?" Sandor asked.

"Here at the base," Wilson told him. "He's working out some financial details with the group from California. I'd better tell them to forget about the ransom, before someone starts sending out funds."

"Hold on," Sandor said. "I have a request."

"We're listening."

"I don't want Cristo to know the hostages have been released. In fact, I don't think you should tell anyone at the base they've been freed, except the honcho from L.A."

"Alan Goldberg?"

"Right. If you think you can trust him, Frank, I can use his help. But he's got to understand he's being read in here only in the strictest confidence. As for Cristo, arrange a soft sequester. Don't give him any idea he's been cut off, just be sure the only people he speaks with at the base are you and Goldberg."

"Go on," Wilson said.

"Tell Cristo there's been a shooting at the warehouse, we've concluded we're out of time. Tell him the State Department has instructed you to act as intermediary to transfer the ransom funds, to expedite the process. You'll take control of all the money and you'll claim that you sent the wires. The key is that he cannot know the hostages have been released. You with me on this?"

"I'm not sure," Wilson admitted. "Putting aside whether my superiors are going to buy into this, how the hell am I going to keep a lid on the hostage rescue? There are all sorts of media vans outside the camp. They saw our trucks rushing in and coming out."

"True, but we loaded those vehicles inside the warehouse, out of view. No one has a visual on whether any of the hostages were being released, and no one has made a statement yet, correct?"

"That's correct," Peter Forelli said.

"Then no one is sure what happened. Shots were fired and people saw an ambulance and a couple of trucks come and go. We only need to hold the press off for an hour or so."

"What are you up to Sandor?" Director Walsh asked.

"Sir, I believe we have one critical issue and a couple of loose ends."

"Go on."

"The immediate order of business is intercepting the UAV's. General Randall is doing all he can about that, and his odds have improved since the hostages are safe and can take full counter-measures. As for Cristo, I'm convinced that part of his deal with Farashi is to see that the ransom gets paid before the drones hit. Craig, we monitoring his calls?"

"All over it."

"Good. Once word is given that the money has been wired, I guarantee you he'll phone in a signal to Farashi or someone else. That's when they'll fly those UAV's into range and launch the missiles. And guess who's going to get blamed?"

"We will," Forelli said. "As you say, they're our drones, our missiles, and our failure to control our own weapons."

"That's my take on it, sir. The world will mourn the deaths of those poor refugees, the hostages, and especially Jensen and Dedalus, while the entire Arab community, and the rest of our enemies worldwide, will be pointing their fingers at Washington. The headline will be, *U.S. Drones Murder Thousands of Innocent People*. Farashi and his ISIS friends in Ansar al-Thar will become a footnote."

"But if I read you right," Walsh said, "you would be deliberately causing Cristo to call in the attack."

"Not really, sir, it's actually a timing issue. As soon as word gets out the hostages have been freed, they'll launch the strike on the camp anyway. Let's face it, we can't keep a lid on the release of the hostages for long."

"Agreed," Wilson said. "Too many people involved here, too many journalists with iPhones."

"As far as the UAV's," Sandor continued, "they can't operate them much longer without the risk that we'll locate and neutralize them."

"All the same," Walsh said, "we have to proceed with caution."

"That's my main point sir. Caution dictates we move quickly. General Randall's men are as ready as they're going to be to shoot down the drones or neutralize the missiles, am I right General?"

"Affirmative. We've got assault helicopters in the air, F-16's nearby, and ground to air hardware in position."

"Sir, I believe Farashi is going to order the strike, with or without the payment, and it's going to happen soon. He's a terrorist, let's not forget that. Cristo is only his banker. If Cristo fails to get the ransom wired out, Farashi is going to hit the camp anyway. In fact, wherever Farashi is, he may try and phone his men inside the warehouse at some point. It's nearly sundown, and there was a beheading on his calendar. If he calls his men and gets no answer, he'll know the game is up and pull the trigger on the drones."

"I understand," Walsh said. "Then why not simply arrest Cristo?"

"For what? Those taped conversations don't prove enough. I want to catch him in a blatant act." Sandor paused. "Then there's a second reason I want him to believe the money has been sent."

"We're listening," Walsh said.

"Because that's how we're going to catch Farashi."

CHAPTER 75

U.S. Army Camp, Mosul

As soon as they signed off, General Randall called the base and ordered his men to locate and detain Eduardo Cristo. They found him in the commissary, where he had gone to await word on funding from Alan Goldberg. Cristo was told by the head of a small detail that there had been new developments in the hostage crisis, and security was being tightened for his own safety. When Sandor and the others returned to base, the two ambulances made their way directly to the infirmary. Orr had lost a great deal of blood, and his injuries were now considered life-threatening. Dedalus was weak, but they already had him hooked up to an I.V. and the color had returned to his face.

Sandor saw to it that Bill Sternlich was also taken to the medical unit.

"It's just a bruise," he protested.

"I want it looked at all the same," Sandor told him.

Sternlich paused. "After all these years, all of the half-stories, all the hints at what you do. This was something, Jordan. Seeing you in action." He paused again, feeling choked with emotion. "You saved our lives." Sternlich shook his head, as if disbelieving what he had just experienced.

"Yeah, well if you get all dewy-eyed over this, I'm coming back to New York and telling Nadine you're a pussy."

Sternlich managed a weak smile. "Hell you will, pal. You're going to tell her how I held a terrorist at bay with a Kalashnikov."

Meanwhile, in the other truck, Amanda Jensen and Shahid Hassan were told there were procedures that had to be followed. They were driven to a building at the interior of the compound, far from the commissary where Cristo was being held, and generally out of view.

There, they were hurried off the truck and taken inside.

Sandor and Garinger wasted no time making their way to Wilson's office. Goldberg was already waiting for them.

"You fill him in?" Sandor asked.

"Thought it would be best if you did it," Wilson said.

Sandor nodded, then faced Goldberg. "What I'm about to tell you is to be shared with no one. It is a matter of national security, and the lives of hundreds, even thousands of people will depend on how you deal with this information in the next ten minutes."

"The hostages—"

Sandor held up his hand. "I don't want to hear anything you have to say, except whether or not you are prepared to do precisely what I ask."

Goldberg, who had been standing, sat down. "I'll do anything I can to help."

"Good," Sandor said, as he and the others took their seats. "Now listen up."

By the time Sandor was done explaining the situation, Goldberg was dumbstruck. "You mean this Dr. Cristo is working with the terrorists."

"I do."

Goldberg looked at Garinger and then Wilson before turning back to Sandor. "And the hostages are safe? You were the one who rescued them?"

"It doesn't matter who rescued them, the point is they're safe, and now we have to deal with the men who engineered this scheme."

"Which is intended to kill thousands of those poor refugees, not just the hostages?"

Sandor nodded impatiently. "You're an intelligent man, I believe you understand everything I've said. By sharing this with you I have also put you in danger. Not only do you have to play your part with Cristo during the next few minutes, but after this is over I would strongly advise that you never divulge to anyone your role in this."

"Because other members of this terrorist group might come after me."

Sandor responded with a grim look. "Precisely."

"All right. I'll do everything you ask, I just hope I can be convincing."

Sandor forced a smile. "You're from Hollywood, for chrissake."

⊙

After they were done, Wilson cleared his office, then had his assistant arrange to have Goldberg brought back in, along with Cristo. He wanted it to appear they were both being treated the same, being given military escorts, and an explanation that the risk factors had increased.

When the three of them were seated, the soldiers were dismissed and Wilson began.

"The task force believes we have run out of time. Farashi is gone and we have not been able to locate him. There has been a shooting inside the warehouse, and it will not be long before the remaining terrorists take further action. We have no choice but to allow you to pay the ransom."

Cristo was both surprised and relieved. He nodded solemnly. "We are prepared to do what is necessary."

Goldberg said, "We're still unhappy about making payment before the hostages are released. We've been going around and around on the issue for the past half hour."

"Let me be candid," Wilson said. "I am opposed to the payment of this ransom, not just as an expression of my country's policy, but on moral grounds. Nevertheless, we are not being given a choice. Farashi is gone and his men will not countermand his order. If payment is not made and confirmed, the hostages will not be released."

Goldberg shook his head.

"I am not at liberty to share everything I know," Wilson informed them. "But I can tell you there have been certain developments. We have spoken with the man Farashi left in charge. He and his comrades blame us for the disappearance of Farashi. They believe we took Farashi and Gabir prisoner after their meeting with you, Dr. Cristo. This man, Elazar, has made it clear that Farashi left orders to proceed with the threatened beheading tonight if he did not safely return. The only alternative is for you to pay the ransom, end the standoff and give these men safe passage out of the camp. Otherwise, I fear all of the hostages will be murdered."

Goldberg appeared positively stricken. "You're admitting these men are liars and murderers. Obviously none of us want to see harm come to any of the hostages, but paying the ransom under these circumstances and expecting them to be released seems little more than a hope and a prayer."

"We share your concerns, of course. In an effort to deal with the issue, the State Department has suggested that we arrange the wires through our accounts."

Cristo's somber look was suddenly informed by a touch of suspicion as he asked, "In what way will that help?"

"According to the wiring instructions given you by Farashi, the banks are in Yemen and Syria." He lifted the Photostat of the list his assistant had made during their earlier meeting. "If you two arrange a series of private transfers and the hostages are not safely returned, you will have absolutely no chance of retrieving the funds. If, however, the funds come from an official channel such as our State Department, I'm sure you can see that would be another matter entirely."

Cristo knew these banks better than Frank Wilson. They were not about to return money to anyone, let alone the Americans. Still, he wanted to temper his skepticism with the appearance of cooperation. "We want to get this done in the manner most likely to result in the hostages being returned safely, but surely you know that these countries have limited diplomatic relations with the United States."

"Limited, it's true, but there are certain avenues of back-channel communication available to us that will never be available to you."

Cristo sat back in his seat. "What about your policy against the payment of ransom to terrorists?"

"As I am sure you can imagine, this was a subject of considerable debate. The conclusion reached was that we are not paying the ransom, we are merely assisting your organization and Mr. Goldberg's group in a humanitarian effort to save lives."

Goldberg had been watching Cristo carefully and, if he had harbored any doubts about the accuracy of what Jordan Sandor had told him, they were now completely dispelled. He turned back to Wilson "I know you do not have a crystal ball and cannot predict the future, but I must ask for your most sincere and well-considered judgment in this situation. Do you really believe we have no choice but to pay this ransom and hope the terrorists will honor their promise to release the hostages?"

"The only way I can honestly answer that question is to tell you that I believe the hostages will be murdered tonight if we do not make arrangements to pay the ransom. As I have said, with Farashi gone we must assume that the worst possible fate awaits the hostages. These are terrorists who have no compunction about killing and no fear of dying. You must also understand that we are all but out of time."

Goldberg uttered a long, deep sigh as if finally receiving some terrible news he had been doing his best to avoid. "My group has been divided over this issue, as I explained, but it is evident we cannot wait any longer, we must move forward. I will provide you with our account information so we can pass the funds through whatever facility you think will best expedite the process." He shook his head. "Call these bastards and tell them our money is coming. Don't allow anyone else to be murdered."

Cristo looked from one man to the other, trying to weigh this combination of good and bad news. On the one hand, Goldberg and his associates were finally being moved off the dime—by Frank Wilson, of all people, the most unlikely of sources—and they were going to release the money they were holding. On the other, he was distinctly uncomfortable with the transfers being handled through the State Department.

Not realizing how deep in thought he appeared, he had to be roused by Wilson. "Dr. Cristo, you have a question?"

"Not a question, a concern. As a representative of WHI, I am not clear that I can simply release fifteen million Euros without proper authorization and paperwork."

"Do you really believe it's less safe to transfer that money to the State Department than directly to accounts controlled by terrorists? If so, I am certain we can get your Mr. Killian on the phone to request authorization. Will that be necessary?"

Cristo reverted to his gleaming smile. "No, of course not."

"Then you see the logic in having us make the transfers?"

"I believe I do."

Wilson stood, forcing the other two to get to their feet. "In that case gentlemen, I suggest you act immediately to get me the necessary information. Meanwhile, I will call Washington and we can begin to make this happen."

"What about calling Farashi's people to let them know the payments are being made?" Cristo asked.

"Of course," Wilson said, wanting to kick himself in the ass. "As soon as you leave, contacting the warehouse to confirm the ransom is being paid will be our first order of business."

CHAPTER 76

U.S. Army Camp, Mosul

There was obviously no call being made to the warehouse, since all of the terrorists there were dead. General Randall assigned a squad at the refugee camp to sweep the interior and roof, and they had already confirmed there were no survivors. Randall ordered them to keep the garage door closed, secure the perimeter and not allow anyone else inside. He also instructed them to be on alert for his further order to return to the command center outside the fence. If a missile strike was coming, he did not need any of the men under his command becoming martyrs. He would leave that to Allah's army of renegades.

Meanwhile, Cristo and Goldberg returned to Wilson's office with their information for the source accounts and routing numbers they needed to wire their funds to the special State Department account that had been established to handle this transaction. Unknown to Cristo, that account was actually controlled directly by the CIA.

After that transfer was accomplished, Wilson allowed them to remain in the room as he emailed the data for the terrorists' list of destination accounts to someone he described as being in charge of international finances at State, but who was actually one of Byrnes' men on the second floor at Langley. It did not take long for the CIA to confirm receipt of the funds from Goldberg and Cristo, then send back fake identification and routing numbers that purported to ensure the outgoing wires to banks in Syria and Yemen had been made. That done, Wilson said he had been empowered to convey this data to Farashi's man Elazar, inside the warehouse.

"Well," Cristo said, "it would seem my work here is done. I will leave you to the business of taking custody of the hostages." He paused. "Might I be provided transportation to the airfield? It's time for me to return to London and report to Mr. Killian. I've just spent fifteen million Euros of the Institute's money, and I believe he'll want me to provide the details in person."

Wilson's respect for Jordan Sandor went up yet another notch. Sandor had correctly predicted several of Cristo's moves, and he was also right about this one—as soon as the money was wired out, Sandor said Cristo would make a hasty departure. According to their script, Wilson promptly agreed.

"I'll have a jeep take you to your plane," he said, "I'll have my assistant escort you to the briefing room. You can wait there while we make the arrangements." Then he directed himself to the man from Los Angeles. "What about you and your group Goldberg?"

Once again, according to plan, Goldberg said, "I think we'd prefer to wait and greet the hostages. Perhaps you could have us transported to the camp, so we could be with them as soon as they're released."

It was clear nothing could make Cristo happier, and he told them so. After all, if there was any chance the coming drone missile strike would also kill these Jews from Hollywood, that would be an unexpected bonus.

The three men stood and said their goodbyes, comrades who had worked together to save five innocent lives. It was all they could do not to embrace. After they shook hands, Cristo turned and was gone.

Goldberg waited a few moments, then shut the door and lowered himself back into his chair. "What do you think?"

"Sandor hasn't been wrong yet. He thinks Cristo will be on the phone in short order, telling Farashi that the money is on the way. Then Farashi will call in the drones."

"My God, that is one evil man."

"Cristo?" Wilson nodded. "Can you imagine, he's at the upper echelon of a foundation like WHI? I would never have believed it if I didn't witness it myself."

"You think he bought everything we told him?"

"I hope so. I certainly don't think he believes the State Department is going to keep money belonging to WHI."

Goldberg did nothing to hide the tension he'd held in check until now. "How did I do?"

"I think you did just fine."

"I've produced dozens of feature films, but there wasn't one premiere that made me as nervous as this." He forced an awkward grin. "Not even the lousiest of them."

"This was different, this was about life and death."

Goldberg nodded. "You're right."

Wilson smiled. "For what it's worth, if they gave an Academy Award for this sort of thing, you'd be a shoo-in."

CHAPTER 77

Outside the Refugee Camp
near the Syrian border

All of the locally available resources of the United States armed forces were now on full display. As Randall had pointed out, there was no longer any reason for stealth. Farashi was gone, the men he left behind were dead, the hostages were safe, and now it was only a matter of whether or not they could prevent a genocidal assault on the refugee camp. The F-16's were in hot pursuit of the drones, Syrian borders be damned. The technicians in Niamey were using their equipment and satellite feeds in an effort to track the UAV flight patterns. Assault helicopters were patrolling the perimeter of the camp. All available surface-to-air missile launchers were loaded and ready.

Shoulder mounted Stingers, such as the FIM-92, were unlikely to be effective. The best ground-to-air equipment on hand was the MIM-104 PATRIOT system. The acronym, "Phased Array Tracking Radar to Intercept on Target" described the technology. The incoming projectile needs to be spotted on radar, the coordinates set and the missiles fired. Timing and accuracy were critical—a miss could be disastrous.

While defensive preparations were being made, Sandor and Garinger traveled by chopper from the base in Mosul back to the camp. If any of the drones got through, they wanted to be on the ground to do whatever they could to help.

General Randall nodded appreciatively when they entered his command tent. "Not what you people normally do, is it?"

"We were all Army before we worked for Langley," Sandor said. "All except Beth."

She was studying the radar monitor. Without looking up, Beth said, "I went to Wharton, which I guarantee you is tougher than basic training."

Sandor smiled.

One of Randall's men walked in and reported, "Sir, there's an uprising in the compound. First the shooting, now the choppers hovering. Probably looks to them like we're going to attack them."

"Damn," Randall said. "Let's have a look." He led the group outside, followed by three of his men.

As they approached the main gate, the situation was clear. People were pushing forward, shoving and jostling each other in a huge crush of bodies, trying to force their way past the armed squadron.

"Don't we have a bullhorn, or some sort of P.A. system?" Beth asked. "We need to calm these people down before they start trampling each other."

Randall shook his head. "They won't hear a thing with the noise from the choppers overhead. Part of me says to let them go, maybe dispersing into the desert isn't such a bad idea." Before anyone could respond, another of Randall's lieutenants came running toward them. "Sir, we have a visual on the first drone."

Their supposition that the drones had been hiding somewhere over Syrian airspace had not been wrong. The first UAV they spotted was coming directly out of the northwest, on a course of dead reckoning with the camp, less than two miles out.

"Alert everyone to fire on sight," Randall hollered to his men. "Lieutenant, call the detail guarding the warehouse and order them to get the hell out of there right now. Jack, have them reposition the two northernmost choppers to see if they can intercept the damn thing before it gets any closer."

Randall then turned and raced back to his tent to check the monitor.

The din from the helicopters was amplified by the arrival of F-16's circling south and coming around, directly above them, flying straight at the coordinates they had been given.

"We're not going to know anything standing here," Sandor said, then led his group at a trot back to the command tent.

The general got on the line with one of the fighter pilots. "Can you get a lock on it?" he asked. He waited, nodding at the response. Suddenly, they heard an explosion in the air, not too far from where they stood. Randall turned to them. "Got one," he said.

"The first one had to be their scout," Sandor said. "We assumed they were coming from somewhere north and the first one came at us from that direction. Gets everyone pointed that way, but we've got to figure one of the remaining two was programmed to circle back around us."

Randall nodded. "Already have that covered. We have two truck mounted PATRIOT systems heading this way from the south, staying behind us if they make that move."

"Sorry," Sandor said. "I shouldn't have—"

"Nothing to be sorry about. I'll take all the good ideas I can get right now."

With that, another call came in. There were visuals on the other two UAV's, and one was already firing.

That UAV was coming from the northeast, and had launched two of its six missiles. The good news was that the projectiles did not have the range to reach the camp, and fell short in a pair of fiery explosions. The problem was that both had gotten through the first shield Randall's men had created. If they did not succeed in shooting down the drone as it continued its approach, the next missiles fired might reach the compound.

As the fight in the sky intensified, so did the panic inside the complex. Soldiers guarding the perimeter had neither the orders nor the intention to shoot any of these unfortunates, and now, with explosions above them and off to the north, hundreds of the refugees broke through the fence, and past the military cordon, and ran into the desert.

When General Randall got word, he said, "Let them go. You men pull back."

Meanwhile, the last of the rogue drones was spotted coming from the south.

A barrage of surface-to-air missiles were launched from trucks carrying radar guided rockets. Two of them found their target almost simultaneously. The group inside the command tent ran outside to witness the fireball in the sky, less than half a mile behind them.

Before the drone had been destroyed, however, it had managed to set off three of its missiles. Two of them were immediately intercepted by strikes launched from truck-mounted surface-to-air systems, causing more fireworks above them, and increased panic inside and outside the camp.

But the third projectile had gotten past the counter-strikes.

Sandor, Randall, and the rest of them watched helplessly as the missile raced toward its target—the warehouse. The structure was obliterated in an instant, but fortunately little other damage was done.

Radar indicated only one drone remained, still coming fast from the northeast.

Randall called off the F-16's. This last UAV was flying too low, and an approach by the fighter jets was too risky—for the pilots as well as those on the ground. He stayed on the radio hook-up, ordering his men in the attack helicopters and on the ground to unleash everything they had.

"Take the damn thing down," he shouted.

The next few moments felt to Sandor as if they were being played out in slow motion.

This last drone successfully launched four of its weapons just before it was blown out of the sky.

All of those missiles were aimed at the defenseless people still inside the compound, and now a deafening roar of counter-strikes filled the air. Sandor and the others standing outside the command tent, watching as one, then two, then a third of the attacking missiles were neutralized, evaporating in fiery explosions.

But then they saw the last missile emerge from the cloud of debris, speeding along its lethal course into the heart of the refugee camp.

Given the angle of attack, the helicopters could no longer fire without raining down a hail of gunfire onto the people below. The surface-to-air strikes resumed, but it was too late. The missile dove toward the ground followed by a loud crash, a sizzling blast, and the screams of men, women, and children.

CHAPTER 78

U.S. Army Camp, Mosul

Word was given that all of the rogue UAV's had been destroyed, and now first responders were reacting, at the order of General Randall.

The number of fatalities was in the process of being verified. Thus far there were seventeen confirmed dead. The random configuration of the tents inside the complex, as well as the way the refugees scattered during the fighting, actually saved lives. After the first missile demolished the warehouse there were no other buildings to hit. The second explosion did damage, but not as much as might have occurred if there had been an occupied structure or a denser collection of people near the point of impact.

Some of the wounded were being treated in hastily constructed triage areas inside the camp, while the most seriously injured were being rushed by helicopter and truck to the infirmary back at the army base.

None of the media vans outside the refugee camp were hit in the attack, and the journalists on hand—shut off from any briefings as the conflict played out over the past few hours—were now in overdrive, spinning the story in whatever way would appeal to their particular constituencies. Cameramen and journalists sought out anyone who had the time or inclination to speak with them.

A videoconference had been assembled from Wilson's office, and leaders of the task force in Washington commended General Randall for his clear-headed leadership. The general, who was back in his tent and connected by phone, responded by admitting he was more than a little disappointed that all of the missiles had not been shot down. There was a general assessment that the casualties might have been worse, but that provided little comfort to those who did all they could to prevent the attack.

"The stakes were high," Forelli told him. "And you had limited time and options. The President feels the job you and your men did was exemplary."

Randall replied with a simple, "Thank you," then informed them that the base in Niamey was asking to be tied into the call.

John Coman joined in, verifying the original assessment by their technicians—four drones had been reprogrammed, all of which had now been downed. "We've cut off their ability to interfere with the codes for any other of our UAV's."

"When you say 'their ability,' does that mean you've identified the source of this sabotage?" Forelli asked.

"Not yet," Coman admitted. "We're working on it."

"Are you at least saying this cannot happen again?"

"Not with the software they used this time."

No one was thrilled with that qualification, and Forelli said so.

"Without our encryptions they cannot invade our system," Coman explained.

"All right, so how do we locate these people?"

"Remmell is working on a method to determine the origination of the signal they used to intercept the drones."

"Go on," Molly Stroup from NSA told him.

"In essence, Remmell has developed a means of reversing their signals to reach the starting point. Since the four UAV's have been destroyed, we can play with their guidance protocols and passwords without any risk they can be used again."

"Without getting too technical about this, do you think it'll work?" Dick Bebon asked.

"We do. We'll be reporting back to you on the final results, but we're fairly certain the signals were generated in Damascus."

"Goddamned Syrians," Bebon snarled.

"We may not be able to say for sure who was behind this," Coman told them. "But we hope to pinpoint the location where the interception was initiated."

"Understood," Forelli said. He then thanked Coman, told him to keep them apprised as information became available, and dismissed him from the call. "It will be helpful if we can prove this attack was engineered from within Syria."

Sandor, who was sitting between General Randall and Craig Raabe, shot his fellow agent a familiar look.

Raabe mouthed the word, "Politicians."

Sandor grinned.

"What about that company in France?" Bebon asked.

"Fronique," Sandor reminded him.

"Right. How do they figure into this?"

"We're working on that," Mark Byrnes replied. "It's highly doubtful they were directly implicated in this scheme. It's more likely someone inside the company was working for Ansar al-Thar. Or perhaps they simply sold the technology after Remmell helped bring it to this level."

Forelli asked, "What's your best guess?"

Byrnes hesitated. "We're not in the business of guessing. Particularly about something this important."

"Indulge me."

"Based on the encounter Sandor and his people had with the men babysitting Remmell in Sophia Antipolis, I would say the company knew what was being researched."

"Well then, Director Walsh," Forelli said. "I believe it's time for your people to get that theory confirmed or denied, so appropriate diplomatic action can be taken."

"Understood," the head of the CIA responded.

"Diplomatic action?" Sandor blurted out. "What if we just send in a team and blow up their goddamn building?"

"That'll be enough of that," Walsh admonished his agent.

The ensuing comments made it evident there were many on the call who shared Sandor's view.

Forelli said, "The White House wants it clearly understood that we will handle the media. None of you is to give any interviews. Not on or off the record, is that clear?"

They all acknowledged their understanding.

"The hostages will continue to be treated by your medics at the base. When they're ready to be moved, they'll be flown to Washington for a meeting with the President. As we all understand, the circumstances of their rescue and identity of the people involved cannot be revealed. Those of us on this call understand the debt that is owed. We will simply have to say that the terrorists were overtaken by American soldiers and the hostages released. We will undoubtedly be asked for the identity of the military involved, but we will say that information is classified."

Sandor and Garinger exchanged an amused look.

Forelli went on. "We assume the hostages will cooperate in not identifying anyone directly connected to the release. In fact, it is doubtful they actually know who those people are."

Sandor thought about Hassan, but said nothing. The Saudi had already proved himself a friend and was not likely to betray him now.

"The injured refugees at the camp should be given the best medical treatment available. Our troops on the ground should increase their protection of these people until a solution can be achieved or more suitable arrangements can be made."

"Suitable arrangements such as what?" Bebon asked.

"The President is exploring all possible options and will be in touch with both the Iraqi and Syrian governments. As I've said, these are matters that will be addressed from the White House and only from the White House." When no one disagreed, Forelli asked, "What else have we got on our plate?"

Byrnes responded. "First there's the matter of the bogus payment of ransom. My agents handling this situation believe that the phantom transfer will give them an opportunity to track Farashi and his lieutenant Gabir."

"Track them to where?"

"Some of the money was designated for accounts in Yemen, but the bulk of the funds were wired to banks in Damascus."

Forelli nodded. "Once these men learn that the funds have not arrived, whatever else they may do, they will surely disappear into the desert rather than risk capture. Am I missing something, Mark?"

Byrnes was uncomfortable divulging the details of a clandestine operation to a group this large. Despite the security clearances each of the participants held, he said, "Perhaps it would be best if I work out the details on my end and report back."

Forelli had been playing the Potomac shell game long enough to know this was not the time to pursue the matter. "Fair enough, keep us in the loop," he said. Then he signed off, ending the videoconference for everyone.

Less than a minute later Byrnes and Walsh were back on the phone with Randall. "It would be helpful if I could speak with my people privately," the DD said. The general had enough to do, and was only too happy to clear out of his tent and leave them to their discussion.

Director Walsh began by asking Byrnes what he had in mind.

"As indicated, we intend to set a trap for Farashi."

"That will take days to set up."

"It will not," Byrnes disagreed. "Our plan is to have the team travel to Syria now and intercept him at the source."

"When you say the 'source,' I take it you mean a bank in the middle of Damascus. Am I getting this right?"

"That is exactly what I am saying."

"Assuming we actually locate and confront these two individuals, what do you propose to do with them?"

Sandor had enough. "I propose to invite them to lunch," he said.

"Knock it off," Byrnes admonished his agent, cutting him off before the director had the chance.

Walsh spoke up again. "You have taken into account, have you not, that Farashi may well be accompanied by armed support, men who participated in the initial abduction and then eluded capture. You must also recognize that a group of Americans murdering a Syrian on the streets of Damascus, regardless of the character or background of the victim, will create an international incident with serious repercussions."

This time Byrnes did not allow Sandor the opportunity to reply. He said, "Given the target, I daresay anyone who would condemn his execution will be hard-pressed to find support in the community of civilized nations. Therefore, I am not sure what sort of serious repercussions we should be concerned about, especially from Syria."

It was not often that Sandor and Raabe got to see their boss face off against the director, and they were finding it difficult to hide their amusement.

Walsh nodded slowly. "All right. Is there anything else we need to address at this time?" Sandor thought about the plans he had for Dr. Cristo, but kept that to himself.

"You make a run at this," Walsh said. "If it works, do what needs to be done. If it doesn't, get your butts out of Damascus."

"Yes sir," Sandor said.

Without so much as "good luck," Walsh ended the call.

CHAPTER 79

U.S. Army Camp, Mosul

As events unfolded at the refugee camp, Cristo had been held incommunicado at the army base, waiting impatiently in the briefing room for his transportation to be arranged. When the door finally opened, the last man in the world he expected to see strolled in and pulled the door shut behind him.

Cristo stood and said, "Mr. Sandor."

Sandor moved toward him. "I have some wonderful news for you."

"Is that so?"

"Yes indeed. First, you should know that the hostages are safe." Sandor smiled. "Come on, Eddie, don't look so surprised. It gets better." When Cristo offered no response, Sandor went on. "Not only did we free all five of them, but we also stopped the transfer of the ransom money before it got through."

As Sandor had already observed, Cristo was a better actor than most of Alan Goldberg's stars. "That is wonderful," he replied, infusing the statement with all the enthusiasm he could muster.

"I have some other news," Sandor told him. "You interested?"

"Of course."

"Let me start you off with a few headlines then," Sandor replied. "First, we know that you were involved with Ansar al-Thar in arranging their kidnapping scheme. We know that you were instrumental in the plan to use Harry Remmell to develop technology for Fronique, which is intended to intercept American drones. We also know that you intended to personally benefit from the ransom money, as well as a number of illegal trades you organized through shell companies set up for you by Corinne Stansbury."

Cristo feigned astonishment. "What utter nonsense."

"Really? Then I'm sure you'll be interested to know we have the recording of your discussion in the mosque with Farashi and Gabir. Oh yes, the recorded prayers were a nice touch, made remote eavesdropping difficult. Thing is, we had your Kevlar vest wired for sound, so we got the whole conversation, up close and personal. Also have a recording of your call to Farashi, a couple of hours ago, when you told him the money had been wired so he had the thumbs up to start the drone strikes."

Before Cristo could reply, Sandor stepped forward and roughly searched the man's sportcoat pockets, pulling out two cell phones.

"What do you think you're doing?" Cristo demanded.

Sandor held up the two phones. "I wonder which one of these is intended to receive the next call from Farashi."

He walked to the door, opened it and handed both phones to a waiting Craig Raabe. When he pulled the door shut behind him and returned his attention to Cristo, it was apparent the man was not about to surrender so easily.

"Who do you think you are sir? Whatever misinformation you may have, you must remember that I have rights."

"And whatever rights you have are trumped by the fact that you are an international terrorist."

"That is slander."

"Not if it's true. You know, you might really want to check out the laws on slander when you have some time. I can call you anything I want, long as I can prove it."

Cristo's scowl spoke volumes, but he remained silent.

"So, let's discuss your arrangement for the payment of the ransom. As soon as that was arranged with the boys from Hollywood, and you left Frank Wilson's office, the first thing you did was call Farashi. As I say, we have the transcript of the call. What you and Farashi did not know at the time was that the hostages had already been freed, and the money you thought you were wiring to the State Department is really sitting in a safe account in D.C. Although your chat with Farashi was in a type of code, the message you gave was clear. You were letting him know it was time to unleash the drone strike on the refugee camp. Am I right?"

Cristo glowered, but said nothing.

"Ah come on, Eddie, give some credit where it's due." He shook his head. "All right, have it your way. Meanwhile, since you made your call to Farashi, you've also tried to confirm the wire transfers of the ransom funds were completed."

"That was my obligation as the chief financial executive of WHI."

"Of course it was," Sandor replied. "Also incredibly helpful to me. I now know precisely which banks you expect to report back to you first. Your test cases, so to speak. Very helpful."

"What now?" Cristo asked. "I suppose you're going to threaten me with physical violence?"

"I almost never make threats."

"Then you have nothing but idle speculation."

"Oh, I have a great deal more than nothing. My problem, you see, is that I understand we'll have to spend millions to prosecute you. Along the way, any number of people and institutions will be embarrassed for not having seen through your charade. The WHI will be ruined, a decent organization that you polluted. Then Colville and his RSL firm will be rocked by scandal, even though they served as nothing more than an innocent conduit. The United States drone program will be tarred and feathered by the media." Sandor shook his head as if saddened by all the trouble Cristo had created. "Then, of course, there are all those innocent lives that were lost. That will always be the worst part."

Cristo was silent again.

"I actually thought about leaving you alone. I mean, think how disappointed Farashi is going to be when his fifty million Euros doesn't show up. And guess who he'll blame?" Sandor paused to think that over. "I decided that's too risky. You're a helluva talker, as we've seen, and I wouldn't want to give you the chance to wriggle out of that mess. No, this is something I'm going to have to handle myself."

As Sandor took a step closer to him, Cristo drew a small pistol from his suit coat pocket.

"You didn't notice this, when you were stealing my phones."

Sandor smiled. "Actually, I did. Hoped you would be stupid enough to pull it out."

"You're a lunatic, that much is obvious, and it will be my pleasure to empty this gun into you."

"Actually, that would be perfect. I mean, you might find a way to explain your calls to Farashi, and you might even claim that your discussion with him in the mosque was some sort of gambit on your part to reduce the ransom demand. But how are you going to explain the murder of a federal agent? That would be the death penalty for sure."

Before Cristo had a chance to respond, Sandor made a quick feint to his left, then moved right, knocking Cristo sideways as he wrapped his forearm around the man's neck and reached out with his other hand, wrenching the gun free.

"There was just one little problem with that approach," Sandor said as he released him with a hard shove forward. "I really don't feel like getting shot."

Cristo stumbled to his knees.

"Get up."

Cristo stood and straightened out his wrinkled suit jacket.

"You've given me an excellent option here," Sandor said. "I could shoot you with your own gun, claim you pulled it on me and then say you died when I fought you off. Self-defense, not a bad story."

"You won't do that. You Americans pride yourselves on your righteous ethics." Cristo smoothed back his hair with the palms of his hands. "That's why, in the end, your people will fail. You don't have the stomach to do what needs to be done."

"See now, I feel just the opposite. I think morality is our greatest asset. You people have this perverse belief that a religion which preaches murder, hate, and the persecution of minorities and women can prevail, but in the long run I don't think it can. Still, there are times when the death penalty *is* appropriate, and some of us have the solemn responsibility to carry it out."

Without another word Sandor drew his Walther. "Fortunately for me," he said through clenched teeth, "with the slaughter of all those innocent people, I don't have a moral dilemma here."

His next move was quick and decisive. He fired two shots into Cristo's head and watched him slump to the floor. Then he bent down, placed Cristo's own automatic in his hand and fired two shots through the ceiling.

By the time Craig Raabe opened the door, Sandor was kneeling over the body.

Sandor turned to him and said, "The sonuvabitch pulled a gun on me, you believe that?"

Then he stood and headed for the door. "We've got work to do."

CHAPTER 80

Damascus, Syria

Time was short, and Sandor's scheme was dependent on key suppositions as well as immediate action.

Byrnes reached out for agency contacts in Mosul, who arranged for Sandor, Raabe and Garinger to be provided forged media credentials. There was no time to create new passports or identities. They used their own names and their civilian papers, which bore no mention of the State Department or any of their other standard covers, then boarded the short flight to Damascus posing as journalists.

Beth, despite her protests, realized that taking a woman into Syria on a mission like this would be a liability, and so she was persuaded to return to New York and wait there.

On the plane, Sandor was seated across the aisle from his fellow agents. He leaned toward them. "Thanks to Cristo's phone calls, we have a good idea which bank Farashi will approach first. It was one of the smaller amounts wired, and I believe they designed the uneven split of money to provide an opportunity for a test case or two, before they go after the larger deposits."

The other two nodded their understanding.

"Once Farashi discovers the money hasn't arrived yet, he'll try to contact Cristo. No telling how soon he'll do that, and no way of knowing how soon he'll figure something is wrong when he can't reach him."

"Why would Farashi visit any of the banks?" Garinger asked. "Why not just track the deposits online, or even by phone?"

"That's not the way Wilson set it up with Cristo. Given the circumstances and the amount of the transfers, we insisted on attaching certain stipulations to ensure the funds would not be released to the wrong people. The reasoning he gave Cristo was that he had to guarantee the money would be received by Farashi so Farashi would order the release of the hostages."

"And Cristo bought that?"

"He had no choice. Think about it. How could he argue against anything that would safeguard the exchange of the ransom for the prisoners?"

Garinger nodded.

"So," Raabe said, "you're telling us we're going to stake out the bank where the smallest transfer was sent in the hope that he shows."

"It became much more than a hope, once we got Cristo's phones." Sandor paused. "Although I don't expect Farashi to be the one to make contact."

"I take it you have a plan to overcome that little detail."

Sandor grinned. "I'll explain that when we get there."

"And if the cheese you lay out doesn't draw the rat?"

Sandor shrugged. "Then we'll go to Plan B."

"You actually have a Plan B?" Raabe asked.

Sandor sat back in his seat. "I'm working on it."

They landed in Damascus and went through the sort of thorough immigration screening worthy of a country continually at war. Posing as employees of a cable news program, the process was completed without too much stress—thanks in large part to the quality paperwork Byrnes procured for them. Making their way out of customs, they grabbed a taxi and headed for the Ahmayd Hotel.

Once again, Byrnes had made preparations. A local agent named Yavin, Jordanian-born and multi-lingual, was waiting for them in the lobby when they arrived. He had arranged their reservations— although the group had no intention of remaining overnight, they needed to properly cover their entrance into the country—and expedited their check-in.

When that was done, Yavin handed out keys and led them to the elevator. They remained silent as they rode upstairs and all four of them went to Sandor's room.

Once inside, Yavin placed the large case he was carrying on the bed, pulled a device from his pocket and swept the room for bugs. Once he nodded that things were all clear, proper introductions were made.

"Glad you're here to help," Sandor said. "What've you got for us?"

Yavin opened the bag and displayed an impressive array of weapons. He began distributing automatic pistols, street maps, and instructions for the escape route they should use if and when they needed an emergency retreat. He told them he had transportation, and the electronic surveillance equipment they had requested. "This is going to be very difficult, what you are trying to accomplish." His English bore the inflection of his native language, but was clear nonetheless. "You might be here for days."

"I don't think so," Sandor said. "You don't expect us to just stand outside the bank and wait for Farashi to come strolling down the street, do you?"

The Jordanian offered no reply.

"Farashi didn't choose any of these banks by throwing darts at a board. He picked places where he has friends. This was the first place Cristo called, the place they have contacts. I believe it was designed for a sort of test run. I realize he is not going to approach them directly. He'll probably use an intermediary, or some sort of pre-determined code. For our purposes it doesn't matter. We're going to force his hand."

"How?" Garinger asked.

"Yavin and I are going into the bank and we're going to find whoever is highest on their food chain."

"And what will you do then?" Yavin asked.

"The key is to identify Farashi's contact within the bank, then we'll set things in motion."

Sandor smiled. "I'll explain the rest of it on the way over. Time's a wasting."

Armed and ready, the four men went downstairs and climbed into a panel van Yavin had parked out front. It bore the logo and phone number of a non-existent plumbing company. The Jordanian got behind the wheel, Raabe in the passenger seat, while Sandor and Garinger climbed in the back. Then they headed for the Syrian Aswan Bank on Tahir Square.

Damascus is an ancient, crowded mess, a jarring combination of the very old and the very new. Westerners, when envisioning metropolitan areas in the Middle East, sometimes have a misguided image of low slung limestone buildings, unpaved roads, and livestock running free through the streets. In fact, there are nearly two million inhabitants crammed inside Damascus, the total swelling to over three million if the nearby environs are included. The downtown area features dozens of modern, high-rise structures which—if not likely to win any Bauhaus awards—are nevertheless contemporary and well equipped. In the midst of this urban sprawl, there is evidence everywhere of the endless fighting the city has endured.

Like most ancient cities, the streets of Damascus are not conducive to the current congestion of cars and trucks. The outer bypass roads are modern, but once Sandor and his team entered the center of town it would not be easy for them to get out quickly. Matters would become even more complicated if they became engaged in a running gun battle and the local authorities became involved. As Yavin said at the outset, this was not going to be easy.

Not unless things broke just right.

Their job was to flush out Farashi and, as Sandor had often observed, waiting was the toughest part of the game. His intention was to foreshorten the timeline, and he explained his plan on the ride over, finishing just as Yavin brought the van to a stop just across from the bank. The four agents took a couple of minutes to double-check that their electronics were in place and working, then Sandor and Yavin got out and made their way across the street and through the front door of the bank.

Inside, tellers were positioned off to the left, behind the protection of iron bars and bulletproof glass. To the right was a reception area where a young man sat behind a desk, not even making an effort to appear busy. Yavin approached and asked to see the president of the bank. The young man appeared surprised at the request, saying the president rarely came to the bank. Yavin then asked who was in charge. The young man said that would be the manager, and asked the nature of his business. Yavin flashed a set of credentials that Byrnes had his people in Mosul prepare, and explained he was on official business regarding an international financing issue.

After seeing Yavin's papers, the clerk stood and hustled into the office area behind him, returning a minute or so later.

"This way," he said.

They were shown into a modestly appointed office where a rotund man, appearing to be in his mid-50s, invited Yavin and Sandor to be seated. He then asked his guests to display the credentials that had been presented to the receptionist. He stood over Yavin, having a look at the card and badge as he asked, "What can I do for you?"

"You speak English?" Sandor asked.

"I do," the man replied, though even that short statement revealed a heavy accent.

"Good, that will save time. As for what you can do for us, I think you know," Sandor said in a firm manner.

The manager blinked, then took a moment to walk back around his desk and sit down. "I'm sorry sir, but I have no idea what you're talking about."

"You recently received notice that a wire transfer from the American State Department was being made to an account in this bank."

This time the man matched Sandor's authoritative tone. "Unless you have a direct interest in any such account, I am not permitted to give out any information."

Although Sandor saw the satisfaction in the banker's eyes as he delivered this defiant response, he took no offense. To the contrary, in that moment he knew he was speaking to the right man, which was far more important than any issues concerning attitude. "The 'direct interest' you refer to with respect to this transaction is going to be yours, not ours, unless you cooperate."

"As far as I can see, you gentlemen are way beyond the limits of your jurisdiction. In fact, your threatening manner gives me the right to phone the authorities and have the two of you arrested."

"You are free to do whatever you please," Sandor told him. "I should remind you, however, that the transfer of funds we've come about relates to several acts of international terrorism. That sort of conduct defies borders or jurisdiction, and you should proceed with great caution before you become implicated in these events."

The manager was silent for a moment, looking as if he might still pick up the phone and call someone, but he obviously thought better of it. "Whoever you men are, and whatever you think you know, this bank has received no such wire."

"I did not say you had received the wire, I said you had been given notice that the wire was coming. We are here because we want anything you have concerning the account that was created to receive those funds, including contact information."

The banker stood, but remained behind his desk. "This meeting is at an end. As I've already explained, I owe you no such cooperation. I will contact my superiors and, if you choose, you may leave *your* contact information with the receptionist and we will be in touch with you if and when we feel it is appropriate."

Neither Sandor nor Yavin moved.

"Good day gentlemen."

They hesitated at first. Then both men rose from their seats and headed for the door, where Sandor stopped and turned back.

"Mass murder, kidnapping, and extortion. If you fail to provide us the cooperation you don't believe you owe us, I can assure you the death penalty will come as a relief by the time this is done." He then stormed out, wrote out a cell phone number for the receptionist, left it on the desk, and the pair exited the bank.

He and Yavin did not return directly to the van. Assuming they were being watched, they instead walked in the opposite direction, circled the block and came around the back of the vehicle where they could not be seen from the front of the bank. Once they climbed inside the vehicle, Sandor asked, "You guys get all that?"

Raabe was wearing earphones and operating a high frequency eavesdropping device.

"Every word."

"Think you'll have any problem picking up his next conversation?"

Raabe smiled. "He was dialing before the two of you hit the street. If this gadget doesn't pick it up, the bug you slid under his desk should do the trick. "

CHAPTER 81

Damascus, Syria

The banker had indeed placed a call. It was to a number he believed to be secure, and he told the man who answered, "We have an issue."

"Say nothing more. We will be there in ten minutes." Then the line went dead.

Yavin translated and the four agents looked at each other.

"Ten minutes," Raabe repeated. "In all this traffic, whoever he spoke with is almost as close to the place as we are."

Sandor nodded. "We'll see." Then, for the third time, he checked the Glock with silencer that Yavin had provided.

The van was fitted with eyeholes that were cut into the bold lettering on the side of the panels proclaiming the vehicle to be owned by a plumbing company. The holes were all but invisible from the outside, but provided a wide field of vision from the inside. They waited and watched anxiously, while they continued to monitor the banker's office.

The manager made two more telephone calls, both sounding innocuous enough, and neither dealing with the visit he had just received from the authorities. The fact that he was not reporting his meeting with Sandor to a superior within the banking organization made it evident that, whatever involvement his bank might have in the scheme regarding payment and transfer of the ransom money, the manager was in it up to his elbows.

A little more than ten minutes had elapsed when the digital receiver in the van came to life with the voices of two men exchanging a cursory greeting. It was followed by the sound of the bank manager's office door closing.

The ensuing conversation was in Arabic, and Yavin did his best to provide a running translation. Whoever the visitor was, it was not Farashi. Based on the preliminary dialogue Yavin also doubted it was his second in command, Gabir. The man was some sort of messenger—highly placed, perhaps—but a messenger all the same.

The banker described his brief meeting with Sandor and Yavin, including several unflattering comments regarding Americans and turncoat Arabs.

"Who do you think they really were?" the messenger asked.

"They posed as some sort of compliance officers for international banking transactions, but they were lying. They were enforcers, not bureaucrats." When the other man said nothing, the banker asked, "Is the money really coming?"

"You tell me," his visitor replied with unmistakable anger in his tone. "You said you had the tracking numbers you required."

"Yes," the banker conceded. "But there were rumors the transfer was being delayed once they announced the hostages had been rescued."

"Nonsense," the messenger said. "You told us there could be no delay. You said once you had the routing number and identification code the money was as good as in the accounts."

"This has never happened before, not in all my years," the manager admitted. "Well it happened now, and you need to tell us what can be done about it. As I am sure you can imagine, our friend is extremely unhappy."

Silence ensued, and Sandor could picture the banker's nervous face, confronted as he was by two dangerously unhappy options. He could not afford to anger a genocidal terrorist, nor could he risk running afoul of men whom he had already concluded were not there to audit his books.

"I need time," the manager said, his voice a plea rather than a demand.

"Time for what?"

"I will contact the transmitting bank as well as the clearinghouse. There must be some way to force a completion of the transfer."

The messenger uttered a short, bitter laugh. "The wires were initiated through their State Department. You think anyone is going to force the United States government to hand over money, now that the hostages are safe?"

"It's all I can think of," the banker said weakly. "Please remember, this problem is not of my doing."

There was the sound of movement, as if the messenger was standing up. "I've stayed here long enough. No telling when your new friends will return, and I need to report back.

Be careful what you say on the phone. When you have any sort of news, signal us."

"I will, I will," the banker said, obviously relieved to see the man go.

There was a pause. "I need another way out of here. This American you described is likely somewhere nearby, and I don't want to walk out the front door."

"Follow me," the banker said.

⊙

Several men had entered the bank during the ten minutes Sandor and his team were watching, and waiting to spot the messenger, but they had failed to pick him out. Now that he elected to leave through a secondary exit, it would be easier to identify him—provided they caught up with him before he got away.

Raabe and Garinger, the two agents whom the manager had not met, immediately climbed out the back of the van, crossed the street, and headed in opposite directions toward the rear of the building.

Raabe spotted him first, a short man in traditional Arab garb who had emerged on foot, apparently coming up from the parking garage below the building. Raabe was across the street and casually turned away, looking into a shop window that provided a good enough reflection to reveal the man checking up and down the street before he headed off to his right.

"Got him," Raabe reported to the others on the digital microphone hidden beneath his shirt lapel. Then he gave a description of their target. "Brandon, make two rights and you'll be behind him. I'll stay ahead, let me know if he turns anyplace."

"Copy that," Garinger said.

Sandor told them they would drive the van around the block and get even further in front, which was a classic surveillance technique—people who suspect they are being followed almost always check behind them, rarely ahead.

Since the messenger was on foot, and since Sandor's team knew he had reached the bank in less than ten minutes after the manager phoned him, they knew he could not be going far. Despite the visit by two officials at the bank, Farashi and his people had no reason to suspect a black ops squad was already in place. He would likely believe the current focus was on retrieving the ransom money, or preventing the transfers before they went through. According to the information the banker had imparted to the messenger, the latter appeared to be true, which was hopefully Farashi's worst case scenario at the moment.

A critical part of Sandor's plan was that Farashi not yet know whether or not the transfer of funds had been blocked. The bank manager had called, was told not to discuss anything on the phone, and the intermediary was dispatched to get an in-person status report on the funds. That meant Farashi still believed there was a chance the payments might be coming through.

"Brandon, any sign he's making a call?" Sandor asked.

"Negative," Garinger replied. "Not unless he's wearing a wireless hookup I can't see. His hands have been at his side the entire time." There was a pause, then, "He's turning left. Get you a street name in a minute."

"Roger that," Sandor said. "You have it covered Craig?"

"The street is Al Okaibah," Raabe said, "just passed it. I'm not doubling back, I'm making the next left and coming around."

"Perfect."

Garinger was now the only one who had the messenger in sight. Not breaking stride as he watched the man hurry along, not more than fifty yards ahead of him, he looked at his watch. "It's been over eight minutes. There appears to be a small hotel, end of the block, across the street on the right. Way he's looking and moving, I'm guessing that's where he's headed."

"Got it," Sandor said. Yavin swung a U-turn that incited a round of horn honking and cursing from other drivers, then sped to the corner and made a right turn. "We're coming around from behind you now. Almost there."

"Do we take him on the street?" Garinger asked.

"No way," Sandor said. "They may have lookouts posted. Whenever he goes inside a building, the hotel, anyplace, don't even cross the street with him, just keep walking past."

"Got it."

In the next few moments, Garinger saw that his guess was correct. The messenger took a few more furtive glances behind him, then wended his way through traffic as he crossed the street and disappeared into the lobby of the cheap looking hotel across the way.

Sandor expected things to happen quickly, now that Farashi was about to receive word his ransom money had not arrived, and also be provided with a description of the officials who had made inquiries at the bank. He told Yavin to stop the van right in front of the hotel. As they had planned, the Jordanian got out with no delay and went inside. Sandor waited in the back of the vehicle, listening on the digital monitor.

⊙

The reception area was small and dingy, not the sort of place a guest or anyone else would be likely to sit around on a sunny day, not unless they had to. Even so, it came as no surprise to Yavin that there were two men there, seated on opposite sides of the lobby, each pretending to read a newspaper, neither doing a very convincing job of it. Yavin nodded pleasantly to the man on his right and got no response. When he reached the front desk, the clerk was busying himself over some paperwork. Yavin introduced himself, identified his plumbing company, and said he was there in answer to a service call.

The two men watched with obvious curiosity as the clerk responded with a look as blank as one of the unused sheets of copy paper he was holding. The young man said he knew nothing about a plumbing problem, and Yavin began raising his voice, upset at having been dragged all the way to this hotel on what appeared to be a bogus request.

The two silent observers were on their feet now, reaching inside their jackets, when Sandor strode through the front door.

"Can I help you gentlemen?" he asked.

The two lookouts turned in the direction of the American who was now standing, feet astride, arm extended, his silenced Glock in his hand. The two sentries pulled out their weapons, but it was too late. Sandor fired through the elongated suppressor, shots spitting out, dropping them both to the floor.

By now, Yavin had his own gun in hand and was pointing it directly between the eyes of the young hotel clerk. "Forget the plumbing," he said, "let's talk about your guest list."

⊙

Outside, Garinger had done as Sandor instructed. He walked past the hotel without crossing the street and continued on halfway up the next block. Then he turned, moved to the other side of Al Okaibah, and hurried his pace toward the hotel.

A rookie mistake, as Sandor would later observe.

As Garinger neared the corner, a man stepped out from a narrow passageway. He came up quickly from behind Garinger, grabbing him by the arm with one hand, the other shoving the barrel of a gun into his ribs. Then, in broken English, he said, "You are walking fast. You have a hurry?"

Garinger froze, then managed to say in Arabic, "I don't understand."

"Then I will make you understand," the man told him.

"This is a mistake," Garinger said.

"I don't think so," the Syrian replied as he began to pull Garinger into the alley. "I have questions about your friends."

A quiet voice just behind the two of them said, "It's good to have friends, don't you think?" Craig Raabe held his automatic right beside the man's ear as he cocked the hammer, so there was no mistaking the sound. Before the Syrian could react, Raabe grabbed the man's wrist and gave it a violent twist, his weapon falling to the ground.

Then he wrapped his arm around the man's neck and dragged him further into the narrow passageway. "You wanted to bring my friend in here, right? Now we're all here."

The Syrian was standing with his back against a brick wall. The tip of the silencer on Raabe's automatic was wedged underneath the man's chin, and Raabe's knee was shoved into his groin.

"I'm going to be the one asking the questions. The first time you refuse to answer, the first time you lie to me, the first time you even pretend you don't understand, I'm going to pull the trigger. Now, tell me you understand, so I don't have to have my friend translate it into Arabic for you."

Fear was evident in the man's eyes, which was helpful. The last thing they needed was to be wasting time on someone eager to die for the cause. "I understand," he replied.

"You are working for Farashi, yes?"

"Yes."

"He is in the hotel just down the street, yes?"

"Yes."

"What room?"

The man's eyes widened. "I, I don't know." Raabe applied additional pressure on the Glock.

"I don't know what room."

"How many of you are out here on the street?"

The man seemed confused by the question and did not reply.

"You are here to protect Farashi, yes?"

"Yes."

"Are you a member of Ansar al-Thar?"

"No."

"Is he paying you?"

"Yes, yes, the other men and I, we are to be paid."

"How many others are there, and where are they positioned?"

"I have already said too much. I will say no more."

"You're sure about that?"

"I will say no more," he repeated. "You have no chance of leaving here alive."

Raabe nodded, then pulled the trigger.

CHAPTER 82

Damascus, Syria

Inside the hotel lobby, the clerk was unable to take his eyes off the barrel of Yavin's automatic weapon, since it was pointed at the center of his forehead.

"I need an answer," the Jordanian told him.

The young man nervously explained that all four rooms on the third floor had been rented a couple of days ago, but he swore he had never seen the men who rented them.

"You must have seen someone coming and going these past two days," Yavin said.

"Yes, but I never know which rooms they go to or who rented them."

"Who's in charge in their group?"

The clerk shook his head. "I do not know. But I understand there are two main men who have not come down at all."

"How do you know that?"

"I hear them talking, the men in the lobby here."

"What about the man who came into the hotel, just before we arrived?" Sandor asked.

"Did he go to the third floor?"

"I'm not sure," he replied. "I think that's where he goes."

"Has he been here before?"

When the clerk did not understand, Yavin translated.

"Yes, yes, he is the one I see most of all. Other than these men who were sitting here."

He looked down at the two corpses on the lobby floor. "Are you going to shoot me?"

Sandor fixed him with a serious stare. "Not if you tell us the truth."

Just then Raabe and Garinger made a cautious entrance into the hotel.

"What've we got?" Raabe asked.

"Just what I was going to ask you," Sandor replied. They exchanged information on conditions inside and outside the hotel.

"So," Raabe said, "can this guy tell you how many men are up there right now?"

They turned to Yavin who repeated the question to the clerk. After a brief exchange in Arabic, Yavin said, "He says there are at least three, probably five or six with the other guards."

"The three presumably being Farashi, Gabir and our pal from the bank," Sandor said.

"We hope so," Raabe agreed.

Sandor leaned over one of the corpses on the floor and plucked a two-way radio from his belt. "Well boys, I figure sometime soon, someone is going to be checking in with someone. What do you think?"

"No time like the present," Raabe said.

"Yavin, bring in your magic suitcase. Craig, give him cover."

Yavin moved toward the hotel entrance, looked up and down the street, then hurried into the van and promptly returned with the large case that appeared on the outside to contain plumbing tools. He set it on the reception desk and opened it. There were several weapons inside, including four automatic rifles. Sandor passed those out, along with extra magazines.

He also placed a couple of other items in his jacket pockets.

"Get our young friend here to drag those two bodies behind the desk," Sandor said to Yavin. "Stay with him to handle any action coming from street level. If we don't make it back and it turns out he lied to us about anything, I mean anything, you shoot him and get the hell out of here."

The Jordanian nodded.

"Ask him if he has any idea which room the two main men are using."

The clerk understood the question. "Don't know," he told them. "But one room is bigger. The one facing the street. Thirty-four."

Sandor nodded. "All right," he said to Raabe and Garinger, "you two take the elevator, just give me a little head start." Then he disappeared into the stairwell.

Sandor took the steps two at a time, his rubber-soled shoes not making a sound, and he quickly reached the landing on the third floor. He opened the fire door, just slightly, and had a look. From his vantage point the short hallway appeared to be empty, no lookouts in evidence.

He waited, not moving, until he heard the *bing* of the elevator arriving and the sound of its doors sliding open.

If that was supposed to bring out any of Farashi's men, they weren't paying attention. Sandor watched as Raabe and Garinger carefully stepped out into the opposite end of the corridor. Sandor now also emerged, had a quick look around and pointed to his left.

Room 34.

Fortunately, the door did not face the length of hallway, through which the peephole would have provided full view of the three approaching men. Raabe and Garinger stayed close to the near wall as they reached Sandor.

There had not been much time to piece together this part of their plan. They had forced an intermediary acting on behalf of Ansar al-Thar to show himself and, hopefully, lead them to where Farashi was waiting. The problem was that they were now on Farashi's turf. They had no idea how many men they were facing or how much warning Farashi and his men had that they were here.

The one certainty was that the messenger had now told Farashi about Yavin and Sandor visiting the bank and flashing credentials, which would put him and his men on high alert. The only good news, as Sandor had already observed, was that there was no place on earth where these terrorists were more likely to feel safe than in their own country.

Raabe had already taken out one of Farashi's lookouts on the street, while Sandor had dispatched the two sentries in the hotel lobby. Farashi and Gabir likely had a protection detail with them. Who else might be in any of the other rooms was a crapshoot.

The current hope was that the clerk was telling the truth, that Room 34 was the largest on the floor, and that Farashi and Gabir were inside.

Sandor pointed to his eyes, then at Garinger, then behind them at the other three doors.

Garinger nodded, turned his back to the other two agents and leveled the assault rifle Yavin had provided him at the other three rooms in the hallway.

Sandor looked at Raabe, then pointed at his own foot and made a kicking motion. Raabe nodded his understanding. He hurried past the door to room 34 in a crouch, then stood and readied himself on the other side.

Sandor moved fast, turning so he could set himself in front of the door, then immediately hit it with two quick sideward kicks. The silence in the corridor was broken by the first loud thrust, followed by the sound of splintering wood and a metal chain giving way as the second kick sent the door flying open.

Neither man hesitated, Sandor charging in first, Raabe right behind him.

The clerk had told them the truth, this room was the largest on the floor. There was a small foyer and a sitting area directly ahead. The first man they spotted was the messenger, who was seated in an armchair. Across from him, to Sandor's left, was Gabir, also seated. Standing behind Gabir was Farashi. No one else seemed to be in the room. None of the three was holding a weapon.

All three Syrians responded with looks of confusion and alarm, and for an instant none of them moved.

Aiming at them with the automatic rifle in his right hand, Sandor pulled the silenced handgun from his belt with his left and fired two shots into Farashi's chest, sending him stumbling backward against the wall where he collapsed in a heap on the floor. Raabe was already taking out Gabir, also opting for his silenced Glock. He squeezed off four shots, the last hitting Gabir squarely in the face, snapping his head back. The messenger tried to get to his feet, but Sandor was already on him, shooting him in the head three times from close range.

Only Farashi was still breathing, and Sandor was now standing over him, aiming the gun at his forehead.

Farashi did not beg for mercy he knew would not be given. All that was left to him, in that last moment before certain death, was recognition of his executioner and a vague awareness of how this had happened. He drew a painful breath and, in a raspy voice said, "You have come all this way only to die, Sandor."

"I don't think so," Sandor said. "I actually came all this way to kill you."

"You should have perished in the explosion in Hartford. You and Hassan, it should have been perfect, avenging your sins against my people."

"Your people are the ones who deserve to die." Their eyes locked. "Let's start with you." Then he fired twice into Farashi's face. "See what all those virgins think when they get a look at that kisser."

"Jordan," Raabe called out, then pointed to the door.

Out in the hallway, all hell was breaking loose.

The sound of Sandor kicking in the door to Farashi's room had rallied the men down the hall. Once they were ready to move, they came out in force, and the corridor was now filled with the deafening sound of rapid-fire gunshots. Fortunately most of the shots were being generated by Garinger before he moved back and joined the other two agents in Farashi's room.

"How many?" Sandor asked.

"Not sure," Garinger told him. "Hit the first three, looks like there were more behind them."

"We need to get the hell out of here. Someone's going to call this in and we can't be dealing with the locals."

"Let's do it," Raabe said.

Sandor led the charge, first sticking the barrel of his rifle out the door and emptying the magazine with random fire. He replaced the magazine as Raabe rushed past him and into the hall, shooting as he went. They were taking return fire now, but none of Farashi's remaining men were showing themselves. They chose instead to fire blindly from behind the cover of door jambs, sending bullets flying in every conceivable direction.

Sandor was in the hallway now, covering the other two agents as he hollered, "Go, go, go."

Raabe led Garinger to the stairway entrance, but one of the shots caught the younger agent in the shoulder and spun him against the wall.

"Come on," Raabe shouted, as he grabbed him by the arm and pulled him to safety in the stairwell.

Sandor was also on the move. From the safety of the landing he turned back. Reaching into his jacket pocket he pulled out two grenades. Yanking out both pins, he lobbed one the length of the corridor, the other toward the nearest open doorway.

Then he followed Raabe and Garinger as they charged down the stairs.

The two explosions reverberated throughout the building as they ran.

In the lobby, Yavin was standing there, his weapon aimed at the staircase door. When Raabe burst through the door, the Jordanian said, "What the hell!"

"Grab the clerk and let's go," Sandor ordered.

"The clerk?"

"We're not leaving the only person here who can identify us. Let's move."

They raced outside, Yavin dragging the terrified clerk, and Raabe helping Garinger.

On the street, two of Farashi's lookouts had appeared, guns in hand. The Americans did not hesitate, Raabe dropping one as he raced toward them from the corner on the right, Sandor taking down the other as he came at them from across the street.

Then they piled into the van and sped away, the sound of sirens growing in the distance.

CHAPTER 83

New York

They had no choice but to make their departure from Damascus via the emergency route Yavin had arranged. Taking their chances at the airport, even to board a private plane, was out of the question. Instead, they drove to a garage in the industrial section of the city, switched to another truck, and made their way to an airstrip just outside Dumayr.

From there they called Byrnes, who agreed they should bring Yavin and the hotel clerk with them on the flight to Mosul—the former because his effectiveness in Syria was now over, the latter because they could not leave any loose ends behind.

"He can take a bus home tomorrow, if he wants to," Sandor said. "By the time he gets back, he'll realize that keeping his mouth shut is the best chance he has of staying alive."

Garinger was taken to the infirmary at the base, where he was treated and cleared for transport back to the States. The injury was not bad, but he had lost blood and needed rest.

Sandor and Raabe stopped by and told him he was cleared to travel.

"Time to go home," Sandor said.

"Not before you answer one question for me."

Sandor stuck out his lower lip and nodded. "Okay, shoot."

"Farashi mentioned something about you scuba diving in the Red Sea. I could see in your face, it was like something made sense to you, a riddle was solved."

"So what's the question?"

"What was he talking about? What did he know about you that registered that way?"

"That's actually two questions," Sandor said with a grin. "But because you're injured I'll cut you some slack." He glanced at Raabe before he said, "I had an assignment that took me to Sharm al-Sheikh. Some Russian thugs made a run at me there, I wound up surviving, they didn't do quite as well. Apparently they were friends of Farashi. I'll tell you the longer version of the story on the plane ride home."

They reached New York late morning the next day and headed straight for Beth's apartment. After she and Sandor embraced, Raabe said, "What, no hug for me?"

Beth indulged both Raabe and Garinger, then the four of them sat and she listened to them describe everything that had happened.

"That miserable bastard," she said.

"Which one do you mean?" Raabe asked.

"Cristo. He was in such a high position of influence and trust, and he betrayed everyone."

"Yes," Sandor said. "Betrayal of trust is the lowest of the low."

No one disagreed.

They spent some time discussing the fallout of the incursion in Damascus, when Beth asked, "What about you and Farashi?"

Sandor shrugged. "I had no way of knowing he was connected to Sudakov and his pals in Egypt. Never saw him before we met that day at the refugee camp."

"Frightening, how far this terrorist network reaches."

Sandor nodded. "You're right about that."

Garinger mentioned the time, and so they all headed for drinks at Morton's on East Forty-Fifth Street. They chose that location, not only because the cocktails were poured with care and generosity, but because the barroom featured several televisions, and they did not want to miss a moment of this afternoon's featured attraction—a press conference from Hollywood.

Regularly scheduled programming was being interrupted for the event, which began with a panning shot showing the front of the room. At the center of the dais were the two superstars, more famous than ever, if such a thing were possible, and Alan Goldberg seated beside Amanda.

As to the other three survivors, Bill Sternlich was waiting at Morton's for the four agents that had been instrumental in saving his life. Hassan was in Saudi Arabia. And Tom Orr was recuperating at home in upstate New York.

There were others on the stage, but all eyes, and most of the camera shots, were trained on the two featured attendees. Dedalus had his arm in a sling, was wearing his usual sunglasses, trendy clothing, and a serious look. Amanda Jensen was at her best, looking impossibly gorgeous in a navy blue dress that was not risqué, but did nothing to hide her obvious assets. Her features were perfect and—as with movie stars at any red carpet style event—she was perfectly made up. Her eyes, however, did not bear the usual vapid look so many celebrities conveyed. There was fire in them, and Sandor understood. Unlike scenes shot in the world of movie magic, the impact of an authentic life-and-death experience does not fade quickly.

The people who were most responsible for the survival of these people ordered their drinks. Even Sternlich, who did not usually imbibe before sundown, relented and had a Macallan 18 year-old, with one large ice cube. The five of them watched as Goldberg was the first to speak. He expressed the gratitude of the entire world that the hostages had been returned safely. He conveyed sympathy for the families and friends of all those who had died so senselessly in an attack by a group of cowardly men. Then, looking directly into the camera, he went on.

"This entire tragedy would have been exponentially worse had it not been for the brave men and women of the United States military, and all the other branches of government involved. Those people who relentlessly, courageously, and without regard for their own safety did all they could to avert disaster. I cannot name names because I do not know them. I can only say 'Thank you' to each and every one of you, because whatever else may be said or written about these events in the days and years to come, you will always know who you are."

The press conference was being held at a large pavilion in Los Angeles, and in response to that statement, the entire arena erupted in sustained applause, even the members of the jaded media joining in.

The four agents looked at each other.

"Go figure," Sandor said, then had a sip of his bourbon.

"I have just one more thing to say," Goldberg told the audience. "Then I'll turn the microphone over to the people you really want to hear from. Our great nation is often criticized by our allies and frequently vilified by our foes, but we can deal with those insults, and do you know why? It's because we know we are the greatest country in the history of the world. We know that we are the shining light of hope for all the people who live with poverty, oppression, and even tyranny. We represent faith, regardless of what others say or do. Today, I simply ask that we never forget, despite the differences we may have here at home—whether it's religion, race, politics, or economics—I ask that we never forget that in the end we are all Americans. The rescue of these people is just another example of our excellence."

There was more applause. Then Amanda Jensen spoke.

After echoing many of Goldberg's sentiments, she said, "No one was closer than the five of us to witnessing the actions that led to our rescue. Nothing in any motion picture I ever see or participate in making will come close to portraying the sort of heroism we saw on display." She stared directly into the camera. "As Alan said, I may never know your names, but I just wanted you to know I will never forget your faces." Then she glanced at Goldberg and the two shared a conspiratorial smile.

Beth glanced at Sandor as he watched the screen. "Come on Jordan, don't try to tell me those lips are real."

Raabe and Garinger began laughing.

"I wouldn't know," Sandor replied as he took another drink. "Never got the chance to find out." Then he smiled at her. "Not that I wasn't interested."

Later that day, Sandor kept another appointment. He and Howard Lerner met on the second floor of Armani on 55th Street where the restaurant manager, an old friend of Sandor's, gave them a small table near a window overlooking Fifth Avenue.

"I thought meeting at the King Cole Bar might be pushing our luck," Sandor said.

Lerner smiled. "They see the two of us together there, they'll evacuate the building."

Sandor laughed.

Lerner had a taste of his scotch. "Kinnie is a good man. I gave him exactly double what you said I owed."

"Nice of you."

"Sorry about his friends, I truly am. I gave him some money for their families too."

"You shouldn't have been using the computer."

"I know that now. I had no idea how dangerous things were."

"When they tried to take you at the hotel, that didn't give you a clue?"

"I figured that was a one-off. Thought I was safe, once I was with your guys."

"You were, if you didn't set up an electronic road map for them to find you."

Lerner was quiet for a moment. "You're the one who rescued the hostages, aren't you?"

"What hostages?"

"Come on Sandor, it's just you and me here."

"Last time it was just you and me, people were trying to blow our heads off."

"A reasonable point, I grant you. But everything that went down is over, right?"

"It is for you. Never is for me."

"I had that last part sorted out when I came to see you." He had another swallow of the whisky. "So, can you tell me about Corinne?"

"She was involved in some bad things, but my guess is she didn't understand how bad they were, not at first. She started to make some inquiries and they murdered her, or that's my take on it anyway."

"Questions about Fronique?"

"That's my guess. Cristo was funneling money to them so they could work on a project that wasn't intended to do anyone any good. That's all I can say about that."

"What about the shell companies?"

"Again, it must have looked to her at first like a clever investment strategy. When she started asking the wrong questions, well, you know the rest."

"When you say 'the wrong questions'..."

"RSL has been cooperating, we've had people checking her history of emails and so forth."

"Damn." He had another drink. "So Charlie Colville was in the same boat?"

"Same pond, at least. Once they got rid of her they had to neutralize him too. Given what she told him, he might have become dangerous."

Lerner shook his head.

"I have to admit pal, there were times I wondered how you fit into all this."

Lerner returned his friend's unblinking stare. "I have to admit, I don't blame you for the thought."

Sandor smiled. "Glad someone else turned out to be the villain."

"I can't believe it was Cristo. Really rotten, huh?"

"The worst. Couldn't tell the difference between ideology and money. Completely warped." Sandor waited, but it appeared his friend had nothing to add. "So, what's next for you?"

"Not sure. Heading back to London tonight to see Freddie. Expect a nasty post mortem."

"None of this was your doing. If you hadn't come to me we would never have gotten the head start we had."

"I know that's logical, but the nature of my business defies logic. If you lose money, it doesn't matter whether it's your fault or not, you still lost. If there's a stench attached to you, doesn't matter if you're not the skunk, you still smell."

"Will you hook up with another firm?"

"Maybe. Or start my own. I've got plenty of dough. Maybe I'll take some time, vacation on the west coast, visit with my girls."

"Nice thought."

"Look Jordan, I really owe you. I don't know how to say this, don't want you to be insulted—"

Sandor showed him the palm of his hand. "Don't even go there."

"Okay, but there's got to be something."

"Actually there is. What time is your flight out tonight?"

"Not until ten, why?"

"Mary O'Hara. Never got to the Old Man's funeral, and neither did you. I figure with all the money you have, you can afford to take us on a cozy limo ride up to New Haven. We can pay our respects, then get drunk on the way back."

"Well sure, but how do you know she's even home, or wants to see anyone?"

Sandor smiled. "Already called. She's expecting us."

Lerner burst out laughing. "You'll never change."

"You can count on that pal."

ABOUT THE AUTHOR

A native of the Bronx, now living in Greenwich, Connecticut with his wife Nancy, where they raised their two sons, Graham and Trevor, Stephens is the author of the Jordan Sandor thrillers, TARGETS OF DECEPTION, TARGETS OF OPPORTUNITY, TARGETS OF REVENGE.